DR VINCENT LAM w̶ ... ̶m
the expatriate Chine... ̶ne
and is now an emer... th
his wife and children. *Bloodletting & Miraculous Cures* was awarded the
2006 Scotiabank Giller Prize for fiction. This is his first novel.

'Vincent Lam's first novel, about Vietnam, has makings of a master-
piece ... [It] flows fast and smooth along an artfully twisting arc full
of drama, intrigue and no small amount of horrifying violence ...
Those emotional truths make *The Headmaster's Wager* a powerful and
engrossing work.'   *The Globe and Mail*

'[A] sumptuously plotted first novel ... Lam goes for the jugular,
combining an operatic love story ... with evocations of Vietnam's
occupation by the Japanese and the later horrors of the Viet Cong's
persecution of the city of Hue.'   *The New York Times Book Review*

'Lam, a Canadian whose family lived for a time in Vietnam's com-
munity of Chinese expatriates, is sensitive to the complexities of allegiance, to the impossibility of being impartial, and to the way that,
in war, every gambit, no matter how well calculated, entails loss.'
                                                        The New Yorker

THE
HEADMASTER'S
WAGER

VINCENT LAM

FOURTH ESTATE · London

Fourth Estate
An imprint of HarperCollins*Publishers*
77–85 Fulham Palace Road
Hammersmith, London W6 8JB

This Fourth Estate paperback edition published 2013
1

First published in Great Britain by Fourth Estate in 2012

Copyright © Vincent Lam 2012

Vincent Lam asserts the moral right to
be identified as the author of this work

A catalogue record for this book is
available from the British Library

ISBN 978-0-00-726383-7

Printed and bound in Great Britain by Clays Ltd, St Ives plc

MIX
Paper from
responsible sources
FSC **FSC™ C007454**

FSC™ is a non-profit international organisation established to promote
the responsible management of the world's forests. Products carrying the
FSC label are independently certified to assure consumers that they come
from forests that are managed to meet the social, economic and
ecological needs of present and future generations,
and other controlled sources.

Find out more about HarperCollins and the environment at
www.harpercollins.co.uk/green

For William Lin

Rocks stand stock-still, unawed by time and change.
Waters lie rippling, grieved at ebb and flow.

LADY THANH QUAN

PART ONE

CHAPTER I

1930, Shantou, China

On a winter night shortly after the New Year festivities, Chen Kai sat on the edge of the family kang, the brick bed. He settled the blanket around his son.

"Gwai jai," he said. Well-behaved boy. "Close your eyes."

"Sit with me?" said Chen Pie Sou with a yawn. "You promised . . ."

"I will." He would stay until the boy slept. A little more delay. Muy Fa had insisted that Chen Kai remain for the New Year celebration, never mind that the coins from their poor autumn's harvest were almost gone. What few coins there were, after the landlord had taken his portion of the crop. Chen Kai had conceded that it would be bad luck to leave just before the holiday and agreed to stay a little longer. Now, a few feet away in their one-room home, Muy Fa scraped the tough skin of rice from the bottom of the pot for the next day's porridge. Chen Kai smoothed his son's hair. "If you are to grow big and strong, you must sleep." Chen Pie Sou was as tall as his father's waist. He was as big as any boy of his age, for his parents often accepted the knot of hunger in order to feed him.

"Why . . ." A hesitation, the choosing of words. "Why must I grow big and strong?" A fear in the tone, of his father's absence.

"For your ma, and your ba." Chen Kai tousled his son's hair. "For China."

Later that night, Chen Kai was to board a train. In the morning, he would arrive at the coast, locate a particular boat. A village connection, a cheap passage without a berth. Then, a week on the water to reach Cholon. This place in Indochina was just like China, he had heard, except with money to be made, from both the Annamese and their French rulers.

With his thick, tough fingers, Chen Kai fumbled to undo the charm that hung from his neck. He reached around his son's neck as if to embrace him, carefully knotted the strong braid of pig gut. Chen Pie Sou searched his chest, and his hand recognized the family good luck charm, a small, rough lump of gold.

"Why does it have no design, ba?" said Chen Pie Sou. He was surprised to be given this valuable item. He knew the charm. He also knew the answers to his questions. "Why is it just a lump?"

"Your ancestor found it this way. He left it untouched rather than having it struck or moulded, to remind his descendants that one never knows the form wealth takes, or how luck arrives."

"How did he find it?" Chen Pie Sou rubbed its blunted angles and soft contours with the tips of his fingers. It was the size of a small lotus seed. He pressed it into the soft place in his own throat. Nearby, his mother, Muy Fa, sighed with impatience. Chen Pie Sou liked to ask certain things, despite knowing the response.

"He pried it from the Gold Mountain in a faraway country. This was the first nugget. Much more was unearthed, in a spot everyone had abandoned. The luck of this wealth brought him home."

It was cool against Chen Pie Sou's skin. Now, his right hand gripped his father's. "Where you are going, are there mountains of gold?"

"That is why I'm going."

"Ba," said Chen Pie Sou intently. He pulled at the charm. "Take this with you, so that its luck will keep you safe and bring you home."

"I don't need it. I've worn it for so long that the luck has worked its way into my skin. Close your eyes."

"I'm not sleepy."

"But in your dreams, you will come with me. To the Gold Mountain."

Chen Kai added a heaping shovel of coal to the embers beneath the kang. Muy Fa, who always complained that her husband indulged their son, made a soft noise with her tongue.

"Don't worry, dear wife. I will find so much money in Indochina that we will pile coal into the kang all night long," boasted Chen Kai. "And we will throw out the burned rice in the bottom of that pot."

"You will come back soon?" asked Chen Pie Sou, his eyes closed now.

Chen Kai squeezed his son's shoulder. "Sometimes, you may think I am far away. Not so. Whenever you sleep, I am with you in your dreams."

"But when will you return?"

"As soon as I have collected enough gold."

"How much?"

"Enough . . . at the first moment I have enough to provide for you, and your mother, I will be on my way home."

The boy seized his father's hand in both of his. "Ba, I'm scared."

"Of what?"

"That you won't come back."

"Shh . . . there is nothing to worry about. Your ancestor went to the Gold Mountain, and this lump around your neck proves that he came back. As soon as I have enough to provide for you, I will be back."

As if startled, the boy opened his eyes wide and struggled with the nugget, anxious to get it off. "Father, take this with you. If you already have this gold, it will not take you as long to collect what you need."

"Gwai jai," said Chen Kai, and he calmed the boy's hands with his own. "I will find so much that such a little bit would not delay me."

"You will sit with me?"

"Until you are asleep. As I promised." Chen Kai stroked his son's head. "Then you will see me in your dreams."

Chen Pie Sou tried to keep his eyelids from falling shut. They became heavy, and the kang was especially warm that night. When he woke into the cold, bright morning, his breath was like the clouds of a speeding train, wispy white—vanishing. His mother was making the breakfast porridge, her face tear-stained. His father was gone.

The boy yelled, "Ma! It's my fault!"

She jumped. "What is it?"

"I'm sorry," sobbed Chen Pie Sou. "I meant to stay awake. If I had, ba would still be here."

1966, CHOLON, VIETNAM

It was a new morning towards the end of the dry season, early enough that the fleeting shade still graced the third-floor balcony of the Percival Chen English Academy. Chen Pie Sou, who was known to most as Headmaster Percival Chen, and his son, Dai Jai, sat at the small wicker breakfast table, looking out at La Place de la Libération.

The market girls' bright silk *ao dais* glistened. First light had begun to sweep across their bundles of cut vegetables for sale, the noodle sellers' carts, the flame trees that shaded the sidewalks, and the flower sellers' arrangements of blooms. Percival had just told Dai Jai that he wished to discuss a concerning matter, and now, as the morning drew itself out a little further, was allowing his son some time to anticipate what this might be.

Looking at his son was like examining himself at that age. At sixteen, Dai Jai had a man's height, and, Percival assumed, certain desires. A boy's impatience for their satisfaction was to be expected. Like Percival, Dai Jai had probing eyes, and full lips. Percival often thought it might be his lips which gave him such strong appetites, and wondered if it was the same for his son. Between Dai Jai's eyebrows, and traced from his nose around the corners of his mouth, the beginnings of creases sometimes appeared. These so faint that no one but his father might notice, or recognize as the earliest outline of what would one day become a useful mask. Controlled, these lines would be a mask to show other men, hinting at insight regarding a delicate situation, implying an unspoken decision, or signifying nothing except to leave them guessing. Such creases were long since worn into the fabric of Percival's face, but on Dai Jai they could still vanish—to show the smooth skin of a boy's surprise. Now, they were slightly inflected, revealed Dai Jai's worry over what his father might want to discuss, and concealed nothing from Percival. That was as it should be. Already, Percival regretted that he needed to reprimand his son, but in such a situation, it was the duty of a good father.

Chen Pie Sou addressed his son in their native Teochow dialect, "Son, you must not forget that you are Chinese," and stared at him.

"*Ba?*"

He saw Dai Jai's hands twitch, then settle. "You have been seen with a girl. Here. In my school."

"There are . . . many girls here at your school, Father." Dai Jai's right hand went to his neck, fiddled with the gold chain, on which hung the family good luck charm.

"*Annam nuy jai, hai um hai?*" An Annamese girl, isn't it? It was not entirely the boy's fault. The local beauties were so easy with their smiles and favours. "At your age, emotions can be reckless."

The balcony door swung open and Foong Jie, the head servant, appeared with her silver serving tray. She set one bowl of thin rice noodles before Percival. She placed another in front of Dai Jai. Percival nodded at the servant.

Each bowl of noodles was crowned by a rose of raw flesh, the thin petals of beef pink and ruffled. Foong Jie put down dishes of bean sprouts, of mint, purple basil leaves on the stem, hot peppers, and halved limes with which to dress the bowls. She arranged an urn of fragrant broth, chilled glasses, the coffee pot that rattled with ice cubes, and a dish of cut papayas and mangos. Percival did not move to touch the food, and so neither did his son, whose eyes were now cast down. The master looked to Foong Jie, tilted his head towards the door, and she slipped away.

Percival addressed his son in a concerned low voice. "Is this true? That you have become . . . fond of an Annamese?"

Dai Jai said, "You have always told me to tutor weaker students." In that, thought Percival, was a hint of evasion, a boy deciding whether to lie.

Percival waved off a fly, poured broth from the urn onto his noodles, added tender basil leaves, bright red peppers, and squeezed a lime into his bowl. With the tips of his chopsticks, he drowned the meat beneath the surface of the steaming liquid, and loosened it with a small motion of his wrist. Already the flesh was cooked, the stain of blood a haze, which vanished into the fragrant broth. Dai Jai prepared his bowl in the same way. He peered deep into the soup and gathered noodles onto his spoon, lifted it to his mouth, swallowed mechanically. On the boy's face, anguish. So it was a real first love, the boy afraid to lose her. But this could not go on. Less painful to cut it early. Percival told himself to be firm for the boy's own good.

From the square below came the shouts of a customer's complaint, and a breakfast porridge seller's indignant reply. Percival waited for the argument outside to finish, then said, "What subject did Teacher

Mak see you tutoring, yesterday after classes?" Mak, Percival's most trusted employee and closest friend, told him that Dai Jai and a student had been holding hands in an empty classroom. When Percival had asked, Mak had said that she was not Chinese. "Mak indicated that it was not a school subject being taught." Percival saw perspiration bead on Dai Jai's temples. The sun was climbing quickly, promising a hot day, but Percival knew that this heat came from within the boy.

The sweat on Dai Jai's face ran a jagged path down his cheeks. He looked as if he was about to speak, but then he took another mouthful of food, stuffed himself to prevent words.

"Yes, let's eat," said Percival. Though in the past few years, Dai Jai had sprung up to slightly surpass his father's height, he was still gangly, his frame waiting for his body to catch up. Though everyone complimented Dai Jai on his resemblance to his father, Percival recognized in his silence his mother's stubbornness. The father's duty was to correct the son, Percival assured himself. When the boy was older, he would see that his father was right.

They ate. Their chopsticks and spoons clicked on the bowls. Each regarded the square as if they had never before seen it, as if just noticing the handsome post office that the French had built, which now was also an army office. Three Buddhist monks with iron begging bowls stood in the shadow of St. Francis Xavier, the Catholic church that was famous for providing sanctuary to Ngo Dinh Diem, the former president of Vietnam, and his brother Ngo Dinh Nhu, during the 1963 coup. After finishing his noodles, Percival sipped his coffee, and selected a piece of cut papaya using his chopsticks. He aimed for an understanding tone, saying, "Teacher Mak tells me she is very pretty." He lifted the fruit with great care, for too much pressure with the chopsticks would slice it in half. "But your love is improper." He should have called it something smaller, rather than love, but the word had already escaped.

Percival slipped the papaya into his mouth and turned his eyes to the monks, waiting for his son's reply. There was the one-eyed monk who begged at the school almost every day. The kitchen staff knew that he and his brothers were to be fed, even if they had to go out and buy more food. It was the headmaster's standing order. On those steps, Percival remembered, he had seen the Ngo brothers surrender themselves to the custody of army officers. They had agreed to safe passage, an exile in America. They had set off for Tan Son Nhut Airport within the protection of a green armoured troop carrier. On the way there, the newspapers reported, the soldiers stopped the vehicle at a railroad crossing and shot them both in the head.

"Teacher Mak has nothing better to do than to be your spy?" said Dai Jai, his voice starting bold but tapering off.

"That is a double disrespect—to your teacher and to your father."

"Forgive me, *ba*," said Dai Jai, his eyes down again.

"Also, you know my rule, that school staff must not have affairs with students." Percival himself kept to the rule despite occasional temptation. As Mak often reminded him, there was no need to give anyone in Saigon even a flimsy pretext to shut them down.

"But I am not—"

"You are the headmaster's son. And you are Chinese. Don't you know the shame of my father's second marriage? Let me tell you of Chen Kai's humiliation—"

"I know about Ba Hai, and yes, her cruelty. You have told—"

"And I will tell you again, until you learn its lesson!

"Ba Hai was very beautiful. Did that save my father? An Annamese woman will offer you her sweetness, and then turn to sell it to someone else."

Percival knew the pull that Dai Jai must feel. The girls of this country had a supple, easy sensuality. It would be a different thing, anyways, if Dai Jai had been visiting an Annamese prostitute. Even a lovestruck boy would one day realize that she had other customers. But this was dangerous, an infatuation with a student. A boy could confuse his body's desires for love. Percival saw that Dai Jai had stopped eating, his spoon clenched in his fist, his anger bundled in his shoulders. "You can't trust the pleasure of an Annamese."

"You know that pleasure well," mumbled Dai Jai. "At least I don't pay for it."

Percival slammed his coffee into the table. The glass shattered. Brown liquid sprayed across the white linen tablecloth, the fruit, the porcelain, and his own bare arm. He stood, and turned his back on his son to face the square, as if it would provide a solution to this conflict. Peasants pushed carts with fish and produce to market. Sinewy cyclo men were perched high like three-wheeled grasshoppers, either waiting for fares or pedalling along, their thin shirts transparent with sweat. Coffee trickled down Percival's arm, over his wrist, and down his fingers, which he pressed flat on the hot marble of the balustrade. When the coffee reached the smooth stone, it dried immediately, a stain already old.

Percival said, "You are my son." The pads of his fingers stung with the heat of the stone, his mouth with its words. In the sandbagged observation post between the church and post office, the Republic of Vietnam soldiers rolled up their sleeves and opened their shirts. They lit the day's first cigarettes. "You must show respect." Percival turned halfway back towards Dai Jai, and squinted against the shard of light that had just sliced across the balcony. Soon, the balcony's tiles would scorch bare feet.

Percival noticed a black Ford Galaxie pull off Chong Heng Boulevard, from the direction of Saigon. He considered it. Who was visiting so early? And who was being visited? Dark-coloured cars were something the Americans had brought to Vietnam, thinking them inconspicuous. They had not noticed that almost all of the Citroëns and Peugeots that the French had left behind were white. Now, many Saigon officials had dark cars, tokens of American friendship. Dai Jai stood to see what had caught his father's attention.

"Where are they going, ba?"

"That is no concern of yours." It was prudent to take note. But he must not let the boy divert the conversation. The Galaxie turned the corner at the post office, floated past the church, and then pulled up at the door of the school. Two slim Vietnamese in shirtsleeves emerged, wearing identical dark sunglasses. Percival felt his own sweat trickle inside his shirt. That was just the heat, for why should he worry? Everyone who needed to be paid was well taken care of. Mak was fastidious about that. Percival watched them check the address on a manila envelope. Then, one man knocked on the door. They looked around. Before he could step back, they looked up, saw Percival, and gestured, blank-faced. The best thing was to wave in a benignly friendly way. This was exactly what Percival did, and then he sat down, gestured to Dai Jai to do the same.

"Who is it, *ba*?"

"Unexpected visitors." Had his friend, police chief Mei, once mentioned the CIA's preference for Galaxies? Perhaps it had been some other car.

"Are you going down, Father?" asked Dai Jai.

"No." He would wait for Foong Jie to fetch him. He preferred to take his time with such people. "I am drinking my coffee."

Percival reached towards the tray and saw the broken pieces of glass. Dai Jai hurried to pour coffee into his own glass, and gave it to his father. A few sips later, feet ascended the stairs, louder than Foong Jie's soft slippers. Why were the men from Saigon coming up to the family quarters? Why hadn't Foong Jie directed them to wait? When she appeared, she gave the headmaster a look of apology even as she bowed nervously to the two men who followed her onto the balcony. They shielded their eyes despite their sunglasses. The balcony now glowed with full, searing morning light.

The younger one said, "Percival? Percival Chen?"

"*Da*." Yes. Dai Jai stood up quickly, but Percival did not. The two men in sunglasses glanced at the single vacant chair, and remained standing. Now that they were here on his balcony, Percival would do what was needed, but he would not stand while they sat.

"This is the Percival Chen English Academy?" said the older man.

"My school." Percival waved at Dai Jai to sit.

"We were confused at first—your sign is in Chinese."

The carved wooden sign above the front door was painted in lucky red, "Chen Hap Sing," the Chen Trade Company. Chen Kai had made his fortune in the Cholon rice trade and had built this house. He could not have imagined that the high-ceilinged warehouse spaces would one day be well suited for the classrooms of his son's English school.

"It was my father's sign. I keep it for luck."

"Your signature here, Headmaster Chen," said the younger man from Saigon, offering a receipt for signature and the envelope.

"I will read it later," said Percival, ignoring the receipt as he took the manila envelope. "Thank you, brothers. I will send it back by courier." He put it down on the table. They did not budge. "Why should you wait for this? You are important, busy men. Police officers, of course."

They did not say otherwise. The older man said, "Sign now." Of course, they were the quiet police. Below the balcony, Percival glimpsed some of the school's students having their breakfast in the square. Some squatted next to the noodle sellers. Others ate baguette sandwiches as they walked. Percival was relieved to see Teacher Mak coming towards the school. Foong Jie would send Mak up as soon as he arrived.

Percival tore open the envelope, slipped out a document from the Ministry of Education in Saigon, and struggled through the text. He was less fluent in this language than in English, but he could work out the meaning. The special memorandum was addressed to all headmasters, and outlined a new regulation. Vietnamese language instruction must be included in the curriculum of all schools, effective immediately.

"You rich Chinese always have a nice view," said the older man, looking out over the square. He helped himself to a piece of papaya. Dai Jai offered a napkin, but the officer ignored him and wiped his fingers on the tablecloth.

The younger one thrust the receipt at Percival again. "Sign here. Isn't that church the one . . ."

"It is." Percival peered at the paper and selected an expression of slight confusion, as if he were a little slow. "Thank you, brothers, thank you." He did not say big brothers, in the manner that one usually spoke to officials and police, or little brothers, as age and position might allow a headmaster. He made a show of re-reading the paper. "But I wonder if there is a mistake in this document coming to me. This is not a school. This is an English academy, and it falls under the jurisdiction of the Department of Language Institutes."

The older one bristled. "There is no mistake. You are on the list."

"Ah, perhaps the Department of Language Institutes did not review this directive. I would be surprised if Director Phuong has approved this." Mak must be downstairs by now. Percival could easily delay until he made his way up.

"Director Phuong?" laughed the younger officer.

"My good friend Director Phuong," smiled Percival. He was Hakka, his name was Fung, though he had come to Vietnam as a child and used the name Phuong. Each New Year, Percival was mindful to provide him with a sufficient gift.

The older one said, "You mean the former director. He recently had an unfortunate accident."

"He is on sick leave, then? Well, I will take up this matter when he—"

"He will not return." The older man from Saigon grinned. "Between you and me, some say he gave too many favours to his Chinese friends here in Cholon, but we didn't come to gossip. We just need your signature."

Percival stared at the memorandum. He was not reading. Just a little longer, he thought. Now he heard sure steps on the stairs, familiar feet in no hurry. Mak appeared on the balcony, nodded to Percival, who handed the papers to him. Mak glanced at the visitors and began to read the document. The teacher was thin, but compact rather than reedy, a little shorter than Percival. While some small men were twitchy and nervous, Mak moved with the calm of one who had folded all his emotions neatly within himself, his impulses contained and hidden. For years he had worn the same round, wire-rimmed glasses. The metal of the left arm was dull where he now gripped it to adjust the glasses precisely on his nose.

"Brothers," said Percival, "this is my friend who advises me on all school business." He continued to face the officers as he said, "Teacher Mak, I suspect this came to me in error, as it applies to schools, but we are a language institute."

Mak quickly finished reading the papers.

"Headmaster," said Mak in Vietnamese, "why not let these brothers be on their way?" He looked at Percival. He murmured in Teochow, "Sign. It is the only thing to do."

Surprised, Percival took the receipt and the pen. Did Mak have nothing else to say? Mak nodded. Percival did as his friend advised, then put the paper on the table and flourished a smug grin at the quiet police, as if he had won. The younger one grabbed the receipt, the older one took a handful of fruit, and they left.

Percival was quiet for a few moments, and then snapped, "Dai Jai, where are your manners?" He tipped his head towards Mak.

"Good morning, honourable Teacher Mak," Dai Jai said. He did not have his father's natural way of hiding his displeasure.

Mak nodded in reply.

Dai Jai stood. "Please, teacher, sit."

Mak took the seat, giving no indication he had noticed Dai Jai's truculence.

"I had to take Vietnamese citizenship a few years ago, for the sake of my school licence. Now, I am told to teach Vietnamese," said Percival. "What will these Annamese want next? Will they force me to eat *nuoc nam*?"

"*Hou jeung*, things are touchy in Saigon," said Mak. "There have been more arrests and assassinations than usual. Prime Minister Ky and the American one, Johnson, have announced that they want South Vietnam to be pacified." He snorted, "They went on a holiday together in Hawaii, like sweethearts, and issued a memo in Honolulu."

"So everyone is clamping down."

"On whatever they can find. Showing patriotism, vigour."

"Hoping to avoid being squeezed themselves."

"Don't worry. We will hire a Vietnamese teacher, and satisfy the authorities," said Mak. "I can teach a few classes." Though he was of Teochow Chinese descent, Mak was born in central Vietnam and spoke the language fluently. Percival only spoke well enough to direct household servants and restaurant waiters, to dissemble with Saigon officials, and to bed local prostitutes.

"Vietnamese is easy," said Dai Jai.

"Did anyone ask you?" Percival turned to his son. "You are Chinese, remember? For fifteen hundred years, this was a Chinese province. The Imperial Palace in Hue is a shoddy imitation of the Summer Palace in Beijing. Until the French came, they wrote in Chinese characters."

"I know, *ba*, I know." Dai Jai recited, "Before being conquered by the Han, this was a land of illiterates in mud huts. Without the culture of China, the Vietnamese are nothing but barbarians."

"That is very old history," said Mak, glancing around at the other buildings within earshot. "Anyhow, let's talk about this inside, where it's cooler." The sun was already high, and the balcony radiated white heat.

"I will say what I want in my own home. Look, this school is called the Percival Chen *English* Academy. Students expect to learn English. Why teach Vietnamese here? Why should we Chinese be forced to learn that language?"

From below came the clang of the school bell.

"What are you waiting for?" Percival said. "Don't you have class? Or are you too busy chasing Annamese skirts?" Dai Jai hurried away, and it was hard for Percival to tell whether the boy's anger or his relief at being excused caused him to rush down the stairs so quickly.

Mak sighed, "I have to go down to teach."

"Thank you for telling me about the girl. He must marry a Chinese."

"I was mostly concerned about the school; your son with a student, the issue of appearances."

"That too. Get someone else to take your second-period class this morning. We will go to Saigon to address this problem, this new directive."

"Leave it."

"No."

"Why don't you think about it first, Headmaster?"

"I have decided." Mak was right, of course. It was easy to hire a Vietnamese teacher—but now Percival felt the imperative of his stubbornness, and the elation of exercising his position.

"I'll call Mr. Tu. He is discreet. But Chen Pie Sou, remember it is our friends in Saigon who allow us to exist." Mak used Percival's Chinese name when he was being most serious.

"And we make it possible for them to drink their cognac, and take foreign holidays. Come on, our *gwan hai* is worth something, isn't it?"

If the connections were worth their considerable expense, why not use them? Mak shrugged, and slipped out.

Had Percival been too harsh on Dai Jai? Boys had their adventures. But a boy could not understand the heart's dangers, and Dai Jai was at the age when he might lose himself in love. A good Chinese father must protect his son, spare him the pain of a bad marriage to some Annamese. The same had destroyed Chen Kai, even though she was a second wife. Now, the Vietnamese language threatened to creep into Chen Hap Sing. Looking out over the square, watching the soldiers clean their rifles with slow boredom, he saw it. The events had come together like a pair of omens, this new language directive and Mak's mention of Dai Jai's infatuation. Under no circumstance could he allow Vietnamese to be taught in his school. He must be a good example to his son, of being Chinese. Percival went downstairs and found Han Bai, his driver, eating in the kitchen. He told him to buy the usual gifts needed for a visit to Saigon, and to prepare the Peugeot to go to a meeting.

CHAPTER 2

AS THE SECOND PERIOD BEGAN, PERCIVAL and Mak climbed into the back of the white sedan and sat on the cool, freshly starched seat covers. Han Bai opened the rolling doors of the front room where the car was kept, eased it out of Chen Hap Sing, and set off for Saigon. By the time they crossed the square, the car was sweltering. When Percival had first come to this place, when it was still called Indochina, he had enjoyed this drive from Cholon to Saigon. It wound over a muddy, red earth path alongside market garden plots of greens and herbs, and sometimes flanked the waters of the Arroyo Chinois. It had reminded Percival of Shantou, except for the colour of the soil. Now, they drove on a busy asphalt road, which each year grew more dense and ugly with cinder-block buildings on weedy dirt lots.

Percival said, "I've heard that Mr. Tu wants to send his son to France before he is old enough for the draft. He must need money. I'm sure we can avoid this new regulation." He fingered the wrapped paper package which Han Bai had put on the back seat.

Mak shrugged. "Even if this is possible, it will be a very expensive red packet. It would be cheaper and simpler to hire a Vietnamese teacher. You won't have to pay nearly what you pay your English teachers."

"Let's see what price he names." Percival looked out the window as they sped past a lonely patch of aubergines. Since the Americans had come, the main things sprouting on this road were laundries and go-go bars. It was a short drive now, the six kilometres covered in half the time it had once taken.

Mr. Tu's office was in a back hallway of the Ministry of Education. In black letters on a frosted glass insert, the door was stencilled, SECOND ADJUNCT CHIEF ADMINISTRATIVE OFFICER OF THE DEPART-MENT OF LANGUAGE INSTITUTES.

Percival knocked on the door. "Two humble teachers from Cholon have come to pay their respects," he said, in a tone that could have been self-mocking.

Mr. Tu answered the door and shook their hands vigorously in the American manner. He made a show of calling Percival "headmaster," *hou jeung*, and held the door. Mr. Tu was the type of Saigon bureaucrat who had a very long title for a position whose function could not be discerned from the title alone. He regularly helped people to sort out "paper issues." He guided his guests to the chairs in front of his desk, and beamed. Yes, Percival concluded, Mr. Tu was clearly in need of funds. Behind him was a framed photo of an official, looking out at Mak and Percival, his mouth set with determination against the glass of the frame.

"Isn't that the new minister of . . . ?" said Percival, as if he might remember the name. "He is the brother of . . ."

Mr. Tu laughed, saying, "*Hou jeung*, I could say it was our new president, and you would believe me."

"You're right. But I take an interest when I have an interest." Percival grinned, and settled into the worn green vinyl upholstery, which had endured in this office through countless changes of the portrait on the wall. Percival told Mr. Tu of the breakfast visit at his school. He said nothing of his personal wish to avoid teaching Vietnamese. Despite being a practical man, Mr. Tu might be patriotic. Instead, in plodding Vietnamese, Percival explained his reluctance to add another teacher to the payroll. "It's just one salary, but once you employ a man, he must be paid forever. He expects a bonus at Tet, and a gift when he has a child. If his parents become ill, he'll need money for the hospital. So I wonder . . . if this new regulation might exempt an English academy, say, with a generously minded headmaster. You know I don't mind spending a little if it helps me in the long run."

Mr. Tu cleared his throat. He slowly spread his fingers as if they had been stuck together for a long time. Had there been the twitch of a frown, though quickly erased by the expected smile? He said, "I sympathize. Deeply. Absolutely. It is so unfortunate that an unimportant person like myself can do nothing about this issue."

Invariably, Mr. Tu's first response to any request was to profess his simultaneous desire and inability to help. Percival placed the wrapped paper package on Mr. Tu's desk. He said, "It may be that language institutes such as the Percival Chen English Academy fall outside the parameters of this new regulation. There may have been a simple administrative mistake. If so, I wonder about an administrative solution. After all, I run an English academy. It's not a regular school."

Mr. Tu opened the package, and thanked Percival for the carton of Marlboros and the bottle of Hine cognac. "The issue of Vietnamese instruction in the Chinese quarter—in Cholon—is . . . how can I say . . . important to some," he said. "It may be difficult to make exceptions." This type of response was also typical, in order to justify a price. But Mr. Tu looked genuinely uncomfortable, which was unusual.

"Please understand," interjected Mak. "The headmaster thinks only of the pressing need to educate English-speakers who will help us help the Americans."

"Surely, the Ministry of Education would not wish to diminish English instruction time when all of our students already speak Vietnamese," said Percival. Of course, many of the students at the Percival Chen English Academy were in fact of Chinese descent and spoke only basic Vietnamese, like their headmaster.

"We have the utmost of patriotic motivations," said Mak. "The American officers whom I know often tell me that they need—"

"No doubt," said Mr. Tu. "What is your tuition now?"

"I would have to check," Percival countered, anticipating price negotiations.

Mr. Tu rubbed the amber bottle with his palm, and placed it, along with the cigarettes, in his desk drawer. From his bookshelf, he plucked a bottle of Otard, and poured three glasses. Lifting his glass to his lips, Percival smelled and then tasted a cheap local liquor rather than the promised cognac. Mr. Tu said with a casual shrug, "I will make inquiries. Further conversations might be required, with my chief, and possibly above him." Mr. Tu looked down. "So you should ask yourself, are such conversations worthwhile? This is not an easy matter."

"But what would make it easy?" said Percival, undeterred, preparing already to balk at a price and counter with half.

"Hard to say."

"Roughly."

"I don't know the price," said Mr. Tu.

"Your best guess." It was better to get a number to start the discussion rather than leave empty-handed.

"Or even if it is possible," said Mr. Tu, and stood. "I am a humble *fonctionnaire*. It may be beyond me. As men of learning, you know that some answers are more complex than others."

"I see," said Percival. This did not seem like mere negotiation of price.

"That is our new ministerial advisor," said Mr. Tu, indicating the new photo. "Thuc is below the minister in theory, and above him in reality. He is very patriotic. Prime Minister Ky chose him personally to oversee education." He tapped the arms of the chair and looked from Percival to Mak.

Mak stood, smiled graciously, and said, "Thank you, Mr. Tu, for your time." He leaned towards the desk and said, "If there is no solution to be found, there is no need to remember that we asked."

Mr. Tu nodded. "Don't worry. It would serve no one."

Percival stood, and they left, closing the door themselves as they went into the hallway.

As Han Bai drove them back along the road to Cholon, which was now quiet near midday, Percival said to Mak, "You had nothing else to push him with? Some favour he owes us?"

Mak turned to face Percival. "To what end? Mr. Tu spoke clearly— this policy is a patriotic and political issue. You know that some in Saigon dislike the Chinese-run English schools in Cholon."

"Because our graduates get the American jobs."

"That ministerial advisor is *Colonel* Thuc. He was just transferred from the Ministry of Security and Intelligence."

"I suppose that was why those quiet police were delivering educational directives."

"It may prove unwise to attract attention over this issue, *hou jeung*."

For the rest of the trip home, they sat in thick silence. What else could Percival say, when Mak's judgment was always sound? He always knew what had become important of late in Saigon.

By the time they returned to Chen Hap Sing, the morning students were gone, and the afternoon students had begun their lessons. Dai Jai had left for his Chinese classes at the Teochow Clan School. Percival went to his ground-floor office, cooler than the family quarters at this time of day. On his chair, Foong Jie had hung a fresh shirt for the afternoon. On the desk, she had put out a lunch of cold rice paper rolls and mango salad. He shut the door, ate, removed his crumpled shirt, tossed it on the seat of the chair, and laid himself down for his siesta on the canvas cot next to his desk.

As Percival's breathing slowed, the blades of the electric ceiling fan hushed softly through stale air. On each turn, the dry joint of the fan squeaked. The fan had been this way for a long time, and Percival had never attempted to lubricate it, for he liked to be tethered to the afternoon. Only half-submerged beneath midday heat, he was not bothered by dreams. After some time, he heard a thumping. At first, he ignored it and rolled to face the wall. The noise continued, and then a voice called, "Headmaster!" It was Mak.

Percival propped himself up on an elbow, his singlet a second skin of sweat, his eyes suddenly full of the room—the grey metal desk, the black telephone. A gecko at the far upper corner of the room looked straight into Percival's eyes, limbs flexed.

"*Hou jeung!*" A fist on the door.

"Come in, Mak."

Mak entered, shut the door, and stood by the cot for a moment, as if he found himself a little wary of actually speaking.

"Please, friend. What is it?"

"I have heard something worrisome," Mak said. "Chen Pie Sou, it is something that your son, Dai Jai, has done."

"Involving the girl?" said Percival, angry already. Had Dai Jai defied him further?

"No."

Mak explained that at the start of the afternoon class at the Teochow Clan School, when Teacher Lai had announced that she would begin the newly mandated Vietnamese lesson, Dai Jai stood up and declared that as a proud Chinese, he refused to participate. Mak said, "Dai Jai's classmates joined him in this protest. Each student rose, until the entire class stood together. Then, Dai Jai began to hum 'On Songhua River,' and others joined in. Mrs. Lai was frantic, but they wouldn't stop."

"How does Dai Jai even know that old tune?"

"Finally, he walked out, and the class followed him."

"Where is the boy now?" Percival rubbed his eyes.

"I haven't seen him," said Mak. Then, speaking deliberately he added, "I got all this from Mr. Tu. In Saigon. He has heard of it already, and wished to warn you. They have eyes in all the schools."

Percival stared at his friend. He had heard and understood Mak immediately, all too well. The delay was in knowing what to say, to do. If Mr. Tu knew, then someone at the Ministry of Education was already writing a report.

"Mak, you know what happens in Saigon these days. Tell me, are they making arrests at night or in the day?" During the Japanese occupation, the Kempeitai preferred to seize people at night and behead them during the day in public view. Before and after the Japanese interlude, the French Sûreté usually made arrests during the early part of the day. The bleeding, bruised person would be left on the street late in the afternoon if a single interrogation was sufficient, so that the officers could make it for cocktails at the Continental patio. If more was required of the prisoner, he or she would disappear for months, years, or would never be seen again. Now, the Viet Cong liked to work at night. They crept into Cholon across the iron bridge from Sum Guy and would kidnap someone for ransom, or lob a grenade into a GI bar before disappearing into shadows. Percival found that he could not think of the habits of the Saigon intelligence.

"They make arrests whenever they feel like it," said Mak quietly.

"Where is Dai Jai?" said Percival, his voice pitched high. "They can't have found him so quickly."

"You don't think so?" Mak caught himself. "No. Of course not."

Rays of light pierced the small gaps in the metal shutters. Dots and slashes. Percival struggled to pull on his fresh afternoon shirt, the starch sticking to his skin.

"We will have to hire a Vietnamese teacher immediately," said Percival.

"Clearly," said Mak.

Percival was about to go look for Dai Jai himself, but Mak suggested that he stay at the school. If the quiet police visited, the headmaster should be there to deal with it. Percival sent the kitchen boys out to help Mak look for Dai Jai, not telling them why. He stood at the front door, scanning the square for either his son or a dark Ford. He stalked his office, glared at the phone. Finally, late in the afternoon, Percival heard one of the kitchen boys chatting amiably with his son in the street, both of them joking in Vietnamese. Percival heard the metal gate clang, then whistling in the hallway. His relief gave way to anger as he shouted to summon the boy. Dai Jai came to the door. "What is it, *ba*?"

Percival rose from his chair. "What were you thinking today at the Teochow school?"

"Are people already talking about our protest?" He stood in the doorway, excited, his white school shirt soaked through with sweat.

"Protest. Is that what you call this stupidity?"

"*Ba*," he said, his eyes wide. "You said yourself this morning that the Chinese should not be forced to study Vietnamese."

"Did I raise a fool?"

Dai Jai's voice fell. "I thought you would be proud."

"For bringing trouble? I heard of your . . . theatre from people in Saigon. Do you understand?"

"Good," he puffed up. "They know that the Chinese will not be pushed around, yes, *ba*?"

Percival's mouth felt numb as he said in a softer voice, "Son, if you wish to do something, it is often best to give the appearance that you have done nothing at all."

The last of Dai Jai's proud stance withered. "But I did it to please you," he said.

"I see." Percival slumped into his chair, the anger flushed out by guilt and fear. His hand went to his temple. "No matter, your father is well connected. I will fix it."

That night, Percival and Dai Jai ate together as usual in the second-floor sitting room. The cook made a simple dinner of Cantonese fried rice. As they were eating, there was a knock at the front door. From downstairs came the shuffle of Foong Jie's feet. Percival could hear the nasal tones of Vietnamese words, a man's voice, but he could not make out what was being said. Downstairs, the metal gates clanged shut. Foong Jie appeared with a manila envelope. She was alone.

Percival exhaled.

She handed Percival the envelope and slipped out. With sweaty, shaking hands, he ripped it open.

"What is it, *ba*?"

Percival waved the letter at Dai Jai. "A note from your mother," he said. "She has heard about your . . . incident. She wants me to meet her tomorrow in Saigon."

The boy picked up his bowl and resumed eating. After a while, Dai Jai broke the silence with laughter, still holding his bowl, almost choking on his food. He swallowed and wiped tears from his eyes. "You thought—" and he was again seized with uneasy laughter. "Well, it was not the police, just a note from Mother."

"This is nothing to laugh about!" said Percival. He pushed away his half-eaten dinner. He stood and turned on the radio. After a hiss and pop, the Saigon broadcast of Voice of America was recounting the day's news, informing listeners that the Americans had bombed oil depots in Hanoi and Haiphong, that the French president, De Gaulle, had announced he would visit Cambodia in September, and that Buddhists in Hue and Da Nang were protesting against Prime Minister Ky's military government.

Percival's spirits lifted. Were the monks setting themselves alight once again? He had often remarked that he couldn't understand these bonzes—they killed themselves to criticize the government, but surely the government must be glad that some of their critics were dead. After news of an immolation, Percival was always relieved to see the one-eyed monk in the square, for he was fond of that one, who seemed to have the intensity that a martyr would require. The suicides by fire attracted a great deal of attention, though, so now Percival listened with hope. Surely, those in Saigon who watched for dissent would take more interest in a new spate of Buddhist trouble than in some trivial incident at a Chinese school in Cholon. Percival turned to Dai Jai. "I will meet with your mother tomorrow. Do you see how serious this is?"

"I'm sorry, Father. I thought it would make you proud."

What to say, that he might have been, if the incident had remained Cholon gossip rather than Saigon trouble? But even if that had been the case, he would have had to instruct the boy nonetheless, that he must learn to pair his best impulses with canny quiet. Percival said, "I will fix this. Until then, you cannot leave Chen Hap Sing."

"I need to go out tonight. I need—"

"No!"

"*Ba*, I have to buy larvae for my fish. They need to eat every day."

Percival was tempted to ask whether Dai Jai was planning to buy fish food from a pretty Annamese fellow student, but that didn't seem so important now. "Someone might be outside, waiting to arrest you. I will send one of the servants for your larvae."

Later that evening, Percival went out on the second-floor balcony where Dai Jai kept his tanks. The boy made no acknowledgement of his father's appearance, but continued to skim the water clear with a flat net. Yes, for the boy to be so moody about staying in, it must have been a rendezvous with the girl. Ever since he was very small, Dai Jai had nurtured gouramis and goldfish, kissing fish and fighting fish. In recent years Dai Jai had renounced most of his childhood toys and games in favour of soccer with his friends, stolen cigarettes, and a French lingerie catalogue that one of the sweepers had found hidden in his room, and which Percival had directed be placed back exactly where it was found with nothing more to be said about it. The one fascination that persisted from boyhood was the fish.

Percival held out two lotus-leaf cones of live mosquito larvae in water. "For you, Son." He had gone out himself to buy them, but did not say so. This was the hour that the casinos were becoming busy and filled with people he knew, but Percival had no urge to gamble tonight. He must stay close by, in case something happened.

Dai Jai took the cones with quiet thanks, and gently tore off a corner to let the fluid out. He began to pour the food into each tank. The fish darted amongst the water plants to take their meal. Dai Jai went from one tank to another, feeding the fish until the whole row of tanks was a shimmering display.

"How do you know the song 'On Songhua River'?" asked Percival. Why would the boy know that old tune of the Chinese resistance against Japan's occupation? It was not a modern melody.

"You often hum it."

That was what Percival had thought. "What you did was foolish, but I appreciate the spirit in it."

Dai Jai put down the net. "Father, you always say that wherever we Chinese go in the world, we must remain Chinese." The words Percival had spoken many times now rang back in echo. Beneath the sky's thick gloom, points of light appeared in the square below. The first lamps on the night vendors' carts were being lit, their flames dancing and spitting briefly until they were trimmed into a steady light. People emerged from their houses, chatted happily and walked with new energy in the cool hour.

"Son, a man can think without acting, or act without being seen. A son should be dutiful. Not reckless."

"Yes, Father."

"We are *wa kiu*." They were overseas Chinese, those who had wandered far from home. "We are safer when we remain quiet." The lamps in the square glowed into brightness—one after another. It happened quickly, as if each lamp lit the next. Cholon was most alive, sparkling with energy, in the early evening. Dai Jai's fish pierced the water's surface and took the tiny larvae into their mouths, leaving behind rippled circles. "Until I have dealt with the problems you have caused, don't leave the house anymore. Don't go to the cinema or the market. Don't go to the Teochow school. Don't even attend school here. Be invisible."

"Yes, Father."

"If there are visitors from Saigon, hide yourself well, but stay in the house. You are safer here." The old house had many dark hallways and secret nooks. It was the house that Chen Kai had built. It would be safe.

CHAPTER 3

AT THE CERCLE SPORTIF, HAN BAI pulled up in the circular drive fronting the club's entrance, stopped the car beneath the frangipani, and went around to Percival's door. The headmaster was not in the habit of waiting for his driver to attend to him, and in most places he would simply open the door himself and step out of the car. However, at the club, Han Bai knew that the headmaster waited for his driver.

Percival ascended the canopied stone steps, nodded to the bows of the doormen, went through the clubhouse, and out to the pavilion that looked over the tennis courts. Since their divorce eight years earlier, this was where he and Cecilia met to talk. The roof of the pavilion was draped with bougainvillea, which reminded Percival of Cecilia's old family house in Hong Kong.

A waiter pulled out a chair, his jacket already dark in the arm-pits. At nine in the morning, one game of tennis was under way. The Saigonese and the few French who remained from the old days played before breakfast, but some Americans were foolish enough to play at this hour. Cecilia was on the court in a pleated white skirt, playing one of the surgeons from the U.S. Army Station Hospital in Saigon. She had always cursed the city's climate, but now did most of her money-changing business with Americans so played tennis when they did. She displayed no feminine restraint as she lunged across the court to return a serve. The surgeon had his eye more on his opponent than the white ball, and Percival could not help feeling the familiar desire.

"For you, Headmaster Chen?" said the waiter.

"Lemonade."

"Three glasses?"

"Two."

How typical of Cecilia, to arrange a game of tennis with an attractive foreign man when she had asked Percival to meet her at the club. In reply, he stared in the other direction. There was no way to turn his ears from the players' breathy grunts, quick steps, and the twang of the ball ringing across the lawn.

Cecilia had played tennis since she was a child in Hong Kong, years before Percival ever saw a racquet. Her name had been Sai Ming until she was registered by the nuns at St. Paul Academy as Cecilia, and thereafter eschewed her Chinese name. When they had been students, he at La Salle Academy, and she at its sister school, St. Paul, she once offered to teach Percival how to play. He was even more clumsy with a racquet than he was on the dance floor. Cecilia had laughed at his ineptness, and Percival declared tennis a game of the white devils.

Percival had come to Hong Kong in the autumn of 1940, just a few months after a fever had ravaged Shantou. During that contagion, Muy Fa became hot, then delirious. Despite the congee that he spooned between his mother's cracked lips, and Dr. Yee's cupping, coin-rubbing, and moxibustion, one morning Muy Fa lay cold and still on the *kang*. The years of his father's absence had put coins in the family money box, but now the silver seemed cold and dead to Chen Pie Sou. It had paid for a doctor, but not saved his mother. There was no question of a Western-trained doctor or medicines, for the Japanese occupation of Guangdong province was two long years old. Chen Pie Sou sent both a telegram and a formal letter of mourning to his father in Indochina, and paid ten silver pieces for it to go by airplane. An exorbitant sum, but his mother deserved every honour. He was shocked to receive a brief telegram from Chen Kai indicating that business matters and the dangers of the war prevented him from returning to mourn in Shantou, that he would pray for his deceased wife in Cholon, and asking his son to go ahead with the burial rites, though sparing extravagance. Soon after the funeral, a letter from

Chen Kai informed his son that he would be sent to Hong Kong for a British education. Chen Pie Sou wrote back dutifully, saying nothing of his anger at his father's failure to return, nor his disappointment at not being asked to join him. As most of the family's cash savings was used for the funeral, Chen Kai made arrangements through a Shantou money trader for a sum of Qing silver coins to be provided for his son's needs in Hong Kong. A forged French *laissez-passer* was smuggled to him, along with a letter of registration from La Salle Academy. These documents would allow Chen Pie Sou to leave the Japanese-controlled territory and enter Hong Kong for his studies.

Intending to dislike Hong Kong on account of the way he was sent there, Chen Pie Sou soon began to think that it was not so bad. The priests and nuns gave him a new name, Percival. People in the colony lived in an energetic jumble one on top of another, the streets filled with constant shouting and scrambling to buy and sell. The tall apartment buildings, he was told, were a Western invention. Afraid to live in such a towering structure of dubious origins, Percival took a tiny neat room in an old rooming house owned by a Cantonese woman, Mrs. Au. At first, it was frightening for him to be in the streets, to see the ghostly white British masters who rolled past in carriages that sputtered along without horses, or to be confronted at a street corner by the terrifying beard of a Sikh policeman. What weapons might they carry in their gigantic turbans if they wore curved knives on their belts? However, the tumult was soon energizing. From the street vendors, Percival bought dishes that he had never known existed. At La Salle, English came easily to him. Why did some boys complain that it was difficult, when there were only twenty-six letters? Percival was soon tutoring slower classmates and had a few extra coins for the cinema. And the girls! They were a different species than those in Shantou.

By the time Percival became captivated by the perfect arc of Cecilia's neck, and by the slight pout which rested naturally upon her lips, she was already going out of her way to defy the introductions that her mother, Sai Tai, coordinated. Wealthy Hong Kong society offered its suitors by the handful to the heiress of the colony's biggest

Chinese-owned shipping fleet. One after another, Cecilia declared them unsuitable. One boy had bad skin, another was too pretty. One did not have enough money, and another bragged tiresomely about his family's wealth. Also, she complained, that last one drove his car too slowly.

Percival heard all this by eavesdropping on Cecilia's gossip with her girlfriends. He didn't stand a chance, he concluded, but that didn't keep his thoughts from being frequently invaded by Cecilia. She was unlike any girl he had ever encountered. She used none of the sup-pressed giggles or blushing avoidance of other girls her age. Cecilia entered movie theatres alone, people whispered. She was spotted at the betting window of the Happy Valley racetrack. She made wagers on new, unknown horses and won. Some of the less affluent students at St. Paul tut-tutted that Cecilia's behaviour was disgraceful, and whispered with smug reproach that great wealth did not buy proper behaviour. Boys either found her strangely threatening or desired her with intensity, as Percival did.

Once, when he was trailing her longingly, she turned suddenly and stared straight at him. She fixed his eyes immediately. How could he have known, at that naive age, that these were the eyes of a cat who had found its mouse? He became hot, flushed. She was ivory-skinned perfection, her lips pursed. Then she tilted her nose up slightly and turned slowly away, so that Percival tortured himself for days afterwards, trying to decide whether she had been amused or offended by his interest.

At Christmas, the chaperoned school dance for the girls of St. Paul and the boys of La Salle was held in a respectable banquet hall on Queen's Road. As the band began to play the easy three-beat rhythm of a waltz under the watchful eyes of the priests and nuns, Percival finally managed to summon the courage to approach Cecilia, resplen-dent in a peony-patterned gown. He crossed the now vast dance floor and managed to get out the words he had rehearsed. "I am Chen Pie Sou, will you dance with me?"

"Didn't the priests give you an English name?" she replied. After a moment, she rescued him from his stunned inability to speak. She said, "Percival, isn't it?" She lifted his chin with a fingertip, the shock of her touch coursing through to his toes. Before he could say anything else, she had his hands and was leading him gaily in the waltz. When the dance was finished, he felt both abandoned and relieved to watch her flit into the distance again. After that, Percival could think only of Cecilia. Her image threatened to crowd out his studies. In front of his desk, he tacked up the letters from his father, formulaic correspondence exhorting him to study. Percival's dreams of Cecilia fulfilled him during sleep, and shamed him when he woke, his underwear stained.

The remittances from Chen Kai had been enough to make Muy Fa and Chen Pie Sou wealthy in Shantou, but once he went to Hong Kong and became Percival, he heard the snickers of his more cosmopolitan classmates. Percival had two school uniforms, which he washed by hand and hung to dry in the tiny room he had rented. His father had written shortly after his arrival in Hong Kong, warning that he must make the small sum of silver last through the school year. That was a surprise, but Percival had not complained. The suitors whom Cecilia had already rejected were heirs to property, and wore uniforms carefully pressed by their servants, but for some reason Cecilia began to seek out the boy from Shantou. She would sit with him at lunch. When he offered to walk her home, saying he was going in the same direction, though this was an obvious lie, she accepted.

They went to the movies, and held hands. Percival worried that someone might see them, but Cecilia conspicuously rested her head on his shoulder. She took her family's Austin Seven and taught him to drive on the twisting lanes of Victoria Peak, urging him to go faster despite the absence of guardrails. Sitting high above Hong Kong's craggy coast, they watched the Peak Tram shunt forever up and down.

Cecilia said one day, "Can you keep a secret?"

"Anything."

"I will see the world. Soon, I will sail abroad. I will meet famous people in important places."

Percival dared not betray his ignorance by asking exactly where these places or whom these people were. He said, "Yes, you can go anywhere. Your family's ships can take you." One of their coal barges was cutting slowly across the bay beneath their feet.

"You are silly," she said, but added kindly, "and sweet. My family's ships only sail the South China Sea. I think I will sail on one of the Messageries Maritimes steamers—those are the most handsome. The suites have silk drapes."

"Maybe I will—" he stopped to unstick the words from his throat, "go with you."

Without a word, she took his hands in hers, as one might console a child. From then on, whenever they sat up high on the Peak, Cecilia told Percival of the places she would visit—Westminster Abbey, the Louvre, the Grand Canyon. Her family owned books, she said, with photographic plates of all these wonders. While she talked, with her eyes on the water, Kowloon beyond, she allowed him to touch her. He stroked her palms, kissed the backs of her hands, massaged her fingers. He explored her perfect forearms. Percival heard his own breath, heavy, as she asked him if he knew of this monument or that museum. In a damp sea wind, he brushed the goosebumps that rose on her skin. Cecilia allowed him to be as passionate as he liked, but stopped him at the elbow.

As a young man of half-decent though backwater origins, Percival was occasionally invited to the same banquets as Cecilia, mostly to occupy an odd single seat at one of the banquet tables. Cecilia never bothered about where she was supposed to be seated, and seemed to enjoy making a minor fuss disrupting the arrangements and sitting next to Percival instead. As pleased as he was by Cecilia's attention, Percival could always feel the wave of Sai Tai's anger pulsing at him from across the room. Cecilia's satisfaction was just as palpable. It was disrespectful to snub an elder, but Percival's wish to please Cecilia was stronger than his desire to uphold decorum, and besides, Percival told himself, it was Cecilia who was angering her mother. While the quiet of their time alone was what he longed for, Cecilia seemed to relish being in public, flaunting her unsuitable paramour, so much so that it seemed to Percival that she almost forgot him in her efforts to display him. She never introduced Percival to her mother.

In the autumn of 1941, a schoolmate of Percival's asked him if the rumours were true. Cecilia, the friend said excitedly, had revealed in strictest confidence to a number of friends that she might marry the poor country boy Percival. It was the talk of the school. She and Percival had never discussed marriage. Percival assumed an offended air and told his chum that no gentleman would answer such an indiscreet question. He did not mention the rumour of their impending marriage to Cecilia. He was both afraid to open himself to her mockery, and worried that trying to clarify this rumour might cause its tantalizing possibility to vanish.

AS HE SIPPED HIS LEMONADE, PERCIVAL watched now as Cecilia served the ball to the American surgeon. A flick of her wrist, and the ball spun. Sure enough, her gangly opponent was caught off guard on the bounce. She called out, "Fifteen . . . love," to the American, but as she turned she shot her triumphant glance at Percival. Of course, he realized with annoyance at himself, as usual he'd been unable to resist looking at her.

The Japanese invaded Hong Kong in December 1941, and by overrunning it in eighteen days demonstrated that it was not the impregnable fortress that the British had promised. Some La Salle students volunteered as orderlies at St. Stephen's Hospital, and only one returned. He told Percival that the Japanese had shot the doctors, tortured the patients, violated the nurses, and burned the hospital down. The school Christmas dance was cancelled, and the British surrendered on Christmas Day. Though some of Percival's friends asked him to join them when they stole into the hills to fight with the Gangjiu resistance, Percival stayed in his room, grateful that his landlady had such heavy furniture with which to barricade the door. All the tenants were hungry and sleepless, for around the clock the shots of executions punctuated the wailing of the girls and women being raped.

When the noise of violence had exhausted itself after a few days, Percival ventured out to try to find some food. White, yellow, and brown soldiers of the British Army swung from the lampposts, their bodies already swollen, discoloured. Those who still lived were being marched away barefoot by the Japanese, many of whom now wore good English boots. For the first time ever, Percival knocked on the door of Sai Tai's grand garden house on Des Voeux Road. He didn't know what he would say, but he wanted to see Cecilia, to know that she was safe. In reply to his knock, there was only terrible silence. Finally, a neighbour appeared, implored him to stop banging lest it attract the attention of the Japanese, and informed him that Madame Sai and her daughter had gone. They had abandoned their house for a rented apartment on the sixth floor of a plain building. Sai Tai, the neighbour said, hoped that after climbing so many stairs, a Japanese soldier would not have the energy to violate her daughter. The neighbour did not know the address of the apartment where they had fled.

La Salle and St. Paul were both commandeered by the Japanese, so there were no more classes to attend. The Kempeitai, military police, arrested and punished suspected members of the Gangjiu with great efficiency, the flash of a sword by the side of the street. Bystanders were commanded to watch. The head was speared on a fencepost, if convenient. Hunger, both of people and beasts, made the days long. One day, as he searched for a shop that had food to sell, Percival saw a pack of dogs ripping with mad pleasure a hunk of meat, perhaps a piece of dead horse or donkey? Normally, he would not think of eating such meat. Now, he wondered how he could distract the dogs or scare them off long enough to grab it. Then he saw the man's body several feet away, clothes ripped open, the stump of neck. The head was nowhere in sight, other dogs must have carried it off already. Sai Tai's handsome garden house was soon taken over by General Takashi, so it was best that it was empty when he came to seize it.

Percival was lucky that he still had a few of the silver coins his father had provided, and with these he barely managed to feed himself. In late spring, as deaths from starvation became common, the Japanese declared that those with foreign papers could apply for exit permits. Percival had the French *laissez-passer* he'd used to enter Hong Kong. He learned that the freighter *Asama Maru* would sail for Saigon in two weeks, and some said that things were better in Indochina. Percival used the last of the Qing coins to pay the bribe for an exit permit, and to purchase a ticket on the boat. All he had left was the family charm, the reassuring lump around his neck, which he was careful to keep out of sight lest he be killed for it by a Kempeitai. Down by the docks, Percival recognized a number of Cecilia's family's ships, which had been seized by the Imperial Navy. They were being repainted in military grey and branded with the Rising Sun insignia. Percival had not seen Cecilia since the invasion. He thought about her often, but Sai Tai was keeping her well hidden.

A week before Percival's ship was due to sail, a woman in peasant dress approached Percival on the street. Sai Tai had sent her maid to summon him. The next day Percival found the apartment building, climbed the stairs, and at the precise time he had been commanded to appear knocked on a green wooden door. The door swung open. Percival was startled to see Cecilia's mother rather than her servant standing before him. She wore a formal silk robe that was incongruous with the modest apartment.

"You are . . . ?" she asked, as if she did not know. As if she had not summoned him. The matriarch fixed him with her narrow eyes, dared him to speak. He was frozen, as terrified as if she were a Japanese officer.

"Is something wrong with your legs?" she said. "Come in. Close the door."

Percival did as instructed.

Sai Tai glided across the room, her feet hidden by generous silk folds. She came to a rosewood chair, its wood so dark that the chair emerged from shadow only when she lowered herself regally into its arms. Percival followed meekly, unsure how close to approach, erring on the side of being a little far away.

"Are you a mute?" she said. "Introduce yourself."

"I am called Chen Pie Sou," said Percival, guessing that she cared more about his Chinese name. "It is a great honour to meet you, madam." He stepped forward and bowed his head.

"I wish I could say the same." She sat intensely straight, as if sitting in such company required immense effort. "Understand that I wanted my daughter to marry someone suitable to her family's stature."

"Naturally, madam."

"My maid tells me your family is in the rice trade."

"Yes, madam."

"However, I have never done business with them. They must not be very important." As she leaned forward, her jade bracelets clicked against the arms of the chair.

"I'm sure you are correct, madam," said Percival.

"But people always need rice. At least you are not completely worthless."

"We have a house in Indochina, which my father built. It is—"

"Your family has a house?" she barked. "You think this is worth mentioning? Then you are very nearly worthless."

"Yes, madam." Percival went down on one knee, his heart pounding, and imagined his head being lopped off.

"Get up!" He reminded himself that it was Japanese soldiers who decapitated their prisoners. Wealthy old women with jade-heavy arms were not known to do this. "Is my daughter running around with a totally spineless wretch?" Percival scrambled to his feet. "You are not bad-looking," she said.

"Thank you, madam."

"Good-looking men are indiscreet. They cannot be trusted."

"Yes, madam."

"So you agree. You are not trustworthy?"

"Not at all. I mean, no. I don't agree. No, no, in fact, I am not very good-looking. That's what I mean."

Sai Tai sat back a little. "At least you make an effort to show some respect. Unlike my daughter. I am told that you have a French *laissez-passer* and an exit permit from Hong Kong. I've heard you have a cabin on the *Asama Maru*, and will soon be leaving for your home in Indochina?"

"Yes, madam." He could barely utter these words, never mind being able to clarify matters. It made no difference, he thought, that he had never been to Indochina. His papers said that he was a resident of that country.

"I am told that the French and the Japanese have some kind of deal, that it dampens the bestial behaviour of the Japanese in Indochina.

They say this year's rice crop was good in Annam, and no one goes hungry, despite the Japanese occupation. Is this true?"

"I have heard the same," he said.

"Your household must have stores of rice?" Only then, he noticed that her cheeks were less haughty than he had seen them before, perhaps a little hollow? Did even Sai Tai, he wondered, feel the hunger of the occupation? "You have the means to care for my daughter?"

Years before, along with peppercorns, cinnamon, nutmeg, and brandy, Chen Kai had brought with him on a visit to Shantou a photo of the house he had built in Cholon. It was six storefronts wide, and three floors high. Within, Chen Kai explained, were high-ceilinged warehouse rooms for fresh paddy and threshed rice. There was no building so spacious and grand in Shantou, he declared. Chen Pie Sou had resented his father's taking of a second wife. Muy Fa had stared at the photo of Ba Hai in front of the house, and criticized the building's extravagant size, saying nothing of her husband's Annamese wife. Ba Hai was a small-boned, dark-skinned foreigner wearing Chinese clothes in the photo. As a boy, Chen Pie Sou swallowed his question; why, if his father had found enough gold to build a house like that and take a second wife, had he not returned to Shantou? But now, confronted by Sai Tai's questions, Percival was glad to think that even Cecilia would admit that his family house was a decent size. "Yes," he said, with a small burst of confidence. "My family has ample means to care for your daughter. Our house is large. Our warehouses are full of rice." This last must be true, he reasoned, as his father was a rice trader.

"Then take my daughter with you to Indochina. Better that she escape with you, though almost worthless, than stay here and be devoured by Japanese dogs. Remember, I am choosing you as an option preferable to dogs. Come tomorrow at the same time for your wedding." She waved him off, not moving from her carved chair.

Trembling, he backed away in stumbling bows, and fled down the stairs. That was how the couple became engaged. Cecilia's mother did not offer her daughter's hand. She commanded Percival to take it. As he left the apartment, Percival rejoiced at his good fortune—that the very rubble and stink that he was picking his way through had led to his engagement with the girl he longed for. The next day, they were married in the sixth-floor apartment by one of the La Salle priests who had somehow survived the Japanese invasion. Cecilia wore the *cheongsam* in which Sai Tai had once been married, and glared at her mother through the whole ceremony.

A few days later, standing on the deck of the *Asama Maru* in formal dress, the newlywed couple waved goodbye to Sai Tai, who sat in a canopied rickshaw on the dock. As Hong Kong retreated across the choppy water, Cecilia said, "I dreamt of Paris, or London, but I have married a country bumpkin who is dragging me into the Indochina mud."

"But you spread the rumour that we wished to marry——"

"Were you stupid enough to believe that I would actually want to marry you?" She whirled away from him. "I fooled with you precisely because it was inconceivable that I could ever marry so beneath me. I did it to keep my mother's suitors away. If it wasn't for the war, she would have agreed by now to send me to England or America—in order to get me away from you!" She stalked towards the companionway, and shouted across the deck, "Now see what I'm stuck with!" She disappeared below. Percival looked around, saw the other passengers turn away.

As they reached open water, Percival clenched the rail at the edge of the deck, fighting down a sick feeling. The shallow-bottomed freighter began to roll. Had Sai Tai plotted a double victory, calling Cecilia's bluff and forcing the marriage to show her control of her daughter as well as send her to safety? He stood, unbalanced by the sea, as flecks of black soot drifted from the smoky stack and ruined his one decent white suit.

When Percival made his way unsteadily down below deck, lurching against the growing motion of the boat, he did not know what he would say or do. He appeared in the doorway of their cabin. He spoke from instinct. "Cecilia, we're married now."

"Look at your suit. What a mess."

"Isn't there something special between us? What about when we were up at the Peak, holding hands and talking."

"A worthless muddy peasant covered in soot."

He closed the door, walked up to her, took her shoulders, and pressed his mouth to hers. In the Western films they had seen together, this was what the man did when the woman was upset, and then the beautiful starlet would melt into the man's embrace. He wasn't sure what to do with his lips or tongue, but he tried to scoop her towards him with his arms. Cecilia bit his lip, hard. When he pulled back she laughed, "You coward, can't even stand up to your wife?" He touched his lip, tasted the salt, looked at his red fingertips. She said, "Is that what you call a kiss? It's like kissing a block of wood." Percival rushed upon Cecilia, they fell to the floor of the cabin with a lurch of the boat, and Percival forced his hands up her blouse. She struck him with her fists, landed punches on his sides. His lip bled freely, he kissed her through her angry insults, smeared her face red with his blood. Until his jacket was off, trousers, and then her blouse, and now they both struggled from their clothing until they began to move together rather than apart.

Afterwards, he rolled on his back, his sex a wet snail curled up on itself, sated and guilty. What should he say? He felt like crying, but a man must never cry. Had he hurt her? But a husband did not apologize to his wife. The ocean slapped the boat over and over. After a long time listening to the water meeting the hull, he said with regret, "Now that it's done, it's not what I thought."

She turned on her side. Naked, she was more perfectly beautiful and terrifying than he had ever imagined—ivory skin and smooth curves. She said, "It's not for thinking, then. And you're not done." She put her hand between his legs.

The second time, Cecilia straddled his hips and reached down to put him inside her, began to move. Once she was satisfied she draped herself over him like a sleepy cat. Percival was grateful for this quiet space which did not require words. Could this peace contain them, however they had arrived here? Tears welled, streamed down his face. He said, "I may not be what you wanted, but I love you." The words were exposed, vulnerable on his lips.

Cecilia had an expression he had never seen before. For a moment she was unsure. Then, her face solidified. He couldn't tell if she had taken a decision or simply defaulted to something in the face of confusion. "Well," she said, "it seems even a peasant is good for the animal things," and climbed off him, began to dress. A steaming, humiliated anger clouded Percival's image of Cecilia. His wife stared at him, defiant, as if demanding that he strike the first blow if he wished to break her shell. He stood, put on his clothes, and went out into the salt spray of the evening.

Cecilia stayed in the cabin for most of the journey to Saigon. Percival spent the time pacing the deck. On occasion, Cecilia would appear there and summon him by saying, "There's something I need from you." Or she might say, "You're still here? I thought you had fallen overboard." He would take her wrist and pull her down to their cabin, the other passengers whispering after them.

Sometimes, he would go below deck telling himself that if only he persisted with tenderness, the peace that came after sex might last. On other occasions, at a snickering glance from a fellow passenger, he'd decide in frustration that he had marital privileges to exercise and storm downstairs. Sometimes, Cecilia led as she had on the dance floor, told him to move his hand or his tongue in a particular way, to go faster or slower. Other times, she alternated between beating him and caressing him. Whether she initiated it or he did, whether he went hoping for peace or to assert himself, their sex often opened a door to a truce, which Cecilia then closed with a torrent of insults.

As the tugboat pulled the *Asama Maru* up the dull brown thread of the Saigon River, Percival and Cecilia stood on the deck of the freighter, watching the dense tropical foliage drift past, listening to the strange, raucous welcome of the jungle birds. He had been twelve years old when he had last seen his father, on Chen Kai's visit to Shantou five years earlier. Now, he was married, and would meet his father again as a man. On that trip in 1937, Chen Kai had promised Muy Fa that the next time he returned to China it would be to stay. He had almost enough gold, he told her. Chen Kai did not say whether he would bring Ba Hai to China, and his son silently hoped that the Annamese woman would stay in the Gold Mountain country. Then, just months after Chen Kai had returned to Indochina, the Japanese had occupied Guangdong province. By 1939, they were in Indochina as well. The birds screeched around them, and Percival realized with surprise that there was no mountain here, golden or otherwise. Small local fishing boats with bright-painted eyes on their prows returned his suspicious gaze.

A bored moustached Frenchman glanced at their permits and Percival's forged *laissez-passer*, and waved them down the gangplank. Saigon was an awkward jumble of European facades sprawled across a mud flat. Before they were off the gangplank a cyclo driver seized their luggage. He saw that Percival and Cecilia were Chinese and offered to take them to Cholon. Bumping along in the cyclo, which swerved erratically to avoid expansive mud puddles, they left Saigon on the road to Cholon.

Cecilia said, "A wretched hole."

Percival replied, "There are fewer Japanese here." Whether it was the collaboration of the French administration, or had something to do with the oppressive heat, the Japanese soldiers they saw seemed slower moving, more calm, than the ravenous troops in Hong Kong.

Upon arrival, despite having seen photos, Percival was surprised at the size of Chen Kai's house looming over him. Was this it? The red-painted sign announced, "Chen Hap Sing," the Chen Trade Company. Surely his father must have collected enough gold to return to China if he had built a house like this? Percival knocked on the door and told the servant who he was. The servant vanished inside. Shortly after, it was Ba Hai who appeared in the doorway. In person, she looked even smaller. After Percival introduced himself and Cecilia, Ba Hai stared at them through a long silence in which it was impossible to say whether she was more shocked or angry at their arrival.

She said to Percival, "You must call me *ma* and treat me with the same respect as you would your mother." Ba Hai spoke the Teochow dialect, but in a way he had never heard, with the accent of her native Annamese tongue. She turned to Cecilia. "You may be young and beautiful, but if you forget that I am the first woman of this house, I will scratch out those pretty eyes of yours." With that, she told a houseboy to take Percival to see his father, turned, and disappeared.

The houseboy led Percival up the stairs to the building's family quarters. The servant opened a door, and Percival peered into the high-ceilinged room. It was well proportioned, the windows tall but shuttered against the daylight. There was a smoky, sweet-scented gloom. Percival recognized the source of the smoke. Some of the old men in his Hong Kong rooming house had been devotees. Why was the houseboy showing him this room? Where was Chen Kai? Then Percival saw that against the far wall, slumped on an ornate bed, was a skeletal figure who wore only a cloth around his middle and whose ribs heaved mightily as he sucked on a pipe of opium.

CHAPTER 4

THE SOUNDS OF TENNIS HAD STOPPED. Percival looked up from his lemonade to see Cecilia at his table, her opponent's hairy arm around her waist.

"The Viet Cong are keeping your knives bloody, Doctor?" Percival could not recall the surgeon's name. If he had remembered, he would have pretended not to.

"Nah. Disposable scalpels. Always clean——at the start of the case, anyhow. Pleiku is hot this week. Choppers bring them every morning. Kids, right? Fresh off the plane, all blown to bits, calling for momma."

"Then you fix them?" said Percival.

"Humpty dumpty," the doctor snorted. "The Cong bury these little jumpers. Charge pops up so high and blows the kid's balls off. Cuts off his legs, too. See, I figure they intended it to rip out a soldier's chest, but the yellow soldier is so much shorter, they calibrated it wrong." He laughed and looked to Cecilia, who smiled obligingly. How did she put up with the smell of white men's sweat, Percival wondered. It stank like river oxen.

Cecilia noticed the two glasses. She caught the eye of the waiter, gestured to bring another.

"Don't worry about me, honey. You've got a business deal to discuss, right? I've got to go." He bent for a peck on the cheek from Cecilia, but she found his lips with hers, made a show of the kiss. Percival drank his lemonade.

"Wow," the surgeon winked at Percival, "a country worth fighting for."

"Bye, love," she called sweetly as he left. Cecilia sat and drank a whole glass of lemonade. Her chest still heaved from the effort of the game.

"A new business partner?" Percival asked in Cantonese. "Or a friend?"

"Everything is business," she said.

"It's like that with you, isn't it?"

She leaned forward. "Dai Jai must leave Vietnam immediately. The mood in Saigon is sour. I heard of one officer in the Rangers who turned in his brother to the quiet police."

"A suspected communist?"

"Supposedly. Or a family feud. But there's no time to waste, Dai Jai is in danger."

"How did you hear of his problem so quickly?"

"His problem? *Your* problem. I'm sure this is your fault, always blabbering on about China. For all the times you talked about returning there, if only once you had actually gone!"

"I tell Dai Jai to marry Chinese, but I should remember to advise him that his wife must also be Chinese inside, unlike his mother."

She laughed. "Is that supposed to be some kind of insult? Pathetic."

"It is from his mother," said Percival evenly, "that Dai Jai learned to speak before thinking."

"His mother thinks about surviving and advancing in this world. As for defying some trivial new rule from Saigon, from whom else but you could Dai Jai get such a nonsensical idea?" She signalled for another lemonade. "Anyhow, when you already teach Chinese students English, why should you oppose teaching them Vietnamese?"

"It's different. English is profitable," said Percival. "We may not have to teach Vietnamese anyway. As you know better than anyone, the right contacts can change any Saigon policy. Mak is making inquiries."

"Mak, always Mak. It's good Mak has replaced your brain, as your own was always so lacking." She switched to English. "Listen to me. I don't give a shit about your school. Think about your son." Then back to Cantonese. "We must send Dai Jai to Europe or America, before he is taken from us. I will arrange it." She drained her glass. Percival watched the beautiful line of her throat undulating as she swallowed. He had loved kissing her there.

"Did you rehearse that vulgar English expression just for me? You would send him to a place full of foreigners?" he said.

"You would say he is a foreigner here."

"Of course he is. But why should he leave, when I am well connected in Vietnam? I'll protect him. Anyhow, if he goes anywhere, it should be to China."

Cecilia laughed. "You are so predictable, both in what you say and what you fail to do. If you really wanted to go home to China, you would have gone by now."

"I stayed for you."

In 1945, after the Japanese surrender, people were moving in every direction. Cecilia had challenged Percival to do what he said he wanted, to return to China. She would not go. He was still in love with her then, hopeful that things would work out between them. He stayed. When he was eager to return in 1949, to cheer Mao's unification of the country, Cecilia became pregnant with Dai Jai and there was no question of travel. They had waited a long time for a child, had thought themselves barren. Then came the school, and with it the money and its enjoyable uses. By the time of their divorce in 1958, Percival, like many other Cholon businessmen, was regularly sending money home to help the Great Leap Forward but knew that to enjoy his own profits he must remain outside of China. Already, by then, it was important to keep such remittances secret, for China had made its full transition from being an ally in the defeat of Japan and fascism, to being a communist threat to America and the free world.

"Bullshit," she replied. "Tell you what—you keep the Saigon dogs from getting near our son. I will speak to my friends about sending him abroad. These days, there are ways to send people to America—for studies, for technical exchanges."

"I will make this little issue vanish. My contacts can easily do it."

"Don't be so sure. Besides, you mean Mak's contacts, your money."

Percival swirled the ice in his glass, rattled the hard, cold cubes.

"Good day, *hou jeung*." She called him headmaster the same way she had once called him a country bumpkin, and walked away swinging her racquet.

LATE THAT AFTERNOON, HAN BAI DROVE Percival into La Place de la Libération. From across the square, Percival saw a dark Galaxie parked in front of Chen Hap Sing. Two men leaned against the hood.

"Han Bai," said Percival, "go the back way." The driver swung the car around, like a great white whale in a sea of cyclo wheels, feet, and vendors' pushcarts. They turned off from the square and went around through the narrow lanes under the tamarind trees and the long, flapping flags of laundry to reach Chen Hap Sing. Percival told Han Bai to stay in the car in case they needed to slip away with Dai Jai in the trunk.

Percival crept in the kitchen entrance, surprised the cook and the cook's boy, who had begun to prepare dinner. He asked where Dai Jai was, and they shrugged. How could he have been so stupid to stay in Saigon all day without having someone watch Dai Jai? He had forbidden his son to leave the house, but he should have asked Foong Jie to keep an eye on the boy. The headmaster passed through the central hallway, and from the classrooms he could hear the voices of teachers and students. He went up the stairs to Dai Jai's second-floor bedroom, calling out to him. But the boy was not in his room. He peeked down through the slanted shutters to confirm his fears. It was the same two men who had visited Chen Hap Sing the previous morning. They leaned back against the hood looking bored, large sunglasses perched on small flat noses. Was his son in another room? Perhaps Dai Jai had noticed the car and hidden himself? Percival crept from room to room through the family quarters, aching for Dai Jai, checking behind furniture, whispering his name. He said a hurried prayer at the ancestral altar. At each window, he peeked out. They were still there. The dark car must have been parked there for some time, as several vendors had settled comfortably into their trade around it.

Finally, Percival went up to his own third-floor bedroom and looked out into the street again. He tried to convince himself that there were any number of reasons, having nothing to do with his son, why these men might have returned to Cholon. Besides, if they had come to make an arrest, why did they sit outside? Unless, he thought with a chill, they had already checked for Dai Jai, knew he was not in the building, and were waiting for him to return.

This was all Cecilia's fault. Had she not made him both angry and lustful, Percival would not have called Mrs. Ling from the lobby phone at the Cercle Sportif. Had he not called, he would not have discovered that, yes, Mrs. Ling did know a lovely girl, a dark Malay beauty newly arrived from Singapore, who was free that afternoon and could use a few extra piastres. Without this temptation, Percival would have returned directly to Cholon instead of going to one of Mrs. Ling's discreet apartments. Were it not for Cecilia, he would have been home earlier, perhaps would have seen the dark car pull up, and could have made sure Dai Jai escaped or was safely hidden away. If he had been here, thought Percival, Dai Jai would not have dared disobey his father's strict orders not to leave the house.

The older man stood up from the black car and had a long stretch. He paced. The younger man lit a cigarette for each of them. They were willing to wait. Below him, on the ground floor, Percival heard the school bell ring. There was the commotion of the students beginning to leave. Ah, thought Percival with relief, the quiet police were waiting for school to let out to make their arrest. It could be any one of his students they were after. Even if they wanted Dai Jai, he would not be coming out with the bell. Perhaps they would grow impatient and leave. The older one yawned. Percival gripped the window ledge, peered out from his shutters, willing them to go.

As the first students appeared below him, Percival surveyed the square. At some distance, a boy and a girl walked towards Chen Hap Sing. He glimpsed them through a row of flame trees, which were in full, extravagant bloom. Through their branches, he couldn't be sure. He stared. Did his eyes trick him? The boy's gait was Dai Jai's. Were the men from Saigon looking in that direction? Perhaps they were drawn to the slim silhouette of the girl.

Percival ran out of his room, down the stairs two at a time. He pushed his way through the jostling, high-spirited students, shoved himself towards the door. Perhaps the quiet police would not recognize Dai Jai, and his son would slip back into Chen Hap Sing unnoticed. When the students saw it was Headmaster Chen, they hurried aside. Down the hall, now almost at the front door. He would distract the two men from Saigon. He did not know how. On their previous visit, they had not wanted money. He must somehow get their attention, perhaps anger them, even if that meant getting himself arrested. He hoped he was mistaken, and it was not Dai Jai whom he had seen from his window.

Percival burst out the front door. It was his son, standing alone. The girl had fled. Dai Jai was within shouting distance, but what should he call out? The men from Saigon were no longer by the car. Percival panted, out of breath. Students streamed around him, out into their afternoon, their freedom. Dai Jai stared at the quiet police, frozen in place, as they walked briskly towards him. The boy held a lotus-leaf cone suspended by a string. He had gone out to buy food for his fish, and to see his girlfriend. The men cut a direct line through the chaotic foot traffic. Percival's instinct was to yell at his son to run, but no words came. Dai Jai did not run. He was probably correct not to, Percival realized. Now that they had spotted him, it would not help.

Percival fought for calm, for confidence, which was always the best place to start, but he had difficulty finding it. He waited by the Galaxie, chest pounding, as the two men returned to the car with Dai Jai. Each of them gripped one arm. Percival struggled to summon an air of authority as he said in Vietnamese, "What's the problem? I'm Headmaster Percival Chen. This is my student."

"Don't worry, *ba*," said Dai Jai in Teochow, shaking his arms as if it would cause the men to release him.

"Speak so we can understand you," said the older one, using his free hand to slap Dai Jai in the back of the head.

Percival found words in Vietnamese. "Brothers, you must be so tired. It is late in the day. Thank you for bringing him back. He should have been in class." He put a firm hand on Dai Jai's shoulder, relieved to touch him. "Dai Jai, go inside." The younger man from Saigon wrenched Dai Jai away towards the car. As if it were a daily occurrence for students to be arrested in front of the school, Percival said, "Big brothers, thank you for returning him. I will take charge of this disobedient student."

The younger man said to his colleague, "This headmaster thinks we are truant officers."

The older one said, "Or he is playing dumb."

Dai Jai said in Vietnamese, "Let go of me."

The younger one twisted Dai Jai's arm behind him. The older one slapped Dai Jai hard in the face. "Stupid Chinese," he said. He waved Percival off with a backhanded gesture.

"Big brothers, there has been some mistake, a misunderstanding," said Percival, all assurance gone from his voice. "Perhaps some additional . . . paperwork will help. I might have some red packets inside, also green paper. Let's go into the school, big brothers." The lotus-leaf cone dangled from Dai Jai's fingers. Percival looked around, as if assistance might be nearby. The vendors watched with some curiosity. There was the one-eyed monk, begging for alms.

"Just like a Chinese. You think that money buys everything. I don't think so." The older man from Saigon retrieved a single-page document from a manila envelope. He squinted. It was not clear whether he was reading or if this was simply a gesture. "These arrest papers are from the Political Security Section. That section has no interest in your green paper."

Percival saw the gold chain peeking out from under Dai Jai's shirt, thought of the charm hidden within. He hoped it would not be snatched from the boy's neck by these men, prayed to the ancestors' spirits that their powers and those of the family charm would keep his son safe. He had clasped it around Dai Jai when he was a small boy, the night before he was to attend the Teochow Clan School for the first time. He had sat on the edge of Dai Jai's bed and told him the same stories that Chen Kai had once offered, of the distant ancestor bringing the charm from abroad, of its protective power. Now he trusted, he had to trust, that the charm could somehow keep the wearer safe even if arrested by the quiet police. But he must not succumb so easily—perhaps there was still something to say. Percival tried to muster some bravado. "Ah, the political section. The new advisor to the education minister is busy, yes? I know Colonel Thuc well. An old friend, a childhood friend." His voice trailed off. Percival thought of the photo in Mr. Tu's office, of a man he had never met. In any case, Mak would know how to get to him.

"Unlikely. He is from Quang Ngai."

"Long live Prime Minister Ky, who will vanquish the communist terrorists," offered Percival desperately. "Listen, big brothers, I know all about yesterday's unfortunate incident at the Teochow School. Is that the problem?"

"So you know all about it," said the older one.

"Yes."

"You know more than we do?" said the younger one. "Is that what you're saying, *hou jeung*?"

Suddenly, Dai Jai burst out in Cantonese, "I'm sorry for causing trouble." His voice was high, his eyes wet. "I was only trying to show you my patriotism."

These words burned. Percival did not meet Dai Jai's eyes or give any sign he had heard him. His smile was frozen, insistent. "Mr. Tu is my good friend at the Ministry of Education. I will call him. Leave the boy here. Tomorrow Mr. Tu can answer any question that you might have. We'll all sit down and talk about it then."

The younger one said, "This matter doesn't concern education or Mr. Tu, Headmaster. Besides, school is over for the day. If you were simply this boy's teacher, why would you tell him to go inside? You are his father. You think we don't remember that the two of you were having breakfast yesterday on your balcony? Don't play us for stupid."

"Never, big brothers." Percival felt a painful strain in his face. "Please leave him with me. I will bring him myself to Saigon tomorrow. We will all sit sensibly and work out an arrangement. Tonight, think about what you would like. You know a father will do anything for his son."

"Ah," said the older one. "You could both be in Cambodia by tomorrow. A day changes so much, doesn't it? This arrest warrant states that Dai Jai is a dissident, and if your son is a dissident, you are right to be concerned." He brandished the paper under Percival's nose.

"A stupid gesture," said Percival, "an immature demonstration."

"Indeed."

Mrs. Ling's Malay girl had a spicy fragrance that Percival had lingered to enjoy a second time. The first time he had been too quick, only satisfying his body, not his agitation. She had climaxed, then dozed a little before the second slow, carnal pleasure in which they had both cried out. What if he had come home after the first time, slipped out while she napped, leaving some money on the bed? He might have got home in time.

On the street in front of Chen Hap Sing, Percival's agony was being monitored by the curious eyes of the shoe-shiner, the woman with the basket of bananas, and the two haircutters who squatted nearby. He wanted to yell at them to go away. A steady stream of the unconcerned—servants pulling on the hands of young children collected from school, the darting flashes of Vespa riders, a cyclo man with a passenger—continued to flow past. The one-eyed monk stood at a little distance, observing placidly. He might be praying, Percival hoped.

"Let's go," the older officer said. He tossed the lotus leaf to the ground. The younger man shoved Dai Jai into the car and closed the door. Once inside the vehicle, he looked wildly about and pressed his hands against the glass. "*Baba*, help!" *Baba*, the word a small boy used. Dai Jai grappled with the door handle, but the door was locked.

"Please!" yelled Percival. "Don't take him!" He lunged for the door, but was casually knocked down by the older man and tumbled into the mud of the spilled larvae. The two men got in the car. The engine coughed to life, and the taillights glowed like hot coals. Percival picked himself up from the ground and saw his son's panicked eyes behind the glass as the boy began to cry. Percival ran alongside the car, pleading. The Ford's big engine revved and the car pulled away, scattering vendors and snack-sellers, who fluttered to each side like birds. Percival trailed after the car, shouting, until it disappeared out of sight.

Percival went in the house, closed the door and stared at it. It took a while for him to gather himself, to put one thought in front of another. It was almost dark by the time Percival telephoned Cecilia and told her what had happened. Did she know anyone in the Political Security Section? When he asked, she became uncharacteristically quiet. Then she cursed, and asked why had he not been able to do the most simple thing—to hide Dai Jai. She yelled at him through sobs. He lied about how it had happened. He said that the police had insisted on searching Chen Hap Sing, as if he had been standing guard there all day since their morning meeting, rather than bedding a prostitute for most of the afternoon.

"What should we do?" Percival said.

"We must both put our connections to work," she said. "There may not be much time." He wished he could contradict her, disagree, which was the norm between them, but he had the same fear.

After speaking with Cecilia, Percival found himself wandering outside. Walking past the spot where Dai Jai had been arrested, he saw his son's face dissolving into tears in the back of the car, thought of the lump of gold tied as always around his neck. Yes, that was something. Percival walked briskly past, into the welcoming darkness. Instead of going to gamble or to find a woman, he went out to buy a new lotus-leaf cone of mosquito larvae to feed his son's fish.

CHAPTER 5

FROM BEFORE SCHOOL STARTED UNTIL AFTER the last students were gone, Percival sat in his office with the door shut and lights off, sweltering by the telephone. Each time it rang, he seized the phone with fear and hope. But it was never Dai Jai. Nor was it the morgue.

It took a few days for Mak to arrange a lunch with Cholon District Police Chief Mei, who was usually eager for a good meal and a red packet but for some reason was now slow to make himself available. On the day of their meeting, Percival and Mak joined the chief in a private room within a quiet restaurant that specialized in Northern Chinese dumplings, Mei's favourite. Percival ordered dumplings filled with beef and young garlic, chicken and bird's nest, scallops and prawns. Mak and the chief made awkward small talk about the new Spanish racehorses at the track—no good in this climate; about mah-jong—a friend had lost a villa in Dalat in a big game; and about where to get the best black market exchange rates for the U.S. dollar. Percival bad-mouthed Cecilia's rates, but otherwise said little, restrained himself. All he wanted to talk about was whether Mei could help. Mak had advised Percival to keep quiet and let him do the talking. They drank beer, dipped dumplings in vinegar, and Mak laughed heartily at Mei's jokes.

When they loosened their belts and put down their chopsticks, the serving plates were still half full. Mei pushed himself back from the table, belched, and said, "It has been good to see you." He glanced at his watch. "So late already."

Percival started to rise, irate that Mei was going to play it this way, as if he did not know the purpose of this lunch. Mak shot Percival a glance, and he sat down, fuming. Mak asked if Mei could spare a further moment and calmly, slowly explained what had happened to Dai Jai. He explained it exactly as if Mei did not know, as if it were not a subject of heated gossip in Cholon.

Mei shook his head. "You have a serious problem."

"Hmm . . ." Mak said. "If we can at least find out if he is safe, where he is . . ."

"There are two main possibilities," Mei said. "There is Paulo Condor, an island prison on the southern coast where the French used to send the Vietnamese who displeased them." He spoke the same way that Mak had, as if what he was explaining was not known to everyone at the table, as if he were talking to some American newly arrived in Vietnam. Mei smirked. "Now, it has both Vietnamese jailers and prisoners. There is also the National Police Headquarters, which is well known because—"

"Yes, I am familiar with its reputation," interrupted Percival, not wishing to hear whatever euphemisms Mei might use for that house of cruelties.

"Of course."

Percival knew there was a third possible fate that his son might have already met, but pushed that fear back.

Mak said, "Brother Mei, what can be done?"

"You should have come to me earlier." Mei shook his head, looked at Percival, and then turned his eyes back to the table. "It would have been easier to prevent his arrest. Now, to free him?"

"Big brother," said Mak, undeterred, "can't your fellow policemen in Saigon help? You are a district chief. They will do you a favour." It was not necessary to say that Percival would, in turn, owe Chief Mei any favour he thought to ask.

"They let us Chinese police control Cholon as long as we don't cross them . . . on sensitive matters."

"And this is sensitive?" Percival asked.

Mei shrugged. "What do you think?"

"But you will try," said Percival, sliding forward a plump red envelope. He had to pay, even for this useless encounter. He could not afford to dismiss the possibility of Mei's help.

Mei slipped the envelope into the ammunition pouch on his belt. It contained no bullets, but was full of cash. "Of course, friend. I will see what I can do."

Each morning, Percival pressed Mak on the situation and the progress of his inquiries. A week after the lunch with Chief Mei, Mak informed Percival that the usual Saigon channels were exhausted. He would have to begin making other contacts. It would require night-time queries. Could he take the car? Percival gave Mak both the car and driver, and often Mak took it in the evening, brought it back spattered with mud in the morning. Percival did not ask where Mak was going to look for help, because it didn't matter.

Cecilia probed her American business connections, but they were of no use. They could get dollars, francs, and change piastres for U.S. Army scrip. But this was Saigon politics, they said, meaning either that it was too deep for them to see what was happening, or they did not wish to look there.

Chen Hap Sing was bearable during the day, when school was in session and the old rice storerooms were full of students and teachers, bustling with English dictation and reading exercises. The nights were more difficult. Percival wandered the familiar high-ceilinged halls and fastidiously tended the ancestral altar. He found himself pacing the rooms and talking, not to himself, but saying to his father, "If you are here, lurking in this house that you built, rescue your grandson. Keep him safe."

Dai Jai's fish tanks became dirty. Percival didn't have the patience to clean them, but continued to feed the fish. Dai Jai would be happy to see them still alive when he returned. Unable to sleep, Percival ventured out to Le Paradis, sometimes Le Grand Monde, anywhere noisy and filled with light. He played small sums to pass the time. He did not bring any girls home, had no taste for it. Several times, he chanced upon Chief Mei, and let him win a sum of money. Each time, Mei took the money, looked into his drink, and told Percival that he had learned nothing about Dai Jai, as embarrassed as Percival was angry.

Twice daily, Percival burned joss sticks and prayed to all the departed spirits of the Chen family, asking them to please keep Dai Jai safe, and to return him home. On the new moon day, then on the full moon, Percival arranged a roast duck, oranges, and kow-towed before the altar of the ancestors with these offerings. Percival implored them to save his son. In the midst of this, he caught himself cursing his father for leaving Shantou and drawing them to the land of the Annamese, but he hurried to push this thought beneath the surface and replace it with prayers to the spirit of Chen Kai. Somehow, as much as he tried to make the feeling go away, being faced with the loss of his son made him angry at his father. Why had Chen Kai left their home in China and led them to this country? Wasn't it better to be poor farmers there than rich foreigners here? Then, in 1944, Chen Kai had suddenly insisted upon travelling overland to China while there was still heavy fighting between the Chinese and the Japanese in northern Indochina. Percival never heard from him again. Couldn't he have waited for the war to end, after being away from home for so many years? Why had he insisted, at the most dangerous possible moment in that war, that he needed to return to Shantou?

In the first years after his father's disappearance, Percival had been tortured by indecision—whether to include his father in his prayers to the ancestors. After all, if he was not dead, it might be disrespect-ful. Finally, he concluded that it would be worse if Chen Kai was dead and not included in ancestral prayers, for then it would be the ultimate neglect. Gradually, he came to assume that his father must have been killed. Did one pray to dead children, Percival wondered? Quickly, he begged forgiveness of the ancestors' spirits for wondering such a thing, and pleaded with them that the bad luck of thinking it would not make it true.

Two weeks after Dai Jai's disappearance, as Percival sat before a bowl of untouched rice congee one morning, Mak burst onto the balcony. "I have found a contact—someone who knows where Dai Jai is and can bring him out."

Percival whispered thanks to the ancestral spirits and the golden family charm around Dai Jai's neck. He said to Mak, "What is the price?"

"He won't name it until you meet him."

"Who is it?"

"It is not one of our usual friends," said Mak.

"Anyone who can help is my friend." Percival would not ask more. Some of Mak's contacts preferred to move within shadows rather than Saigon offices. Discretion must be respected, for it was also part of the friendship and trust between the headmaster and the teacher.

"You must go alone," said Mak. He gave Percival a scrap of paper, written directions.

Percival read it. "He wants to meet at a graveyard?"

"Today. Don't be superstitious. It's just a secluded place."

"How much money should I bring?"

"He wants to talk first."

After a few forced mouthfuls, Percival set out in the Peugeot. He drove up to Saigon, past the National Police Headquarters, where Mak had told him Dai Jai was being held. He continued through the city, and then northeast. Since he did not often drive, he concentrated on manipulating the pedals and turning the wheel. At a checkpoint on the city's outskirts, two South Vietnamese soldiers held up their palms, and Percival stopped the car. The leaves shimmered in the heat, and the clatter of cicadas surrounded him. A faded French sign pointed the way to Cap St. Jacques, though the Vietnamese had renamed it Vung Tau a decade ago. Percival always thought of the beach town by its French name. The soldiers began a half-hearted search of the car. Percival waved them over and gave them each a hundred piastres. They smiled, nodded, and he drove away, directing the car through the low hills.

This road to the sea wound its way through the methodically planted avenues of the Michelin rubber plantation, and the trees flashed past in perfectly spaced rhythm. Before the divorce, Percival and Cecilia had often taken Dai Jai this way for holidays at the beach. Today, however, Percival would not go all the way out to the coast. After an hour of driving, he saw the first of the landmarks Mak had described—an old French stone bridge near a road marker which indicated fifty kilometres to Cap St. Jacques. He fished the paper from his shirt pocket, just to be sure, and watched his odometer. Three kilometres later, he saw the stand of bamboo on a hill, then, at the top of the hill, an abandoned graveyard pavilion barely visible from the road. He turned the car onto the red dirt path that twisted through the bamboo, flanking the graves. The path became too narrow to drive. Percival stopped the car and continued on foot until he found the shack of cinder blocks and galvanized roofing set within the bamboo. As described, it was well back from the road.

There was no knocker or bell. He rapped his knuckles on the low steel door. The only reply was the rasp of cicadas. He tried to shift it. The heat of the corrugated metal stung his palms, and the door rattled but did not move—it was fastened from within. His shouts were answered by the bamboo chattering in the slight breeze. Standing in the sliver of shade provided by the short overhang of the roof, leaned against the prickly hot blocks, Percival scrutinized the scrap of paper. This must be the place. Through the bamboo, he could see the shape of his car parked near the pavilion. It glowed like a smooth, bright stone. Untended graves were being swallowed by the earth and vegetation. Had the nearby village been emptied during the partition? When General Giap's 1954 victory over the French army at Dien Bien Phu had led to the division between north and south, people were swept in both directions, as jarring a rearrangement of the country as the military victory itself. Many had thought their dislocation temporary, that they would be home in a year, once the promised national election took place. Now, thought Percival, enough time had passed that small children who had been relocated might not remember the villages from which they came. Travel between north and south was impossible, now that they were at war. That must be the reason for the overgrown tombs. Why else would the dead have been so neglected? A strange place for a hut, he thought. Bad luck to build anything so close to a graveyard. Somewhere nearby, a stream gurgled, hidden in the bamboo. He heard the clanking of some inner latch undone, a scraping noise behind him, and then the steel door was dragged open. From inside, a voice invited him to enter.

The shack was stifling. A thick smell of tamped earth, a distinct odour of urine, and another scent mingled in, which Percival couldn't quite place. Percival thought of the inside of a crypt, and he told himself to force down his rising fear. No lamp or window. A stingy rectangle of light entered from the door. At first, Percival saw nothing else. He advanced into the darkness, stumbled and fell to his hands and knees, a sudden panic, and stood up again. The ground was uneven.

"You are Mak's friend?" said Percival.

"What is friendship, in these difficult times?" said the voice who had called him in. "You are Headmaster Chen, I suppose." Percival could barely see the man. He was just a shift in the gloom, a voice, now a sing-song lilt that said, "Chen Pie Sou, Percival Chen, Headmaster Chen. These are all you?"

Percival tried to muster cool defiance but the constriction of his voice betrayed him. "Who are you?"

"Don't worry about that. You have enough to worry about, yes?"

"I hope I have found the person who can help."

"You must think so if you came to meet me. Or, you simply have no alternative."

As Percival's eyes adjusted, he began to see dark shapes within the shadows—suggesting storage crates, a rough bench, an oil drum, and the dark outline of a man pacing. A stocky frame, a restless way of moving and speaking. He could navigate this shack with ease, Percival realized, for he knew where everything was. Think of the mah-jong table, Percival told himself. When the odds delivered by the tiles weighed heavily against him, he knew to draw his opponent out, gain some feel for the situation, and be attentive for any small advantage. He would hold his words and wait for a clue. He would not be the next to speak. The silence grew, filled the room. He would win. Force the man to give away the next word.

The man stopped and stood directly before Percival. His breath stank of betel, his voice was flat. "I hope you did not come here to play the silence game. I know every game—better than you."

"My son played a prank. That's all." Percival couldn't keep his words from tumbling out, from sounding like an apology.

"A political gesture by a dissident."

"Ridiculous. Arrested for a childish joke."

"A protest."

"The boy has no politics."

"Everyone does. Or perhaps better to say, everyone's actions have political meaning, whether or not they have political intentions."

"A small misunderstanding."

"Some acquire their politics by accident," said the man.

"That's right, it's not his fault."

"Or for some frivolous reason, perhaps to impress a father." He let the words settle. Percival realized that the man already had the upper hand—knowledge—while Percival had nothing, no leverage. "In Saigon, it is always politics somehow. But what shall we talk about today—the reasons for your son's arrest, or the prospects for his future? It's amusing, but useless that you try to defend your son's actions to me. It's irrelevant, don't you agree? You are afraid, and not thinking clearly."

Percival hated having been read, and then the insult of it being displayed. "I will do what is needed to address this problem." Percival was aware of the man circling him.

"You will." The man nudged Percival lightly. Just to see what would happen? "I am a simple man," he said. "Are you?"

"What do you mean?"

He pushed Percival hard, nearly knocked him over, set his heart pounding. "Since I love simplicity, I think the best approach to any particular situation is to know exactly what the issues are. I dislike ambiguity. Do you share my simple view?"

"If that is best," said Percival, fists clenched.

"It is. Today, the issue is your son."

"Yes."

"Who does not wish to learn Vietnamese and has been arrested for his political theatre."

"But my son was born here. He speaks Vietnamese better than I do," said Percival. Why was he once again justifying? Because the man in the shadows was in control.

"True. He speaks like a native Vietnamese," said the man. "Your own use of our language is clumsy. Like a child's."

"Dai Jai is a child." Had this man seen Dai Jai? How else could he know the boy spoke well? Was the boy alright? Had he been given enough to eat? Did he still have his lucky amulet? But Percival did not ask. He did not wish to reveal anything more of his desperation.

The man continued. "Since you are not comfortable with the language of my country, we can speak in French, or English, as you prefer, Headmaster. You Chinese look down at us, but we are more flexible people than you."

Percival said in Vietnamese, "Children get silly ideas. How can I remedy the situation?" He wondered what the price would be—a thousand American dollars, or two thousand perhaps. He would bargain. Even a thousand would be a fortune for a rough man like this, he thought. Perhaps he could be persuaded to accept piastres.

"Boys get their ideas from their parents," said the man in Vietnamese.

"I am a simple teacher."

"Don't embarrass us both. You say that Dai Jai's demonstration of loyalty to China was a youthful indiscretion. Next, you will tell me that he plans to join the South Vietnamese Army, unlike so many Chinese boys whose fathers send them to Australia or Canada before they can be drafted. Go on, spin some fanciful story, but before you do, should I tell you something about my practical nature?"

"Please."

"I'm not concerned with your politics."

"Fine."

"Yes. It is."

On the road outside, Percival heard a truck gear down as it prepared to climb the small hill towards the graveyard. It was the sound of grinding, mechanical determination.

"Ambiguity is worthless," the man continued. "For instance, Mak must have told you that Dai Jai is at the National Police Headquarters? Yes. But what does this mean, exactly? Is he being held in the section for criminals, or the section for suspected communists—the political section? Do you know?"

"No."

"It doesn't seem like he committed a simple crime." The man's pacing stopped. "The political section would seem to be the right place."

"Have you seen him there?"

He began to walk again. "I see many people."

Percival's restraint crumbled. He had to know what was happening to Dai Jai. "I would be most grateful if you would tell me."

"At least you possess some polite phrases. Let us say, for the sake of discussion, that he is being held in Room 47A. There are many political prisoners there. The room is no bigger than this one but contains over a hundred men, all waiting for questioning. Your son would be one of the younger prisoners, which does not mean he would be shown any special kindness. He would be taken for his sessions in one of the east interrogation rooms. What are those like? Small, with two chairs, a little bench, a table, and a bucket. Sometimes there is other equipment, as needed."

Percival heard a machine's high-pitched cry—the truck, cresting the hill, then its gears screeching down past the graveyard.

"Two chairs would seem normal, yes, so that the official and the prisoner can sit while chatting? The bench, you might think, is for the prisoner to rest. Perhaps to take a little break from the discussion in order to reflect upon issues at hand? A bucket, you assume, provides a cooling drink? These rooms are hot."

As the man spoke, Percival noticed, as if they had materialized from the darkness of the shack, the outlines of two chairs, a bench, and a bucket on its side in the corner. Nearby sat an old table.

In the manner of an administrator, as if boring himself by explaining the need to fill out a form in triplicate, the man continued. "Did you know that sometimes a person being questioned must be bound to a chair?" He kicked one of the chairs, which skittered away. "The National Police Headquarters is busy. There is a schedule to be followed. If the prisoner has a tendency to fall asleep, which can happen after many hours of focused discussion—attempts at retrieving memories of crimes—it may be necessary to keep him sitting up and alert." The man continued in English. "You'll recall I mentioned ambiguity?

It is so difficult to avoid, for not all things are what they seem. Take this bucket, for instance. Obviously it is a bucket, but what is its real purpose?" He rapped the metal pail and handed it to Percival. "Feel the bottom. Run your finger over it." Percival did so. "Ah, you found the little hole?"

"Yes." A tiny gap in the metal.

"It is not an ideal bucket for holding water," he said, now in English. "It has a hole. But if one wishes to keep someone who is bound in a chair awake, one cannot be forever prodding him and shouting. This tires the interrogator, who is a busy man and has other prisoners to attend to. Hence, this bucket can be filled with ice and suspended from above." The man pointed to the ceiling. Percival saw nothing, but imagined the type of hook from which an electric fan or light was often suspended. "As the ice melts, cold water drips onto the head of the man or woman, though we will say boy, if you like, in the chair. You would think it is merely a chair, and only a bucket. Not so. The cold dripping of the water becomes a dagger thrust into the skull, though more rhythmic and merciless. It seems like nothing, but a boy with this water dripping onto his head soon vibrates with pain. His entire body quivers like the strings of a violin. Or the strings of an *erhu*, as you are Chinese." He must have switched to English to be sure that Percival understood.

"I take your point . . ." said Percival, feeling a wave of nausea.

The man gave no indication of hearing him. He said, "As this goes on, the skin on the head becomes red. With each slow, patient drop, the prisoner—the boy—cries out, as his scalp becomes a deeper colour, eventually purple. This continues for hours. As the ice melts and the droplets fall more quickly, the screaming becomes ever more hysterical. He tries to move his head, but the water still falls on him somewhere—forehead, eyes. He cannot keep his head away from the water, so he gives in—sitting in the drip. Now he is broken. He will remember whatever he is supposed to. No one even needs to touch him."

"Enough. You have explained this. I see your—"

"This is a new Vietnam. We strive for modern efficiency. The interrogator can leave to do something else and return hours later."

Percival tried to interrupt, but the man shushed him and continued, energized by his own words. "Finally, with one important drop, the boy's head tears open like paper. The skin splits wide open, and blood flows down the scalp. For a little while, this gash actually seems to relieve some of the pain, and sometimes sleep comes. But not for long, and soon it is worse as the water falls on the open wound, runs down the face, and mingles with blood and tears."

Percival fought down the sick in his stomach. He wished it would stop, but the man continued, his words beating down like drops of water. His English was good, somewhat formal, accented by French. His phrasing, Percival realized, betrayed an education. An elite one. He was more than the rough thug Percival would have expected in this place. He spoke in a slow, pedantic manner, like a teacher who admires his subject, saying, "Water shapes the earth. No one can resist it. This is the difficulty you are facing. The facts may be simple—that your boy is in a room with a chair and a bucket—but there is such ambiguity in these facts. I am here to clarify." The refinement of his language gave softly spoken words even more venom.

The man picked up a policeman's baton from somewhere in the gloom and swung it as he talked, as if in warning. Percival closed his eyes, tried to slow his racing heart, saying, "Where did you study, if I might ask?"

"You may not!" A loud bang shocked Percival's eyes open. "This is not your school! I ask the questions." And then another bang, as the man struck an oil drum with the baton. "Consider oil drums such as these—a boy can be put in a drum filled with water, and the drum beaten with wooden clubs. Amazingly, all the force and pain are transmitted without leaving any marks on the skin. The shock reaches the internal organs, like beating a person from within." Percival felt his hearing close in. His vision hazed with white fear and anger as the man detailed the use of the bench—the way in which the prisoner was tied, face up, nose plugged, a rag stuffed into his mouth while water was poured onto the rag. It combined the sensation of choking and drowning, the man explained. Percival's impulse was to seize him, to close his hands around his neck, to squeeze the hate through his fingers. But then how would that help Dai Jai? The baton swung, a whistle as it sliced the air. This man was his only contact. Now a soft voice, "You are angry with me. I understand."

Percival asked, "What is the point of this?" He hated his own voice, its impotence.

"I am explaining your boy's situation to you. Isn't that what you wished to talk about?" The baton swung, a bang; swung, another, laughter reverberated with the howling drums. Now Percival recognized the other smell in the room, the faint but definite scent of stale human shit.

"What is your price?"

"Ah, yes. Let us turn to concrete issues." He slapped the baton lightly against his own palm.

This was a transaction, Percival told himself. He must think of it in terms of money. The idea put ground beneath his feet. The point of this theatre was the price. Already, he felt a bit more calm. He would give whatever was asked—two thousand, five thousand dollars.

"A thousand."

"One thousand dollars." Percival almost laughed, but did not. His father was right. The Chinese were smarter business people than the Annamese. "Done. A thousand dollars. Can I give it to you in piastres? At a good rate, of course."

"A thousand taels of gold."

"A thousand . . ."

"Taels."

Percival finally lost his restraint. "What is my son's condition? Has he been beaten? This . . . all of this . . . is simply a threat, yes? Once I pay, I will have my son? I will bring it to you in American dollars, I can get it faster, that would be—" The sum was staggering, about fifty thousand American dollars.

"You will bring me gold."

"But that amount—"

The man sighed as if he were a rich jeweller with a stone so rare and beautiful that there was no need to discuss its provenance or price. "Is there a problem?"

"Of course not. Yes, a thousand taels." There was no point in negotiating. He had already been deprived of anything with which to bargain. "Yes, I will pay."

"Then get out of here." With that, the man retreated into a corner of the hut. He was not that far away, but he was invisible. Percival hurried towards the open door, stumbled out of the hut and squinted into the light. He thrashed his way through the bamboo, swatted aside insects and vegetation that grasped at him. From the direction of the sea came a surprising cool gust. He opened the door of the Peugeot, sat down in its furnace heat, and placed the key in the ignition.

Safely in his car, Percival felt a surge of defiance. The man's display was theatre, sheer dramatics. Dai Jai was fine. That thug had taken Percival for a fool, easy prey. Why would anyone harm the boy if he wished to obtain a ransom? Perhaps he should go back to bargain, to show he was not a sucker. The sum was more than twice the value of Chen Hap Sing. The shack was a short walk away, he could go back. Surely he could get the man down to seven hundred and fifty, or to fix a price in dollars. It would be easier to obtain the dollars. He should go back. The wind rustled the bamboo leaves. Percival did not get out of the car. Instead, he started the engine, put the Peugeot in gear, and allowed it to go forward. He told himself that Dai Jai was safe, that it was all about the price, nothing more.

CHAPTER 6

PERCIVAL GUIDED THE CAR OUT THROUGH the bamboo, past the graveyard, his fingers seized on the wheel. He turned onto the road, a rope of ochre dirt that wound through the forest. As if driving itself now, the car gathered speed, followed the path. Percival saw before him a line of dry blood, the skin of a shaved head split open, water falling drip by drip. He rolled the window down, greedy for fresh air.

He forced himself to focus on the trees, a comforting green curtain of leaves. As the car crested a hill, he caught sight of a dark shadow above in the canopy. The Peugeot glided past an old French army watchtower high on stilts. When they had driven to Cap St. Jacques for family holidays, Dai Jai had often asked to stop so he could climb one for the view. One of his school friends bragged of having done so and had dared Dai Jai to do the same. Percival had always refused to stop, telling Dai Jai that there wasn't enough time. He did not tell his son that it was often to the watchtowers that villagers had been taken for night-time abuses by the black-skinned soldiers whom the French marooned in these remote places. Screams travelled farther from a height. It would be bad luck to visit such a place. Following the withdrawal of the French army from Vietnam, the stations soon became obsolete. As the next war found its rhythm, the Americans fought differently, jumping from place to place like grasshoppers in their helicopters. Percival noticed his hands aching, willed them to loosen.

Around a bend, the road folded down once more out of wild jungle, into the marching rubber trees. In the very early years of the school, before the departure of the French, when Percival was scrabbling for a few students and a little money, they drove along this road in an old Deux Chevaux. The low hills had strained that car, so Percival drove with one eye on its temperature gauge. They stayed in a single-room beach cottage so small that, when lowered, the mosquito net covered not just the bed but the entire floor. In the evenings, once Dai Jai was asleep, Percival and Cecilia sat on the verandah, listened to the surf, allowed themselves to gradually disappear into dusk. They drank rice beer and, using a charcoal brazier, cooked skewers of fresh squid and prawns that Percival bought from the fishermen's baskets for a night-time snack.

Cecilia's family fortune was gone soon after the war. Much of it had been sunk with the Imperial Japanese Fleet, the remainder lost in risky ventures that Sai Tai had pursued to regain the family's position. The news had come that Sai Tai was reduced to living in the servants' quarters of her house on Des Voeux Road and renting out the house itself. Percival was secretly glad. This turn of events had dampened Cecilia's criticism of his own modest business advancements following the war.

Enjoying the simple pleasures of these beach holidays, having capitulated to exhaustion, they were better to each other. It was a relief, as if the patient noise of the water substituted for the racket of their usual fighting in Cholon. Even after they had divorced, Percival remained glad to have memories of Cap St. Jacques, though on the few occasions he had mentioned it, Cecilia pretended she had no recollection of the good times.

When crew-cut Americans in civilian clothes became more common in Saigon, the Percival Chen English Academy began to make decent profits. Once U.S. Army uniforms became a common sight, the school was soon making more money than Percival and Cecilia had ever imagined it could. They took a membership at the Cercle Sportif, an extravagance Cecilia had long coveted, now a minor expense. Percival bought a new Peugeot 403. The gears were changed by means of pushing square white buttons on the dash. Sometimes, when he reached to change the radio station, Percival would instead shift gears, causing the car to struggle and stall. Dai Jai thought this was very funny. But even with money, Percival and Cecilia fought just as much, perhaps more. Cecilia wished to holiday in Europe, and Percival had no interest. She would go alone, she said, and he told her not to bother coming back. When she discovered that he had sent thousands of piastres through the Teochow Clan to support China's Great Leap Forward, she dismissed him as a fool. She had headaches at night, and Percival discovered the charms of Mrs. Ling's introductions.

For their holidays, they began to rent a seaside villa from a Frenchman. The house's cook prepared at least five courses every night. He could cook French, Vietnamese, and a little Chinese, in keeping with the languages he spoke. His specialty was sea emperor's soup—a hot-and-sour broth heavy with pineapple, taro stems, prawns, and scallops. Dai Jai asked about this soup for weeks before going to Cap St. Jacques, and Percival would assure his son that the cook would make it. The villa was big enough that Cecilia and Percival could avoid one another, and they found it increasingly easy to do so.

Dai Jai was happiest during those beach holidays, for it was the only time he was able to attract his father's attention. In town, Percival was always preoccupied with the school, mah-jong games, money-circle dinners, and lovers. Each morning at Cap St. Jacques, Dai Jai was anxious to rush to the beach, and each morning Percival checked that his son's charm was securely fastened. Once, he said to his wife, "It will keep him safe."

"He is a boy. He will lose the lump of gold. Then, because you are so superstitious, you will mistake it for a terrible sign rather than simply a waste of money."

Through a gap in the trees, Percival saw a flash of sun, blue water in the distance, then took a breath of salt air. Percival realized he was driving towards the sea rather than towards the shanties that fringed Saigon. Not thinking, he had taken this direction. The car had brought him almost to the ocean. Percival eased on the brakes, let the car coast down a gentle slope and looked for an open spot to turn around. Then on a flat section, he took his foot off the brake pedal and put it back on the gas. It must be good luck to revisit these memories, for why else would the water be coming into view? Why else would his hands and his car have taken him here?

He tried not to think of Dai Jai, with the height of a man but the fragility of a boy, in an interrogation room furnished with a bucket, chairs, a bench, and an oil drum. Push it away. To dwell upon danger might itself bring bad luck. He made a quick entreaty to the ancestral spirits, forced himself to stare at the road. Beneath the wheels, the ground became a softer mix of earth and sand blown up from the sea. Through the open side window his eyes traced the line of searing white beach. With Cap St. Jacques just around the corner, he stopped short, parked beneath a tall palm. The fishermen's boats were pulled up after their early morning work, long since dry. Percival removed his shoes and got out of the car, walked a few steps and worked his feet into the warm sand. The palm fronds whispered reassurance.

Hadn't they come to this stretch of beach during the holiday before the divorce? He tried to pick out the spot where he had once feared the worst, unsure now of the precise location. He never brought up that day with Dai Jai for to do so would be bad luck, but he thought of it sometimes at the ancestral altar, when he thanked the ancestors and offered roasted meat and oranges.

One afternoon during what was to be their last family trip in 1958, the beach was empty at siesta time, but Dai Jai did not wish to return to the villa. He wanted to swim. Over the course of summers at Cap St. Jacques, Dai Jai had learned how to swim from the local boys, and he spent every possible moment in the water. Cecilia was stretched out on a lounge chair beneath an umbrella, complaining of the heat. There were no beach boys to run and bring cold drinks, and the air burned the inside of Percival's nostrils. He, too, wanted to escape the sun and lie beneath a fan, but since Cecilia wished to return to the villa, he declared that the boy should swim. Dai Jai bragged to his father that he could swim out to the open ocean, to where the waves no longer broke. He ran in and plunged headlong into the surf. Dai Jai darted beneath the waves as they crested. Cecilia asked Percival to call their son back, but Percival retreated beneath an umbrella and said nothing, pleased that Dai Jai had taken his father's permission as enough.

The heat caused time to stretch, and Cecilia closed her eyes. Percival half-watched Dai Jai for a while, expecting that he would soon turn back towards shore. The boy paused, waved, and continued to go out. Big for his eight years of age, he was becoming a good swimmer. After some time, Percival remarked, "He is swimming very fast, isn't he?"

Cecilia sat up and stared. They could see only Dai Jai's back bobbing up occasionally. Then Cecilia stood, shouted at their son, but already he was too far to hear. Between the peaks of the waves he disappeared. His arms were little punctuation marks in the ocean.

As they watched, Dai Jai shrank into the ocean. "He is being swept out!" she said. Although Percival's reflex was to disagree, it was true. The boy was going out faster than he could possibly be swimming. A large wave broke over him and he vanished in a long expanse of water. Cecilia yelled, "Go out after him!"

Percival stood, and then stopped, frozen. "I can't swim." Neither of them could.

"You are his father. Go!"

There was no doubt. The boy was being swallowed by the ocean. Percival ran out into the water, and was surprised at the force that tugged and buffeted him. He waded ahead. "Son! Come back, you're being pulled out!" His voice was lost in the crashing surf. Percival swung his hands high above him like flags, struggled forward into water that surged up to his neck. "Turn around! Swim back!" He threw the words uselessly into the ocean. Soon he was unable to see more than a few feet around him. A wave smashed over his head. Salty brine filled his mouth, stung his eyes. Percival looked into the moving walls of water, trying to see through them where Dai Jai had gone. He was caught by another wave, a larger one, that pushed him off his feet. He lost all direction as the wave roiled over him and carried him towards shore. He staggered up onto shore, coughing, his throat prickling with salt. Again, he ran into the surf, called, waved, but was unable to see the boy. Behind him, Cecilia yelled, "Go get your son, you useless man!"

Vietnamese children learned to swim as soon as they learned to walk, in the creeks, lagoons, and in the sea, but Percival had grown up in Shantou. During all these trips to Cap St. Jacques, he had never been into water deeper than his knees. He liked the look and smell of the ocean, but had never been interested in swimming. Now he flailed desperately into the water again, could not see Dai Jai. A crest lifted him up, his feet off the sand. He made the wild motions with his arms and legs that seemed to be what swimmers did, and felt his head submerged once more, a fist of water rammed down his throat. A swell gathered him, tumbled him over in white and blue, until he felt his knees scrape on the sand near the shore. On his hands and knees, sputtering, Percival vomited sea water.

Cecilia did not look at him. Her eyes were fixed on the horizon. "There he is! Look!"

Percival staggered a little way up the beach, searched in the direction of her pointed finger. At first, he saw only breaking waves and the line of the horizon.

"Where?"

Then he saw the black dot of his son's head appear. He was treading water. He had been pulled beyond where the waves were breaking, far enough that if they had not seen him swim out, they would never have known he was there. The boy began to swim towards them. He must have just realized how far he had been taken by the sea.

"He's fine, he's coming back," said Percival, his spirits surging like the water. They stood motionless in the sun. Percival stared at the horizon as the salt water dried to a fine itchy powder on his skin. Dai Jai swam towards the shore, but though his arms churned desperately in a small commotion, the boy continued to grow smaller.

Cecilia said, "He's being dragged farther out. The water is taking him away."

"He has his good luck charm," said Percival, a near whisper.

Cecilia stared at her husband, her fury beyond words.

Then Dai Jai vanished for a long few seconds. He appeared again, struggling now to stay afloat it seemed, his movements tired. Percival wished he had told the boy not to swim, that he had agreed with his wife that it was time for a siesta. He said, "I'll get a boat!" and clambered up the sandy incline. He looked up and down the deserted beach. It was midday, and the boats had already been pulled up high. He tried to shift one, but it was too heavy for him to budge. He cursed his soft city muscles. The sand shimmered, indifferent. Percival ran from boat to boat, hoped to find a fisherman taking a siesta. Finally, he found a man mending nets in the shade of a palm.

Percival's Vietnamese was worse when he was under pressure, and now he mingled vanishing words with panicked gestures. After he had managed to make himself understood, the fisherman looked at the horizon, squinted at the waves, "Swimming? Now, with the undertow? No one swims at this hour." He shook his head. "You Chinese city people." He rose slowly and chucked the nets into his boat.

The small outboard soon buzzed them out to where the water was quiet but heaved with deep, forceful swells. The fisherman cut the engine, and they sat on the wet thwart, bobbed up and down, peering into the shifting strokes of light on water. There was only the empty slap on the hull, and the boat itself creaking mournfully.

"He was out here," said Percival. "I saw him here last."

"The current is strong," said the fisherman uncomfortably. "Sometimes it sweeps north. He could have been taken up that way." He pulled the starter cord, and the engine coughed to life. They headed north until they came to a long, rocky arm that extended from the land into the ocean. The fisherman said he dared not go close. Percival watched the waves smash against the rocks and did not ask whether swimmers were sometimes pulled into them. They turned south and searched back and forth several times. After an eternity, the fisherman said that they must turn back. He was almost out of fuel. They returned, and pulled the boat up the beach. Silently, Percival pleaded with the ancestors' spirits. Surely they did not want Dai Jai to die in this foreign land.

The fisherman looked away. He commented upon the price of petrol. Dazed, Percival gave him a hundred-piastre note, far too much, and regretted doing so once he saw that the money seemed to make the fisherman so happy. The smile gave Percival a pain in his chest. The man ambled up the beach with his jerry can.

Cecilia ran up, touched Percival's arm. "Where is he? Where is our son?"

"I don't know," said Percival, close to tears. He imagined his son limp and motionless, drifting beneath the surface of the sea, eyes fixed open. "He disappeared in the water, but don't worry," said Percival, forcing out the words, as if by saying them it would make the image of Dai Jai's drowned body vanish. "He will be fine. The ancestral spirits will save him."

"Why didn't you find him?" Tears welled up in her eyes.

"They will protect him. And the sea goddess . . ."

Cecilia struck Percival with both fists, and then buried her face in them. She wept until the fisherman came back and began to fill the fuel tank. She turned to the fisherman. "Take me out into the water." The fisherman hesitated. She pleaded, "I will pay you a thousand piastres." He hurried to launch the craft.

Percival helped push the boat out. Cecilia was already inside, urging both him and the fisherman, weeping at the same time. Percival was about to jump in, but the fisherman told him that the small boat could not carry more than three people. Percival was about to say, "But we are three," when the fisherman cut him off. "We must leave a space for the boy."

Yes, of course. The third space. The fisherman still had hope, and for this Percival forgave him his happiness at the money. Percival trudged back to the water's edge and sat in the sand. His wet clothes clung heavily to his limbs. His mouth was dry, his lips swollen with the salt and sun. Now Percival felt the blood pulsing in his temples, and prayed to Chen Kai and all their relatives' ghosts to save Dai Jai. He opened his eyes, and the sight of thin brown legs filled him with joy.

"You want ice-cream-Coke-Heineken-young-girl? What you like? Suck-fuck-very-tight, I get for you quick-quick?" the beach boy asked in English.

He swore at the boy, who gave a single-finger salute and ambled away. From a distance, muffled by water, he could hear Cecilia's plaintive calls for Dai Jai from the small boat.

At the opposite end of the beach from the jagged rocks, there was the tiny outline of a figure. A boy. Was the figure familiar, the profile like his own son? Probably another beach runt, hawking drinks and his sister. At first, Percival wanted to stand, to run down the beach. His legs wouldn't move, did not want to carry him to disappointment. He was drawn by hope and paralyzed by fear. Percival closed his eyes and appealed to the ancestors' spirits not to play any more tricks. If they returned his son to him, Percival promised, he would redouble his efforts to honour the ancestors. He would offer whole roast ducks. He would burn real American dollars at their altar. He would return to China. He would bring Dai Jai with him. A promise, a bargain. He opened his eyes and got to his feet.

Did the figure wave? It shimmered in and out of the heat from the sand. After some long minutes, he thought he could just make out the face of his son, but how could he be sure of any features at this distance? Then a flash. A brilliant golden reflection winked from the boy's neck. The figure grew close, and larger, waved with both hands, and ran. Dai Jai embraced his father, arms around his waist, then tears came to Percival's eyes. He held his son to him, clasped the birdlike frame of his shoulders and arms. He could not remember ever having been so happy and grateful.

"*Ba*, why are you crying?" said the boy.

Percival calmed his heaving shoulders. He said, "I thought you were . . ." and then stopped himself. "I thought you were swimming very well," he said instead. He still had his arms around the boy, did not want to let go, worried that Dai Jai might prove himself a ghost if he did. But when he summoned the courage to loosen his grip, Dai Jai was still there. Percival said in a near whisper, "Dai Jai, how did you come back?"

The boy spoke matter-of-factly, as if he were talking about someone else. "I swam too far and got pulled out."

"Did you . . ." he wanted to ask if the boy had perceived the spirit of Chen Kai, if he had felt his grandfather's hand pull him to shore. Had the boy known the danger he had been in? Percival couldn't tell, but if Dai Jai had not realized it, why should he frighten the boy now?

"You must be tired. Did you learn your lesson?" Percival drew back a little, his hands on the boy's shoulders. He was not yet ready to let go of him.

"The ocean was so strong. Even when I struggled against it, the land got farther and farther away, and I was tired, scared too. Finally I realized that the best thing was to rest. I lay on my back and stared at the sky. I'm good at floating on my back. I decided to rest and figure out what to do. After a long time, the waves began to break over me once again. The tide had turned. It began to push me back to shore, and I swam with it, until I was swept up on that beach over there— beyond the rocks."

"We must return to China, we should go back home," said Percival. "If we had been in China . . ."

Dai Jai screwed up his forehead, "You always say that."

Percival could see that Dai Jai didn't understand him. Suddenly, he ached to be in his childhood home, to hear people speaking the Teochow dialect on the street, to lie on the old *kang*. He was being shown the dangers of being a *wa kiu*. He should take the boy home.

"Where is Mother?"

"She has gone to look for you, in a boat."

Soon, the fisherman landed the small craft. Percival let go of Dai Jai. Cecilia jumped out and ran to embrace her son.

With Cecilia standing there, Percival felt he should be stern with Dai Jai. He said, "Did you thank the ancestors?" Cecilia looked at her husband as if he was speaking a foreign language. He turned to Cecilia, on the verge of shouting without knowing why. "Did he? I want to know—is he grateful to his ancestors for saving him?" Dai Jai looked from his mother to his father and back again.

"Let's go to the villa." Cecilia turned away from her husband, her arm around their son. "The cook will make you anything you like." For the rest of the holiday, she said nothing else about the incident, and Percival began to feel that Cecilia's silence spoke more clearly than any criticism of him. After they returned to Cholon, she would often announce that she was going to Saigon for the day, and say noth- ing of what she had done when she returned. Percival pretended not to notice or care, and he often called Mrs. Ling. He thought on occasion of China, but the strong impulse to return there faded in the face of Cholon's distractions. The school was busier than ever, and money came easily. He had a run of good luck at the mah-jong tables. It had been only in the dizzying emotional height of the moment, he told himself, that he had promised the ancestors he would return. It was not practical. He offered two ducks, and burned fifty dollars. That should be enough. Several months later, when a raft of new legislation in South Vietnam included legalized divorce, Cecilia enjoyed a front-page photo of her own smiling, immaculately made-up face in the *Far East Daily*, a Chinese-language daily newspaper. The accompanying article explained that she was the first woman in Cholon to divorce her husband.

CHAPTER 7

PERCIVAL DROVE UP THE COASTAL HILLS away from the beach. He took a different road than the one he had arrived on, avoiding the graveyard. Daylight failed, and he pressed on into darkness. When he reached the rubber plantations, which were known for night-time kidnappings, he cut his lights and drove as quickly as he dared by moonlight. Entering the city, he was stopped at a checkpoint and paid the soldier to ignore his curfew violation. He went straight to Cecilia's villa and pounded on the door until a light appeared. A few seconds later Cecilia's voice asked who it was.

"Your first lover," he said. The door cracked open.

A bit of leg, her hand up against the door frame. "Oh, it's you," she said. Cecilia rubbed her eyes. She lowered her arm and uncocked the pistol that she usually kept in her purse. She stood blocking the doorway and pulled her silk kimono around herself. She had been ready to seduce or to threaten, but Percival required neither.

He said, "Let's go inside?" Now that he was here, he realized that he had not made his usual careful plan of what to say to Cecilia. He was just here, a blank impulse.

She did not move. "You must have news of Dai Jai," she said. "That had better be why you're here."

"You're not alone?" Percival peered into the darkness behind her. He longed for her now, not for sex, but for them to deal with this situation together.

"Is that any of your business? Is there something about our son?"

"He is being ransomed."

"Then he is safe?" She breathed relief.

"They want a thousand taels of gold. How much do you have?"

"But how is he? Has he been hurt?"

In the hallway there was a movement, an American voice. "You're up. Everything alright, honey?" She waved the man back to bed.

"Yes, he's fine, I'm sure of it," said Percival, lying. "Is that your surgeon friend back there?"

"Who are the kidnappers?"

"I met one. He didn't give a name."

"You expected him to? But you must have got some idea of who he was, some impression? Did he give you a letter from Dai Jai, a picture, some kind of proof that he is unharmed?"

"He did most of the talking. I met the man outside Saigon. I couldn't change the price."

"I don't care about the cost. I care about our son. Where did you meet this mysterious man?"

"Near the rubber plantations."

"Is he Viet Cong? The Americans are afraid of fighting there—they say that area is a rat's nest of tunnels."

"No. A simple gangster. Just a profiteer. He can get Dai Jai out, and we have to pay." Was he Viet Cong? Percival didn't care, but he felt embarrassed that he had not fished for more clues, for some idea of who the man was, and where there might be hazards. "Dai Jai is safe. They just want the money," he said.

"Then we will find it," she said. "Meet me tomorrow evening at the Cercle."

The next morning, having hardly slept, Percival pounced on Mak as soon as he arrived at the door of the school. "Who is that contact of yours?"

"Was there a problem?" Mak said, clearing his throat. He took off his glasses, which were clean, and wiped the lenses carefully with his handkerchief. "He can rescue your son." He lifted the glasses by the metal arms, held them to the sun outside the doorway, and examined them minutely.

"He was a little blunt." Was it worth pressing? Mak always came through, and in this instance was doing Percival a large favour. He had his ways, and his contacts. It had taken him a while to get to this man, so whatever Mak knew of him he must be obliged to keep to himself. The most valuable friend was a discreet one. Percival said, "As long as he can do it. He wants a thousand taels of gold. I must find reliable dealers, not the kind who dilute the metal or shave the edges of the bars. They must deliver quickly!"

Mak put on his glasses. "I will make inquiries. We'll get this done."

That afternoon, Mak brought a Cantonese gold dealer to the school office, for whom Percival emptied the school safe of all its American dollars. Percival counted the seventy-five paper-wrapped tael leaves jealously, put them in a slim valise, and sealed them in the school safe. The safe held about seven hundred and fifty thousand piastres as well, perhaps another hundred taels' worth, but the gold dealers did not accept piastres. They would have to be changed to dollars first.

That evening, Percival and Cecilia met at the Cercle and agreed that Percival would scour Cholon while Cecilia raised money and bought gold in Saigon. Then, when she heard that Percival had paid fifty-two dollars per tael, she complained that his obvious panic had allowed him to be gouged. "Why did you let yourself be cheated? I can get an even fifty. If you buy too much like that, it will force up the market price."

"You said you didn't care about price."

"That doesn't mean I want to get rates that some dumb GI would get. Just bring me your dollars or piastres or whatever, and I'll make them into gold."

"No, that's alright, I'll handle it myself." Percival had brought the piastres with him to have Cecilia change them into dollars. Mak had promised to bring another gold dealer in the morning who wanted those dollars. Percival had also hoped it would be a reason to go to her house, in order for her to get dollars from the safe. They could speak quietly, though he wasn't sure what he wanted to say. "I have to go now." He stood, not mentioning the money that Han Bai was guarding in the car.

He had a better use for the money, anyhow. He told Han Bai to take him to Le Grand Monde. When he arrived at the raucous, incandescent casino, Percival ignored the croupier's call and the girls who sidled up to him. He accepted a highball glass of whisky from a hostess but only took a small sip. He found a seat at a quiet mah-jong table where he recognized the players and knew that a big-money game must be under way. He took fifty thousand on the first game. Luck would be with him. One good night and he could get enough for all the gold that was required.

THE NEXT MORNING, PERCIVAL LAY IN bed holding his pounding head. A banging on the door.

"Chen Pie Sou!"

"What?"

"I'm sorry to disturb you. Where are the dollars? The gold dealer is here."

"Send him away, Mak. Apologize. We'll call him." Percival rolled out of bed and vomited into the porcelain basin on the nightstand. After he had gone bust last night, there was nothing to do but drink. Now his stomach was empty, his mouth sour, and he drank a little water from the pitcher on his desk. He said, "I don't have any dollars. I'll come down in a bit." The floorboards creaked as Mak went slowly away.

Mak did not express anger at Percival. Even if he had, it could not have made Percival sink any lower into his deep pit of self-loathing. In the school office, Mak said quietly, "*Hou jeung*, you must not play mah-jong anymore. Not until we have dealt with this problem. We must conserve money." Not lose it. He did not say that, a good friend always. "Alright, I will arrange a money-circle dinner. You still have enough to pay for a small banquet, don't you?"

"Of course I do." He would have to run a tab at the restaurant.

Each day, Mak had new contacts. He helped Percival find money circles and loan sharks to lend him piastres and dollars, and other people to sell him gold. Percival conducted the deals hastily, agreed to six percent monthly interest, fifty-three dollars per tael. He met with Chinese and Vietnamese businessmen and mafia, with French jewellers who spoke Vietnamese, and with Sikh gold merchants who spoke Cantonese. Percival preferred to do business with Chinese, but now the only colour he saw was gold. At Chen Hap Sing, he slept only in fragments. He dreamt of Dai Jai and woke just as his son's head split open, screaming out of his nightmare, again and again.

Cecilia had her gold jewellery melted into bars, the gems pried out and traded for more gold. Her American business contacts were more helpful in finding gold than they had been in finding Dai Jai, and she was able to squeeze better deals from her transactions than Percival. They met every couple of days at the Cercle to make an anxious tally. In ten days, they had over five hundred taels between them. Cecilia complained that a thousand taels was enough to buy herself a better ex-husband, and cursed him for the boy's arrest. "People are starting to whisper about how much gold is at Chen Hap Sing," she said. Under the table, she slipped Percival a snub-nosed, double-barrelled, two-shot Remington pistol. It had the weight of a palm-sized stone, and it fit in his pocket. "You see? Now you are in the money business like me," she said. "It's only good up close. You have one shot to scare someone. If you need the second one, aim for the belly. That way you'll hit something."

From then on, Percival took the hoard of metal out of the safe at night and slept with it under his mattress. This required two trips up the stairs, lugging one valise each time. He kept the pistol under his pillow. Two weeks after the meeting in the hut, the night before an ancestor worship day, Percival dreamt of his father. It was an old dream from his childhood, one of flying. They soared high over a cold, jagged peak. It was the Gold Mountain for which Chen Kai had abandoned his home, a mass of sharp glittering angles and dagger crags of lustrous wealth. Percival congratulated his father on his success, but bragged that he himself would become yet more wealthy. Even as Chen Kai nodded with approval, saying that a son must surpass the father, Percival began to fall from the sky. His power of flight was gone. He hurtled towards the ground, calling out in terror to his father, but falling alone to be impaled by gold shards. Gasping, Percival woke already clutching the pistol, jumped out of bed and pulled out one valise. He fumbled open the clasps, caressed the gold. He turned on the light beside his bed and counted it, his fingers dropping the pieces. Then the other case. All there. He put it under the mattress and lay on his back. He stared at the fine teak beams in the ceiling, in the house that Chen Kai had used his fortune to build.

In 1933, on his first visit back to China after three years away, Chen Kai brought enough silver coins with him to buy two *li* of stream-fed rice paddy. He rented it out so that Muy Fa would have an income even without his remittances. He hosted a dinner for the village and roasted two fat pigs and three geese to celebrate becoming a landlord. He poured liquor freely for the village men, and gave everyone red-dyed eggs as if he were celebrating a birth.

During that visit, Chen Kai lavished his son with Annamese treats and hard English candies. They went for walks in Zhong Shan Park, where they watched the fat goldfish in ponds and snacked on candied peanuts. Chen Kai gave Chen Pie Sou painted French lead soldiers and took him to play with them on their newly bought land. They played "Manchuria," making the red-and-blue figurines the Chinese and using lumps of mud for the Imperial Japanese Army. Chen Pie Sou liked to be General Ma Zhanshan, and he always defeated the Japanese at the 1931 battle at Nenjiang Bridge, stomping gleefully on the lumps of mud. They played this so often that Chen Pie Sou came to believe this was what had actually happened. At night, Chen Kai made a point of filling the *kang* with heaps of coal, making it so hot that it was difficult for Chen Pie Sou to sleep.

Chen Kai doted upon his son during the day, but was distracted in the evenings. Every night he greeted visitors as if he were holding court—men who sought advice about travelling to the Gold Mountain, men who hoped to borrow money, and men who wished to taste French brandy. His success abroad had transformed Chen Kai from pauper to landlord, a celebrity in his own village. Chen Pie Sou longed for his father to sit at his side while he fell asleep. He lay on the *kang* each night listening to the words of his father and the other men become slurred with drink, excited with ever wilder and grander stories of sublime foreign pleasures, and fortunes of property and gold. Chen Pie Sou toyed with the lump at his neck. How could such a small, rough piece of metal be so valuable?

Before departing, Chen Kai paid his son's school fees for the next year. He had noticed that his son liked eggs, and promised to leave enough money that the boy could eat an egg every day.

"Must you leave again, Father?" Chen Pie Sou asked.

"I must go back to earn money. For your eggs."

"But I don't need so many eggs. And you have bought two *li* already. We are wealthy landlords now."

"You think so because you've never seen wealth, real wealth." He tousled Chen Pie Sou's hair. "Son, amongst the Annamese it is so easy to make money. We Chinese are smarter than they are and can get rich from them. It would be foolish for me to stay in Shantou."

"But when you have enough, you will come back."

"Yes, yes, I will, but . . . I don't have enough just yet."

"How much is enough?"

In his father, Chen Pie Sou now sensed a hunger for something that he could not understand. Perhaps his father could not express it. When he had first left Shantou in 1930, Chen Kai had been desperate to find a way to feed his family. He had been agitated by a need that Chen Pie Sou knew in the gnawing feeling in his belly each morning, in the careful rice portions and small pieces of bony meat that they sometimes ate. Now there was enough money to eat eggs every day, but his father wanted something more. Chen Kai had an empty space that needed to be filled, but Chen Pie Sou could not understand what must be obtained to satisfy that void and bring his father home.

"I'll know when I have it. Then I will return to China for good."

Now, staring at the ceiling beams of Chen Hap Sing, Percival remembered Dai Jai as a small boy. Percival had often sat at his son's side at bedtime. Even after Dai Jai no longer needed someone to be at his bedside, Percival would sometimes sit listening for Dai Jai's breathing to slow. After the breaths became deep and measured, the boy's limbs would shift. Arms and legs relaxed into sleep, the alertness of day drained out of them. On some nights, particularly if he and Cecilia were not talking, Percival would then go out to fill his eyes with light, his hands with money, his lap with a girl. He consumed all of these voraciously, because they promised to fill a void. But then after these fleeting ecstasies, he emerged more empty.

It occurred to him that he could get out of bed, go find a game and a girl. This thought came like a sign on a road, to a place that he had no wish to visit just now. All of those distractions which had been so enticing in their moment felt like nothing, not even their promise of satisfaction could be summoned. If only he could sit at Dai Jai's bedside, watching him fall asleep.

PERCIVAL OBTAINED ADVANCES ON TUITION FOR the next semester. He went to money-lending circles, took as many shares as he could, and then used this cash to buy gold. His monthly repayments would be huge, but he would worry about that later. The Peugeot went to a garage as guarantee on a loan. Percival visited the Teochow Clan Association treasurer and was able to borrow two hundred and fifty taels, though only by signing a promissory note on Chen Hap Sing. This was a worry, for the head of the association had always admired the old trade house. Even with Percival and Cecilia's combined efforts, it was not easy to find so much gold on short notice. His nightmares—of Dai Jai's splitting skull, or of falling towards the Gold Mountain—woke him nightly in a panic. Daytime was the painful daze of sleep deprivation, as he desperately traded everything, anything, for more gold.

Three weeks after the meeting in the shack, and over a month following the arrest, Percival obtained the last few taels one evening by pawning his Tissot wristwatch. He called Mak. He had accumulated five hundred and ninety taels. He phoned Cecilia, who he knew had raised four hundred and ten, and went to her house. She had her portion wrapped in two cloth bundles. She handed them to Percival. "I'm counting on you to get our son back."

"I've sent word to Mak, to arrange a meeting."

Cecilia embraced Percival, but when he put his arms around her, she pushed him away, tears in her eyes. "Go."

The next morning, Percival ate his breakfast on the balcony. Below, on the pink stone steps of St. Francis Xavier, the Catholic priests and Buddhist monks chatted amiably. Percival wondered if he should donate to the church. He had already given especially generous alms to the local temple and lit one of the gigantic incense coils in prayer for Dai Jai. Percival had never been interested in the white man's faith, but perhaps he should give the church something, just in case it might help. He ate without tasting. Foong Jie was putting a sliced boiled egg in his noodles every morning. She must have noticed how little he was eating. He picked at the egg. He stared at Dai Jai's vacant chair. Foong Jie had tried to put it away when Dai Jai was arrested, but Percival stopped her from tempting such bad luck. Each morning, he willed himself to sit across from the empty chair. Mak arrived early, well before the start of classes. The fortune in gold sat on the table, two briefcases, two cloth bundles. Percival did not dare let them out of his sight. Mak glanced at the hoard, sat down, and said, "The meeting is today. In the same place."

"In the countryside? How will I get there?"

"I've borrowed a car for you—Chief Mei's. It has a police plate, so they won't search it at checkpoints. Safer for the ransom. I told Mei it was the least he could do for you."

"You think of everything, friend."

"Get that gold off your hands," said Mak. "All of Cholon knows what you have here."

Percival pulled the small pistol out of his pocket and checked the two rounds.

Mak said, "*Hou jeung*, leave it with me."

"I have to be sure to get Dai Jai."

"You will. That won't help you." When Percival did not reply, Mak said, "Just do as he says. He could easily turn the gun on you, old friend. Have you ever shot one?"

"No," said Percival, searching Mak's face. He wanted to ask, Who is he? Why do you trust him?

Mak realized the question in Percival's eyes. He said, "A friend of a friend."

Percival opened one of the cases. He looked at the gold, the smaller leaves tied together in ten-tael bundles, the bars glistening and cold, a fortune in metal, about seven and a half million piastres' worth, most of it borrowed. He was trusting Mak with this, and more importantly with Dai Jai's return. "You are sure that he will give me Dai Jai?"

"Have I ever led you wrong?"

Percival closed the case, clasped it shut. To pay for its contents, he would have to return more than he had borrowed. That was the nature of debt. These were sums that his own father could only have dreamed about when he left China. It did not matter, as long as Dai Jai was safe.

"Mak, will you take a few thousand piastres to the church for me? I'll pay you back."

"But you're not religious. Don't worry, you'll be safe at the meeting."

"It's not *my* safety I'm thinking about." He handed his friend the gun.

After breakfast, with the gold in the spare tire well of Mei's Citroën DS with police plates, Percival set off and drove northeast out of the city. He nodded to the soldiers, only slowing at the checkpoints, which is what a district police chief would have done. They saluted. When he arrived at the bamboo grove, he turned from the main road, drove past the graveyard, walked through the bamboo to the concrete shack, and found that the door was already open.

He called out, "Dai Jai?"

A voice, not his son's. "Come into the centre of the room." It was the same man as before.

He went in. He hesitated, his eyes slow to adapt to the dark.

"Please walk forward, Headmaster Chen. Where is the gold?"

"Where is my son?"

"This is not your school. I ask. You answer. The gold?"

"In the car."

"The keys."

"I want to see my son."

"Do you suppose, Chinaman, that you are in a position to make demands? Walk forward three paces," said the man.

His orders had military precision, thought Percival. He still could not make out a face. It figured that the ransomer was a soldier, for how else could he get to Dai Jai? All of the South Vietnamese Army could be bought, thought Percival scornfully, gratefully. Percival walked into the middle of the room, his feet nervous on the uneven ground. Emerging from darkness, the bench, the oil drums, the stocky figure. Where was his son? There was only one silhouette.

"Put down the car keys."

"I want my son first." Percival heard his voice rise.

Quick footsteps, and then from behind an arm curled like a snake around his neck. Cold metal pressed into Percival's ear, a metallic click. The arm tightened, choked.

"Let's not complicate this," said the man, squeezing. "Where in the car is the gold?"

"Under the spare tire." Lightheaded, almost fainting, Percival felt the keys snatched from his hand.

"You Chinese always find money. Just like rats find garbage. Sit down on the ground."

He half-fell down. "Where is Dai Jai?"

"Put your hands on your head." The man backed away from him towards the door.

"I have brought you the gold." Percival could not keep himself from pleading. "Where is my son?"

"Go home." He stood at the door, blotting out the light. "My advice is that the best thing for you is to go home."

There was a clang of metal. The door slammed shut, and then darkness. Percival was alone. He heard the man doing something to the door, and then a rustle in the grass going away from the shack. He rushed to the door. He pushed on it, but it did not open. It was blocked from the outside. Booby trapped? He pounded it with his fists. But even if it was wired with a grenade, why should he care, if he did not recover Dai Jai? Percival took a few steps back and ran into the door with all his weight. It shifted a little. He felt a cold sweat, furious with himself. He had been cheated of a fortune and did not have his son.

He cursed in the Teochow dialect, then in Cantonese. He struck the corrugated metal with his shoulder, and heard a slight crack, felt a little give. From farther back, he ran at the door again. There was the sound of wood splintering, and the door opened enough to allow a crack of light. He backed away, ran at it once more and struck it with his other shoulder. Again and again, each time rewarded by the sound of wood splitting, until something snapped and the door sighed open. It had been blocked from the outside by a rod of green bamboo hung on hooks.

Through the leaves of the grove, the Citroën shone white hot. He stumbled towards it, batting away the heavy growth. The trunk was open, the spare on the ground. Only now, his limbs ached with the effort of his escape. Percival felt empty. His hands bled. Then, as he saw the car better through the shafts of bamboo, he noticed that the passenger-side rear door was ajar. He heard a plaintive sound, a muffled voice, and ran towards the car, ignoring the sharp leaves which drew quick lines of blood on his forearms. He shouted, "I'm coming!" Dai Jai was on the floor, blindfolded and bound. "You are here!" Percival rushed to pull his son up and helped him sit on the back seat. Dai Jai was dirty, and he stank. Percival fumbled to pull off the blindfold. Dai Jai's right eye was swollen shut, a shining dark egg of bruised eyelid. His head was shaved, but not split open. He wore the same school clothes in which he had been arrested, now stained with blood and torn into rags. There were bruises on his arms and body, some older and some fresh. As he had years ago on the beach, Percival embraced his son with relief and happiness at having him back. He seized him in his arms, pressed his face to the boy's stubbled scalp. The hard lump of gold was at his neck. Percival whispered his thanks to the ancestors' spirits, to Chen Kai's ghost.

"I'm so happy, son. I thought you were . . ." He must not say it. He thanked the ancestors' spirits again, for he had feared that he would next see his son in their world. The strength of his fear now transformed itself into joy. "I didn't know when I would see you again. You are safe now, I will keep you safe."

"Oh, no," said Dai Jai. "They arrested you, too, *ba*?"

"No, I have ransomed you."

"I don't understand." Dai Jai looked around wildly.

"I've bought your freedom."

"Then I am not going to be shot? Where are we?"

Percival clawed at the cords on Dai Jai's hands. They were loosely tied, easy to unwind, not meant to hold him for long. "We are near the rubber plantations, outside of Bien Hoa."

"Where is the guard?"

"We are alone. We are halfway to Cap St. Jacques," said Percival, smiling through his own wet eyes. He said hopefully, "Should we go there? Should we go and have your favourite, sea emperor's soup?"

Dai Jai stared at his father with his left eye as if he were a stranger. Then he began to shake. "They said they would kill me today. They took me from the cell, yelling, hitting, and said it was my turn to die." Dai Jai cried, tears flowing freely from his left eye and welling out from between the swollen lids of his right.

Percival embraced the boy again, held his shoulders. "It was just to scare the other prisoners." If only they were with their own people, in China, none of this would have happened. Here in Vietnam, they were vulnerable, made to suffer and then to pay for relief from it. "It was an act for the other prisoners. To make it look like you were being killed, not freed. You are safe. Your father is here. I paid a huge ransom." He would have paid any sum.

Dai Jai looked around, crazed. "We are in a graveyard, Father. We are two ghosts in our graveyard. They said I would die today."

"No, don't say that, it's bad luck," he whispered, shushing the boy as if someone might hear. For an instant, his own joy swung back to terror. Then he calmed himself and said to the boy, "I think you are hungry, yes, so hungry that you can't think clearly. No one is dead. There are no ghosts here. You will feel better after eating and resting. It will be as if you were never arrested." If only they could go back, to a favourite soup, a villa near the sea.

After a moment, Dai Jai said, "Yes, of course, Father. Eating and resting. You're right." He nodded mechanically, obediently.

Percival helped his son lie down in the back of the car, settling him in a way that was least painful for his wounds. He began the drive back to Saigon. Soon, Dai Jai fell asleep. Percival saw the wisdom of this car. The soldiers saluted him at checkpoints, and he drove through. Even if he had been stopped, they wouldn't think twice about a beaten prisoner in the back of a police chief's car. He would bring a doctor and make sure that Dai Jai received the very best care. He would have Foong Jie pamper the boy and nurse him around the clock. Once Dai Jai regained his strength, and once his scars faded, Percival assured himself, it would be as if none of this had ever happened.

CHAPTER 8

THE NEXT MORNING, PERCIVAL SENT Foong Jie to fetch Dr. Hua, the most expensive doctor in Cholon. He arrived in a short-sleeved shirt of fine white cotton, open at the neck, pressed white trousers, and excellent sturdy brown shoes in the fashion of an old French plantation manager. He carried his heavy leather bag and stopped short in the doorway when he saw Dai Jai's condition.

"Do everything you can to mend him," said Percival to the doctor.

The doctor looked skeptically at the boy's bruised face. "Yes, *hou jeung*, I shall do the very best." He extracted a starched white lab coat from his bag, pulled it on with a flourish, and buttoned it up the front. He pried open Dai Jai's swollen right eyelid, shone a flashlight into the bloodshot membranes, and made a clucking sound with his tongue. The physician opened Dai Jai's shirt, prodded here and there with his stethoscope, and flitted over the boy's abdomen with his hands. He pulled Dai Jai up from his bed into a seated position, seemed not to notice the boy's gasp of pain, and continued his examination. Finally, he held his stethoscope in his hand and proclaimed that beneath Dai Jai's bruised face, the eyes and brain were intact. He said that the boy's nose had been broken but was straight, that several ribs were fractured but the lungs beneath were breathing, and that the three teeth which had been knocked out would never give him cavities. He alone laughed at this joke. Foong Jie glared at the doctor as she gently helped Dai Jai to settle back into bed.

The Cholon-born, Paris-trained, Chinese doctor recommended an American medication that he had conveniently available for sale in his bag. He wrote a prescription in Chinese for a herbal infusion, and requested payment in American dollars.

"I will have it sent to you tomorrow," said Percival.

"I'm so sorry to be a bother," the doctor bowed, "ah . . . I have obligations that I must pay today. Might I impose upon you to settle up now?"

Percival felt his face redden. His credit was no longer any good. In Cholon, it was impossible either to gain wealth or owe it without it being widely known. Perhaps his stature remained—the doctor was at least being polite. Percival went to his room, retrieved his last few American dollars, and brought them to pay the bill. As the doctor was leaving, Percival looked at the American medication. He wanted to call down the hallway, *And he will be as he was before?*

As if he had heard Percival's thoughts, the doctor turned and bowed. "*Hou jeung*, time never reverses itself, but he will heal if you allow him to." At the top of the stairs, the doctor was nearly knocked over by Cecilia rushing up. She stopped for a moment and put her arms around Percival, then, as if she did not want to be caught doing this, she let go of him and hurried into Dai Jai's room.

Percival stood alone in the hallway. From the doorway, he saw Cecilia leaning over their son, holding him silently, stroking his forehead. Dai Jai's tears flowed freely, and he clung to his mother, who reassured him with a steady, calm voice. She must have hurried over as soon as Percival had called to say that Dai Jai was home. Her hair was hastily tied back, and there were dark circles under her eyes, which she must have carefully hidden with powder for their recent meetings at the Cercle Sportif. She, too, had been losing sleep during their son's absence, Percival realized. He felt as sheepish and unsure of himself as when he had once admired Cecilia from afar at the Christmas dance on Queens Road. Without makeup, her naked face betrayed its creases and lines of worry, the years and troubles that had passed. They had been Dai Jai's age when they met, and not much older when they married.

Cecilia sat with Dai Jai until he fell asleep. When she came out into the hallway, where Percival had remained, she said, "Thank you for bringing him back."

It was so strange to hear her thank him, that he had no words with which to reply.

She allowed herself to be folded into Percival's arms, and now her tears were released. "Why did they have to hurt him?"

"I don't know."

"Wasn't the money enough?" Tears streamed down her cheeks, and Percival found himself stroking her hair. It was thinner than he remembered. What if they had grown up a little before they met, he wondered.

"We have him back, that's the main thing."

"But look what they've done to our baby," she sobbed.

"Best to forget . . ." said Percival. "He is back with us, whole. He will heal."

She nodded, buried her face in his shoulder. Percival moved a little, thought of kissing her forehead. She pulled back. Of course, if they had been older, if Cecilia had been more free from her mother, she would never have even looked at him. She withdrew from his touch and said, "When will you repay me my four hundred and ten taels?"

"But that was . . . your share," said Percival.

"I'm not sharing in your stupidity," she said. She wiped away the tears, sniffed, he could see her making her face hard. "Your idiocy got him arrested. But I'm thankful that you rescued him. I'll give you a break on the interest." She turned, and fled down the stairs.

UNDER PERCIVAL'S WATCHFUL EYE, Foong Jie nursed Dai Jai, spooned lukewarm rice congee to his lips and cleaned his wounds with a washbowl and cloth. Cecilia visited frequently. She brought chocolate éclairs and lemon tarts from la Patisserie St. Honoré, but Dai Jai could only manage a few bites. One day, she brought a tremendous bouquet of gladiolas for his bedside, but their beauty seemed only to make Dai Jai look worse. Percival hovered around him constantly at first, but found that he didn't know what to say. He wished he had not opposed the directive to give Vietnamese language classes and would have done anything to take that day back, but he could not apologize to his son for that. Not after what had happened when Dai Jai tried to impress his father with his own patriotism. Percival was amazed at Dai Jai's strength in having survived his imprisonment, but how could he say anything positive about such a horrible ordeal? How could he even mention it, when the main thing was to forget? Let it go, he decided. It would fade with time, like the bruises.

More crucially, he told himself, after a few days of uncomfortable hovering over his son, he must find money to pay his debts. Foong Jie had the care of Dai Jai well in hand, and he would leave it to her. Time was chasing him, as he had borrowed at high rates. He added an evening class and another full daytime class to the Percival Chen English Academy's schedule, both of which he discounted for students who could pay a full year's tuition immediately. Though it had been years since he had actually taught on a regular basis, he took the new classes himself to avoid having to pay another teacher. This gave him enough money to pay back the Sikh lenders, whose debts bore the highest rates. He sent drips of money via Mak to the Teochow temple, keeping Chen Hap Sing out of the creditors' hands. He did not want to go himself, lest they call him on the whole amount. After the evening class was over, Percival sat at Dai Jai's bedside as he fell asleep. This was the best time, for in the dark it was not necessary to say anything. Dai Jai could pretend that he was asleep, and Percival could pretend that he believed this was so.

Once Dai Jai was actually sleeping, Percival went out to work the casinos. He did not drink or take girls to bed. He counted his cards at blackjack and played poker only with weak players whom he knew he could read. He had promised Mak to stay away from the mah-jong tables with their large stakes and unpredictable emotions, and he did. Normally, Percival was propelled by the excitement of possibility, the belief that the next hand might contain a big win. Now, he felt a sobering motivation, a fear of losing. He disciplined himself to play for moderate amounts and pushed aside his usual taste for large risks and payoffs. When he was down, he worked his way back methodically. By the end of each night, he came out ahead.

The school had been at capacity with five hundred or so students, and now it swelled with almost a hundred more. For the new Vietnamese classes, Mak took the job of instruction upon himself, careful to fulfil the Saigon directives to the letter. To help his friend generate some extra cash, Mak advertised tutorials for job-seekers, HOW TO WIN AMERICAN FRIENDS AND JOBS. These were so popular that one morning, as Percival returned from a long and reasonably profitable night at Le Grand Monde, Mak came to him with a proposition. "If your students could be exempted from the English proficiency exams that American employers require, I'm sure we could increase tuition. What if we got a special designation for the school, a certification?"

Percival rubbed his eyes, exhausted. "Do it. Anything that will bring more money."

"It might take a while."

"Mak, I need cash now," said Percival. He collapsed on the cot in his office, still in his shirt. Each morning, he closed his eyes until his classes started. Brief siestas sustained him between teaching, gambling, and sitting at his son's bedside. He managed to get the Peugeot out of hock from the garage, but soon was forced to use it as collateral again, to keep the Clan Association at bay. He bought lotus leaves of mosquito larvae when he remembered. The tanks were filthy, but the fish lived.

For several weeks, Dai Jai stayed in bed. He observed the square quietly from the window, but as his appetite and a little of his strength returned, he devoured the French cakes and snacks, as well as the expensive pâtés and rounds of La vache qui rit cheese that his mother brought. There was a growing stack of American comic books that she bought for him in Saigon. Normally, Percival would have criticized the cheeseburgers, French fries, and pizza that Cecilia brought from the U.S. Army PX, and banished the cans of Coca-Cola and the Marvel comics. He would have admonished her that the Chinese stomach could not tolerate very much of this Western food, and why should their son read about superheroes in ridiculous costumes when there were so many real Chinese heroes of history? In the face of Dai Jai's enjoyment of these things, Percival held his tongue, and responded with a steady stream of pork buns, fresh papayas, custard apple, ginseng infusions, sweet Chinese bean soups, and kung fu novels.

At the time of the divorce, Percival had given Cecilia a sum of money to buy a house and start her own business. In exchange, Dai Jai would live with him. Now, when he saw the natural tenderness between mother and son, Percival combatted his jealousy by telling himself that it was certainly best for Dai Jai to live at Chen Hap Sing with him. What kind of example did Cecilia provide, taking men to the house and answering the door with a gun?

Once he had enough strength to walk a little, Dai Jai drifted through the house with a halting gait. He carried a small bowl in which to spit the blood that he coughed up. When Percival listened to the radio, Dai Jai often lingered nearby. The radio sheltered them from having to speak to one another. When Percival glanced at his son, he could see only his scabby wounds and the discoloured bruises smeared up and down his arms.

Life would be better after the bruises healed. Then, he would be able to look at his son without imagining blows landing, without thinking of the methods of the National Police Headquarters, without replaying once more what he should have done differently to avoid this trouble. Dai Jai asked one morning if he might come and join his father for breakfast on the balcony. "But you should rest," Percival said reflexively. "You must heal."

"It is too quiet in my room."

"I cannot let you climb the steep stairs to the third floor. You are not steady on your feet. What if you were to fall? No, you must rest until you are better."

"Yes, Father," said Dai Jai in a near-whisper.

Percival longed for the boy's return to the chair across from him at the breakfast table, but he wanted everything to be exactly as it was before. He wanted to sit across from his healthy, though headstrong, son. Soon enough the boy would be healed and would join him at the table.

Dai Jai had always been bold, given to boisterous statements and gestures. Now he was quiet. The only time he was loud was when he screamed in the middle of the night. Sometimes there were no discernible words, and sometimes he cried out, "Stop! No!" his eyes still closed, his arms raised to protect his head from phantom assailants. At the ancestral altar, the only place it was safe to express both gratitude and fear, Percival now thanked the spirits for saving Dai Jai both from the sea and from prison. He also begged that his son's nightmares would stop. Often, when Percival heard screams escaping from Dai Jai's bedroom door, he fled to the casinos. After all, he told himself, as he hailed a cyclo, he was going out into the night to help pay the debt.

It took the remainder of the school semester for Dai Jai to be physically well again and finally join his father for breakfast on the balcony. His bruises were gone, but he remained hesitant, easily startled. Percival offered to take him out to the places he liked—for an ice cream in Saigon, or perhaps a lime soda at the Cercle. With the onset of the mid-year heat, Percival suggested hopefully that they take a beach holiday. This sounded a little ridiculous even as he heard himself voice the idea. Dai Jai always replied that he still felt weak and wasn't quite ready to go out. In the late afternoons, when it was sweltering upstairs, Dai Jai retreated to an empty ground-floor classroom of Chen Hap Sing to read. Once, from behind closed classroom doors, Percival thought he heard a girl's gentle voice as well as Dai Jai's. Percival asked Foong Jie about it, for she saw everything that happened. Foong Jie shrugged. It must be Dai Jai's Annamese sweetheart, and Percival realized that he did not care. It was better to allow Dai Jai this comfort. Then, one day, Percival looked out from the balcony and thought he saw Dai Jai and a girl on the other side of the square, their backs to Chen Hap Sing, buying young coconuts with crushed ice. The boy turned, yes it was his son. Percival was overjoyed that Dai Jai had ventured out. In the evenings, Dai Jai resumed tending to his fish. Early one evening, Percival found him feeding them on his balcony, the tanks meticulously cleaned.

"They're beautiful," said Percival.

"They need attention."

"Sorry, I let the tanks go. While you were away."

"Thanks for feeding my fish."

A slight breeze had arrived with the evening, a hot wind but still a relief. "Do you want to go out for a good dinner in a restaurant? Let's go for lobsters, Cantonese style, somewhere air-conditioned."

"I'm still recovering."

"Though I noticed that you went out today."

Dai Jai looked down into a tank.

"Maybe I was too harsh about the girl before," said Percival. "You are a young man, after all. You must still marry a Chinese, but for now . . . The Annamese are free spirited. If you don't feel like lobster, what about oyster omelettes for dinner—Teochow style?"

"I had better stay in. My appetite's not great. Aren't there a lot of police out at night?"

"It's fine to go out," said Percival. It was safe, he assured himself. If anyone was still after Dai Jai, he should have heard about it by now. Mei had promised to warn him if anyone in the police even whispered about Dai Jai. How could he convince the boy? Percival said, "There are fresh scallops at the Golden Dragon. They are delicious."

"Yes . . ." said Dai Jai, but his face became closed, "but my stomach is still sensitive."

Percival used the school break to drum up business, to encourage early registration. He bought more desks and crammed them in, to increase the class sizes without hiring more teachers. He spread the rumour that his school would soon have a special certification with the Americans. Soon, Dai Jai could resume his studies at the academy and at the Teochow school. Seeing his old friends would improve his spirits.

When Percival submitted the official registry for the new semester of the Percival Chen English Academy, he received a phone call from Mr. Tu. "Dai Jai has been placed on a 'not eligible for school enrolment' list. Routine—political lists," Mr. Tu said. "But don't visit me on this problem. Stay away for awhile, actually. I attracted attention with your last visit, coming so near to your son's antics."

It was not a big problem, Percival decided. It was his own school. Dai Jai could attend classes without being registered, and later, when they fixed the papers, Percival would backdate the registration. A few days later, Percival saw the headmaster of the Teochow school at a money circle. He told Percival that he could not register Dai Jai at his school either. He began to explain.

"I know," said Percival, "he's on a list. I haven't had a chance to fix it yet."

"I'm not so sure it's easily fixed, old friend. I've had a few 'inspections' by the quiet police." Not about Dai Jai, he assured Percival, but the officers asked about their curriculum and seemed to be looking for anything outside the official guidelines. "They asked me why we teach Chinese history rather than Vietnamese history. They said they might have us replace the calligraphy classes with basic military training—I think they were joking, but I'm not sure. Anyway, please keep Dai Jai away from his old Teochow classmates and well away from the school grounds." He added apologetically, "The Chinese schools are an easy target. We are only one step away from being closed."

So, they were putting extra pressure on the Chinese schools. Mak had advised Percival well in 1950, when he suggested that Percival open an English school. They might close the Chinese schools, but not an English one, he had said even then. Not as long as the Americans were in Vietnam. That year, French bureaucrats had taken the rice and transport licences from the Chinese and given them to Vietnamese. It was to prevent those vital industries from being infiltrated by Chinese communists, they said. In giving the licences to the locals, the Chinese grumbled, the French hoped to buy their allegiance after nearly a century of abusing them. This was how Percival became an educator, exaggerating the extent of his British education in Hong Kong and relying upon Mak to cultivate friendships for the school in Saigon. Cecilia always said that it was best for Chinese to be in the money-exchange business precisely because it was the black market. It had no regulations. A school was different—even English schools needed licences to issue diplomas.

Percival did not immediately ask Mak to fix this problem, because he was tight for cash. He had the Peugeot back and was making progress on the Clan Association debt, but the weekly interest payments dogged him. They had extended his loan at eight percent monthly. Dai Jai still hesitated to leave the house, so there was no rush to get him to school. For a routine political list, there should be a similarly routine solution but it would still have a price. Once he had worked off a little more of the debt, Percival would ask Mak to find a contact to remove Dai Jai from the list.

With the new semester, Dai Jai began attending classes at the Percival Chen English Academy even though he was not registered. He began to venture out of the house regularly. Since the boys from the Teochow school had been told to stay clear of him, Dai Jai played soccer and basketball with the Vietnamese houseboys, and Percival excused them from their work. Occasionally, Percival saw Dai Jai retreat into an empty classroom after school. A few times, as he marked papers in his office, Percival heard a girl's small laugh, quickly muffled. He did not even get up to investigate.

"Is she kind?" he asked Foong Jie. The head servant pretended not to hear.

Then, one day after Percival had missed an ancestor worship day because he had passed it at the Continental Hotel with a lovely young thing from a nearby village, a letter arrived for Dai Jai. Foong Jie brought it to Percival in the school office. Mak was with him when it came, going over the monthly receipts and the debt repayment list. It was a South Vietnamese Army envelope. Percival tore it open, read it twice.

"What is it?" said Mak.

Percival handed it to him.

"This must be a mistake," said Mak. "Students are not eligible for the draft."

"I meant to have you inquire. About Dai Jai being on a list of students not to be registered for school."

"He is to report for basic training in three weeks' time. Near Cu Chi, a dangerous place," said Mak, rubbing his forehead. "That is a problem. It would have been easier to deal with this before he was drafted. Now it's an army matter . . ." Percival picked up the phone. He asked Cecilia to meet him at the Cercle Sportif in an hour, to discuss a small complication. This was how he put it, and then said he could not elaborate on the phone.

This time, she did not stage her theatre of a tennis match. She sat waiting for Percival in the pavilion near the tennis courts, drumming her nails on the table. After she read the draft notice, she said, "He must go to France or America. A Chinese boy cannot be in the South Vietnamese Army."

"Of course not. You think I'm so naive?" He thought of several former neighbourhood boys. When their bodies were returned home, the bullet wounds were often in their backs. "Our son must return to China," said Percival. "It is the only safe place for a Chinese person."

"Don't you know what is happening in China?" she said.

"What do you mean? They are moving forward. They are making steel now. Tons of it. Sometimes, I don't even think you are Chinese."

"Sometimes, I don't think you are even awake." Cecilia had taken little interest in the victory of Mao in 1949, but after the land reforms she criticized everything about the People's Republic with as much fervour as she found fault with her husband. For years afterwards, Cecilia continued to complain bitterly about her family's estates of several hundred *li* having been seized and given to the tenants. Percival had declared that he was proud that his family's land would serve the people of China. Cecilia had ridiculed those two *li* as the size of her family's vestibule, and cheered the Americans in Korea. "Do you still send money to China? I'm sure whatever you send ends up in a vault in Geneva. You think the communists don't steal?"

Every year, the Clan Association took up a collection for schools and hospitals in China, and Percival was one of its most generous supporters. He said, "I don't know anything about communists. I am a patriotic Chinese, and I send money to help my country." He also sent money every year to a poor cousin in Shantou to maintain Muy Fa's grave, and the cousin sent letters that both praised Percival's generous remittance and listed the wonderful developments in the new China. "My cousin writes that things are better all the time in China. Dai Jai should be in his own country. Mak says he might be able to get him there."

"Don't you ever wonder how Mak can do these things? Is it normal for a school teacher to know everyone of importance in Saigon? And how could he get Dai Jai to China?"

Percival signalled the waiter. "That's Mak's private business. I don't involve myself." He ordered a Martell and Perrier, didn't ask Cecilia if she wanted a drink. Mak lived exactly as one would expect a teacher to live, comfortably but modestly. He did not siphon even a little money from the school, as many right-hand men in successful businesses would be expected to do. So what difference did it make to him what Mak used his contacts for? Perhaps the school gave Mak cover, a legitimate reason to have connections through which he found other business. However he profited from his connections was his own affair. The waiter brought the drink, a twisted napkin around the stem beneath the frosted glass. There were discreet men in Saigon and Cholon who, it was said, had all their gifts and envelopes deposited in overseas accounts. That would be like Mak—the kind who did not need to taste and touch his profits. For some, Percival supposed, the existence of money was its own satisfaction. Percival lifted the glass, enjoyed the tickle of mineral-water bubbles in the cognac. He did not see the point of such asceticism, but some did. "Oh, did you want a drink?" he asked Cecilia.

"Not with you. One day Mak will be arrested for something, or he will turn up dead. He is deep into something, and you just don't know what it is."

"And why should I ask? He always comes through." He hoped Mak could find people who could get Dai Jai to China. If they were criminals, what well-connected person did not step in and out of the law as the occasion required? Percival put the glass down and repeated, "What I know is that Mak can get Dai Jai back to China."

"Just as your father tried to return, while there was still a war under way," she shot back. "To this day, you don't even know where his corpse lies."

Percival's anger flared in his stare, so glaring that Cecilia looked away, a rare flinch. "Sorry."

"Let's not get into our own battles again," he said. Cecilia usually reserved this painful barb, the journey of Chen Kai, for the height of an argument rather than its beginning. "I'm trying to get our son away from this war."

"America would be even safer."

"They can draft him there, too."

"France, then."

"Besides, how will *you* get him out? Half of your clients sell the guns Dai Jai is now being called up to carry. You think your business partners can get him a visa just like they get you military scrip? They wouldn't even help you find him in a Saigon jail."

"The piastres you get as tuition are printed in the same press. You think Mak can do something beyond bribing Saigon officials?" she said. "Let's see who can find a way abroad sooner."

Since Dai Jai's appetite had returned, Percival directed Foong Jie to serve rich dishes—wheat noodles in pork-bone broth, pickled eggs, dry shredded meat—to build Dai Jai's strength. Percival tolerated the smell of *nuoc nam* at the table, which Dai Jai liked to flavour his soup with. During breakfast a week after the draft notice came, Percival said, "Son, a minor issue has come up. I don't want you to worry, because I'm going to fix it." He slipped the envelope across the table.

Dai Jai read the paper. He pursed his lips slightly, but his face barely reacted. The boy was still in shock, Percival decided. His reactions were still numbed by his ordeal. Clearly it would be dangerous for him to be in the army.

Percival said, "I will find a way to keep you out of it."

"I know boys who have gone into the army."

"Vietnamese."

"Some people buy safe postings. The post just over there is all people who paid for it." Dai Jai pointed to the quiet army post across La Place de la Libération, in the shadow of the church. Connections and money should be able to manage that, but now Percival was not sure of his influence in Saigon.

"The best thing will be for you to get out of Vietnam. Mak tells me he has already found a possible route to China."

At this, Dai Jai sat up straight. "Leave Vietnam? After being drafted? They check the draft lists at the airport."

"Your father has lots of *gwan hai*," Percival said. "You know, when I was a small boy, my greatest dream was to study in Shanghai, or in Beijing. You could have the opportunities I never had. You could be a real scholar."

Dai Jai resumed eating as a worried look spread over his face.

Cecilia made inquiries in Saigon about sending Dai Jai to France or America, but Percival had been right. It could not be done. The draft notice blocked every avenue, trumped every favour that she tried to call in. Every Frenchman sent her to another office, to pay another bribe, to find another dead end. They shrugged, ever polite, blamed bureaucracy with Cecilia's money in their pockets. Her American friends told her that if her son had not been drafted, they might have been able to do something. As it was, they could hardly interfere with the South Vietnamese Army's draft. They had enough problems in America with their own draft dodgers.

Meanwhile, Percival made only the monthly money-circle and minimum loan interest payments as he put away cash for the expense of sending Dai Jai abroad. Mak said he was getting close to settling the route for the journey abroad, but it would be expensive, at least five thousand American dollars. Cecilia mocked Percival's gullibility when he told her the price. She refused to contribute to it. Clearly, Mak was taking a cut, she said. When the garage owner saw Percival driving up to pawn the Peugeot again, he laughed and called out a price even before the headmaster stepped out of the car.

Two weeks after the draft notice, Mak came and explained the details of the plan to Percival and Dai Jai. Dai Jai, dressed in shabby clothes, would pretend to be a local trader and travel with a snake-head on a local bus to Cambodia with several suitcases full of transistor radios. It was a bus that traders often took to sell U.S. Army PX goods in Phnom Penh, and Mak would pay the officer in charge at the border to simply collect his usual bribe from the traders without checking their documents. He did that often enough anyway, but Mak would pay the officer to ensure it. Once across the border, an old friend of Mak's would take care of Dai Jai, arranging documents and air tickets. From Phnom Penh, there were flights to China. Once he was in China, Dai Jai would be fine. Every Chinese had the right to return. Mak had been in touch with an educational cadre at a secondary school in Shanghai who had agreed to register Dai Jai. Had Percival raised the cash? Mak asked. Cecilia might be right, but Percival did not mind. Mak deserved a cut, after all. Percival handed him the money. He did not look to see what Dai Jai's reaction might be—taking his silence as agreement.

That evening, Percival sought out Dai Jai on the balcony. To see him in the half light of dusk carefully tending his fish, his bruises healed and his hair grown back, one might forget that he'd ever gone to the National Police Headquarters. Percival did not dare stir up the recent past by saying how much better Dai Jai looked, or by saying how happy he was that his son moved with some of his old confidence.

Percival said, "You must be excited, about your trip to China." He said it as if it were a trip to Dalat, the resort town, or a holiday in Paris.

Dai Jai hesitated before saying, "I didn't think it was possible. Not with the politics here, or even the situation in China."

Was the boy's expression one of alarm? "Don't be scared. You won't be caught. Did you think I was going to let you enlist in the South Vietnamese Army? Everything is arranged for you to return home."

Dai Jai stopped skimming the surface of the water. "How can I return somewhere that I've never been? I don't want to go."

"You are Chinese," said Percival with finality. Dai Jai stared deep into the fish tanks without a word. It seemed he was expecting Percival to say something else. Perhaps the boy did not understand the situation, the dangers of the South Vietnamese Army for a Chinese. Or was this Cecilia's fault? Finally, Percival said, "Has your mother given you the idea of America? Even with many so-called American friends, she cannot arrange it. Impossible, now that you've been drafted. Your name comes up on lists. Or does she talk to you now of France? What good have the French ever been to us Chinese, or any white people? You would be miserable in a land of the *gwei lo*." How could the boy even contemplate living amongst the white ghosts?

Dai Jai looked straight at his father. "It's not that I want to go to America or France. I just don't want to leave." Dai Jai nudged a fish with the net, gently. It skittered around gracefully in the tank. Percival saw how fearful Dai Jai was of saying this, and this tempered his response.

He had come up to the balcony expecting Dai Jai to be excited, perhaps thrilled. Or at least appreciative. He said quietly, "I wish I could go to China myself, but I must stay here, pay the debts, and save the house that your grandfather built. When he left Shantou, Chen Kai only intended to make his fortune and return. He got stuck here—he stayed longer than he intended, and built Chen Hap Sing. But in the end, after finding the Gold Mountain, the only thing your grandfather wanted was to return to his home village. He regretted not going back sooner. Now, you have that chance. Maybe I'll join you, even. Maybe after I've paid the debts and saved up some money."

"How much?"

"Once I have enough," said Percival reassuringly. "You can't imagine how happy your grandfather would be, to know that you are returning to China."

"But you never heard from him again. Obviously, he must have been—"

"Shh!!! My father picked a terrible time to make the journey. That was because he waited too long. He travelled towards danger, but you are travelling away from it. The ancestors' ghosts will be happy for your return."

"I heard on the radio that the People's Committees have banned the Parade of Deities celebration. They say people must stop worshipping the ancestors, because in the new China—"

"You are very lucky that Mak has been able to arrange for you to study in Shanghai. This is not easy. I am still struggling with my gold debt, but I will send you with ten taels to pay your expenses."

Percival could see that Dai Jai remained doubtful. He struggled for something to say and could only come up with platitudes that suited any Teochow primary school lesson. He used them regardless. "Don't you know the greatness of the Chinese civilization? We conquered Annam two hundred years before Christ was born. We invented paper money and gunpowder."

"And now the Americans are the masters of both of those things, and this place."

Percival did not know what to say. He was terrified to think of his son in a South Vietnamese uniform. "The greatest minds of all civilization—Emperor Wong, Confucius, the Cheng brothers—all derived their wisdom from their mother China. You will thrive in Shanghai. You will get a better education than you could ever hope for here in this muddy backwater." Percival searched Dai Jai, who still seemed unconvinced. He added desperately, "The girls there are prettier than any here, and far more elegant."

"I'm supposed to report to the army in a few days. Maybe I will get a post in Saigon. Even if not, I can try to get home for the festivals."

"I don't want you fighting amongst Vietnamese. Chinese soldiers don't last long in their army. Look, they fight a war against their own people. For what reason? I can't tell you why. No one can. How stupid."

"Are we Chinese better? What about Mao and Chiang Kai-shek—"

"Believe me, if they can kill their own brothers, they aren't bothered by shooting us Chinese, even if you wear the same uniform."

"I know what people say . . . but what if I just report for training and speak only Vietnamese? I will never speak Chinese, and that way I will blend in."

This was the boy who had protested the new Vietnamese language regulation, and suffered so much for it? Now, he declared so casually that he would never speak his own language? Percival was frustrated, about to yell at him, but found the words stuck in his chest. Perhaps the beatings his son received had affected his views, had made him decide it was wrong to declare himself Chinese. All the more reason to send him to China. Percival found his voice cracking. "You want to crawl in the jungle and wait for a bullet in your back? In China, you can study. Here, you are forbidden to register even in your own father's school. Mak has found a way for you to leave, and you must use it!"

Dai Jai caressed the side of a tank, which attracted the angel fish to come and kiss the glass. "I am at home here."

"For what reason?" asked Percival. He seized the skimmer from his son's hand and waved it. "Is it for your girl? There are girls in China. You will find them anywhere."

"You should know," said Dai Jai.

Percival raised the skimmer, as if to hit Dai Jai with it, and saw the boy recoil. He threw the skimmer across the balcony, heard it skitter on the marble.

"I will go as you wish, Father," Dai Jai said, his words quivering.

"*Gwai jai*," said Percival. Obedient boy. He said softly, "This whole episode will turn out to be a blessing in disguise, for spurring us to send you to China. You will visit my mother's shrine, and in Shantou you can enjoy Zhong Shan Park, the most beautiful park in the world." Percival walked across the balcony, retrieved the skimmer, handed it to his son apologetically. Dai Jai resumed tending his tanks with shaking hands. Percival fled. He felt relief, a lifting of a weight. One day, soon, in fact, the boy would thank him for forcing this. What else should a father do? He found Foong Jie downstairs, gave her the ten taels of gold that he had bought for Dai Jai, and instructed her to sew it into Dai Jai's most sturdy trousers and show him where it was hidden.

Two days later, five days short of Dai Jai's date to report for basic training, Cecilia came early in the morning to say goodbye to their son. It was still dark. Dai Jai clutched a bundle of his favourite foods, which Foong Jie had prepared for him. Cecilia held him in her arms for a long time in the front hallway. The smuggler arrived with their props, two large boxes of cheap Sanyo radios. Percival had intended a bright send-off, to be as cheery and celebratory as possible. He had chosen a verse of classical Tang poetry. He would wait for Cecilia to finish her embrace. Then, Dai Jai squirmed out of his mother's arms, his own face wet, suddenly in a hurry to leave. He went out the door, and everyone followed him. An overnight rain had left the square freshly rinsed, cool. Once they were out of the house, Percival called for Dai Jai to wait a moment, found that his poetic quote had been erased from his mind, and fumbled awkwardly in the dark to embrace his son, throwing his arms around the boy's shoulders. Mak stood a little way off in the dark. He had come to make sure everything went smoothly, and was acting as lookout, scanning the square.

Percival had a wild thought. What if he told the smuggler to go away, that he was not needed? But if Dai Jai were to stay, he did not have time to buy a safe post now. Another idea flashed before him—he could go with Dai Jai and leave the school and house in Mak's care, but no, there were the pyramids of debt. To leave Chen Hap Sing would almost certainly be to lose it. No, this was correct, the best possible action. These speculations vanished as quickly as they had arrived. He must let Dai Jai go. The boy would be safest with other Chinese. He loosened his hold, held Dai Jai's shoulders in his hands.

"Why are you sad?" asked Dai Jai. "Are you disappointed in me, Father? For what I did, and all the trouble?"

Percival said, choking on his own tears, "No. Don't say that—you are our only son. It hurts me to send you away, but I think it's best."

"I know, that's why I'm going."

"Because it's the best thing. Yes."

Dai Jai said quietly, "I'm going because you think it's best."

Against the first glow of an ashen sky, the limbs of the flame trees seemed oppressive, and dark. The smuggler murmured that they must not miss the bus. Dai Jai nodded and hoisted his box of radios.

Cecilia wanted to go to Dai Jai's room. They stared at his empty bed, his desk. They went out onto the balcony. The fish tanks had been scrubbed spotless and shone like gems beneath the pre-dawn sky. When the light appeared, they looked out into the square below. Percival was fearful and hopeful—if something went wrong perhaps he would see the smuggler returning with his son. Perhaps they would miss the bus. Perhaps the bus would have a mechanical problem. But the square began to fill with vendors and cyclo men, without any trace of Dai Jai.

Percival said to Cecilia, "Do you remember, when we arrived in Cholon, this was the first room in the house that we saw."

"How could I forget? If the *Asama Maru* had been returning to Hong Kong, I would have gone back to the wharf."

The bedroom that was emptied by Dai Jai's absence was the same room that had once been Chen Kai's. It had the best view of the square. It received the most breeze, through the two French doors that opened onto the balcony. Through it, air moved through the whole family quarters.

The first time Percival set foot in this room, the doors and shutters were closed tight against the light. They had just met Ba Hai, and she had shooed them up the stairs. They had fled Hong Kong's starving unfortunates, those who had been reduced to begging for rice on the street. Indochina was to be their refuge, a place of lush paddies and full bellies, but when Percival's eyes adjusted to the dark room and the opium smoke, he was shocked by a figure who was as thin and fragile as the carved lattice headboard on the mahogany bed where he lay. Skin draped loosely from the contours of cheekbones. Veins undulated over the back of a hand. There was no movement except for breathing, and with that effort the clutched opium pipe moved slightly. After a long pause, Percival said, "It's me. I have come, Father."

Chen Kai moved lightly, like a feather. "Who is it?" he said.

"It is Chen Pie Sou, your son."

"No, my son is in Shantou."

"I have come from Hong Kong with my new bride." Percival tried to pull Cecilia towards the bed. She should kowtow to her new father-in-law. She pulled her hand away and stood near the door.

Chen Kai snored, wheezed, then roused and with a great effort, succeeded in putting the pipe to his lips. "You are a ghost. Tricking me! No, my son wrote. He would not come. He is in Shantou, angry with me. He stayed with his mother's grave, a dutiful son." He sucked on the pipe, realized that the drug no longer burned within, and let it clatter to the floor. He turned slowly, his eyes closed, his words slurred. "As soon as I am better, I must return to Shantou."

A cough at the door—it was Ba Hai. She said with syrupy sweetness, "When he learned of his first wife's death, he could not sleep, and so we tried this medicine. Now, the opium pipe is the only thing that gives him comfort."

"He looks worse than dead," said Percival. "Why does he say I am in Shantou? I never wrote any such letters."

"Look at him, he has lost his mind."

Percival stood in the centre of the room. Cecilia lingered near the door. The room was very warm, an old heat stale with layers of opium smoke and darkness. He looked to Ba Hai. "Did you forge those letters to me, as if you were my father? Did you send me to Hong Kong and tell my father I had stayed in Shantou?"

"Don't you come here, Chinese boy, and think that this is your house," spat Ba Hai. She turned and left.

"He will have no more opium!" Percival shouted after her. He went to the shutters and threw them open. Light flooded the room and Chen Kai recoiled, shielded his eyes, begging that the shutters be closed. Percival jerked the doors open so that the noises and smells of the square invaded. He snatched the wood pipe from the floor and flung it out the window.

Now, the same room was full of Dai Jai's things, the good clothes which he could not take with him to China, the carefully squared piles of Marvel comics and kung fu novels, books which were painful for him to abandon. Percival looked out on the square and imagined where the opium pipe might have landed. He said to Cecilia, "Dai Jai is going home. Just as his grandfather Chen Kai once wanted."

She said dully, "This is the only home he ever knew. All he knows about China are the stories you've told him. You are right about the *gwei lo*. I can't believe how useless my American friends have been. They're happy to change money, but when I really needed their help . . ."

"Why can't you believe it?"

She did not answer.

After Cecilia left, Percival tightly shut the windows and doors of Dai Jai's room and told Foong Jie not to open them. From then on, the family quarters of Chen Hap Sing were close and stifling. Those first nights, Percival would pause at Dai Jai's quiet door, and then slip past, outside into the cool damp darkness.

After a week, a telegram came from Shanghai. "Arrived. Registered for school."

So it had worked. Percival was both lonely and relieved. There was the debt, diminished but not discharged. Perhaps after securing the safety of the school, he would go to China himself. Or maybe he would go to visit. After all, there was still money to be made. Even before making money, he must pay back what he owed. It was somehow comforting to have these practical problems to address. He slept soundly and deeply, awoke determined to fill his thoughts with dollars, piastres, gold, and the challenge of saving Chen Hap Sing from the creditors. The house echoed a hollow quiet—perhaps he would call Mrs. Ling.

PART TWO

CHAPTER 9

1967, CHOLON, VIETNAM

Several days after Dai Jai's telegram arrived, Mak caught up with Percival in the school hallway. He said, "I have met an American, a Mr. Peters, who is newly arrived at the State Department in Saigon. He might be the person to help us with our certification."

"How much will you need?" asked Percival. They had already judged that if the graduates of the Percival Chen English Academy could be exempted from the American English proficiency exam, it would be worth a red packet of considerable size. They could probably increase tuition by half.

"Mr. Peters is the type of American who needs to be convinced," said Mak. "I will nurture the idea slowly, but it may not be a matter of simply giving a gift. If you meet him by chance at the Cercle, don't raise the issue. If he knows who you are and brings it up, speak as if it means very little to you—that it is simply a way for us to make things easier for them to hire staff." Mak's words were cautionary, but his tone was excited.

Percival nodded. "He needs to feel it is in their interest, a favour we are doing for them."

"Even better if he thinks it is his own idea."

"Then he is complicated, or even worse, political?"

"I'm just getting to know him. If you somehow meet him, remember what I said."

"The certification means nothing to me. We would be helping him out with it."

"I think I can make this work—but please don't spend what you don't yet have, *hou jeung*. Focus on your debt. Whatever you do, stay away from the mah-jong tables."

The following week, Mak instructed Percival to attend a particular cocktail hour at the Cercle. Mak brought over an athletic-looking American with excellent posture, saying to him what a nice coincidence it was that the headmaster of his school happened to be here. After being introduced, Percival inquired about Peters' work, which the American described as "cultivating innovative channels of communication." Percival nodded as if this meant something to him. He talked a little about the school, asked for nothing, and offered nothing, a neutral stance, as Mak had prescribed. They had a whisky together, and each paid for his own.

One morning, a month following Dai Jai's departure, Percival received a letter from his son. Dai Jai described the French Concession in Shanghai, where he had taken a room. He related some of the strange expressions of the Shanghainese. He wrote that being in China made him understand how small and backwards Cholon really was, and thanked his father for sending him to his motherland.

Percival slipped the letter into his shirt pocket, almost as pleased as if he were with his son. He felt lucky, and went to the garage where the Peugeot was in hock. They would flip a coin, he suggested to the garage owner. If the owner won, he would keep the Peugeot free and clear. If Percival won, he would take it back, and the loan, which was about a third of the car's value, would be cancelled. Percival said that he would otherwise pay off the loan immediately with full interest and take the car away. A bluff—his pockets were empty. The garage owner eyed the big Peugeot, which he had been driving and enjoying, and agreed to the wager. A few minutes later, Percival slipped into the seat of the car, and with the engine purring to life felt the ballooning pleasure of his own good luck.

The good-luck feeling weakened later that day, when the Teochow Clan Association's treasurer visited the school and insisted upon a payment of a hundred thousand piastres by the next day, threatening foreclosure on Chen Hap Sing. That night Percival braved the clinking glass negotiations of a money-circle banquet at the Jade Orchid Restaurant to borrow more cash—yet more debt, guaranteed by promises, and propped up by his strained smile. The rates he was obliged to pay were now the highest in Cholon, nine percent monthly. It could have been worse, but Mei vouched for him, confirmed that there was strong demand for English-speakers in the police. "Bottoms up!" said Percival, and he poured a round of cognac from the bottle of Remy Martin XO that he had ordered for the table—swallowing the rich amber warmth, and the expense of the cognac. It was expected that the borrower be generous. After the dinner broke up, Percival drifted through Cholon in the back of the car. Despite his luck earlier that day, debt circled him like a relentless predator.

"Home, boss?" said Han Bai, as he guided the car through the fluid night.

"It's early." He thought of the family quarters of Chen Hap Sing. The still heat and the closed rooms would remind him of Dai Jai's absence. He would gain some relief if he opened the doors, but it was the lesser discomfort to keep the room shut off. Dai Jai's letter in his pocket was good company.

The car's headlights arced over the flashing legs of the fragile street girls, their bright-coloured butterfly dresses, lipstick slashes on their tired grandmother mouths. Percival wondered what the night was like at Le Grand Monde. Were people in a good mood at Le Paradis, or the Sun Wah Hotel? He rolled down the window and put his hand into the night air. He rubbed the cool humidity between his fingers—was the joy of luck to be his tonight? He had been compelled to borrow for the snakehead's fee and to send ten taels of gold with Dai Jai. Tonight, another hundred thousand owed. All he needed was a few good rounds of mah-jong.

The big Peugeot floated through the streets, and Percival reflected on his luck at winning it back. The Americans were close to giving them the special certification, Mak had recently reported, and good luck came in threes. The Sun Wah Hotel was just a few blocks away.

The proceeds of the money circle sat in an envelope next to Percival. It was due at the Teochow Clan Association by the end of the next day. In the glancing headlights, a girl's smile flashed, plucked out of darkness. Others walked nearby. Through his fluid cognac haze, he saw their light steps, their slender thighs quick in darkness. If nothing else, this war had brought miniskirts to Saigon.

"To the Sun Wah Hotel," Percival said to Han Bai.

Han Bai did not change direction. "*Hou jeung*, you said you wished to go straight home."

"I've changed my mind. I want to see if anyone I know is at the Sun Wah Hotel. It's still early."

"Ah, boss, that's a dangerous place. There are no little games there, just big-money mah-jong. Maybe you want to go somewhere else. You've been doing well with blackjack. Or let's find you a girl, some pretty company. Do you like that one?" Han Bai slowed the car a little, and Percival considered the crossed ankles, the bare shoulder.

"I don't go with this kind of girl. Anyhow, I feel very lucky tonight."

"Look, boss," said Han Bai. "You are already lucky. You got the car back. You've got tomorrow's payment."

"The car, yes. But the money's not mine, it's borrowed." Percival thumbed the thick layers of cash. The envelope tingled in his hand, excited the fingers. Borrowed money, however, was a sing-song girl in a bar. It could be touched but not possessed. The sweetest money was delivered by good fortune. The car had given him a taste. "I don't want a night like this to be wasted."

"Mak said that you promised him not to gamble big money." Han Bai, an old employee, took more liberty than most drivers.

Tonight, there were no flares or bombardments, which often agitated the southwest sky. A lone military helicopter beat the air as it passed above the car, the single eye of its spotlight peering here and there. Then the sky fell silent again. Beneath it, Cholon was noisy and alive. Pungent food smells, oil and garlic, meat and ginger, drifted through the window. Percival was hungry for the night, to touch the girls who leaned in doorways with hands on thighs, to caress the smooth ivory tiles, and to sweep up piastres from a table.

He did not want more debt, but what of the freedom that could come from some cash?

"Mak is practical. He knows how to get things done in the way that someone arrives at a place by walking—one step at a time, much work. I respect that. But the gods of luck can change everything. In a moment, you are blessed with everything you want, like flying."

"Or you are ruined. Your money vanished. And worse, that money's not yours. You just said so."

If he was ruined beyond hope of recovering, he told himself, he could abandon Chen Hap Sing, he could go to China. "I will win tonight," said Percival. It was not for his driver to say otherwise. "You have passed the road to the Sun Wah Hotel. You must turn back."

"As you wish, *hou jeung*."

Han Bai pulled up outside the folding metal gates of the hotel. Percival got out, breathed the night air, thick and damp like a wet cloth. He knocked. Soon, a maid peered through the gates, recognized Percival, scraped a key through the lock and let him in. She knew that he could find his own way up, and lay back down on her cot in the lobby.

Upstairs, Room 28, *yee ba* in Cantonese, the numbers that sounded like easy fortune. Three tables played, each in a corner. A hotel boy dozed on a cot in the fourth corner of the room, near the purser who sat next to the safe drinking tea. Percival knew some of the players, and others were strangers to him. Mrs. Ling looked up. "Percival Chen, now there's a lovely sight."

"As are you," he bowed.

"We have missed you—I was concerned that you had lost your taste for beauty," said Mrs. Ling. She gave a high, tinkling laugh as she swept a pile of chips towards herself. She wore her necklace of pale jade, the clasp a carved dragon, over a well-tailored black silk dress. Pale jade was for a young lady, but she managed to wear this adornment elegantly. She clothed herself in a precise way that allowed her desirability but placed her respectably beyond reach. "Do you have any new teachers? Does any of them need a wife? Perhaps a girlfriend?"

"Do you want to marry one of my teachers, Mrs. Ling?" he asked.

"All my young friends have soft skin, and tender hearts," she murmured. "If your teachers want anything special, I can provide." Mrs. Ling dealt in specific appetites just as other business people procured Levi's jeans and Rolex watches. The Australians and American ex-servicemen who taught alongside Percival's local teachers were good customers of hers. "Marriage or fun, either. American dollars or military scrip." She turned again to the chips she had just won, counted attentively. These were good times for Mrs. Ling. In addition to the usual hotel work, there were foreigners who wanted to meet nice girls rather than bar dancers, and families who paid to have their daughters married away to America. In the best of these transactions, Mrs. Ling made money from both sides.

Police Chief Mei sat opposite the matchmaker. Chang, a scrap metal dealer, sat at the same square mah-jong table. Huong, the importer of Italian shirts, sat a little behind Chang and sipped a drink. There was a bald stranger in the game as well. He wore a banker's shade gripped tightly on his forehead—a green plastic halo. On a nearby couch, a *métisse* girl in a light-blue dress was half-reclined, her legs crossed. Her hands were slender creatures nested in her lap, and her elegance made the furniture cheap and shabby. She had strong French bones and warm Vietnamese skin. Her poise made it clear that she was better than the dress. The garment was slightly small for her, a cut which made Percival think of what was beneath, and yet was not so tight as to be vulgar. It was the way that Mrs. Ling typically dressed her girls. Percival had to remind himself not to stare. Mrs. Ling was a decent mah-jong player, but when she went out to gamble she often brought a girl with her, doubling her chances of making a profit.

Mei said, "Percival, so good to see you again. Maybe I'll have a chance to win back some of the money I lent you. Are you sure you should be gambling with that?"

"I assure you, I will leave with more than I've brought."

"Well, the head of the Teochow Clan has always admired Chen Hap Sing."

"Is there anyone in this town who does not know my business?"

"You don't even try to hide it." The police chief tipped his head towards the bald stranger. "This is a new friend, Mr. Cho. Someone told him the Sun Wah was the best place for a big game."

Cho's eyes twinkled at Percival, his lips pressed in a grin. He joined Mei and Chang to wash the tiles, swirled them around in preparation for the next game. The smallest finger of Cho's left hand had a delicately curved fingernail that was as long as the digit itself, which he protected within his palm as he mixed the tiles. Mrs. Ling lit a mentholated cigarette. She always insisted that the men should wash the tiles, so she wouldn't ruin her perfect hands. Percival saw how she took this moment to assess her opponents' unmasked expressions, to see if they were nervous or confident in the way they moved. The players began to stack their ivory pieces into the four walls that would frame a new game.

"It's been too long since we've seen you, brother," said Chang. "I hope you bring me some luck."

Percival felt the touch of the girl's eyes on him. When he summoned the courage to glance over, she had already turned away. A beautiful girl's presence invigorated a room, like the energy that came from a pile of valuable chips sitting on a table. How much would her introduction cost? The girl was aware of herself, carefully beautiful, not one who stood on the street anxiously watching car windows. She might cost more than Mrs. Ling's usual ten thousand—fifteen, perhaps even twenty. He could not afford twenty thousand piastres for a girl right now, he scolded himself, not even this one.

"Let's get some food," said Percival. Chang lit a Gauloise, inhaled, exhaled deliberately and offered the pack around. Percival waved him off, the stink of it already settling upon the table. Cho plucked one out, cupped his hand to light it though there was no breeze or fan, and grinned at Percival with amusement but without a word.

"We just ate, brother," Chang said, glaring at the tiles.

"Ah, he's in a bad mood," said Huong, smiling and gesturing towards Mei. "Chang is already losing to the chief. I'm always ready to eat. I try to set an example with my good spirits. You see, I've lost my stake already, but I'm smiling."

"Because you mark up your shirts tenfold," said Chang.

Percival woke the hotel boy from his cot and told him to fetch sea-food noodles, roast pork, braised lobster, rice, and to open a bottle of cognac. Mei won the dice roll to be the dealer for the new game. Chang sat to his left. Mei began, taking his four tiles from the wall. The boy showed Percival the unbroken seal on a bottle of Hennessy XO, then opened it, put out snifters on the table, and poured. The boy slipped out the door and went to wake the hotel cook. The enve-lope of cash was heavy in Percival's pocket.

The play began. Mei withdrew into himself as he usually did, moved slightly to collect and discard his tiles. His eyes were lowered, so that while playing it looked almost as if he were asleep. Chang folded his hands over his ivory pieces, occasionally rubbed his fingers.

After a few draws, Mei laid down an early triplet. "*Pong*," he said.

Mrs. Ling discarded noisily, made a fuss of it, almost tossing the pieces. Always a hint of theatre with her. As the play went around the table to the quick rhythm of pieces thrown away and new ones chosen, the tiles clicked softly. Once in a while Mei murmured con-tentedly, smiled, and focused on the empty space within the circle. Did he have a good hand, or was it a bluff?

Huong said, "Hey, any word from Dai Jai?"

"He's arrived safely in Shanghai," said Percival, annoyed at Huong for bringing it up.

"You must be happy."

"A Chinese boy should study in China," said Percival.

"He is a smart boy," said Chang. "Best for him to study."

"I'm worried about how he will do in China. He is headstrong." Being critical of Dai Jai, as a good father should be, might help crowd out the ache of the distance. He had an impulse to reach into his pocket, to touch the letter. No, if he was going to gamble he should forget about Dai Jai tonight.

"He will be fine," said Huong. "Nothing to worry about."

"The schools in Shanghai are top notch. He will have to apply him-self," said Percival. What if they had missed the bus, that morning? It was no time to think of his son, he told himself, for emotions like regret and worry were the enemy of the gambler. Better to think of the girl in the corner. Let her occupy his attention. Desire could bring luck. Even without looking, he was aware of the handsome line of her legs, one hand on a knee now, and, was he right, was she watching him? He wasn't certain that she was available. Mrs. Ling had said nothing about her, had not looked in her direction at all.

Mei won the game. Chang had not even had a chance to put down a triplet. He said he was sick of playing. "Headmaster, if I lose another game you take my chair." They washed the tiles, and built the walls. The newcomer must be a careful person, thought Percival, watching him build the walls with his dainty nail tucked in.

Mrs. Ling said, "Hey, Chang San, you can't step out now. You must play the headmaster. He has debts. Give him a chance to benefit from your bad luck, too."

"You three have my money now," said Chang. "Let him take it from you."

Mei won the last game of the round and dealt again for the next. Chang muttered that he would have one more try. Soon, using a tile that the stranger had discarded, he put a set of three down on the table. He drew a piece from the wall, cursed, and placed it back into the pile in the centre. It was the tile of six bamboo sticks, and Cho took it and put down a set of three. His head gleamed in the light when he leaned forward to draw his next piece. Chang had only put down one set, and the rest of his tiles were all still standing, when the bald one suddenly made mah-jong and won the game. Chang cried out in frustration and took the few chips he still possessed off the table. "I've had enough." The tiles were tumbled into the centre, and the other two men began to wash them for the next round. The tiles chattered like a hundred teeth.

Huong clapped Chang on the shoulder. "It serves you right for winning that ten thousand from me last night."

"Complain to Chief Mei," he said, standing.

"I would ask if you needed some company to console yourself," said Mrs. Ling, "but I doubt you can afford it now." Her eyes passed over the girl, who smiled politely. So, the girl was indeed Mrs. Ling's.

Percival stood, went to the purser, who asked him how much he wanted to change. He had intended to say fifty thousand, but with the girl watching, he heard himself say one hundred and soon changed it all for bright plastic tokens. He sat in the chair that Chang had vacated. Just sitting at the table, he felt the tingling excitement of possibilities. The first round of games went quickly, with small, cautious wins from each mah-jong as the new mix of players settled into a rhythm. They began with ten piastres per point. Percival won a few hundred, lost a thousand, and won it back. He lost a few hundred more and kept his eyes down, watched Cho's hands. The newcomer was doing well. A cocking of the left wrist betrayed nerves, the light drumming of the fingers of his right hand hinted that he was waiting for just one or two important pieces to make mah-jong. People made the effort of controlling their faces, but often let their hands talk.

The clicking of the tiles counted out the passage of the night. Around and around went the play, small money. Yes, Percival decided, he felt the brush of the girl's eyes on him. He tried to find something that might catch her reflection. There was no mirror, and there were drapes on the windows. He commented that the hotel boy was taking a long time with the food and glanced over at the door, looking at the girl sideways. Percival suggested they make it a hundred piastres per winning point. The other players agreed. Percival made the Great Snake Suite, and won three thousand piastres. He was pleased with the feel of the chips in his hand but cautioned himself not to react. He must not appear to be a man who cared much about three thousand piastres. Now, determined to test his luck, Percival ignored an early mah-jong to work for a more elaborate sequence, a bigger win. He felt certain that the right tiles would come. He soon lost two thousand piastres and felt betrayed. Where was the luck he had felt? He lost three thousand in the next round, when Mei went out.

Ignore the worry, he thought. The fear of loss could make itself true. He must have only confidence. The *métisse* girl smoothed wrinkles from her dress with the back of her hand. Briefly, he remembered the money due to the Teochow Clan Association the next day. All of that was far away. He was short a few thousand from losses, no matter. He drank his cognac, sought its glowing assurance that he was poised for a big win. He could not stand up after losses and expect to win a girl. There was nothing attractive in a man who lost money and walked away.

In the next round, Percival proposed to double the points' value. The table banter hushed. Now he would see what this night was about. "With a five thousand minimum," he added. To wager five thousand on a round was to demand a change in the mood of play. No one withdrew. The stranger touched his fingers to his lips. Quiet play circled, pieces were drawn and discarded with conviction. Soon Percival won thirty, with a hoard of two pongs, one kong, and a pair. There it was, the luck! Another wash of the tiles, another serious, silent game, and he lost six. That last loss brought him back down to a hundred and fourteen.

New walls were built, and after several careful turns, Percival knocked over his row of tiles, showed his finished mah-jong, and collected his winnings from the others again. He had a hundred and sixty-four thousand piastres. Cho groaned and showed that he had been close. An amateur, thought Percival, revealing his hand after the round was done. As if it mattered. Mrs. Ling turned her pieces face down so that no one could see.

"The teacher is giving lessons," called Huong, and raised his glass. Percival lifted his cognac, sipped it, and savoured the intoxicating feeling of money. A table could not back down on the size of wagers. Those who won wished to swallow more. Those who lost needed another chance to win. The tiles were washed again, the four walls built. With these stakes, Cho seemed to become clumsy and played erratically, his left wrist cocked up a little. Mei moved precisely, calculated his risks. After a win and then a loss to the silent man in the green eyeshade, Percival was at a hundred and eighty. Cho was inexperienced, but bold.

Percival saw the girl lean over to speak to Mrs. Ling. Mrs. Ling would have been offended to be called a pimp, for she prided herself on her discretion, taste, and judgment. She took her girls' preferences into consideration, for both the situation and the price varied from one introduction to another. The confidence of winning money strengthened Percival's desire. Soon, he made another complex hand, and two hundred thousand sat before him. He drank his cognac and looked directly at the girl. She looked away. He felt his face flush. Had he been too forward? He was afraid that he had offended her. The boy came with the food. Percival had ordered enough for everyone in the room, and offered it, saying, "*Dai ga, sic!*" He gave the boy a big tip.

The game paused. The boy placed the dishes around the jumble of tiles and people helped themselves to food and cognac. Mrs. Ling took a bowl and began to eat. The girl remained seated and ate nothing. She crossed one soft hand over the other, so that together they were a perfect seashell.

"Headmaster Percival Chen," said the man with the green eyeshade. "You have sent your son to China." He spoke in Vietnamese. He ate as he talked, unconcerned if his food showed through his words, crunched a lobster thorax and sucked on the stringy insides. A piece of lobster claw tumbled from Percival's chopsticks to the tablecloth. He knew this man, now that he heard his voice. "It was wise for your son to leave our country, since he doesn't like to speak our language." Cho scooped out the red eggs with two fingers, shoved them into his mouth, the pinky discreetly extended. Was that why he had been silent until now, had he been deciding whether to let himself be recognized? Cho drained his glass of cognac. "Anyway, your son is lucky. He has bad politics but a father who can raise money." He lifted a bowl of noodles to his mouth and ate noisily, shovelled with his chopsticks.

"You joke with me as if we were friendly," said Percival.

"You didn't recognize me at first. I'm not offended. This country changes so quickly that one may not remember who one knows. Some say friendships are out of fashion. That may be the reason you Chinese love money so much?" The other players continued eating, smiled politely but uncomfortably at this conversation. Was Cho revealing himself because he was losing at the table? Was it to unsettle Percival, put him off his game? Of course, the man in the bamboo grove had been more shadow than substance, but there was no mistaking the harshness of the voice, the elegant phrasing. Percival was surprised at the roundness of his features, the ample cheeks. The man was muscular, as Percival had thought, but older than he imagined. He had the pale complexion of a creature that spent its time hidden from the sun.

"I have never seen you here before. But I do know you."

"Well said," Cho laughed, and continued to eat. He looked directly at Mrs. Ling, and then at the girl. Mrs. Ling acknowledged Cho's interest with a slight nod. The girl shifted awkwardly, pulled the edge of her skirt out smooth, clasped her hands, focused on the mahjong tiles. It made her even more attractive, a girl's shyness within a woman's body.

As he lifted his glass, the rich cognac fragrance of old flowers filled Percival's nostrils. Rising through his body came the impulse to lunge at Cho and seize him by the neck, to smash his head on the table, to smear the ivory tiles with blood. Cho stared openly at the girl, as if he were enjoying her already. Did he stare to show that he dared? wondered Percival. Was it just to throw the game off balance? The girl looked away, now flushed. Percival's fingers wrapped tight around the stem of his cognac glass, near to crushing it into shards. He would grind the cutting fragments into Cho's eyes with his own bloody palm, and pummel the blind, shredded face with his fist. Instead, Percival sipped the amber from his glass. He would crush Cho's throat in his hands, feel the cracking of the windpipe, hear the whistling scream. He willed himself to loosen his grip on the cognac snifter. His mah-jong luck was strong tonight and he did not wish to waste it. Mrs. Ling glanced at him, questioning. She disliked situations that she did not understand. He stretched, yawned, to reassure her that it was alright, just a game of mah-jong.

When everyone had satisfied themselves with the meal, and pushed away the now cold and greasy dishes for the hotel boy to collect, Percival said, "It's late. Let's make something of the evening. Let's have ten thousand per player per game." Mei squirmed a little but did not give up his seat. Not to play big would be to lose, for his money was already in Cho's hands. "First mah-jong takes the pot." Huong whistled, rubbed his hands together, amused. "I was lucky to lose early," he said. "I couldn't afford to lose now."

"Let's make it twenty," Cho said. He had the casual manner of easy money, which he had taken from Percival. Percival nodded his agreement to twenty-thousand and looked around to solicit the other players. Mei made no comment but remained at the table. Mrs. Ling gestured to get on with it. The four players rolled the dice to see who would deal. Mrs. Ling won the roll, counted out the place to start, and took four tiles from the wall.

Percival soon won the first game's pot of eighty thousand. He thought of the letter in his pocket. Dai Jai was safe. He had nothing to lose except Chen Hap Sing. He could always return to Shantou, he reminded himself for courage. They washed the tiles and built the wall to play again. Mei won the second round, eighty thousand, but was uncomfortable. Mei played well until the sums began to bother him. After Percival took another pot of eighty thousand, Cho flinched, and then seemed relieved to take the next round of eighty himself. Cho won another game and drained his glass.

"I'm surprised your pockets are still so deep," said Cho. His hands were more calm, Percival noticed. Percival must ignore him. Yes, he told himself, Cho was indeed a beginner—too eager to celebrate his wins. A half-hour later, Percival had three hundred and forty thousand before him. He scolded himself for being as pleased as he was. A good gambler must be detached from the money and focused on making the right sequences, not the pots won or lost, he reminded himself.

The other games in the room had ended. Everyone gathered to watch the big-money table. Mei grumbled that he was tired, that he had been playing for a long time. He counted his chips nervously. He looked around, but no one offered to replace him. The *métisse* beauty stood a little behind Mrs. Ling, watching the game with concern. Percival turned his pieces face down, kept them in memory lest someone be inclined to give signals to his opponents. The others did the same. They cupped their pieces secretly when they drew them. With something that sounded like desperate bravado, Mrs. Ling proposed they up it to forty per player per game.

Again, the players washed the tiles and built the walls of chance. Percival took a round of a hundred sixty. He had four hundred and sixty thousand. There was almost enough to discharge the Teochow Clan debt. A bit more luck and there would be money for himself as well. Mrs. Ling pulled more notes from her purse, the last of her money, it seemed. The purser came to the table to change it for chips.

"How do you think this evening will go?" Cho asked Percival, a mocking growl, but one in which he tried too hard, showed his own nerves.

"The tiles will speak."

"Ah, a percussion of wealth. Like music."

"To the winner's ears." Percival tipped up his cognac and poured another, a warm comfort within the circle of electric light. The shade above them corralled the players into its glow. Alcohol did not impair his play. If he kept his emotions level, he assured himself, it permitted him to follow the instincts of his hands.

Mrs. Ling took a game. Within another two plays, she was broke. The first tin glow of morning glanced in shyly through the drapes.

"Alright, now I will win it back," said Mrs. Ling, hastily pulling forward the girl in the blue dress by her hand. "I need a few piastres. Who would like to be introduced to my beautiful friend?" The young beauty looked down as Mrs. Ling extolled her charming spirit and eagerness to please.

"I will have the introduction," said Cho.

"Can you afford it?" asked Mrs. Ling in a sing-song taunt. "It seems that your luck has shifted tonight, Cho, since the headmaster began to play. Don't feel badly. He is good at this." The girl looked up. "Besides, whoever takes the introduction will have to do some teaching. She is especially fresh, you see?"

Cho retrieved a fat, sealed envelope from his pocket. He ripped it open with his fingernail and tossed fifty thousand piastres across the table at Mrs. Ling's heavily jewelled hands. There was the gold Percival had sought desperately, begged for, borrowed against everything for. Mrs. Ling did not even look at the money. Cho said, "The schoolteacher has loans to pay. You would have nothing yourself were it not for the meat you have brought to market." He reached over to grab the girl's enticingly bare arm, and instinctively she stepped back.

He had to put out a foot to stop himself from tumbling out of his chair. Mrs. Ling put a hand on Cho's shoulder. It was an attractive woman's hand, but her grip was firm nonetheless, and she eased him back into his seat with a teasing smile. She laughed, absolving everyone, and then shot a look of reproach at the girl. "Does the headmaster wish to bid? I believe this has become an auction."

Percival said, "Do you think we are in an American bar, Mr. Cho?"

"Ah, *hou jeung*, he is merely showing us how keen he is for the prize. Who could blame him? You can show your interest with, say, eighty thousand?" Mrs. Ling's fixed smile played one man off the other as she looked from Percival to Cho. "Mr. Cho, I appreciate your enthusiasm, but I have not agreed to any introduction, so please. A gentleman keeps his hands to himself until such a matter is settled."

Percival counted out eighty thousand piastres' worth of chips into a little stack. Tonight, he would win back some of the ransom, keep Chen Hap Sing, and he would also take the girl. Early in the evening, he might have toyed with the idea of losing Chen Hap Sing and being free of it, yet it was only a mental trick to allow himself to gamble. He would never want to lose his father's house, his house. Now that he knew his opponent, he was even more determined to win. The girl smiled almost imperceptibly at Percival and rested her eyes on the chips beneath his hand. Had the smile really been intended for him alone to see? He tidied the stack of tokens as if undecided, but before he could slide it forward, Cho threw out more bills, some landing at Mrs. Ling's feet.

"There, fifty more. Enough for a whole street of whores. I hope she is worth it."

Mrs. Ling kicked off a ten-thousand-piastre note that had landed on her toes and inspected her fingernails, then looked to Percival. The room became alive with speculation. Once started, it somehow became permissible, and the men eyed the girl's hair, her breasts, her legs, and whispered their appraisals. She blushed. Mrs. Ling glowed. Percival placed his eighty thousand back with the rest of his stacks of chips. Mrs. Ling was discomfited by this. The headmaster was usually predictable in his desires. "Let's play one more game,

Mrs. Ling," said Percival. "The girl will be your bet. Mr. Cho? Does that suit you?"

"I would rather pay for what I want than be tricked out of it," said Cho.

"Tricks, Mr. Cho? Isn't this a mah-jong table?" said Percival, as he began to wash the tiles. "The only tricks are those of luck. Two hundred per player, then?"

"If you want to play, let's play." Cho looked up from under his eyeshade.

The spectators whispered, laid side bets on the game. Cho's eyes bulged angrily at Percival. He took back the money that he had tossed at Mrs. Ling's hands and ignored the ten thousand that was on the floor. Mei pushed himself back from the table, apologized sheepishly, mumbled about a policeman's salary. The room was alert again.

Percival said, "Alright, Mrs. Ling's bet will be the girl, and each of us will bet two hundred thousand piastres."

The four walls were built and broken, the pieces divided into the players' hands. Because Mei had bowed out, they dealt a fourth hand which sat unplayed, face down. Percival took a tile from the wall—it was four circles, a piece that he needed. A good draw to start. He reminded himself to betray no excitement.

On his second turn, Cho hesitated, coughed a little, and sipped his cognac. He cocked his left wrist back, settled the piece he had drawn in his hand and cleared his throat. Then Percival said, "If you are happy to wager two hundred on this girl, let's just make it four hundred each."

"Now you want me to decide if that is a bluff."

"You think that naming your problem will draw out an answer?"

Cho glared, furious at Percival, said nothing.

"As long as you don't mind such a big bet on a Chinese game," said Percival. "I know you don't like us Chinese, so if you want to fold for half the bet, if you don't want to play this last round of a Chinese game, I'll understand that it's not because you're afraid of losing. Your fingernail confuses me though, it's such a typical Chinese affectation—old-fashioned though."

If he lost the half million now, Percival would not be able to make his payment and would also have a new debt. Cho tapped his fingers, scanned the backs of the ivories. Chen Hap Sing would be gone, thought Percival, and it surprised him that there was still a tantalizing, terrifying freedom in that idea. He rubbed his chest where the letter was folded. The ancestors' spirits would decide.

"Spare me your tricks. Four hundred each," said Cho.

"I won't give another half of a girl," said Mrs. Ling. There was laughter from the circle of spectators. "But if I win this, I will still have her, and it will be the best introduction I never made."

The play went around. Percival drew a piece that was not what he needed, and was obliged to discard. The same once more. Even the spectators were tense, silent.

One by one, each of the players put down a triplet. Luck answered, and Percival was soon just one piece short. Several pieces came through Percival's fingers which might have helped him if he tried to build his hand a different way, but he decided to hold out for what he needed—the five circles. Cho tapped furiously at the table with his long, sculpted fingernail, drawing and discarding one tile after another with his other hand. Percival touched the next tile in line to be drawn, felt the blood surge in his ears, and slid the tile towards him.

"What are you doing? Take it! You must take it now that your hand is on it! You cannot draw another," barked Cho.

"You think I can see through it with my fingers?" said Percival. He pressed the piece into the table face down, as if trying to divine its identity, pushed it around in a lazy circle. "You think you can tell me what to do?"

Cho whispered, "I have already, haven't I?"

Percival took the piece, made it his. He tilted it up to see. The five circles. "Ah!" he cried, a half-scream, for now it was unnecessary to conceal his greed and the pleasure of this revenge. He showed his hand, but did not hurry to take his money. The room applauded, calling out that the headmaster was teaching, suggesting lewdly that he had more lessons to give.

Mrs. Ling stood, directed the girl delicately by the elbow, and guided her hand to Percival. "This is Jacqueline." It was only once there had been a flurry of excited congratulations, once Cho had cursed, thrown his chair down, and stalked away, once a new cognac bottle was opened and poured, and once the envious, aroused men in the room had finished crowding around Percival, that Percival looked up at Jacqueline's face and allowed himself to see that she, too, was pleased with the evening's outcome.

CHAPTER 10

PERCIVAL TOOK JACQUELINE'S HAND AND LED her out of Room 28, along the hallway, down the stairs. The lobby bustled with hotel boys busily serving the guests bowls of congee and putting out salted eggs, pickled radishes, and dried dace for breakfast. They had already heard about the game and called out to Headmaster Percival Chen, bowing, thanking him for the thousand-piastre notes that he distributed like leaflets as he went. The bundle of money was heavy inside his jacket, the girl on his arm delicate.

Outside, sun baked nighttime mud into the hard earth of day. Jacqueline stood next to Percival. Had he once dreamt of her? Now that it was just the two of them, hesitation mingled with his desire. He could tell her to go home, say that he was tired. What a strange thought, to doubt his pleasure. After a night without sleep, his instincts bled together just as night bled into morning. He touched the letter in his pocket, which now made him sad. He scolded away his melancholy. It was simple. He had won her, an uncommon beauty, along with a large sum of money. Nothing could be better.

The white Peugeot's nose appeared down the street, edged its way forward from an alley, nudging through the morning crowds. Percival gestured and Han Bai saw them. Other girls whom Mrs. Ling had introduced to Percival appeared more attractive half-masked by darkness, their faults glaring in sober daylight. Jacqueline was the opposite. In the morning light, she was too beautiful for the makeup and borrowed dress she was wearing, the shoulders of which were a little narrow, the waist a bit high. A man should follow his desires, Percival reminded himself. It was unhealthy not to, especially in this climate.

In Vietnamese Percival said, "Do you want to come with me?"

"Isn't that the idea?" she replied in English.

The car pulled up. Han Bai came around and opened the door for his boss and the girl. Percival helped her in, for there was nothing else to do, despite his knot of uncertainty and self-consciousness. Fatigue, nothing more.

"Do you want the windows down?" asked Percival.

"No," she said. "I like being on the inside. Looking out, like this."

Han Bai eased the car forward, crept slowly through the growing bustle of people.

"Are you tired? Do you need to rest?" Percival asked. Before she answered his first question, he nervously asked her another. "Where do you live?"

"It's better that we go to your place."

"Of course. Jacqueline . . . you have another name?"

"Do I need one?"

"What I mean is, I would like to know about you."

"Why?" She met his eyes briefly, then released him.

"Forgive me," he said, his words trailing off, drowned out by his beating heart. Had he somehow offended her? "It's not necessary."

Jacqueline took his hand, her fingers light but sure. Was this her first time, as Mrs. Ling had implied? Did she clasp her hand to his in determination to go through with it? They reached the quiet leafy stretch of Chong Heng Boulevard. Percival sat forward a little, began to turn towards her, felt he should speak but had nothing to say. Instead, he looked at Jacqueline's arm, extended over the glaring white territory of the starched cotton seat cover. She caressed his wrist, then his fingers, and rubbed them one by one.

She said, "These are lucky, yes?"

Jacqueline laced her fingers into the spaces between his. As they drove alongside the canal that ran into the heart of Cholon, Percival took shelter in silence. He wished to touch her face, to kiss her, but worried that to move might disrupt her hand, which rested in his. He found himself scared to do anything, a strange feeling. The water in the canal shimmered bright with clean morning light.

Once they reached Chen Hap Sing, Han Bai did not need to be told to drive around the back, where Percival could use the rear entrance to slip into the house with the girl. From there, he could steal upstairs without crossing through the school, like a thief in his own home. The students gossiped anyway, but the headmaster should not be brazen. The effort at discretion was important. The kitchen servants did not give any sign that they noticed as Percival led Jacqueline through the back of the house.

In the quiet of Percival's room, Jacqueline stood beneath the spinning fan. The fan traced its quiet circles of breeze. Her shoulders rose slightly as she inhaled. She closed her eyes and exhaled. That was her only invitation. They kissed, the intimate shock of tongues.

She stiffened a little where she stood. Her closed eyes made him bold, and he reached around, inched the zipper down the back of her dress, pressed his lips on her neck, then collarbone. Percival's hands shook as he ventured within the fabric. The muscles of her back tensed to his touch, her body warm, a film of sweat. He peeled the blue dress off her shoulders and down around her waist, slid one hand up to her shoulder. He could smell her hair, also the stronger scent beneath her arms. He kissed the hollow in her neck, then filled it with his tongue, traced down, licking the salt from her skin.

Percival circled around. Her eyes remained closed. Did she know that he wanted to look without being observed? Had she known this before he did? Was it her seriousness that both frightened him and drew him in? He stood before her, cupped her breasts, gliding lightly on their underside, stumbled on the nipples. As she breathed in, she tilted her head up, a little. He ran his hands down, over the curve of her hips, pushed the blue garment to the floor. He moved forward, so that he felt her breath on his lips. He held his own, wanting to be aware of hers only.

She opened her eyes, kissed him, pressed into him and folded her arms around his waist. Offering and possessing at once. His sex already anxious against hers. The inundation of skin, of wetness, a familiarity, of having found what he did not know he was looking for. Years ago, he might have thought he was falling in love. He hadn't slept, that was it. She undid the buttons of his shirt, down from neck to navel, breathing hard.

He said, "But you seem like a well-raised girl."

She fumbled with the clasp of his belt. "You talk like an old man. Or a shy virgin boy—and you are neither."

She knelt before him, took him with her lips. He shivered with her tongue's stroke, pleasure seeping out from his centre.

He took her face in his hands, brushed her cheeks, and held the back of her head softly, the fragrant brown hair in his fingers. She had light freckles on pale cheeks, and strewn over her white shoulders. Exotic marks. He had never been with a woman who had freckles. Were Jacqueline's Western-shaped lips different from an Asian woman's? Of course she was attracted to him, he thought, for a boy her own age would have already finished, unable to slow himself or give pleasure in return—age brought many benefits. He should have said more to Dai Jai on the subject of women, and lovemaking. He had only told him that he must marry a Chinese girl. The boy would learn the rest with time.

Percival felt the flickering of Jacqueline's tongue and the deep warmth in the back of her mouth. Her strangeness excited him. He should have told Dai Jai that he must not mistake the kind of woman suited to be a lover with the kind meant to be a wife. For a less experienced man, it could be easy to become confused. She came up a little, circled her tongue on the sensitive place on the underside, nearly pushed him beyond, but he wanted to save himself. He pulled her up gently, gasping, "You've done this before."

"What did you expect?" she asked, a worried look, her lips wet.

"Please lie down," he said. She did so, her thighs crossed like long, beautiful white scissors.

"Will you be sorry?"

"You ask this now."

Percival took in the translucency of her skin, lines of blue within the curve of her breasts, nipples hard in his mouth. His lips followed his hands down her flank to her thighs. He nudged open her soft white thighs and tasted her centre. Tongue, then his whole mouth, until she began to arch her back. He slid his body against hers. Both slippery with sweat, then his mouth to hers so that they shared each other's fluids, and he entered her. Her sharp inhalation. A moment of stillness. Then, slowly, slowly at first. Percival moved until he became captive, nearing the point where he might not be able to avert the end. He stopped, perched upon this precipice. Only their breathing. Then, languidly, as long as was possible. Gradually faster, until he gave in, abandoned himself to it, spilled over the edge of himself, knew that she had also done so. Although a man could be selfish in seduction, he must be considerate in pleasure.

A CAR HORN BLARED. PERCIVAL WOKE, sweating into the heat, kept his eyes closed until the horn relented. In the street, curses and shouts, an argument about the price of a chicken. A car door slammed, a Vespa buzzed past. The bright light of early afternoon had invaded. From below he heard his students going out into the street. It was the hour of the midday meal. Hawkers yelled out their dishes, morning already forgotten, from somewhere below came the scent of prawns and green onions in the same pan, the stinking sweet odour of durian. Percival looked around the room. The girl was gone, of course. He got up, found shorts and a singlet, stood surveying the emptiness. Felt an ache for her, a sadness at her absence. He did not usually feel that for Mrs. Ling's girls. But there was something he had forgotten. Something that had been so important last night, though now it lingered just out of his memory's reach.

The money, of course, the money. It was not on his desk. She was gone, and therefore the money must be gone as well. His keys were on the side table, but not the money. He could not remember what he had done with the envelope when he came home. The girl must have paid attention, though. Cursing himself, Percival lifted his mattress, nothing. She could be anywhere by now. That money was Chen Hap

Sing. He flung his clothes off the chair—only an empty chair. She had not told him where she was from, had eluded his question when he asked. Had she already planned to rob him?

Perhaps Mrs. Ling could locate her, but maybe not. Percival opened the shutters to see if he might catch her walking across the square, a small chance. In the thick grey of the clouds, a storm approached. The street was still dry, but the sky flickered with lightning. Distant rumbles of thunder mixed with those of artillery, both from the southwest. The market girls rushed along with their carts. He scanned the room. His jacket lay in a heap by the door. He seized it, and in the pocket was the thick envelope of bills. He felt guilty now. How could he think that she had robbed him? He had not paid her, he realized. Was she so new to this business that she neglected to be paid? He went slowly to the window again, wanted to ask her to return, to come back often, to ask any price. A plaintive prayer bell rang. A cool gust came through the window in advance of the rain, swaying the smaller branches of the flame trees. It blew the girls' *ao dais* around their waists and ankles. The cars and motorcycles honked more impatiently in a sudden rush to reach their destination. The one-eyed monk looked to the sky, a prayer bell in hand. Percival did not see Jacqueline.

There was a splash of water. From the bathroom, the sounds of washing, water scooped from the blue clay jars, then after a moment trickling down the drain. He saw her clothing, neatly folded on a side table. He folded ten thousand piastres into the dress, a normal rate. He thought about it, and added another ten. He wanted to leave more but was scared to show how much he wished to please her, how badly he wanted her to come back. The soft padding of feet, the creaking of the bathroom door, and Jacqueline returned to the room. She had a sheet pulled around her. She closed the door and stood in front of it. He looked at her, and then again out the window. The wind caused the row of trees along the sidewalk to shiver, their leaves flailing. It did not occur to him to speak. It somehow felt normal to see her there.

Jacqueline said, "What are you doing?"

"I am waiting for the rain."

"Can I wait with you?"

"Please. It will be here soon. Can you smell it?"

Jacqueline walked to the window and stood so that they touched.

There was the rising scent of wilted jasmine flowers and burned rice in the bottom of pots. A flashbulb of lightning burst close by, and thunder chased it. Rain surged through tree leaves, reddened the roof tiles like fresh blood. Water rippled over the curved clay, spilled to the terrace below, flooded the gutters and coursed along the street of men and women huddled in thin plastic ponchos. It fell from the top of the window and splashed on the sill, sprinkling Percival and Jacqueline.

"Why are you here?" he said.

"A strange question."

"Will you come back?"

"If you like."

He said with sadness, "What else would you say, I suppose?"

"As if you wished for any other answer." She squeezed his hand and pulled him back from the window. "You think too much. You should feel more." She guided him towards the bed.

"But you are too precious for this. You must have a reason."

She let the sheet fall around her feet. This time, neither hesitated.

When he woke from a subterranean sleep, almost evening now, thick wet air hung over Cholon's mud. He lay still for a long time, hoping that she was there, scared by his need for her. He heard nothing. This time, she was gone.

Percival stood and dressed. He should visit the Teochow Clan Association while the treasurer was there. He counted out his entire debt to them and put the remaining cash in the school safe. He found the letter from Dai Jai. He took it out, examined it closely, slowly read over Dai Jai's descriptions of Shanghai. There was a good description of trees, "the pruned branches like knuckles on a worker's hand . . ." He observed some grammatical mistakes that he would correct in his next letter to Dai Jai, but the boy's written Chinese would improve now that he was in his motherland. Percival put the letter safely in his desk drawer. He recognized the urge to test his good luck again. No, it was important to respect gifts that arrived with such impeccable timing. He would pay off the Teochow Clan Association rather than gamble his winnings. He imagined the treasurer's surprise and consternation. Even though he had insisted that Percival must make an instalment today, he would be annoyed to now receive the full sum.

Percival tallied the debts that remained. They were spread between creditors, he reasoned, as he went out into the square, therefore less dangerous. He was on solid enough ground that he could hire teachers for the new classes now. He waved for a cyclo. He would not summon Han Bai, for he would be resting, having sat outside the Sun Wah Hotel all of last night. In the distance, he heard mortars. He got into the cyclo, and told the man to take him to the Teochow temple.

He tried to think of what recent news corresponded with the shelling. He could not bring it to mind. A few helicopters passed in fast single file, the start of a night of fighting. He attempted to calculate the interest he was saving through this payment.

It was no use.

As much as Percival tried to fill his mind with other things, he could not stop thinking about her.

THE NEXT AFTERNOON, PERCIVAL WENT TO his own room rather than taking his siesta in the office. It couldn't hurt to be upstairs, though his wish to see Jacqueline was unlikely to be fulfilled. She had probably moved on to another assignation. He hoped she would come back, but it would be easier if she didn't, safer. This was a vulnerability he had not known since Cecilia, being scared of his own desire. Now, within the shuttered room, unable to sleep, did he hear someone in the hallway? A servant, no doubt. Even as he looked anxiously to the door, Percival scolded himself for hoping. The morning students were departing noisily downstairs. He saw the door peek open and a hand on its edge, the chestnut hair, her face in profile like a thief or a lover. Something he had not expected—Jacqueline looked as nervous as he felt. Of course, she had waited for the students to be let out. In the commotion, she entered the school and slipped up the stairs.

If Dai Jai were still here, he might have made an effort to impress upon the boy, by way of example, that this was a matter of pleasure rather than love, that a man should make these distinctions. He might have arranged regular trysts with Jacqueline in a nearby hotel. As it was, he told Foong Jie that, from now on, there would be a change in routine. The afternoon meal should be left in his private quarters on the third floor rather than in the headmaster's office. He explained that he needed time alone to reflect upon school business. Foong Jie nodded. Each day, she left a meal for two.

For weeks, Percival feigned surprise at her arrival. Afterwards, as she washed herself from the clay jars, he put money under her clothing. The true surprise, of which he said nothing, was the deepening of his pleasure, beyond simply that of a beautiful girl's favours. Each time she crept through the door, he felt happy that she and no one else was with him. With most of Mrs. Ling's introductions, the enjoyment was contained within the few hours removed from the rest of his life. To be satisfied by a woman and to forget her by paying was complete. He might see her again or not—he did not think about her. With Jacqueline, he thought about her constantly when she was not there, and this longing was merely suspended by her arrival. He still paid, of course, for why else should she come back? The money offered him some assurance that he understood what this was about. She was not Chinese. Whatever he felt for her did not change that.

Even as an ease grew into their time together, Jacqueline never said when she might return, nor did he ask. On days that she did not appear, Percival stood at the window to see if she might come down the street, despite knowing that if she had not arrived by the time the school quieted for the siesta, she would not come.

Though the most dangerous financial pressure had been relieved, Percival's days were still taken up with trying to recruit new students whose parents could pay advance tuition, meeting with certain impatient creditors, and making payments to those who could not be put off. Mak reported that he had managed to get Peters to come up with the idea of a certification of schools, but they would have to wait for him to pursue it further. The press of these problems fell away from Percival during the middle of the day. He anticipated his lover and read letters from Dai Jai as he waited. Dai Jai wrote twice a week, dutifully, and the first month of letters arrived singly, each about a week after being written.

He wrote about his landlady and his school. He wrote about things that were unfamiliar to Percival, neighbourhood committees and cadres. He wrote about the small problems that he faced. There was a difficulty with his clothing not being suitable. Apparently, everyone in China had begun to dress identically. In another letter, there was mention of some friction with the neighbourhood authorities when he tried to sell one tael of gold. Selling gold was anti-revolutionary, Dai Jai wrote, and he was a bourgeois for possessing it.

There was no mail during the second month he was away, and then a bundle of letters—bound with a rubber band after having been cut open and read by censors—arrived together at the end of the month. Percival had the impression of pages missing, for there seemed to be gaps in the text, but the pages were not numbered so he couldn't be sure. He wondered whether the censors had been in China or Vietnam, or both. Percival did not know how Dai Jai's problems had been settled and wrote to ask, but his questions went unanswered.

Over the following letters, Dai Jai began to repeat himself, described the school where he had enrolled, the lane where he lived, the weather. There were fewer grammatical errors, but Percival learned nothing about whether Dai Jai liked the place, was interested in his classes, or was making friends amongst his classmates. He regretted his first response to Dai Jai, with its corrections of the boy's Chinese. He felt as if part of himself had gone with his son to China but was now fading, its feelings becoming opaque. But when Jacqueline visited, Percival felt whole, for everything was contained in their skin, their breathing, in the progression towards climax and the quiet that followed.

After their sex, with desire stripped to satisfaction, he was able to connect one thing to another: sex with loneliness, luck with fear, emotion with memory. Thoughts of the past were fresh. As they lay naked, Percival found himself telling Jacqueline his early memories from Shantou, of the time before his father first left for Indochina. The train passed through the village twice a week in each direction, and when Chen Pie Sou was very small, Chen Kai often took him to see it, tantalized him with wild stories about its routes. It was bound for the coast at night, and Chen Kai said it was going to heaven to bring food for the ancestors' spirits. It passed through again the next morning. Chen Kai pointed to the smoke from the front, the breath of the spirits, he would insist. When he grew a little older and no longer believed these tales, Chen Pie Sou would go to watch the train with the village boys. Often, they would gather to bet on what would happen when it appeared. Would it stop, or simply sound its horn? If it stopped, would it be for cargo or a passenger? If for cargo, would there be a mail package from one of the fathers who was away in the land of the Gold Mountain, or a shipment for Shantou's only merchant? All these possibilities were wagered upon. Chen Pie Sou's friends complained that his luck was too good, that he won too often. He did not tell them that he assessed the odds, studied the patterns, in order to bet. He checked to see if the merchant's shelves were full. If so, he wagered against cargo. Was a packet ship due in port? Then more likely there would be a passenger or mail from the Gold Mountain. Because he won more than he lost, Chen Pie Sou accumulated old chipped mah-jong pieces, marbles, sometimes a copper coin. One day, when he proudly showed his father his stash of treasures, Chen Kai said, "My son has excellent luck! Good for you. Just remember, never wager more than you can afford to lose. Leave yourself room to recover. Have something for the next bet. That's how you'll come out ahead in the end."

Jacqueline listened, and stroked Percival's head, considering the story. She laughed, "His lesson didn't take, then?"

He had already revealed to her that if he had lost that night to Cho, he would have lost Chen Hap Sing. It had been worth it, he said, to win her. Why did he tell her so much? It had been a relief to confess his dread of losing that mah-jong game, and his terrified hope that he would flee to China if he did. To say such a thing made it real, and then allowed it to pass away. She laughed at his convolutions, so he did, too. She was not even Chinese, he admonished himself. But then, he had to admit to himself, he was all the more free because she was not. She had no relatives or neighbours in Cholon to spread rumours. She was not a friend of a teacher who could undermine his authority, had no connection to some servant who could gossip, and was not linked to some local business family that could use knowledge to take advantage of him.

Even with Mak, Percival did not reveal his doubts or emotions. After all, he depended upon Mak and did not want him to have the power of knowing everything. Theirs was a relationship of trust, not of intimacy. Jacqueline had no other connection to his life, and so Percival soon found that he could tell her anything. He related the stories of his childhood that he had told Dai Jai many times, but now he recounted them without their lesson, their moral, which he had applied for his son's benefit. Instead, Percival remembered how he had felt at the time, and told his lover. He told her about Dai Jai's favourite foods, that not a day went by when he did not wonder if the boy was eating well. He confessed his pain that his son was far away in China and the guilt of having opposed Saigon's Vietnamese language directive. If only he had signed the document receipt and shut his mouth. Was he a good father, though? He wasn't sure now. Percival was on the verge of tears. Jacqueline saw that, and cried on his behalf.

In the afternoons that followed their lovemaking, Percival began to tell Jacqueline things from long ago that had never been buried. He thought of his favourite teachers at La Salle, even now, when he was approaching a difficult lesson. In comparison he was a fraud, and would be ashamed if any of his old teachers knew he had the best reputation amongst English headmasters in Vietnam. They would never know, for they had all died during the war. He told Jacqueline about the Japanese invasion of Hong Kong, and confessed his own cowardice. His finest classmates had tried to hide girls to save them from Japanese gang rapes. They had run off to join the Chinese resistance. Few of these brave ones had survived the war. He had sat in his room, the walls pierced by screams.

Percival confided the shameful truth of his father's last years in Cholon. He had pieced it together from the household servants. With the news of his first wife's death in Shantou, Chen Kai had become unable to sleep. For days, he wept with guilt at not having returned to China while Muy Fa was alive. He spread word that he sought a buyer for Chen Hap Sing and the rice business in order to return to China for good. Ba Hai pretended to cooperate, but in reality stymied these inquiries. She gave Chen Kai an opium pipe and suggested that he smoke it in order to rest. Desperate for sleep and for relief from his guilt, he soon came to depend upon the narcotic. Without Chen Kai's knowledge, Ba Hai made all the arrangements for Chen Pie Sou's French *laissez-passer* and his studies in Hong Kong. She forged letters to Chen Pie Sou pretending to be Chen Kai and signed them with his red chop. She forged letters to her husband from his son. Sometimes, when Chen Kai was under the spell of sweet smoke, Ba Hai took the Annamese warehouse foreman to her bed in the middle of the day. Until then, she had crept to him at night. Now, she wanted to show the household what she dared to do. Soon, she began to fire Chinese workers on the smallest pretext and hired only her own relatives for the rice warehouse. She made sure that there was a constant supply of the purple boxes of Thai Royal Grade opium for her husband.

Though Ba Hai gave Percival and Cecilia a room of their own when they arrived in Cholon, it was at the far end of the family quarters, away from Chen Kai. Percival insisted on sleeping on a cot in his father's room, to prevent anyone from sneaking in opium. On the advice of one stoop-backed servant, Percival purchased a case of cognac. He filled a bottle halfway with black balls of opium paste, and then the rest with cognac. He slept with his head on the bottle for fear that Chen Kai might seize it and eat the opium balls. Hour by hour, day after day, when Chen Kai began to shake, Percival poured him a glass of the cloudy liquid and then topped the bottle up with liquor. "One more pipe. Please," Chen Kai would whimper. "What kind of a son are you, to disobey your father?" For days, he protested loudly, howled and sweated. He ran to the toilet to expel his spasms of watery stool, and shook with his need for the drug. The worst of the withdrawal was dulled by the infusion, and after a painful few weeks he no longer pleaded for his drug, but suffered in acceptance, trembling.

"Drink," Percival would say, putting the glass in his father's unsteady hands. This continued over weeks, and the infusion became more and more clear.

Ba Hai engaged in loud copulation with the foreman every afternoon. One day, as Chen Kai and Percival sat in the second-floor room, they heard the rhythmic groans begin. Chen Kai had begun eating again, and he was in the middle of a bowl of noodles. Although his skin was still loose, there was some flesh returning to his bones. He continued to eat.

In the room above them, Ba Hai moaned, and there was the slap of bodies meeting. Chen Kai seemed oblivious to his ongoing humiliation. He said to his son, "I came to this country with nothing, and soon became a rich rice merchant, eventually the biggest trader in Cholon. When I arrived, I was homesick and wanted only to return to China. But once I had money, it stretched me between two places. I knew all these years that your mother missed me. But then, with money came pleasures. As I began to enjoy life here, I felt sad to leave it. There are fruits here, like the custard apple, that we do not have at home. The rain is different, and so are the women." He drained his glass of cognac and held it out. "Every year, I promised I would return to Shantou for good, that I would take just one more year's profit." Percival took the glass from his father's hand. Filled it. Upstairs, the foreman grunted breathy impatience. "I married Ba Hai to have a simple country girl in my bed, and this made it seem less pressing to return home. The Japanese invaded China, which gave me a fresh excuse not to return. Of course, they have come here, too, and Ba Hai wishes to steal my wealth and be rid of me."

Percival put the glass down. "I'm here now, Father. I will protect what is yours."

"Yes, I'm counting on you." Chen Kai gestured for another glass of the infusion, and Percival hastily poured it. "Meanwhile, I'm just starting to realize what I've lost."

Percival swallowed hard. As a child, he had imagined his father suffering to accumulate a large enough sum of gold for his family's sake. It was not a son's place to be angry at his father. Percival felt ashamed, and poured a glass of the cognac infusion for himself.

Chen Kai sipped. "You see, I was confused." Ba Hai and her lover cried out together, and Percival began to tremble a little. Chen Kai continued calmly, almost primly, "The only place for Chinese is in China, and the only suitable wives are from the motherland. You have done well—you have taken a Chinese wife and will have a harmonious marriage."

THE HEADMASTER'S WAGER • 151

"Yes, Father," said Percival, though Cecilia had been complaining relentlessly about the room they had been given, about the house, about the heat, the country, everything she laid eyes on.

Chen Kai seemed to take no notice of his second wife reaching the height of her pleasure in the room above them. "Do you think that your mother's ghost will ever forgive me?"

"I don't know. It is not my place to know, I am your son."

"*Gwai jai*," said Chen Kai, and sighed, closing his eyes. An obedient son.

As his energy returned, Chen Kai began to make his plans for returning to China. Percival thought that he would allow his father to study the map, even to prepare a bag, if this occupied him. He would stop his father from actually making such a dangerous journey. He would restrain him if necessary. For almost a year, this idea seemed to disappear. Later, Percival realized that his father had been waiting patiently, gaining strength. One night, having long since returned to the room he and Cecilia had been given, Percival was woken by the faint creak of floorboards. He got to the hallway in time to hear the front door, ran down the stairs, dashed out and was confronted by the oily black night into which Chen Kai had disappeared.

"So you see," Percival said to Jacqueline, "I weaned my father from opium, but perhaps, if I had been more protective after he recovered, he would still be alive. I failed. I should have protected him better. He could have returned to China after the war. He would be enjoying his old age in comfort."

The more he told her of his secrets, and as she accepted them along with the familiarity of their bed, the less Percival could deny that he hoped for Jacqueline each day. He must be careful that Cecilia didn't find out. He wouldn't put it past her to write to Dai Jai that his father was with a *métisse*. The boy might misunderstand. After all, he was too young to know that being lovers was not the same as love.

HE SAID ONE AFTERNOON, "IT'S STRANGE for me, to be with you."

"Why? Am I strange, or are we strange?"

He thought for a moment, and embraced her, teasing, "You taste like milk. Yes, that's it. A yellow woman tastes only of woman."

Jacqueline laughed and said, "Of course you think so. Your tongue is Chinese. Perhaps that is the difference, rather than anything to do with me. Besides, if what you say is true, I should taste half of milk and half of woman."

"That's it, then." He stroked her arm. "You are half-foreigner. It confuses my mouth. How should it know what to taste?"

She stiffened. "I'm a foreigner? What a strange thing for me to hear from you, when I was born here and you were not." She twisted her hair in her fingers.

"I didn't mean anything . . ."

She shook her hair out, smoothed it back, and laughed. "The yellow think I am more white. The white see the yellow. People always see the portion of other more clearly than that of self." She pulled the sheet up over her bare chest.

"You've never told me about your parents."

"Have you asked?"

"Would you tell me something about them?"

"My mother was a Vietnamese peasant who played at being European. My father was a French engineer who was bored of French women. My mother dreamed of Paris, but never saw it. So there is my story. I am here." She looked out the window.

"Lucky for me, then."

"That I am here?" She placed her hand on his arm. "I am with you, a Chinese, so why do you care what my parents are? You enjoy me, regardless."

"If your father knew you were here, he would be angry."

"He doesn't know."

"Of course, you come here, to keep this secret. They are in Saigon then, your parents?"

"A long time ago my father broke his promise to send for us."

She explained to Percival that her father had to go ahead, he said, when he left for France in 1955. It was easier to get the documents in Paris, supposedly, and would take no more than two months. He had left enough for them to live on for three months, to pay the rent, the dues at the Cercle Sportif, to eat in restaurants, to buy goodbye gifts for friends and greeting gifts for his family while he arranged their passage to France. He had left money for them to have travel clothes made. The money would have been a decade's expenses for an Annamese peasant, but it was just a few months of their costs in Saigon at the time. After three months, the French embassy still knew nothing of the visas and immigration documents that he was supposed to arrange. His former employer claimed to have no French address for him. Another month passed. The rent was a month over-due, and they ate only steamed rice and vegetables. The day before the next rent was due, Jacqueline and her mother slipped out of the bright, spacious apartment in Saigon, each with as much clothing stuffed into suitcases as they could carry away, to move back with her mother's family in the village of Thanh Ha.

"Before we left Saigon, we used to go to films at night. They screened them on the patio at the Cercle. I intended to become a famous French actress and learned all the lines. The pure-white girls made fun of me for it, but I knew they were wrong. I would wear pancake makeup, which I had read all the great stars used liberally, and no one would see my mixed blood. Then, when my father aban-doned us, I realized they had been right all along. I had been the fool."

In their home village, Jacqueline's aunties snickered that her mother was no better than them in the end. In any case, how could she have let her Frenchman go ahead to France? Open legs and empty hands, they laughed. The fool. Jacqueline's cousins used to snatch the rice from her bowl and say, "We can't let you eat such rough native food. Wait until we find you some biscuits and milk." Soon, Jacqueline and her mother returned to the city, to the squalid Sum Guy district, in the mud flats across from Cholon.

"Many French were leaving in '55," said Percival, as if this excused the abandonment. "Or perhaps something happened to him."

"When she realized he was not coming, my mother cried over all the money we had thrown away. I felt so bad about all the ice creams, films, lime sodas, and frites that I had enjoyed. I had loved those things, but suddenly I hated them, hated myself for missing them. I hated everything French for a while, but I could not stay that way forever—as you say, I taste of milk. My mother believed he must have died. She made me pray to him at the ancestral altar. A year later, we heard that he married again in France. A French girl with bad teeth, from a good family that owned a factory. His mother had a bride waiting, they said."

Percival said quietly, "I'm sorry for your mother. For you."

She laughed. "I have become serene about my situation. One looks forward. It's the only way to survive."

"What did your mother do?"

"After my father, no Vietnamese would ever marry her. Because of me, there was no hiding her involvement with a Frenchman. She was tainted. Men thought her pretty enough, but she could never be a wife. My mother decided that if men were going to leave her alone in the bed after having what they wanted, they should leave some piastres."

"Was it your mother, then, who brought you to Mrs. Ling?" Was that all he was? A customer in an inherited profession?

"Oh, no. She wanted me to study, to be educated. She would be ashamed, if she knew what I was doing." She blushed. "Although this is not how I expected it to turn out."

Percival wished, as he often did nowadays, that he had not met her in Room 28 of the Sun Wah Hotel. "Well, you have chosen me," he said. "I was wrong if I ever thought it was the other way around." He would have paid her ten times more, and he wished that he wasn't paying her at all.

She nodded. "Yes, and I come and go as I please."

"I'll keep it secret," he said hastily, afraid already of losing her. "Will your mother stop us . . . if she learns of it?"

Jacqueline looked to the window. She said, "My mother has been gone a few months now."

"Where?"

"She went to visit our relatives in the village. In Thanh Ha. It was at the end of the dry season. There was a gun battle that night, between the Viet Cong and the government soldiers." Jacqueline's eyes fell to the crumpled sheets between them. She turned away slightly.

"I'm sorry," he said, feeling the uselessness of the words. Thanh Ha was often in the news, with repeated announcements that it had been "pacified." He put his arm around her. "She was political?"

"Not at all. A stray bullet. I wasn't even with her when she died. I was in Sum Guy studying for exams. I had to borrow for her funeral."

"And now you are here."

"With you." She began to dress.

"My father . . . He ran away from this house across the square into a moonless night, into a war," Percival told her. "That was the last time I saw him. He was trying to get to China. I often wonder if my father might have been mistaken for someone's enemy—a bystander victim like your mother. Along the border, the Japanese and the Chinese were fighting viciously at that time."

"Shooting someone can be a simple mistake." She stopped dressing, allowed herself to cry. He stroked her hair. His cheek became wet with her tears. And then his own, he realized. He had only sought a girl for a night.

He did not possess the words he needed. Finally, their arms released one another. The only thing he could think to say was, "Do I give you enough money?" More tears came from her eyes, but she said nothing. He fumbled for money, seized a handful from his wallet without counting, some more, put it down before her, could not bear to look at it. She dressed quickly, tucked the piastres into her pocket. She touched her lips to his cheek, and vanished out the door.

Percival watched her from the balcony, as he did each time she left Chen Hap Sing. The afternoon light was beginning to soften. She wore a simple conical hat, and as it drifted down the street he saw how she wore it low to keep her handsome face out of view. Soon, she disappeared in the crowd, like a cat moving unseen, away from danger. What had wedged between his desire and its fulfilment? Where did regret creep in between the two? Regret at having found love in this way, with this *métisse*. That's what it was, he might as well admit it to himself. Meanwhile regret at having gone too quickly. At having paid for something priceless? Usually money made things clean. Now it filled him with a sadness for everything else that he wanted from this girl. He should rest, lie down to calm his wild emotions, which were bleeding into his thoughts—a dangerous thing.

Percival tried to lie down but could not stay still. He got up, went down to the sitting room and paced until it was dark. When the night had cleared the air, he stood up, went to the radio, and tuned in to the shortwave broadcast from home. There was a news report on the triumphant progress of the revolution of culture, a clip of an address by Mao. It sounded just like many others. He listened attentively, trying to guess what might be happening to Dai Jai beyond the bland words of his letters and the radio news, which seemed to be more predictable, more formulaic each month. He had turned the radio on for something reassuring, something solidly Chinese, but the Mandarin-speaking announcer reminded him that he ought to feel embarrassed about Jacqueline, that he should be ashamed to be in love with a foreigner. She was mixed, yes, and neither part was Chinese.

CHAPTER 12

ON AN AFTERNOON OF THICK BREEZES and grey clouds, Jacqueline appeared in Percival's room just as he was choosing a tie to wear with his white tussore silk suit.

"You look very handsome."

He was startled. "I'm sorry. I have an important meeting today." He was genuinely sorry, and wondered if they had time for a brief tryst—but Mak had warned him that Peters was very punctual.

"Wear a red one, for luck," she said.

He held one up, too gaudy. "I should appear respectable." He selected a thin black one.

"Who is it with?" she asked, kissing him tenderly on the corner of the mouth.

He stepped back and began to do the tie. It choked him. "An American. About a school matter." Who else but an American would wish to meet at the hottest hour of the day? Mak had said that it was almost a *fait accompli*. Peters had been carefully led by Mak to come up with the idea himself of certifying schools. At first, he had been put off by the prospect of having to assess all the English schools in the area. Perhaps it would be easier to embark on a trial with one school, Mak had suggested, offering up the Percival Chen English Academy.

Even better, Mak had explained to Percival with obvious relish, Peters was involved in new State Department projects that might require hiring many graduates of the school. American jobs were what gave their diplomas value. It was essential, Mak had told Percival, that Peters felt confident in Percival. Today was their first formal meeting. Percival also knew that he still owed half of the original debt, still a large sum. He had repaid a fortune already, but the interest payments ran away ahead of him.

"It's at the Cercle Sportif, and I must be there in half an hour." He looked at his watch. "There's just enough time to get to Saigon."

"May I come along?" Jacqueline said. "I haven't been to the Cercle since I was a child." Had he ever seen her there? Her mother would have given up their membership around the time that he and Cecilia had taken one.

Percival hesitated. He would like to take her, but no Chinese would bring a woman to a business meeting. Then again, Americans sometimes appeared at lunch with their wives or their secretaries. Jacqueline was wearing a simple, presentable skirt and blouse. A beautiful girl could improve the mood of any discussion. "Of course you can," he said, and they went down to the waiting car.

Han Bai seemed surprised to see Jacqueline, but said nothing. He held the door open for her. She was happy during the drive to Saigon and told Percival some more of her memories from the club. At the Cercle, with Jacqueline on his arm, Percival squinted out from beneath the awning across the patio of the inner courtyard. Even under the overcast sky, Mak's pressed shirt glowed brilliant white. Mak had chosen the most discreet table, at the quiet end of the patio, nestled near a little clutch of oleanders. He sat with his guest, laughing with uncharacteristic enthusiasm. The tall American must have made a joke. Percival saw the *gwei lo* lean forward with a further remark, and Mak dutifully roared with laughter. Mak looked up, saw Percival, and nodded. The American looked up and smiled that wide-open smile so many of them wore for all occasions. Percival stepped out from the shade of the awning, and after two steps he saw Mak's face fall into confusion. Halfway across the patio, as he tried to decipher Mak's expression, he realized that he was walking alone. Jacqueline's hand had slipped from his arm, and he looked back to see her standing, frozen. Percival retraced his steps. He took her hand and whispered, "Don't worry, just smile. I'm going to say you are my secretary."

"Why is Teacher Mak here?"

"He arranged the meeting, of course," said Percival.

Jacqueline said, "I must leave now."

He stared at Jacqueline, his beautiful lover who spoke native Vietnamese, a little French, and very good English. "How do you know he is a teacher?"

"I will find my own way out," she said softly. "I just wanted to see the Cercle again. I didn't think . . ."

She was a student at the school. She slipped into his room when the morning classes let out. It was the one rule he held to, that he did not bed the students. But how could Percival have imagined that a student of his school would be at the Sun Wah Hotel? Percival tried to think through his panic, to think of what was best, what needed to be done. It would not look right for the headmaster to appear with a girl and for her to suddenly flee. The American must have a good impression of this meeting, must feel confident in the Percival Chen English Academy.

"I didn't know Teacher Mak would be here." Then she pleaded, "You go to your meeting, it will be successful. Go."

"You can't leave now," he declared. "What kind of secretary would leave her boss before an important meeting?" He put her hand firmly on his arm, and proceeded across the patio.

Mak's face was stone. He said, "Headmaster, we are here to do business," looking straight at Jacqueline.

"Which is why my secretary has joined us, in case I need her to take notes," said Percival. "A pleasure, Mr. Peters." The waiter approached.

Percival managed to remember one of Mak's pointers, that many American officials did not drink alcohol in the daytime. A pitcher of cold lime water sat on the table, and Percival flagged the waiter for two more glasses. Peters was clean-shaven, and his blond hair was clipped in the neat, too-short fashion of American military officers and junior government officials. He wore his shirt open, and Percival regretted wearing a tie. He felt as if he were being strangled.

"*Rat vui mung duoc quen biet ban, ong giao su*," said Peters. He was pleased to see the esteemed teacher again. He bowed slightly, his eyes on Jacqueline, who sat between him and Percival.

"Please, call me Percival," said Percival in English, "and your Vietnamese is very good." Mak sat opposite.

"*Toi noi duoc chut it*," said Peters, making an obvious but reasonably successful effort with the language.

"You speak it very well," said Percival. "It is also a foreign language to me." Mak shot him a look. Perhaps he shouldn't have said that, or maybe it was the girl that earned this reproach. There were so many students, he told himself. How could Mak expect him to know them all? He hadn't taught regularly for years. It's not as if he went down to the classroom to seduce a student.

"This is Mr. Peters' second visit to this country," said Mak. "Decorated for bravery. Nineteen sixty-four, am I right, Mr. Peters?"

"Yes, I was in uniform last time I was here," said Peters. "Went back stateside, went to college, got a nice quiet government job with the State Department. Guess where it landed me?"

"At least you are in Saigon instead of some firebase," said Percival. He avoided Mak's eye. Percival absolved himself. He did not look at students in that way, had learned not to, so of course he had not recognized her at Mrs. Ling's side. It was not his fault. "This is a civilized place."

"Some say it is," said the American. "Except for the odd grenade, and the politics."

The waiter brought the two glasses and poured from the sweating pitcher of water.

Mak handed Peters a glass. The American couldn't keep from eyeing Jacqueline.

"How is your work going?" said Percival. "You told me a little about it when we met at the bar. I've been wanting to hear more."

Peters said, "When I was in uniform, up near Pleiku, we had two enemies—the Cong, and the guys issuing crazy orders from desks in Saigon. Now, I'm a desk. There are advantages, of course. Saigon contains much beauty." This, he addressed to Jacqueline, Percival was convinced. Why had he agreed to let Jacqueline accompany him? He could have brought her to the Cercle anytime she wished. There had been no need to bring her now. Percival was tempted to ask the American whether the feminine beauty of the country had also drawn him back to Vietnam, but this was certainly not what Mak wished him to say.

Mak donned a smile. "Headmaster, Mr. Peters has come up with an idea. I might have mentioned it to you. It would be easier for him to hire staff if he knew that all graduates of a certain school had consistently good English abilities. I wondered if your school might be able to help?" Mak ignored Jacqueline, as if she were invisible to him.

"We need a lot of translators in our new spheres of activity. I'm going be involved more on the ploughs, less on the swords," said Peters. "Health, education, community-building, only a little intelligence and military liaison. There'll be half a million Americans in this tiny country by the end of the year—most of them armed—but I think it may be the unarmed ones who bring the little man on board. Good translation is at the heart of every partnership."

Percival nodded. "We can supply excellent English-speakers. It would be our way of assisting our American allies." He raised his lime water to Peters, who clinked his glass in response.

"Headmaster, I have to ask you, what do you think of this war?"

Percival had met enough Americans to know that Peters was not trying to be rude. That's just how they were. He sipped his water, turned to the guest, and considered his English words carefully. What was the most intelligent way to claim indifference? He said, "This war is difficult for me to understand. People have varying opinions, which themselves are clouded by numerous biases. Recently the war has been so . . . confusing, and so quickly changing, that I have not been able to follow it very well." He sat back, hoped that his response had been intelligible, and empty.

"And what do you think about us Americans being involved? Some say that we interfere with Vietnamese politics. What is your opinion?"

Mak cleared his throat uncomfortably.

"Well, I look at it perhaps with the same eyes that you do. In that . . ." he struggled for what to say next, "I am an outsider to this place. For me, politics here have been confusing ever since . . . in fact, ever since Le Loi achieved independence from us Chinese five hundred years ago." That should be sufficiently distant.

"That's right, you Chinese had your time occupying this country." Peters grinned and sat back a little. "As the French did? I assume you are part French, *mademoiselle* . . ."

"Jacqueline," she managed to say.

"The most beautiful women in the country are half-French, don't you think?" he asked Percival. Then to Jacqueline, "Does it seem to you we have occupied the country, we Americans?"

Why was the American pressing so hard for their opinions? wondered Percival. He felt as if he were at a gaming table, except that he did not know what was the winning hand. Jacqueline couldn't manage a reply. Percival said, "It is for you Americans to decide whether your presence is an occupation—but this does not change what I teach."

Peters laughed. "You should be a diplomat, Headmaster. Did you know that Roosevelt offered Chiang Kai-shek control of Indochina at the end of the Second World War? He didn't want the French to get it back. Didn't think it was good for the region and didn't think they deserved it after bending over for the Japs. Thought the Chinese should manage the situation."

Percival knew that Chiang had refused Roosevelt's offer. The Annamese, Chiang explained to the American president, would never accept Chinese control, for they resented outsiders.

It must be a compliment, if Peters called him a diplomat, since Peters' bosses were diplomats. Equally, Percival realized, that might make it an insult. The winning hand, Percival intuited, was to allow the American to feel that he knew more. This should be coupled with impartiality. He said, "Is that so? Fascinating. Mr. Peters, you are interested in history."

"Smart guy, Chiang, to stay out of it. Of course, history twists in every direction, doesn't it? I met a guy in D.C. who used to advise Ho Chi Minh, Uncle Ho was our friend for awhile. Our Office of

Strategic Services once backed him. Yeah, incredible, the guys who became the CIA."

Percival had read some of Ho Chi Minh's early speeches, written by his American advisors, and modelled on the Declaration of Independence. He said, "Well, there is your expression, history twisting: Half of the officers in the South Vietnamese Army were once Viet Minh, yes?" Percival heard Mak take a deep breath. He wondered whether the American understood that this also could equally be a compliment or a criticism. In any case, complete naivety did not suit Percival.

"Some say so," agreed Peters, narrowing his eyes. "They speak good French, too, embarrasses me when I try."

Having run out of words, Percival settled on a tight-lipped smile. The difficulty with this game, if that's what it was, was that not only did Percival not know the winning hand, but the American would decide whether he held it. Finally, he broke the silence by saying, "I don't pay much attention to Vietnamese history. What I do hear is like hearing some other family's troubles. After all, I am Chinese. It is not my country, nor my war."

Mak interrupted with forced enthusiasm, clapped Percival on the back. "Our English teaching is the best in South Vietnam, Mr. Peters, and Headmaster Percival Chen ensures that all graduates are excellent conversationalists. There is no politics in our curriculum. No history, either."

"I see. Yes, of course. You are Chinese. That is ideal, to observe this mess from the outside. I would like to come to Chinatown one day, to visit your school." Peters looked into his glass and said, "Tell me something else. Do people in Cholon think that the bombing of North Vietnam will draw the Chinese into this war?"

This time, Percival's smile was wide, for the correct answer was obvious. "I'm too preoccupied running my school to consider such things. In any case, wouldn't China be foolish to fight with America, the world's greatest power?"

Peters laughed. "I suppose that's who we are, isn't it?" He turned his eyes to Jacqueline. She looked into her lap. Why did he think she would improve the mood, Percival berated himself.

"What prompted you to start an English school, Headmaster Chen?" asked Peters.

Now, Percival paused for a moment. Should he say that he had been at a loss after the rice trade was forbidden to the Chinese? Should he say that it was Mak's idea, that to attract students they could print advertisements saying that Headmaster Chen was a graduate of a British school? Almost true, a few semesters shy of it. Should he say something grand, perhaps? That it was because the Chinese believed that the highest calling was to teach and to learn?

Percival said, "To make money."

Peters gave a broad and relaxed smile. "It's so refreshing to meet someone in Saigon who cares about sensible things. We'll get along fine. Making money is the American way." He signalled to the waiter, who came over. He said to his companions, "Have a beer?" and before they had answered told the waiter, "*Bon bia hoi.*"

When the chilled beer came, the men clinked glasses, and Peters took a long swallow. He turned to Percival and said, "We've got the Cong beat in the shooting war. When I was looking at this place through a rifle, orders were to frag them first and sort them out later. We blasted the villages, the countryside, made life a living hell. Problem is, all those peasants we're trying to keep free from communism . . . more and more want to slit our throats. I get that. The rice farmer doesn't care that I'm defending his freedom by burning down his hut. You have kids, Percival?"

"A son."

"And you want the best for your son? You want an education for him, right? A future? What is he doing?"

Mak interjected, "He has finished at the headmaster's excellent school and is studying abroad."

"Right, smart move," said Peters. "The American dream. An education, a profitable business, the free world. That's what we're trying to bring to this country! I'm going to speak frankly. Up until now, this war has been one great big frigging miscommunication of the American spirit. We try to show a village democracy, they betray us to the Cong. Platoon leader stabbed in his cot. We send a good-hearted soldier out to a firebase, he loses his mind after a month, frags a bunch of kids playing soccer yelling they're gooks. Goes home to momma in a straitjacket. Terrible press, again and again. Makes me sick. So, I got a chance to come back without a gun. Farm assistance, village schools, rural clinics, a little military liaison. Not too much, they promised me. My job is to win the hearts and minds of those people out there who this damned war hasn't yet killed. All this bullshit about destroying villages to save them . . . look where that's got us." Peters was nearly done with his beer.

"Very wise," said Percival. He nodded seriously. "And honourable." He articulated each syllable of the last word.

Peters enjoyed the last swallow of his beer. "I love the place, you can probably tell."

"A true friend of our people," said Mak, gesturing to Peters as though he were an auction item.

Jacqueline didn't even sip the beer in front of her, both hands clenched tightly around the glass. Peters explained that he had been seconded to USAID, which was expanding its programs in the central highlands as well as the Mekong delta. They were opening new offices and would need translators both in Saigon and the field stations. Partnerships in South Vietnam would deprive the Viet Cong of their village support. The American explained, "We need as many good English-speakers as you can graduate. The salaries will be good, and we can swing draft exemptions for the boys we hire. Mak suggested that. But they have to be good. No bullshit English translators who say, 'Hello, how are you, give money.' There's too many of those around. Your graduates have a good reputation. They'll need to live up to it."

Mak nodded. Percival smiled genuinely, and wondered if he should increase the tuition by fifty percent at first or just double it immediately. They ordered lunch and a bottle of Chablis. The clouds pressed down, darker and fast moving. Mak seemed relieved to see that Percival and Peters had begun to speak easily, laughing at each other's jokes. Jacqueline barely touched her food and remained silent. Perhaps her presence was not such a big deal, thought Percival, topping up the wine glasses. As they finished eating, Mak said cautiously, "Then, when shall we certify the Percival Chen English Academy?"

"I'll visit your school, sit in on some classes, talk to some kids. If it looks good, we'll make it happen. I'll set that up with your secretary?" Peters eyed Jacqueline.

"Actually," said Percival, sitting up straight in his chair, "Jacqueline is more of a personal assistant." She looked beautiful, uncomfortable with the attention, as he had first seen her at the Sun Wah Hotel.

"Right, sure," said the American. He sat back and winked at Percival. He patted Mak on the shoulder. "Not to worry, Mr. Mak. Doesn't bother me. Every man of substance seems to have an 'assistant' in this place."

As they came to the end of the meal, thunder cracked above them. The afternoon rains descended like water bursting from a dike, and waiters scrambled around with umbrellas. Percival and his party left the drinks where they were and hurried to the clubhouse, soaked through by the time they reached the awning. After wiping the rain from his face, Percival saw Jacqueline fleeing across the lobby of the clubhouse. Peters' eyes followed her.

"She has a number of errands to run for me," said Percival weakly.

"Then, we are agreed?" said Mak to Peters. "We will move forward."

"I'm feeling very good about this," said the American. "I will visit this week."

"Anytime," said Percival.

They shook hands with Peters and watched him go. When he had departed, Mak turned to Percival. "Have you gone crazy?"

Percival whispered to Mak, "*Gung hai se yew lai see.*" He must need a red envelope?

"In fact, it might put him off, if you don't manage to do it with your behaviour," said Mak stiffly in Cantonese.

"I swear, I didn't know she was a student."

"Isn't that the one rule you keep to? You can screw any girl from here to the demilitarized zone, but not your students! If we get this certification, you can pay the rest of your debt by the end of next semester."

"Yes, I hope so."

"Then why did you bring your student, our student, to this meeting?"

Percival stared into the rain. He felt his embarrassment rise.

Mak went on. "If you parade her around and he sees her in the school, he will conclude that we are just like all the other schools where a diploma can be bought, or paid for in bed."

"Mr. Peters must not see the girl." Percival nodded.

"Say goodbye to her. You need this certification."

"Yes, it is very important to the school, yes, for my debt and the progress of the school. You certainly must take a *lai see*, Mak, for all you have done."

"I don't need a red packet. We need this certification. End it with this girl. Have I ever given you bad advice?"

"No, old friend, you haven't. I'm going to go and find Han Bai. You will need a ride back to Cholon." He escaped Mak and headed towards the kitchen, where the members' drivers waited. He found the driver and told him to go and take Teacher Mak wherever he wanted. Percival had planned to go out the side door, but Mak had trailed him to the kitchen entrance, so the headmaster was unable to slip his teacher and friend. Han Bai brought the Peugeot around, and the two men each climbed in one side.

CHAPTER 13

THUNDER SWELLED, AND RAIN POUNDED THE roof of the car. The traffic was slow, and the car stopped often. The wipers flashed back and forth, and still the rain blurred everything so that they saw only coloured shapes through the front window. Mak began to drum two fingers in a staccato, but said nothing.

Already, when they had met as young men, Mak had this way of holding himself in. In 1942, while Percival was struggling to wean Chen Kai off opium, the Japanese declared that all rice could only be bought and sold through Imperial rice procurement agents. They offered Chen Hap Sing such an agency, but Percival refused, apologizing that he must care for his sick father. Ba Hai ranted at his stupidity. The merchants who collaborated soon became rich in both piastres and Japanese yen, and their households were well fed. Despite their new unemployment, all the Chinese workers of Chen Hap Sing and some of the Vietnamese cheered Percival's discreet manoeuvre. Other Vietnamese warehouse men said amongst themselves that the Japanese might not be so bad, if they would one day get rid of the French for good. At least they had yellow skin. They said this in their own language, not realizing that Percival was beginning to understand a little of it.

Without a business to run, Percival often sat on the balcony when Chen Kai napped, observing the square in front of Chen Hap Sing. The Japanese had made it into a stable, paddock, and camp for the cavalry, with the post office as their Cholon headquarters. The doors of St. Francis Xavier were barred, and the priests had been arrested on unspecified charges. The flame trees were carefully pruned by some of the Japanese soldiers who took an interest in such things, so that in their season of blooms in 1943, they were more spectacular than usual. The square was otherwise listless. A few vendors with shoddy goods dickered with customers who were slow to part with money. The hot portion of the day lasted forever. One such afternoon, Percival looked out the window and caught a glimpse of a neighbour on the balcony of the next building, who seemed to be watching the Japanese soldiers and their horses very intently. It was a young man, roughly Percival's age. He was writing notes on a piece of paper.

Percival went out to his balcony. "*Wai*," he offered in friendly greeting. "I am Chen Pie Sou. What are you doing out at this time of day?"

The stranger palmed the stub of pencil and the paper and looked around. "My name is Mak."

"You like the horses?" asked Percival.

"They are handsome."

"Are you an artist? You are drawing them?"

"I am from out of town," said Mak, as if a different question had been asked. "What do you do?"

"Our family was in the rice business," said Percival. "Now, I sit here."

"Oh, then I've heard of you. You rejected an offer to become a procurement agent," said Mak, relaxing visibly. He explained that he was renting a room in the house next door, with a group of Chinese who had fled to Cholon from the countryside. "We Chinese must stick together, right?"

"How could I collaborate with these devils?" Percival gestured out at the square. "Did you know that in Nanjing, two Japanese officers had a competition. It was like a sports event, to see who could be the first to behead a hundred Chinese prisoners."

"You must have a shortwave, if you know that," said Mak warily.

"Yes."

"Well, don't ever admit to it." Mak looked from side to side and lowered his voice. "I'm glad to be amongst patriots, friend, but in these times it may be worth keeping your opinions quiet. If I am asked, of course, I haven't heard your thoughts on the Japanese." Later that afternoon, Percival hid the radio in a giant wedding cabinet—his new acquaintance had a point.

After that first encounter, Percival saw Mak from time to time, and they chatted from one balcony to another. They were both Teochow, though Mak was born in Indochina and spoke Annamese as well as he spoke Teochow, Cantonese, and French. He sidestepped the usual polite questions about his family and education. Between Chen Hap Sing and the building where Mak rented a room, there was a Cantonese refugee family living in a shack in the alleyway. The couple had two daughters—girls with deep, beautiful eyes. The alley did not lead anywhere, a natural advantage for the family, since it could use the walls of the three adjacent buildings. They had added a supporting frame of bamboo, a thatched roof of straw in the village style, and a stack of wooden crates for the front wall. This gave them a home that was better than those of most other refugees, and more comfortable than the Japanese soldiers' tents in the square. The family started an egg hatchery in the crates in front of the shack. All day, the mother and daughters checked the wooden boxes and turned the eggs over in their straw beds. The father fetched eggs and delivered chicks in pole baskets throughout Cholon.

From the balcony, Percival sometimes saw the Imperial Army cook from the cavalry mess come to the family's door to demand eggs. The mother explained that the eggs did not belong to her but had been entrusted to her for hatching, but the cook was not deterred. Some of the Imperial officers had a taste for the delicacy of a boiled egg with the chick inside. At night, drunken soldiers lewdly taunted the woman and her daughters. This was the disadvantage of the otherwise cosy shelter. After a while, Percival saw that the family had been hired, or likely compelled, by the Japanese to feed their horses and sweep up the dung, so all day they would be turning eggs, minding horses, fetching eggs, and delivering chicks.

Once, just as Percival came out onto the balcony and greeted his neighbour, Percival saw Mak stuffing a notebook into his pocket. Was he taking notes on the soldiers' activities? If the notebook were a personal diary, there would be no reason to hide it. It was better not to ask.

There was a bumper rice crop that year, which the Japanese soldiers put in guarded warehouses and shipped down the Saigon River to their armies throughout Asia. Soon, there was widespread hunger in Cholon and Saigon. Even some French looked thin. No one dared complain, though it made people bitter to see the Imperial Army horses so well fed while people starved. If they were lucky, people ate thin millet gruel. Children picked through the Imperial Army's refuse heap. Cecilia lamented having married Percival to escape to a place of rich rice fields, only to be starved there by the Japanese just as they had been in Hong Kong. Ba Hai traded silk clothing, good furniture, and antique scrolls in return for expensive canned foods which only she and the foreman ate. Percival organized the household workers to smuggle tiny quantities of illicitly bought paddy into the smallest, most hidden threshing room at Chen Hap Sing, just enough for the household and a little bit with which to barter.

One day, the egg-hatchery woman from the alleyway came to see Percival. She asked if he could spare some rice husks. Since Percival knew that she worked for the Japanese, he was suspicious. "We don't have any rice husks," he said. "Why would we? We have not been threshing rice for a long time."

"Don't worry, Chen Sang," she said, addressing him respectfully as Mr. Chen even though she was several years his senior, "I will not betray you. I just smell sometimes that your cook burns rice husks. I don't know where you get them. If you ever have extra, I can use them in the beds where I hatch my eggs."

Percival told her to come back after dark. It was the least he could do, to give a few rice husks to a neighbour. Percival could even spare a little rice, but he was afraid to give that to her right away. If she were spying for the Japanese, the rice would be clear evidence that he had been threshing paddy in Chen Hap Sing. The husks could be explained, that they were scavenged as fuel.

Perhaps one night he could secretly leave a few kilos of rice for her hungry family. That would be safer. First, however, he had to be sure that nothing bad came of giving her the husks. There was no such thing as being too cautious when the Imperial Japanese Army was camped just outside the door. He told the cook to give the bags of husks to the neighbour when she asked—but only at night, and only after checking to make sure there were no Kempeitai around. The woman began to come regularly for husks, and somehow, over several weeks, her daughters' faces brightened. Colour returned to their cheeks, and they no longer had the anxious look of constant hunger. So, Percival did not take the risk of giving them rice. Somehow, they were being fed.

Some months later, on a dry, bright day, a stone-faced Kempeitai knocked on the door of Chen Hap Sing. Percival was terrified that their tiny amount of black market trade had been discovered. Was it better to deny the truth or offer a bribe? People were executed for doing either.

But this was not the reason that the Kempeitai had come. He ordered everyone in the house to attend a public trial, even Chen Kai. Percival and Cecilia walked slowly, blending in with the servants. There was no question of refusing. Percival was shocked to see that the family from the alley were on the top steps of the post office, the parents and their two daughters kneeling before an Imperial Army officer.

The square was full of people forced to attend this gathering. The crowd was hushed, and the only sound was that of the charges being read. They were interpreted by the army translator, an educated Vietnamese who had taught classical Chinese and Japanese literature in Saigon before the occupation. Percival was terrified that he might hear rice husks mentioned. Was the family accused of black marketeering? He thought of taking Cecilia's hand and trying to slip away, but the Kempeitai policed the crowd carefully.

A Japanese colonel who had recently arrived to take charge of the stables was conducting the trial. He shouted in Japanese, and the translator shouted in Cantonese, seemingly trying to match the vigour of the colonel. "This man and his wife were found feeding horses rice husks, having stolen the rice that was meant for the animals. Two horses have recently died from stomach ailments. These people are on trial both for theft of rice and the murder of two Imperial Japanese Army horses." The colonel shouted at them, "They weren't just any horses. Those were my personal horses, from Spain! Do you know the value of the horses that died?"

"Whatever it is, sir," said the father, "we will repay it. We will work day and night and starve ourselves to repay it." What would the panicked father say, Percival wondered, if asked where the husks had come from?

Percival looked around. There were soldiers in every direction. Cecilia shook with fear. The colonel shouted at the poor refugees, "Did you steal my horses' rice to sell on the black market?"

"No," the husband protested. "We only took a little for our daughters."

The colonel was pleased with his trick. He shouted, "Then you admit to having stolen the rice!"

The mother began to sob. She prostrated herself on the steps of the post office and crawled to the colonel's feet. "Have mercy, I only wanted to feed my hungry children."

The girls also fell on the steps, shivering with fear. The father was frozen in silence. The colonel kicked the mother away, and the translator struggled to keep up with her wailed pleas and the colonel's annoyed responses.

Suddenly the father lifted his head and cried out, "Spare our children, I beg you! We will pay with our lives, but spare our daughters."

The Japanese colonel paced back and forth. The only sound was his boots on the stone steps. Finally, he said, "I cannot ignore my responsibility. But I do wish to be fair."

Cecilia closed her eyes and drew close to Percival, sheltered behind him. There was a murmur of general relief. Perhaps the family would only be flogged. To one side, Percival saw Mak watching the trial, seething with rage while all around him others only cringed in fear.

Then, from somewhere in the crowd came a laugh. Or simply a gasp. It was very brief, so quickly suppressed that the soldiers could not tell who had made this offensive sound. It might have been a swallowed cry of distress, but the new cavalry colonel yelled at the crowd, "Whoever laughed, step forward!" The translator repeated the order. No one moved. A minute felt like hours. Finally, the colonel said through the translator, "If no one will admit to their disrespect, all you dirty Chinese can pay! Fix bayonets!" The soldiers hurried to fasten their blades on the end of their rifles, made ready to lunge upon the crowd.

Cecilia pressed herself against Percival's back. When the bayonet charge came, he would fall over her, protect her with his own body. She might survive. Then a young man stepped forward stammering, "It was me! It wasn't a laugh, I just made some noise, I didn't mean——" But before he could finish what he wanted to say, the colonel had drawn his pistol and shot him in the face. He crumpled where he stood.

"Alright," said the colonel, turning back to the family on the steps. "I won't behead the girls."

"*Arigato kojaimaste, arigato*," the mother cried, bowing at his feet.

"Instead, they will be fed rice husks." It was not clear what he meant, but it sounded better than beheading. There would likely be no escape for the parents.

At the colonel's next orders, the translator was stunned into silence. The Kempeitai bound the girls' hands and feet behind them, laid the children on the top steps, and cut open their shirts. It was commanded that no one in the crowd should look away. Both mother and father wept as their daughters' bellies and the small beginnings of breasts were exposed to the neighbourhood. The colonel barked in Japanese, at which the Kempeitai drew their short swords and held them at attention.

The colonel gave another order, now yelling directly at the translator. The translator's voice cracked as he shouted, "The order has been given that the Kempeitai shall cut the girls' bellies open and fill them with rice husks." The colonel drew his own sword, held it aloft, and with a few curt words from the colonel one of the Kempeitai rushed forward and plunged his knife into the younger child, just below her navel. She screamed, eyes wide open, as the soldier drew the blade up towards her chest. She tried to curl herself away, even as the bluish coils of her intestines spilled out on the steps.

The Kempeitai then rushed upon both girls. They stabbed, slashed, unable to wait their turn now that it had begun, as if each man was determined to prove that he, too, was capable of madness. The colonel yelled encouragement, and the girls' bowels were pulled out by his soldiers. Their agonizing voices filled the square, penetrated the buildings.

Percival began to retch. He tilted forward, felt his knees buckle. His hands found the solidity of earth, and he expelled the contents of his stomach into the dirt. He saw undigested rice from breakfast, felt guilty both for having possessed it and for having vomited it. He saw quick feet, Cecilia's shoes kicking dirt over the incriminating grains. Then he heard a commotion and looked around to see yelling Japanese soldiers, their bayonets pointed, blood-thirst in their eyes. Cecilia's body was warm, crouched over him, and Percival heard her strangely calm voice, felt hands on his shoulders, then felt himself yanked up. Cecilia helped him to his feet. She was repeating a few words in Japanese in an obsequious tone with her best smile. They might both soon die. Cecilia bowed submissively from the waist, reciting apologies in Japanese even as the wails of the girls stained the square forever. The butchery was ongoing, and no officer was available to give these common soldiers orders to kill Cecilia and Percival, so they shoved them to the ground and turned their attention back to the performance of the Kempeitai.

The Kempeitai were triumphant in their violence. They tore organs, clumps of life, out of their victims, stabbing, slashing, outdoing one another in cruelty. Finally, the girls' last weak moans stopped. Their blank eyes stared out of dead faces, pale and drained of blood. They were mercifully still. The colonel hoisted a bucket of rice husks and poured them into the girls' empty bellies.

Some of the common Japanese soldiers cheered, and others looked frightened into paralysis, clutched their rifles to their chests. The Kempeitai bowed to their commander, who bowed in return and sheathed his sword. One young soldier had turned away from the bloody mess to weep, and a Kempeitai came over to him, took his rifle away and clubbed him in the head with it so that he fell to the ground unconscious, then struck him a few more times. Blood trickled out of the young soldier's ear.

Several other Kempeitai volunteered to behead the parents, and the colonel granted the honour to two whose hands were already covered in the blood of the children. The parents knelt without protest, wailing but not for their own lives. The soldier who brought his sword down on the father's neck must have been inexperienced, and the sword got caught in the vertebrae. The man collapsed forward, blood flowing from the wound. The soldier pulled out his sword, and with his foot on the father's back hacked with several short strokes at the neck to sever the head. He apologized, embarrassed for his lack of elegance, to his superior. The other soldier raised his sword high before bringing it down in a fast whistling arc upon the kneeling mother, and it was a terrible relief to see her head severed in one clean stroke. The colonel turned to the crowd and said via the translator, "I am in charge of the stables. There will be respect for the Imperial Japanese Army, its horses, and its food."

Then he ordered the crowd to disperse, and that the refugee family's home be cleared of their belongings, as the space would be given over to the Army. Their few possessions were burned, the eggs were boiled, and the place swept out.

That evening, Percival could hear the colonel and several of his Kempeitai singing and raising toasts in the house of the murdered family. All the eggs, with the partially grown embryos, were a special treat for the colonel and his officers to enjoy with sake. After several hours, they fell quiet. There was no moon, and there were no stars. Percival heard the snoring of the men lying very drunk in what had been the refugees' shack. From his window, he could see that a little light fell out the front of the house between the slats of the wooden crates. They must have left an oil lamp lit, a dangerous thing to do, thought Percival.

From the balcony of the house next door, Percival heard a voice say, "Is that you, Percival?"

"Yes." He went out on the balcony, where they spoke in whispers.

"It's Mak here. I need a favour."

"What is it?"

"I need some rice husks."

Percival's heart thrust itself against his chest. How did Mak know about the rice husks? Was he trying to extort money from Percival, to make him complicit in the crime of the horse-killing? Was he going to betray him to the Japanese? "Meet me downstairs. I'll give you anything you want."

In the kitchen, Percival opened a bottle of cooking wine. He took several long swallows of the fiery liquid, and it gave him some courage. He heard a gentle rapping at the door and went to unlock it. Without being invited in, Mak slipped into Chen Hap Sing and shut the door.

"Don't light any lamps. Where are the rice husks?" he asked. "And do you have a bucket?"

In the kitchen, Percival found a bag of rice husks and the tin bucket into which ashes were emptied from the stove. He gave them to Mak, expecting him to leave.

"Good, you are thinking. Give me that bottle," said Mak. Percival handed it to him, and Mak tucked it under his arm. "Up to your balcony, quickly."

As Percival followed Mak up, Cecilia whispered from their darkened doorway, "What are you doing?"

"A favour," he said, and rushed past her. It occurred to him, as he hurried to catch up to Mak, that he did not know what he was doing, or why.

From above, they looked down on the little thatch-roofed dwelling, heard the snoring, and saw the light from the oil lamp still spilling out. Mak poured the rice husks into the bucket and then poured the cooking wine over it. He paused to survey the square, empty. He took a match from his pocket, lit it, and tossed it into the bucket. There was a satisfying burst of blue flame. Then Mak tipped the burning husks over the side of Chen Hap Sing. The two men peered down on the little dwelling, whose thatch roof was now punctuated by the burning pinpricks. Already they could smell the first whiffs of smoke. Chen Hap Sing and the adjacent houses were built of thick mud-brick walls, but the refugees' house was all wood and straw.

"We had better go downstairs," said Mak. "We don't want to be seen in the light of the fire." Percival showed Mak out the kitchen door and then ran from room to room to be sure there were no lights in Chen Hap Sing.

"What have you done?" asked Cecilia, when he got to their bedroom.

"Justice," he said. "Quick. Get into bed. If anyone asks, we have been in bed for hours."

"My god, you must be crazy. You want us to be cut open next? I don't know what you've done, but go to your father's room. I don't want to be arrested with you. I'll deny we're married, if I have to."

Percival got up and went to Chen Kai's room, where he lay on the floor across from his father. Not long after, there were screams and shouts in Japanese. There was the soft roar of a fire, like a wind blowing.

In the morning, a scent of roasted meat lingered. Throughout Cholon, it was whispered that the ghosts of the dead family had taken their revenge. The surviving Kempeitai investigated, conducted several days of interrogations and beatings, withheld the meagre millet rations in order to extract a confession, but in the end declared the death accidental. Even if they didn't believe this, thought Percival. It saved face, and there seemed to be an unspoken relief, even amongst some of the Japanese soldiers, that this colonel and several of the most violent Kempeitai who had passed out drunk in the hut were gone.

CHAPTER 14

ABOUT A WEEK AFTER THE ARSON, Mak came over again. He said nothing about the incident and instead asked if Percival would like to earn some money helping in the struggle against the Japanese. He said, "One of my duties is to monitor this regiment and to count their troops and horses. You have noticed, I suspect. I have been given another assignment as well, which will help the patriots in the countryside."

"An assignment, as part of your duties . . . for patriots?"

"Yes, friend," said Mak, looking at Percival. He added, "It may even help our Chinese allies in the north."

Percival could feel Mak trying to read him. He must be careful to keep some distance. Mak continued, explained that a French pharmacist at the Gral Hospital was willing to divert medications from Japanese supplies to the resistance.

"But how can I trust you?" said Percival.

"From time to time, I might ask you a small favour, not often. If you will be sure to help me at these times, I will always be loyal to you, as if we had been brothers by birth." As he had already participated in the murder of a Japanese colonel, and he needed to earn money, Percival could think of no reason to refuse. He agreed, and then realized that Mak must have made the same calculation of Percival's situation. He wondered if Mak was lonely in whatever work he did, and although he wished to know as little as possible about that work, he, too, was lonely in this foreign country. He was glad to have this pledge of loyalty from Mak.

"Alright," Percival agreed.

Mak insisted that since he was a few months younger than Percival, he should call Percival "elder brother." During the dull days of the Japanese occupation, Mak learned English from Percival. After Chen Kai fled to travel north towards China, there was a point in the war when it looked like the Japanese might permanently rule the Pacific. Ba Hai struck a deal with Percival to leave Chen Hap Sing, and Mak helped him to negotiate it. Everyone knew that in most of what the Japanese called their Greater East Asia Co-Prosperity Sphere, desirable houses like Chen Hap Sing had been appropriated by high-ranking Japanese officers, the owners thrown out or killed. They had only moderated their seizures in Indochina because of the French. If the war ended in favour of the Japanese, everyone said, even the Vichy French would have their mansions taken. It was better to own utilitarian rather than showy property, some said. In the deal with Ba Hai, she took the business's village warehouses and all the river barges. Percival kept Chen Hap Sing and the docking rights on the Arroyo Chinois, which at that time were useless. Smug with the bargain she had struck, Ba Hai returned to her village, Long Thang, taking all the Vietnamese workers with her. There, she and the foreman became Imperial rice agents and were soon the most prosperous people in the village.

Percival's part in Mak's medicine smuggling scheme was simple. He met the pharmacist weekly in Saigon, had coffee with him, and took a package of medicines back to Mak in Cholon. Mak gave him money, enough that the Chen Hap Sing household—Cecilia and the workers who remained—ate throughout the occupation. A small portion of the medicines were sold on the black market to pay Percival and Mak. Percival assumed that most of the drugs were smuggled into the jungles for the Viet Minh, who fought a night-time campaign of skirmishes and ambushes against the Japanese. How did it help the Chinese? Mak never said any more about this. Perhaps it had only been bait to convince him, thought Percival, but he didn't ask about it. He did not ask for any details that weren't necessary, for knowledge could be dangerous.

Mak always knew which families in Cholon were suffering the most under the Japanese. He somehow found food to give them, although Mak himself wore threadbare clothing and appeared half starved. As the first favour he asked of Percival, Mak brought Foong Jie to work in the Chen Hap Sing household. Cecilia protested that they could barely feed the people they had in the house already.

"I will make sure you have enough money to feed her," Mak said. "If you don't take her in, she will starve or be found dead one morning. The Japanese arrested her for spying—they violated her, then cut out her tongue as a lesson to others."

Cecilia hesitated, her face softened for a moment, but then she said, "Why don't you hire her yourself, then, if she is a Viet Minh and you feel such sympathy?"

"I did not say she was Viet Minh. Only that she was arrested. What do *you* feel? She is a country woman, and the stump of her tongue is still bleeding." He turned to Percival. "So please take Foong Jie into your house, as a favour to me." He said this with a finality that indicated that the conversation was over. Cecilia was furious, but did not protest further, knowing that Percival would do it anyway. From then on, Foong Jie dutifully ran the household with silent efficiency.

AFTER THE JAPANESE WERE PUSHED FROM Indochina, Chen Hap Sing jumped into the Cholon rice trade again. Percival resumed the business quickly with the help of the remaining employees, and the berths on the Arroyo Chinois allowed them to seize market share. Saigon was overrun with celebrating white, black, brown, and yellow soldiers, and their money. It was as if all the lights in the gambling places, opium dens, and brothels had suddenly been turned on, and their kitchens boiled sack after sack of fragrant Mekong rice. Percival chuckled when he heard that now that the Japanese were gone, no Chinese would do business with former collaborators, including Ba Hai and the foreman. Cholon hummed, Chen Hap Sing's warehouses were full and busy, and Percival discovered the mah-jong tables.

After Cecilia learned that almost all her family's ships had been sunk in the war, she attacked Percival more relentlessly than ever. If only she hadn't married him, she said, as if she could have prevented the family's ruin if she had been in Hong Kong. Meanwhile, Percival ventured into the incandescent pleasures of Le Grand Monde, Le Paradis, and other places that winked and promised.

Percival offered Mak a share of the rice trade in gratitude for the deal with Ba Hai, which had worked out so well, but his friend refused. He said he was too busy with his own affairs. Mak moved out of the rented room next door to Chen Hap Sing and took an apartment nearby. Percival did not see him as often, and when he did, Mak gave only vague hints about what he was doing to earn a living. He looked more preoccupied and worried than he had during the war. Occasionally, Mak asked for a favour, that Percival deliver a valise in Saigon, or for a few crates to be hidden amongst the rice bags in Chen Hap Sing for a week or so, unopened, of course. They were always collected at night, by people that Percival had never met.

For a week after the nuclear bombing of Hiroshima and Nagasaki and the Japanese surrender to the Allied Forces, the Saigon casinos and brothels hummed in a constant state of inebriation and carnal exuberance. Early one evening, Percival, drunk, went to find Mak in his small apartment. "Cecilia threatened to leave me tonight, but it's alright, because we are growing to hate each other. She would have left me already if her family's ships weren't at the bottom of the sea. Come with me to enjoy the night!"

"No, you should go home," said Mak.

"We will gamble and win fortunes. We will dance with sing-song girls and screw the prettiest ones."

"I'll make you some tea, and then bring you home."

"The war is over, my friend, be joyful! Come out with me."

"We have been cheated. The *gwei lo* will give the country back to the French."

"What country?"

Mak grabbed Percival's shoulders. He yelled. "Vietnam. What we fought for, the Allies will return it to foreigners." It was the first time

Percival had heard him raise his voice. Mak was wild, as grief-stricken as if someone had been killed. "Those French parasites did not even try to defend us from the Japanese, but now they will rule us again! For what? Because they have the same skin colour as the Americans and the British."

"Who cares? We are Chinese. Make money, do business. The bar girls all have new dresses, and they all know how to take them off. I'll find you a sweet one."

"You go. I have some business to attend to." Mak urged Percival out the door.

Percival stumbled away, climbed into a cyclo, and said, "Take me to Le Grand Monde, I feel lucky tonight." On the way, he muttered to the driver, "My friend just lied to me! What kind of business happens at night? He must have a girl waiting."

NOW, PERCIVAL SAT WITH HIS OLD friend, the rain thrumming a drumbeat on the roof of the Peugeot. Just outside of Cholon something had brought traffic to a standstill, and outside was a cacophony of honking and yelling, the grunts of oxen. Percival wiped the corner of his mouth where he thought he could still taste Jacqueline's kiss from earlier that day. The rain had relented a little, but the noise on the roof remained loud enough that they had an excuse not to talk. Mak turned and faced Percival. He said, "Do you remember how your school was started in the first place?"

They had been friends for so long their minds went to the same remembered era. "Of course I do," said Percival. "I had debts to pay and I was grateful. I am grateful."

When the rice trade was snatched away by the French, Mak suggested the English school. Despite the distance that had opened between them, Mak remembered his promised loyalty, and worked relentlessly to make the school possible. So, it was natural to offer Mak a share in that business, and when he refused, to hire him as a teacher.

"You would have been ruined. The Binh Xuyen gangsters would have taken Chen Hap Sing to pay your gambling debts. They would have cut off your fingers for good measure. I did everything to help you. I used all my *gwan hai*." It was true, Mak had kept the mafia at bay, had dealt with all the tricky matters of obtaining licences and permissions. He had used angles, advantages, and subtle blackmail to persuade the necessary friends in Saigon. Only a brother would do this for him, Percival thought. As a Chinese who still spoke the Annamese language badly, and without sufficient connections, Percival could not have done what Mak did.

"Now listen to me," Mak said, "that girl will ruin you worse than losing the rice trade. Worse than losing your school. Leave her. If you need to, pay her to go away."

But Mak didn't know about the heart, thought Percival. "You feel strongly," said Percival, staring through the water, barely hearing his friend.

"I did the near-impossible twice—ransoming Dai Jai and getting him to China. Now, I am close to saving you from the debts that this incurred. Am I not a faithful friend?"

Percival nodded, ashamed to appear ungrateful. "Yes, and I appreciate it."

"On rare occasions I ask you for a favour, but those favours are never harmful to you. In fact, they are often good for you." This was true. If Percival hired a teacher Mak had recommended, he was invariably good. If Percival allowed a refugee from North Vietnam to study for free, he was a credit to the school. Percival always agreed when Mak asked for a favour, for these opportunities to show his friend gratitude were so rare and small in comparison with the ways that Mak helped him. "As a favour to me, break it off."

Percival squeezed his eyes shut. "I cannot."

"I understand it is difficult, *hou jeung*. She is very pretty. She must be fond of you, and you of her. But she is our student, and it is your own school rule. The teachers must not love the students."

"Sorry, old friend, but it's a private matter. Forgive me, I can't say anything else."

"You are the headmaster, elder brother. What of the school's reputation? You must escape from your current debt. This American certification could double your income. I've told Peters that the Percival

Chen English Academy is strict—that we pay the teachers well and that they don't accept bribes or pleasure from the students. I've explained that this sets us apart from the other schools."

"Good. It does set us apart, certainly." Percival wished he had been able to slip away at the club. "You've been working hard on this. I understand. I will be discreet. No one will know."

Mak seemed to be at a loss, but after a moment found his words. "I need this certification. Everyone knows that I've used all my connections to find Mr. Peters, to convince him. People will laugh if I fail. Think of my honour. Think of yours."

"I will, friend." Percival looked out at the rain, which splashed into the broad puddles in the street and churned them into commotion.

"I'm saying this as your brother, as your—"

"Do you think if you say it again, it will sound different?" Percival snapped.

"Break it off." The rain ran in sheets down the windows. Mak opened the door of the car, got out. In a step, he was a blurred form, and in a few steps he was gone.

When Percival arrived at Chen Hap Sing, Foong Jie was waiting in front of the building. As he got out of the car and approached the door, she gestured up at Percival's window, which was open.

Could it be an officer of the quiet police? Percival did not see any dark Galaxie, though they must use other cars as well. What would they want with him? He had hired a Vietnamese teacher. Did they have questions about Dai Jai's disappearance? He crept up the stairs, aware of Foong Jie behind him.

He peered into his room and saw Jacqueline, went to her and kissed her.

"I didn't know what to do, so I ran off. Then, I realized it was no good running, and I came here." The tears welled in her eyes. She looked up, saw Foong Jie at the doorway and turned away, burying her hands in her face.

Percival turned to face the door. Foong Jie stood there, gesturing desperately for Jacqueline to leave. The girl was more stealthy than he had realized, thought Percival, if she had until now managed to slip in and out of his room without being seen by the head servant. When Foong Jie saw Jacqueline stealing up to Percival's room today, however, she would have understood that this student of the school was the headmaster's discreet lover.

"Foong Jie, it is not your concern." He went to the door, urged her out, and closed it.

Jacqueline said anxiously, "You have been speaking with Teacher Mak. What did he tell you?"

Perhaps Mak was right. He had never led Percival astray. Percival stepped back a little, as if afraid of his own words. "I have a rule, which I enforce very seriously, that there are to be no improper relations between students and teachers. It's my fault. I should have recognized you . . . and I never asked why your English was so good."

Jacqueline stood with arms wrapped around herself, tears spilling freely. "I was so happy, when you won me at the Sun Wah Hotel. That other man seemed rough. I would have gone with him if I had to, but I thought it was the kindness of fate that you won."

Percival said mechanically, "We have the best reputation of any English school in Vietnam." He wanted to hold her, to comfort her. He cleared his throat. "We are modern, professional, uncorrupted. An American will give us a special certification. It will help us make more money." Already the words were ridiculous, irrelevant. He couldn't go through with it, and he took her in his arms with relief. "There is a school rule. But I can't let you go."

They embraced for a long time. She stopped crying, began to breathe more calmly. She began to unbutton her shirt. He stroked her hair. She slipped it off her shoulders and stood before him. Instead of undoing her brassiere, instead of engaging him with seduction, she cradled her belly. "Do you see?" she said.

He had noticed the slight fullness and thought happily that she was eating well when she visited him. The tears flowed again down her face. "You were worried about what they would say about you sleeping with your student? What will they say about the child in my belly?"

Percival held her closely, as if he wished to press their bodies into one, took a deep breath, and allowed himself to be happy.

CHAPTER 15

WHEN PETERS VISITED CHEN HAP SING, he parked his dark Chevrolet just in front. Percival and Mak went out to greet him and ushered him inside. He admired the building as if it were a strange artifact. "Was this an old Chinese house before it became a school?" he said, as he looked at the scrolls of brush-painting and the carvings over the doors.

"My father built it when the family was in the rice business," explained Percival.

"Why no more rice trade? Seems like a good business," said Peters. Without waiting for an answer, he said, "I guess English schools are a better one."

Mak interjected, "We Chinese value education above everything else. As you know, the Percival Chen English Academy is the most respected English school in Vietnam."

"When was it built, Percival, which dynasty?" asked Peters. Percival was unsure how best to reply. After all, the house was less than forty years old. He wasn't sure if Peters was curious about the Vietnamese or the Chinese dynasty. Chen Hap Sing was built after the fall of the Emperor in China, he thought, but while the Vietnamese Emperor Bao Dai was on the throne under French control. As Percival was considering how best to respond, Peters said breezily, "I would love a tour," and continued walking down the hall. Sometimes Americans did not care much about the answers to their questions.

They visited the classrooms that had once been rice storerooms. The students remained focused on their lessons, as they had been instructed to do when warned of the visit. Peters smiled and waved at the students as if he were a boy in a train passing a rail platform.

"Please, come into the office," said Percival. They all sat down beneath the fan.

Mak asked, "Mr. Peters, would you like a drink? Coke? Iced tea?"

"An iced coffee with condensed milk, please." He looked up. "Hey, your fan needs some oil. Easy to fix that squeak."

Mak called a kitchen boy, who went to get the coffee. "Some schools are run like any other businesses in Vietnam—selling diplomas— but never at the Percival Chen English Academy. We are absolutely merit-based."

The American was energetic, well groomed, and wasn't too much older than some of the senior students, Percival realized. He spoke restlessly and at length about the things that were wrong with the war. "There're so many simple problems with this war. I came back to help find solutions. Good translators are part of the answer, which is why I'm here with you."

"Please tell us more. How can we help?" said Mak earnestly.

The kitchen boy brought iced coffees for all three of them.

"The army is good with sticks, but they're not handing out enough carrots. That's where USAID comes in. The villages are everything. As a soldier, I was part of the Strategic Hamlets Program. Sounded great. We figured that the Cong were harassing the villagers at night, right? So we built big, fortified villages, moved a bunch of smaller villages into the ones we built, gave them some rifles, and the villagers hated us for it. What a mess. They let the Viet Cong in at night because they were their cousins. They couldn't grow anything because they were too far from their fields, so they left and went back to their own villages. The rifles that we gave them to defend the hamlets? I got shot in the ass. Surgeon showed me the bullet, said it was an M-4 round. That's why I came back without a rifle. People want to have schools, health clinics, and better rice crops. Lots of carrots. If we win those villagers, we win this war. To do it, we need translators."

Mak said, "If you are able to certify our school, our graduates will speed your work." Percival had never seen Mak smile so much, as if his face was frozen that way.

Mak handed Peters a folder and went through the school's curriculum plans, marking schemes, and letters of praise from several Americans in Saigon who employed graduates of the school. He spoke about the academy's modern ways—the standardization of curriculum, the rigorous marking of examinations, and the uniform English fluency of graduates. As he always did when discussing school matters, Mak attributed the school's achievements directly to Headmaster Percival Chen.

"It will be a great help," said Peters, after they had perused the folder. "I like what I see here."

Mak and Percival accompanied Peters out, waved him off as if he were a close relative going on a long voyage, and returned to the headmaster's office.

With Peters gone, Mak's smile fell. He closed the door behind them and said, "Headmaster, the girl has not attended school for several days. I suppose you have dealt with this issue?"

"You mean Jacqueline?" said Percival. He looked distractedly at the papers on his desk.

"Yes."

"I have found a solution," said Percival. "She is withdrawing from the school so that there is no conflict." He was nervous, he realized, as if he were one of Mak's students rather than the headmaster. "Is there something else we need to discuss, Teacher Mak?"

"Don't tell me she is still your . . . sweetheart?"

Percival replied only with silence.

Mak said, not unkindly, "Old friend, this situation will cause you problems."

"You have always been wise and correct, but I have fixed it. I withdrew her from the school."

"What about Ba Hai?" said Mak sternly. "You have always said that your father's greatest mistake was to take a local woman for his second wife. If only he had taken a proper Chinese girl—here I'm repeating your words—who would have shown proper respect for your mother and been faithful to your father, perhaps he would be alive. *Chen Pie Sou*. For years, you've drummed it into Dai Jai's head that he must marry a Chinese. I think that's half the reason you sent him to China."

"She is going to have a baby."

Mak stood stunned for a moment, and then struck the table with both hands. "Then pay her to go away," he said. "Pay her more, to take care of the child. A girl like her won't cost too much."

"What are you talking about?" said Percival.

"I'm sorry, *hou jeung*," said Mak, sitting down, leaning forward and speaking now with concern. "I'm just very worried about this certification. A scandal won't help."

Percival felt his own voice rise. "I know it would have been a problem if Mr. Peters had come to the school and seen her here. But he did not. If he comes again, he won't. What is it, Mak?" He could not imagine that Mak loved the girl. Mak strictly adhered to this school rule, and probably many others that Percival had forgotten. What did Mak know? Percival thought of the death of Jacqueline's mother in Thanh Ha. The village was only geographically in the South, for everyone knew it was controlled by the Viet Cong. Mak heard things, rumours searched him out. Perhaps her death was not as innocent as Jacqueline thought. Could her mother have been a Viet Cong spy in Sum Guy? Or perhaps someone she knew in Thanh Ha was Viet Cong and she had betrayed them to the quiet police. If in addition to her body she had been selling her eyes and ears to support Jacqueline, of course she would not have told her daughter. But it was like the stolen Japanese medicines, Percival decided. Some things were better left unasked, and if Mak did not tell Percival whatever else he knew, then what could he expect Percival to do about it? So what if the death of Jacqueline's mother had not been so accidental? It changed nothing. He said, "Mak, thank you for your concern."

A few days after Peters' visit, Percival found a copy of the new hiring policy at the State Department and USAID sitting on his desk. Graduates of the Percival Chen English Academy were "certified" and exempted from the English proficiency examinations. When Percival stopped Mak in a hallway full of students to thank him, Mak said, "I'm doing my best to help you, but . . ."

In a loud voice, Percival said, "This is a happy day! We can raise our tuitions!" The words were of celebration, but the voice was one of anger. Percival put fifty thousand piastres in a red *lai see* packet and left it in Mak's desk drawer. The following day, Percival found that the red envelope, unopened, had been returned to his own desk. He went out that night and lost the money playing baccarat and drinking champagne at Le Grand Monde.

THE APARTMENT THAT PERCIVAL FOUND FOR Jacqueline was just off Tu Do Street in Saigon, on the eighth floor, a lucky number. It was an exclusive modern building with elevators, and housed both Americans and wealthy Vietnamese. The apartment had hot and cold water, a refrigerator, a gleaming white bathtub, and green-painted shutters. When Percival went there, he told Han Bai he did not have to wait, that he would either call him later or take a cyclo home.

Jacqueline had at first seemed sad when Percival said that he would support her on the condition that she quit the school, but the sadness passed quickly. She liked the apartment's view, the morning shade and the afternoon light. As her pregnancy progressed she mentioned how much she appreciated the elevator, and in the middle of the afternoon she enjoyed sucking the ice cubes which the freezer provided. Percival filled it with ice creams, and was relieved that Jacqueline was pleased with her new surroundings. She told him, when asked, that she had been very careful that none of her fellow classmates knew about her relationship with the headmaster. His solution should satisfy Mak, Percival assured himself.

As Jacqueline's belly grew, so did her sexual interest. The moment he arrived, the seduction began, with soft fingertips, moistened lips. This, like the pleasure he experienced once he had accepted the idea of her pregnancy, was a surprise to Percival. When Cecilia had been pregnant with Dai Jai, she had avoided Percival as if he had cursed her with a baby. She and Percival fought constantly. During that time, he gambled and drank even more than usual. Now, waiting to become father to a child with Jacqueline was something new.

After their lovemaking, Percival began to stay at Jacqueline's apartment through the afternoon, into the evenings. He would ask Jacqueline, shyly, if he could bathe her. He put his hands on her belly. She expressed delight with the bathtub, and wistfully recalled the apartment of her childhood. She thanked Percival for giving her this place which was so similar. In Sum Guy, she said, they had washed by means of a section of the tin roof, which could be pulled open to admit rain. Often, night arrived, and there was no reason for Percival to go home. In the morning, he rushed to get back to Chen Hap Sing before class.

He soon realized he was more comfortable with Jacqueline in Saigon, six kilometres and a world away from Cholon. In Saigon, they went for walks along the river where the American battleships were anchored. They ate quietly in French restaurants, and saw only each other. He never would have walked outside with her in Cholon. It was normal there that one would be talked about. To eat in a Cholon restaurant was to eat with ten friends. Hoping to make up for the debacle at the club, Percival paid for Jacqueline to become a member at the Cercle Sportif. At first she hesitated, but soon thanked him for it. She would sometimes translate a comment between a French and an American woman, and everyone laughed that a yellow person translated between two whites. She was accepted into the little clusters of women who laughed conspiratorially in the wicker chairs on the patio, where she was not the only mistress of a wealthy man. Cecilia said to Percival one day, nodding at Jacqueline across the patio, "I see your lover is pregnant. She looks like a gourd."

"The most beautiful gourd in Saigon," said Percival.

"I'm surprised you can support your mistress when you owe me so much money," Cecilia said, loud enough that anyone nearby could hear. "You must be confident you are the father. A girl like that has many friendships, doesn't she?"

Percival dismissed any doubts about that. After all, Jacqueline was not like Mrs. Ling's other girls. She was a student of his school, forced to sell herself when her mother was killed.

IT WAS TWO MONTHS BEFORE TET when the new semester's tuition was due. Mak wanted to increase the amount by half. Peters had been right about the new American presence. Lately, there were more American civilians looking lost and requiring directions in Saigon than ever before. Even in Cholon, the sunburned giants were no longer enough of a curiosity to be followed by gaggles of children as they sought out brothels and Buddhist temples.

"Double it," said Percival.

"Double? It's too much. People will go elsewhere."

"Make sure everyone in this graduating class gets a job interview with an American agency or company. If people see this, we can charge twice as much."

Enrolment was soon fully subscribed, with an even longer waiting list than usual. The fat lump of money was a great relief to Percival. Interest on the debts had been growing steadily, loans to pay loans lining up like dominoes. There was also the expense of supporting Jacqueline. Now, he was able to discharge debts one after another. He wished he could send some money to Dai Jai, but recently foreign remittances were being confiscated in China. It was part of the revolution of culture, explained the shortwave broadcasts from the People's Republic. The Chinese people must not be subservient to tainted foreign money. Loyal overseas Chinese who wished to remit should send their funds directly to the treasury of the People's Republic for the good of all Chinese people, suggested the youthful female broadcaster. That was well and good, thought Percival, but he wanted Dai Jai to have something in his pocket. Even in the new society, didn't parents wish to ensure the well-being of their children?

After the rest of the debts had been dealt with, Percival and Cecilia arranged to meet one morning at the Cercle. He brought a nondescript bag containing a large sum of dollars and gold. The debt he had left to the last was Cecilia's. She had given him that small courtesy, and had made it interest-free. She had lost none of her attractiveness, he thought, as he approached the table. He was glad that she did not come with her usual accessory, an American lover. He was surprised when she said, "I've met your new girl around the club. She seems intelligent, and carries herself well."

Percival was speechless for a moment. Then he slid the bag under the table. "You were introduced?"

"I introduced myself. I wanted to see how your taste had evolved. She seemed a bit shy, but I told her that there's no reason she and I can't be friendly. It's just you and I who are in a habit of fighting. She laughed. I like her."

"You have never asked if I liked your men."

"As if I care. I am confused, though. All these years you have been so bitter about Ba Hai. As if whatever happened to your crazy father was her fault. Now, you and a métisse. And you insisted Dai Jai must marry a Chinese. She is very pretty, I grant you. Even in her condition, she has the eye of half the men in the club." Cecilia clucked her tongue.

"Who said anything about my marrying Jacqueline?" Percival shifted uncomfortably. "You wouldn't write about this to Dai Jai, would you?"

"Of course not," Cecilia laughed, a high tinkle. "I'm not going to take it that seriously. She is only your sweetheart whom you put up in an apartment. Whatever. Your love affairs don't interest me."

"Obviously not. And I see you have come alone, so there must be something you want to discuss. Do you think I can't read you as well as you can read me?"

"I received a letter from Dai Jai."

Percival signalled the waiter and asked for two gin and tonics. He folded one hand over the other and said, "His letters have been a little odd lately."

Dai Jai's letters had become more sporadic. At first, Percival had waited anxiously for them, and now he did not expect to see a note more than once a month, which when they arrived were on thin, dirty-looking paper.

Percival wrote to him inquiring whether he was eating enough, and whether he was able to buy coal. Better to stock up before the change in weather, he wrote. Shanghai would soon be cold. Dai Jai did not answer these questions. Instead, in a letter that arrived seven months after his departure, Dai Jai wrote that his new Red Guard teachers were teaching excellent lessons, much better than the previous bourgeois lackeys of the foreign devils who had been employed in the colleges. The writing was stiff, formal. Percival was shocked— how could they have replaced the teachers? Who had replaced them, were these guards qualified educators? The letter read as if Dai Jai had copied it, or it had been dictated. Previously, even when he wrote about mundane matters, such as the changing weather or his daily problems, there was nuance and description in his phrases. Now, the words were stark rhetoric.

"A little odd? In the latest, he wrote to me that Saigon is the whore of America, that the imperialists are subjugating the masses, that the people must rise up and crush their oppressors in order to be free."

"Yes, same wording in mine. Headstrong youth. In that letter, my son writes that I teach the language of capitalist dogs."

The waiter brought the drinks, and Percival took a long swallow. Cecilia raised her glass. "Congratulations, by the way, on your new American certification. Everyone says you have been given a licence to print money."

In the same cramped page, Dai Jai had written that he was thankful for the revolution of Chinese workers, that previously he was imprisoned by lazy bourgeois colonialists. "It is disrespectful, but what can I do?" said Percival. "It's shameful that my son writes to me in this way."

"I don't care if he insults you. I do it myself, haven't you noticed?"

"He writes that I am a profiteer who drinks the lifeblood of the working people. I am the comprador of the warmongering Americans. But you know, it must be the Red Guards telling them to write such things. The boy writes about politics, but it doesn't even read like his own words. I am afraid of the Saigon censors seeing his letters, though."

"Never mind the censors. What is happening to him? This is our son. The boy loves American comic books. Something is wrong."

"Young boys can be easily influenced."

"I want you to bring him home," she said. "Haven't you heard that things are turning in China?"

"How can you trust the news? Everything is fake."

It seemed that it was well under way, before the radio broadcasts had given it a name, the Cultural Revolution. It was hotly though quietly debated everywhere in Cholon, whether it was good or bad for China, whether it would throw off the influence of the foreigners for good or whether it was merely pandering to Russia. Some said Marx would free China, and others declared this impossible of a foreign devil, even a dead one. Percival had asked Mak what he thought, and Mak had spoken cryptically about the evolution of society. Some in Cholon were sending money to support this new revolution, and others had applied for Taiwanese citizenships.

"I don't follow the news," said Percival to Cecilia.

"Bring him home," said Cecilia again. She spoke in a vulnerable tone, rare for her. "My connections are American. They can't help."

"And they couldn't, before."

"Mak got him to China. Ask Mak to bring him back. Please. He's my son, and there's something wrong."

"What, bring him back here to be drafted by the South Vietnamese Army and shot? The way things are going with the war, he might even be shot by the enemy rather than his own comrades. They say the fighting has become more deadly than ever."

Cecilia gripped the table. "Then have a snakehead smuggle him out to Hong Kong. I will pay half the cost."

Percival stood. "With the gold I've just returned? And I suppose you would make me repay that to you afterwards? I saved him from prison. I saved him from the South Vietnamese Army. Now, you are bothered because he writes strange letters."

That afternoon, after his siesta, Percival smelled something foul. He followed his nose, and found that it came from Dai Jai's room. Could the ghost of Chen Kai have returned to his old room? Did ghosts carry an odour? He summoned the courage to open the door, but the room was undisturbed. The odour was strong—something like *nuoc nam*. Had someone played a trick on him by spilling Vietnamese fish sauce, knowing that he hated it? Percival followed it to the doors to his son's balcony, where he saw the dry tanks, fouled by rotting fish. The glass was coated with algae. He had forgotten them as soon as Dai Jai had left. Had they lived until recently? It looked like it, that they had survived on the downpours of the rainy season, but over the last few weeks it had been dry. They could be replaced, should Dai Jai ever return home. No, he was at home, Percival corrected himself. Dai Jai had returned to China. Percival checked his watch and realized that if he left now, he could get to Jacqueline's place before dinner. He told the servants to clean the tanks, and found Han Bai to drive him to Saigon.

CHAPTER 16

ON THE EVE OF TET IN 1968, Percival sat on the edge of the bathtub. With his cupped hands, he scooped water over Jacqueline's shoulders, and watched as the rivulets traced her body. From the street below, the staccato explosions of firecrackers chased away bad ghosts of the old year and prepared the way for the Year of the Monkey. He lifted the heavy sheet of her hair with one hand, rinsed away the soap. There was singing from the streets, the revelry of soldiers who had come home to Saigon for the Tet ceasefire.

She said, "Some rich women have a maid to help them bathe. I have you, which is much better."

A year earlier, Percival could not have imagined that he would now be in this quiet apartment in Saigon, bathing this brown-haired beauty—pregnant with his child.

"You are not angry about the Tet banquet?" Percival asked.

"No, of course not. I understand, about discretion."

Percival wished that she could be at his side, but it was not possible under the circumstances. The banquet was to be a celebration of Mak's achievements at the school, for Percival still hoped to win the warmth of Mak's friendship back. Percival had decided to say nothing to his friend about this special honour until the night itself. He had hired Sheng Hing, the most expensive chef in Cholon, and told him to make the best of everything, ignoring cost. He had bought Mak a gold Rolex, to present to him at the meal.

If only Dai Jai could be there. He recalled a previous Tet. Two years ago, Dai Jai had helped him arrange a simple meal of a broth fondue and rice wine for the school staff. The whole meal had cost less than one of the courses he had ordered for this year's feast, but he felt wistful for it. The Ministry of Education had not yet issued its memorandum concerning Vietnamese language instruction, and Dai Jai had not yet made his foolish gesture at the Teochow school. One year ago, Dai Jai had just been rescued and Percival barely noticed Tet. In the letter just arrived, Dai Jai had said nothing about the New Year, only rambled that his district cadres were rooting out the land-lords and other class enemies who had oppressed the people for gen-erations. Despite the tone of his letters, Percival hoped that Dai Jai was preparing a celebration with his classmates.

"I'm sorry you will be alone," said Percival. "We'll have a Tet dinner together." He put his hands on Jacqueline's belly. He felt a movement as subtle as a shift in the light. Then a sudden urgent kick, followed by the entire belly convulsing as the child squirmed within.

"He is clever and quick, our little monkey," said Jacqueline.

"Are you so sure it's a boy?"

"I hope so. It's very hard to be a woman."

On Tet morning, Percival returned to Cholon. He had Han Bai drive him to the Teochow temple. Great pyramids of pomelos and tangerines lined the tables along with baskets of holiday sweets. The carved murals were freshly painted. Before them, people kowtowed, prayed, and burned joss sticks. Percival presented fifty thousand piastres to the donations secretary, who kowtowed and called a boy to paint an extra-large red banner to announce this generous gift. The names of the donors fluttered on the walls.

Percival always consulted Mr. Tai, the fortune teller at the Teochow temple, on the first day of the New Year. When Percival first arrived in Indochina, many people were still in this habit, and he would wait a long time to see Mr. Tai for just a few moments. Now, he did not need to wait, for few people kept up this tradition. In the difficult early years, Percival had paid close attention to each word Mr. Tai uttered. In recent years, he found that he attended more out of routine, and yet he would not wish to risk the displeasure of the ancestors' spirits by skipping the visit or the special New Year's donation to the temple. Had he actually followed Mr. Tai's advice over the past year? Visiting Mr. Tai was the one Tet habit he had kept last year. He realized that he could not remember what had been recommended to him, but now he found that he entered the soothsayer's chamber attentively, perhaps even with anxiety.

"Chen Pie Sou," said Mr. Tai, "do you have any debts or obligations?" It was best to resolve loans and problems before Tet, but if they could not be discharged, the fortune teller would give advice about them.

He said to Mr. Tai triumphantly, "I have no debts. In fact, this year I have paid off the biggest debts I have ever faced."

"Good, good, the ancestors' spirits are on your side, then. You should have no worries."

"But I am worried about my son, Dai Jai, whom I sent to China."

Mr. Tai sighed and shook his head sympathetically. "Many who have sent their children home have the same worry, these days. As long as I can remember, and I am an old man, China has been in upheaval. And yet it is China. It is your son's home, and it is where he should be." He took the box with the ivory fortune-telling sticks, shut the lid and began to rattle it. The old man handed it to Percival. Percival shook the box and thought hard of the future as the ivory clicked and chattered within the wood container. He imagined Dai Jai eating dumplings and bean cakes. When the end of a stick protruded from the hole in the lid, Percival drew it out and gave it to Mr. Tai. After two more had emerged, Mr. Tai laid them out in front of him and considered their carved symbols. He rolled them slightly in his hands. "The sticks indicate that just as those of us Chinese far away have questions, Dai Jai's feelings are not unique to him in China."

Percival stared at the old man. What sort of useless comment was that? His own annoyance made him see how desperate he was for prediction and advice regarding Dai Jai. So, he had donated fifty thousand piastres, only to be told the obvious. Percival said, "Thank you, Mr. Tai, *kung hay fat choy*." Good fortune in the New Year. He remained silent, aware that the ancestors would be aghast at any frustration directed at the fortune teller. He could not risk their displeasure. He put his hands together and kowtowed to the old man.

Percival returned to Chen Hap Sing late in the afternoon. The large kitchen was crowded with both Sheng Hing's staff and Chen Hap Sing's cooks, all washing, chopping, and preparing for the evening meal. Under the direction of Sheng Hing's *maître d'hotel*, the servers were decorating one of the larger classrooms, transforming it into a banquet room.

As Percival discussed final details of the banquet with the chef, Han Bai came and found Percival. "Headmaster, Mak asked me to pass you a message. He will not be able to attend the banquet."

"What? Where is he?"

"I don't know where he was heading, but he seemed to be in a rush, Headmaster, and he sends regrets."

The square was raucous with firecrackers and excited celebrations. Percival made his way through the crowd and walked to Mak's apartment a few blocks away. He knocked on the door, and there was no answer. He called out, thinking that Mak might be inside avoiding him. Still no reply. He banged the door with his fists. Was it possible, this insult? Was Mak trying to show the depth of his displeasure, having somehow learned that the banquet was meant to be in his honour?

He called into the door, "Mak, don't be so proud! Just once, I couldn't take your advice. I'll make it up to you. Tell me how." She was no longer a student. It must have to do with Jacqueline's mother.

A neighbour yelled, "Be quiet! People live here," and then appeared on the landing.

"Oh, it is you, *hou jeung*," she said, red-faced when she saw Percival. "Sorry for yelling. Happy New Year."

"Have you seen Mak?"

"I don't think he's been home today. Over the past few weeks he has been in and out at all hours, with many visitors coming and going. I thought you were one of his strange guests making a commotion."

Percival returned to the school and told Han Bai to go looking for Mak.

"But where should I look?"

"I don't know, but Mak *must* be at the banquet tonight."

Soon after, the guests began to arrive. Neither Han Bai nor Mak had yet returned. The room was crowded with the school's teachers, important parents, and Percival's gambling friends. Cecilia, who always attended such events, showed off the naval officer whom she had brought with her. At the sight of the captain's uniform, one of Percival's best teachers, an awkward young American who claimed he had been discharged, but whom Percival suspected was a deserter, slipped out and did not reappear. Percival seated Peters next to himself at a place of honour and saw that the American noticed one of the waitresses, an outgoing *métisse* girl.

The first course was squabs stuffed with cave swallows' nests. Glasses of champagne were raised with loud proclamations congratulating Percival on all he had done to make the school a success, and lengthy rambling about the privilege of working at the best English school in Vietnam. With the doubling of tuition, Percival had recently increased their salaries twenty-five percent. In response to teacher's toasts, Percival praised the quality of their English instruction. There was no sign of Mak or Han Bai.

Next came scallops in a cognac reduction, alongside braised and truffled lobsters. Another round of toasts began, with the teachers praising Peters and the headmaster on their fine example of co-operation between yellow and white in the service of freedom and democracy. "Hear hear!" yelled Cecilia's naval officer. New bottles of champagne were popped, poured, and drained. Police Chief Mei gorged himself, as usual. By the time they were finished with the dainty courses of shark's fin soup and braised goose, almost everyone at the gathering was slurring their words.

There would be another six dishes to follow, plus rice and noodles, enough time for Han Bai to find Mak before the last course. Percival had the Rolex in a gift box under a napkin before him. The servers brought giant abalones with fragrant mushrooms and freshly picked jasmine flowers. The household staff and the teachers began to shower each other in accolades, glasses hoisted unsteadily, clinked, refilled. The popping of champagne corks mingled with the explosion of fireworks outside in the square.

When the champagne was done, the servers opened cognac. Peters proclaimed drunkenly, "*Sun neen fai lok!*" Happy New Year, and Percival grinned broadly, slapped him on the back, and looked around for Mak. The *maître d'hotel* ensured that the American's snifter was never empty as Percival had asked. Noticing the direction of the young man's gaze, the *maître d'hotel* waved the *métisse* waitress over to sit and chat. She did not protest as Peters pulled her onto his lap.

One of the locally hired junior teachers stood, tilted slightly to one side, then caught a chair in his hand and managed to remain upright. "I would like to say thank you to the American army," he said in English. "You have come to do brave battle against small yellow people, and to make the English language a success. Therefore, you help us become rich! Thank you, America!"

Percival winced, but the foreign teachers roared with laughter and Peters was preoccupied making use of his laborious Vietnamese with the waitress who giggled on his lap. She swatted his hand away from her thigh, but accepted the cognac glass that he pressed into her hand.

The same drunk teacher raised another toast, "To young love!" At first, Percival thought to wave him down, assuming he was toasting Peters. The American must not be humiliated, thought Percival, suddenly annoyed. Then he realized the teacher was toasting the *hou jeung*. "To the headmaster, whose heart and love is young!" The other teachers pulled the drunk one down into his seat, and yelled the standard toasts to the headmaster—great fortune, every success, gratitude for his leadership. Reflexively, Percival stood, raised his glass, spread out his best smile, and said, "Everyone, bottoms up!" Even if his relationship with Jacqueline had become known, he must ignore such an inappropriate toast. Thankfully Peters, toying with the wrist of the girl on his lap, had not taken notice.

Where was Mak? Percival poured cognac into his teacup, emptied it in a single swallow, and reached for the bottle again to douse his frustration. Had his old friend bowed out tonight to avoid Percival's efforts to mend their friendship? The cognac bottle was empty, and Percival signalled for another. The alcohol hollowed him out, but offered no relief.

It was past midnight by the time they had eaten the giant chilled crabs, the raw fish salad, and the *kuay teow terng* soup of egg noodles containing eight meats and seafoods. The servers were bringing poached groupers each as long as a forearm, steaming in sauce, to each table when Sheng Hing came to the headmaster and said, "*Hou jeung*, fighting has broken out. I must send my staff home."

"Come on, there's no need for such stories. I'm sorry we've kept you so late. I know they want to go home to celebrate with their families. I'll pay for the staff's trouble, but let me save face and finish the banquet."

"No, I'm sorry, *hou jeung*, there really is fighting. Listen to the noise." The chef swam before Percival's cognac eyes. Outside, there was a burst of explosions.

"Haven't you ever heard firecrackers? You know I give a good tip," said Percival. "Have you seen Mak?"

"Who?"

"My friend. The one who runs this school," he said with the relief of truth-telling that came with drink. "This banquet is to honour him. It cannot end until we toast him."

"I'm serious, no stories. There has been an attack by the Viet Cong."

"Silly—there is a ceasefire. The Viet Cong are celebrating the New Year."

"Yes, I heard about that on the radio. But they have violated the ceasefire, they have attacked."

Percival focused on the noise from outside. It was remarkable, he thought, that a string of fireworks could sound so much like a machine gun.

Percival struggled to his feet, the effort reminding him of his inebriation. "The evening cannot end until I toast Mak."

"Then toast him now, *hou jeung*. This night has become dangerous."

"He is on his way. My driver has gone to fetch him. He will be here shortly."

"*Hou jeung*, he will not come on a night like this." There were several louder explosions outside. "Everyone should go home. Can't you hear?"

Percival laughed. "Can I hear those fireworks? Those big sounds must be the colourful ones." He wavered, steadied himself on the table. He had drunk enough that he should plan before moving.

"No, *hou jeung*," said the chef. There was a single, tremendous blast that shook the room, and the room's attention shifted, guests looking around, tense questions amidst the laughter. Some were too drunk to notice. The waitress slapped Peters, but playfully, as his hand slid between her knees.

Percival said, "Sheng Hing, master chef, you are so serious. You need a drink." He poured another glass, put his arm over the chef's shoulders and sighed. "You know this country. Blood falls in predictable torrents like the monsoon rains. Again and again it drowns everything, and then is swallowed by the earth. You are a chef. Tell me, the food that is grown here is so tasty—do you think it is the blood that makes the earth so full of flavour?" But before Sheng Hing could answer, a rocket-propelled grenade whined somewhere nearby, followed by the crack of the explosion. Close, that one. A waitress screamed. Cecilia stood, regally, and pulled her scarf around herself in leisurely preparation to go. She seemed to have forgotten her naval officer, who sat ashen, gripping the table. Still, many guests continued to laugh and drink.

Percival slowly, deliberately, hoisted his glass and proclaimed a toast. "To Mr. Peters and to Mr. Mak, who will be arriving soon," he exclaimed.

The room shouted in answer to his toast. He gestured to the waiters, who rushed to splash cognac into snifters, and called out, "Bottoms up!"

Sheng Hing stood behind Percival, whispering that his staff were panicking and wanted to leave. Still to come were the fried rice and braised noodles, Percival pointed out to the chef. Didn't he want to be paid in full? As Percival moved through his slow, simple, alcoholic thoughts, one word after another placed itself before him. "Well. You must feed the guests. Do you think I can send people out hungry? If they are to be killed? What kind of host would have guests die with empty stomachs?"

At a flustered word from Sheng Hing, the servers scurried around with bowls and serving dishes. Cecilia sat down. She would not be less brave than a bunch of waiters. Even drunk, Percival knew her.

For the last courses, which were usually very plain, Percival had arranged that they be made more special with the addition of fresh, sweet prawns, which were brought live and wriggling in bowls to be cooked at the side of the table. They had just been scooped from the water. Dai Jai's fish tanks had served as the temporary holding tanks that afternoon.

Now the servers wheeled in the carts, upon which perched bowls of the quivering translucent creatures and burners with their pots of oil and broth. As each guest preferred, the shrimp were either deep-fried or dunked into boiling water. The hissing and popping of the dying shrimp competed with the sound of gunfire from outside. Glasses clinked, and again Percival called out a toast, another bottoms-up. He was feeling good, now that he had finally passed through the dark place of drink and reached the warm, floating place. Words and sounds drifted selectively, he ignored the fearful voices, pulled up the silk sheet of laughter.

But it was during this last course that one of the houseboys rushed over to Percival, saying, "*Hou jeung*, your friend is here, at the kitchen entrance."

"Send him in!" Percival turned to Peters. "Mr. Peters," he said, "our good friend Mak is here."

"No, it is not Teacher Mak. It is a student," said the houseboy.

"Not now," said Percival, irritated that it was not Mak. What student would have the gall to interrupt the teachers' banquet? He delicately manipulated a shrimp, turned it with chopsticks to peel the creature with his teeth, then spat the empty shell onto the tablecloth.

"But *hou jeung*, she is going to have a baby."

Percival stood up too quickly, wavered at the side of the table. The birth shouldn't be for another month. Why was Jacqueline here?

"She asked me to fetch you," said the boy. "She says that she is going to push out the baby tonight."

"What do you know?" Percival began to weave his way across the room, concentrated on putting one foot before the other. He was both worried for Jacqueline and afraid she would make an appearance at his banquet. He had to steady himself against the wall, moving slowly. "Take her up to Dai Jai's room. Tell her I will come soon."

"Also, *hou jeung*," said the boy, "the war has arrived. It is outside in the square."

The boy dashed away.

There was the forlorn cry of a soldier in agony, and then an ear-splitting explosion. The voice was silenced. Peters caught up with Percival halfway across the room, and said, his words slurred, "Do you Chinese have fireworks that sound like artillery? Sounds like a barrage out there. Can we get a look at what's happening outside?"

"Let's go see," said Percival as if it was the first mention that had been made of the fighting. He wiped his mouth with the back of his hand and made his way to the staircase.

Percival climbed up the stairs, aware of Peters behind him. In his intoxicated haze, everything seemed to be of equal yet mild interest—the banquet, the fighting in the square, Mak's absence, and his pregnant lover. Where should he go? He needed some fresh air, a moment of night's clarity, he thought. He crept past Dai Jai's room, where a thin blade of light sliced under the bottom of the door. Jacqueline must be waiting for him.

He would show Peters up, breathe a little of the fresh evening air, and then go to her. They went up to the third floor and out onto the balcony. At that moment, the square had fallen quiet. Glowing moonlight was caught in a column of grey smoke that exhaled from the post office windows. Within those windows, a soft lick of flame. The silhouetted spire of St. Francis Xavier loomed, surveying the square. Framed by the soft edges of inebriation, the scene seemed almost pretty to Percival. Then there was the solo clatter of an engine. A South Vietnamese Jeep sped into view, the clatter rising as its soldiers fired at the post office from a mounted gun, and the Jeep slid to a halt where it was shielded by the corner of the cafe next to the post office. A soldier climbed out of the Jeep, shouldered a grenade launcher, crept to the corner, peered around with the long tube of his weapon, and set off a thin hissing sound like a string torn in half. Then the grenade reverberated within its target, and the corner of the post office crumbled. The Viet Cong must be in there, thought Percival, if the government soldiers were attacking the building.

The sudden shock of an explosion, this one very near, so that he felt the impact in his skin and his ears rang with pain. As the smoke cleared, he saw that a hole had been ripped into the street very near Chen Hap Sing. The Viet Cong's reply had wildly overshot the government soldiers, almost reaching the school. His guests must have felt this. He wondered if they had finished their prawns. He was fortunate to be drunk, he thought, for this gave him a sense of calm.

A flare shot into the sky and hung there for a moment before falling in a harsh, phosphorescent arc. In the spitting yellow light Percival saw something he recognized. It was his Peugeot. It rolled through the night into the square, without headlights. As if driven by a ghost. The car slowed at the end of Chong Hang Boulevard, stopped at the far side of the square. The doors opened, and two people got out, crept along near buildings, within moonlight's shadows. Mak and Han Bai. There was a distant explosion, farther, perhaps on the next block. Percival heard the door swing behind him, someone on the stairs, and then Peters came out on the balcony. Percival hadn't noticed that he had slipped away for a moment. Peters said, "I put on your radio." He considered the column of silver smoke, the soldiers huddling for cover, and the burning post office, as if whatever he had just heard on the radio explained the meaning of what was happening before them. Without the girl, he seemed to have returned to his official self, though his words still bled into one another. He said to Percival, "Percy, they're playing 'Jingle Bells' on the radio."

"What kind of bells?"

"It's a Christmas song. It's a pre-set code. It means there is a general attack. I have to get back to the embassy."

There was an angry crackle. Gunfire spat from the windows of the post office, and the government soldiers replied with the same. From their high vantage on Chen Hap Sing, Percival and Peters could see that a dark figure was creeping over the roof of the cafe, towards where the government soldiers had taken cover. Peters cursed, but it was too far to shout to the government soldiers. On the other side of the square, Mak and Han Bai crouched near a small car, not drawing fire but not out of its reach. Then the dark figure leaned out from the cafe roof, and began to pick off the government soldiers with a single shot each. Two fell in quick succession, and two others jumped out of the Jeep and ran towards the post office. As the men ran up the steps, wildly firing their rifles, one was shot and fell. The last one was struck in the arm and held it as he ran back to the Jeep. His weapon was left behind on the steps. He must have misjudged the direction of the sniper fire, for he took cover on the wrong side of the Jeep, where his enemy on the cafe roof shot him again, and he crumpled inert next to the vehicle.

A second Jeep sped across the square, firing its mounted gun high until the dark figure fell off the edge of the roof and landed motionless on the ground.

"What is happening?" Percival said.

"Bastards. There's a ceasefire!" said Peters.

"It has been cancelled, then."

"I have to get back to the embassy. Where's your car?"

"Over there," said Percival, and pointed across the square to the parked vehicle. Mak and Han Bai advanced from one bit of cover to another, but then there was a wide open stretch to Chen Hap Sing.

"They need covering fire," said Peters. "We have to do something."

"This is a school, Mr. Peters. Not a firebase."

"I need a gun. When I went down to listen to the radio, that policeman refused to come up here to help and wouldn't give me his gun. He looks more scared than anyone else in the room."

"Police Chief Mei? He knows the Viet Cong will shoot him first, on account of his uniform."

"He's wandering around in his underwear, clutching his revolver. They've sent two Jeeps? Isn't there a whole army division nearby?"

They watched as Mak and Han Bai abandoned the small protection of a clump of trees to make a dash for Chen Hap Sing, long strides, arms flailing, to cover the ground. The army and the Viet Cong's bullets erupted at each other. There was a loud explosion. Men within the post office screamed, and still Mak and Han Bai ran. Then another blast, and Peters was already flat on the balcony. He tried to pull Percival's feet out from under him to topple him down, but Percival grabbed the railing of the balcony like the rail of a listing ship. He had to watch his two friends run, as if to stop watching would be to betray them. They were more than halfway across the square. One of the Jeeps burst into flames, and the surviving South Vietnamese soldiers charged up the steps of the post office with their guns spraying wildly before them. Flashes replied from within. Then, suddenly, it looked as if Han Bai tripped. Get up, get up, keep going, thought Percival. Mak noticed that he was alone and stopped, hurried back, rolled Han Bai over. And then once more Mak was running towards the school.

Percival rushed down to the door to open it for his friend, thought of Jacqueline as he went past the second floor, but he had to get to the front of the building. A few guests were milling about on the landing, and Percival rushed past, ignored their questions. He struggled with the locks, his hands now clumsy with alcohol and fear. He got it open and pulled Mak in, saying, "What about Han Bai? We must save him." Percival was halfway out the door but Mak grabbed him, tackled him to the ground. The servants pulled them both in, slammed the door, and bolted it shut.

"He is not there to save, *hou jeung*," said Mak, breathless.

"He is just outside. I saw where. You are hurt, your hands are wounded. I will run and get him."

"This is Han Bai's blood, *hou jeung*."

Percival stared at Mak's hands, the dark blood glossy wet. He said, "But how can this be?" He saw his driver's look of disappointment at being sent out on an errand at the start of a sumptuous meal. Han Bai must have died hungry.

"It's my fault," said Percival, looking at Mak's stained hands. His own hands were clean, undeservedly. Mak seemed to be paying no attention to him.

Mak scanned around. "Have you had any visitors? Are there strangers in Chen Hap Sing?"

"No, only our friends who have come for the Tet banquet," said Percival.

The servants dragged mattresses and beds from the bedrooms and propped them against the windows of the school. The guests huddled in the kitchen, which was in the centre of the building. The foreigners lamented their lack of weapons. Peters brought the radio down from the sitting room so everyone could listen for news, but after "Jingle Bells," the Saigon radio went dead. Nothing came except shortwave from abroad, cursory mention of some fighting in Vietnam. Percival climbed the stairs to Jacqueline. She squatted in the centre of Dai Jai's room, panting, elbows on her knees. A few of the house's female servants had already gone to her. For now, even Foong Jie seemed to have put aside her animosity.

"Are you crazy," Percival said to Jacqueline, "to come to Cholon at such a time?"

She gasped, "I had to come."

"You were safer in your apartment than here."

"It is time for me to have the baby." She panted, went to her hands and knees to crawl towards the bed.

Percival went to her, helped her to her feet and then onto the bed. "It's a month early."

"I think the fighting has shocked the baby—he wants to be born now."

As the night wore on, the women servants gave Jacqueline contradictory advice. One said that she should lie still and drink tepid water in order to slow her labour, for it would be bad luck for the child to be born in the middle of a battle. Jacqueline tried to do this, and the contractions came just as insistently. Another said that the best thing was to walk around and chew ginseng, as this would excite the baby and make it hurry out. She insisted that a prolonged labour and the squeezing of the loins might produce a child with a deformed head and damaged brain. Jacqueline was scared to do this at first, but after having spent hours with no sleep, she felt impatient and began to stamp around vigorously with slices of ginseng in her cheeks. During lulls in the battle, the night was occupied by Jacqueline's low, guttural cries, which became longer, more frequent. Each time the volleys of gunfire came, Percival imagined the rounds ripping apart Han Bai's body, and prayed to the ancestors that the bullets would not reach them in Chen Kai's old room, in Dai Jai's old room. It must have some luck. Mak sat outside the room cross-legged, even though Percival urged him to get some sleep. He had a small kitchen cleaver in his back pocket, the blade wrapped in newspaper. Percival had seen Mak angry before, but never as tense as he was now.

Towards morning, when the Saigon radio finally resumed broadcasts, President Thieu gave a public address. He announced that cowardly attacks by the Viet Cong throughout South Vietnam had been put down by the government soldiers. Order had been restored in Saigon-Cholon. At the moment that he said this, there was a burst of gunfire on the street outside Chen Hap Sing.

Fortunately, the house was full of pomelos, tangerines, sausages, and smoked ducks that had been prepared for Tet, so the guests could be fed. Mak insisted that Peters stay, saying that the Viet Cong would likely kill foreigners on the spot if they saw them. The electricity died, and the radio went silent. The servants sang old Chinese songs, and it felt something like a Tet celebration, except for the now sporadic spasms of noise made by weapons outside.

Percival asked one female servant what would happen if the baby came now, a month early. She said that they should have a white mourning cloth ready to wrap it. After all, if they had made no provision for its possible death, the spirits might be displeased and more likely to take the child's life. Percival ignored this advice and asked another servant. She felt Jacqueline's belly and declared that the baby would be especially vigorous, for it was such babies who were born early.

As daytime heat filled the house, worse with the shutters closed, the contractions set in steadily. Jacqueline's water broke, and she said that she felt something had moved within her. Percival decided to risk going out on the balcony upstairs to see if it was calm enough for him to take Jacqueline to a hospital for the birth, or to bring someone to help.

The post office across the square was now ringed by green army vehicles and green-uniformed soldiers, their guns pointed towards the old French brickwork and the gaping hole in the corner. There were shouts back and forth. Percival hoped that the government troops would quickly kill whomever they were after. He kept his eyes away from where he knew Han Bai's body lay, but saw that the Peugeot was gone. Then, a single shot from somewhere else, a distant scream. The scream continued for a while, begging for mercy. Another shot, silence. No, Percival concluded, they would have to stay here.

He went down to the second-floor room again. Jacqueline's contractions seemed to have become almost constant, one leading into the next with only a moment between for her to snatch a breath. Percival held her hand, whispered encouragement. By now, he was sober. Each pain was longer, more intense than the one before it, and when it came she pursed her lips slightly as she pushed and made no sound until the contraction reached its end. Then, she released her cry of relief and small victory.

Jacqueline panted, "It will be soon."

There were footsteps on the floor above, unfamiliar and distant. Percival forgot them as soon as he heard them. Jacqueline closed her eyes during the pains, and when she opened them between her contractions, she stared through to her lover's centre. Percival held her forearms and through them felt the strength of her woman's body.

Then, shouting voices. Why were there men on the top floor of the house? he thought. There should be no one there. Jacqueline took no notice. Voices shouted urgently in Vietnamese. Percival had not fully heard it, but thought there was something about moving aside. Then, a barrage of feet rushed down the stairs.

He heard Mak. "Big brothers, stop, be calm, there has been a misunderstanding."

Just as Jacqueline gasped, the voices argued with Mak on the landing outside the room. They spoke rapidly in Vietnamese, something was said about a list, about orders. Mak said that there had been a mistake. The strange voices insisted that they had orders. Mak spoke kindly, evenly, telling them that there had been an error. The *hou jeung* was a good man, he was about to become a father, said Mak, soothing. Then Jacqueline reached the end of a contraction and screamed. One of the Vietnamese voices shouted angrily that the oppressors were torturing a Vietnamese sister.

"No, no," said Mak, "she is about to have a baby."

Four men in city clothes burst through the door with the weapons of war. They clutched rifles, and bandoliers of ammunition and grenades were draped over their dirty shirts and poorly fitting slacks. They looked exhausted, ragged. When the men saw Jacqueline, they stumbled over their embarrassment and apologized in Vietnamese, averted their eyes. Mak appealed to them, soothing words as if he were addressing a wild animal. His back was turned to Percival, who could see that one of his hands clutched the handle of the cleaver, still pocketed. One of the intruders asked angrily if Percival was the headmaster, levelling his gun, but before Percival could decide upon his answer, another ordered him out. Then, they were gone. Their footsteps thumped away as they ran down to the ground floor and towards the door.

"It's now! It's now!" said Jacqueline, and a contraction seized her entirely. The swelling between her legs, the purplish top of the head, grew and pushed forward until an entire baby's face emerged like an impossible growth from Jacqueline's own body. She gasped quickly for breath and again began to push. Her face was livid with the effort, and her hands were clamps around Percival's. Slowly a shoulder appeared, with agonizing effort it grew. Then, with a final push, everything seemed to come. In a great hurry the arms and then the body slid out. Now, Foong Jie pulled out the legs, and then lifted him up. It was a boy, his hair matted in bloody fluid, his skin wrinkled, his eyes wide open in amazement and protest. Jacqueline, her whole body quivering, took the boy from the woman with a sudden, possessive grasp and brought him to her, the umbilical cord still snaking down into her. Percival kissed Jacqueline, ecstatic with love for her and their child.

As the boy suckled at Jacqueline's breast, they heard four single shots nearby, outside the school. Mak went white. He went to investigate. He was gone a few minutes, and when he came back he said, "They were Viet Cong—an assassination team. They are no more."

"Why are you sad, then?"

Mak looked up as if startled. "They were men, too."

"Thank you, friend. You saved me."

"Your son saved you," said Mak. "What a waste, this war. Four more dead young men. And Han Bai, too."

Percival said nothing about the banquet having been in Mak's honour. He felt embarrassed now for having wanted to make a gaudy show of their friendship, ashamed of himself at Han Bai's death. He held his new son, clung to him, for it was a fragile blessing to be whole. Later that day, the government soldiers secured the post office and the remaining guests were able to leave in relative safety. The Rolex was gone—some guest had pocketed it. Before she left, Cecilia cast her eyes over Percival's new child and surprised him by sniffing, "It does look like yours."

CHAPTER 17

PERCIVAL HEARD A NOISE FROM DAI Jai's room. He rose from his bed and crept down the stairs, through the hallway, which stretched into the darkness of an empty night. The bedroom doors were all closed. Strange, as lately he had ordered the doors to be left open at night, to allow air to circulate through the house. Again, he heard the noise, movement within Dai Jai's room. He remembered, Jacqueline was there. She must be awake with the baby. But why had she closed the doors? He called out to her. No reply. He crept forward, chest pounding—he did not know why he was so scared, could only hear the creaking of the floors surrounding him. He called out her name, "Jacqueline?"

He flung the door open in case an intruder crouched behind it. The door swung freely, and Percival saw Jacqueline and the baby asleep in the bed. Before he had time to feel relief, he saw the dark figure which stood, its back to him, staring at the sleeping pair. Percival knew that this intruder had come for both mother and child, and he yelled, told the man to step back from the bed, but even as he did so, he couldn't hear his own voice. Percival ran towards the spectre, but could not get any closer, the floors creaking louder, enveloping him. The figure did not move, did not seem to hear him. He ran and ran without advancing, as if in a web. The bed remained at the same distance no matter what he did. His screams were trapped, silent.

Finally, Percival woke—his sheets soaking.

Again, the same nightmare. Each time, he thought it was real until it was over.

THEY NAMED THE BABY LAING JAI, meaning the beautiful child. Percival was grateful that the baby was healthy despite the circumstances of his birth. It was all he wanted. During daytime, it was as if only Jacqueline and the boy were real. Everything else was a dream. Percival would gently cradle the child close to him and let him fall asleep on his chest. As Laing Jai rose and fell lightly with his father's breaths, Percival inhaled deeply, took in the milky floral smell. Dai Jai had once had that scent. When Percival had last smelled it, the rice mills still churned and clanked in Chen Hap Sing, and he had thought it was the rice dust settling on the baby's skin. But Laing Jai smelled the same. Perhaps it was an odour emitted only while babies dreamed. If he could know his ancestral home by a scent, this would be it.

Percival would watch Laing Jai nurse, both mother and child satisfied by the feeding. When the baby paused and took a deep breath, he inhaled with the effort of the whole world. When he let his tiny breath escape, so too did the world's worries. Jacqueline refused Percival's offer to hire a wet nurse and instead fed the baby herself. Her breasts grew heavy, her nipples thick, and Percival allowed himself the intoxication of being in love with both mother and child. Occasionally, he cautioned himself to at least try to preserve his judgment. After all, she was not Chinese. Yet, more and more it felt that he was forcing this thought upon himself.

About a week after the birth, Percival said to Jacqueline, "Today I am having Dr. Hua come to examine the boy."

"That's not necessary. He's fine, don't you think?"

"But what if something is not right with him? He arrived under such difficult circumstances."

When the doctor arrived, Percival welcomed him. Dr. Hua whispered nonsensical reassurances to Laing Jai in French and Cantonese. He poked and tapped, all the while making strange facial contortions that seemed intended, without success, to amuse the screaming child. He listened with his stethoscope and pushed on the baby's flesh with his fingertips. Finally, he said, "Everything is in order—ten fingers, two testicles, and all the appropriate portions are present." The child wailed. Jacqueline snatched him to her breast and retreated to a corner.

"Any concerns, then?" asked Percival.

"I recommend a special syrup of concentrated vitamins. I happen to have a vial of this excellent medicine with me, and will offer it to you at a good price. Only fifteen thousand piastres for a full month's supply—it is all you need."

"Good, good," said Percival, taking the brown glass bottle. "This is a special mixture for babies born under stressful conditions?"

Dr. Hua took his stethoscope off his neck and absently folded it into his brown leather bag. "It's good for any babies." He looked up. "He is a beautiful, healthy boy." He smiled at Percival. "Congratulations, Headmaster."

Percival returned the smile with considerable relief. "We were worried," he said, bowing and offering a red envelope, "since the fighting shocked the child into the world."

The doctor accepted the red envelope and nodded.

Laing Jai had a reassuringly solid build. A shock of rippling brown hair had been passed to him through Jacqueline. Percival thought the boy had his nose, and he made a long examination of himself in the mirror to be sure. Yes, it was. The baby had Dai Jai's bright, darting eyes, and Percival often found himself staring into them. The baby returned Percival's stare with neither cunning nor expectation. Percival resented the idea of Jacqueline going back to Saigon. Why should she? In any case, it seemed their secret had leaked to the teachers even before she appeared during the Tet banquet. He liked her and the child being here. Wasn't this his house?

It had been different when Cecilia gave birth to Dai Jai. She had handed the baby immediately to Foong Jie to care for, leaving Foong Jie scrambling to find a wet nurse. Cecilia had bound her breasts with strips of cotton to discourage them from producing milk, and complained bitterly about what Percival had done to her by making her bear a child. He spent more of the first few months of Dai Jai's life at Le Grand Monde than at home. Meanwhile, the servants were on edge, hurrying to fulfil Cecilia's wishes—to sniff the baby's feces to see if he was sick, to prepare foods that she requested, to bring the boy because he was crying for her, to take him away because she had heard enough crying.

With Jacqueline, the servants did not know at first whether they should attend to her or discreetly pretend she was not there. They did what they thought would be helpful, and found it was well received by Jacqueline. But when Percival appeared, the servants stopped talking to her, as if they would be faulted for having noticed the headmaster's lover. Percival instructed Foong Jie to have Dai Jai's old room scrubbed clean for Jacqueline and the baby. Foong Jie waved her hands before her, a rare objection. He must show that the head of the house did as he saw fit. "I am the boss. It must be spotless for Jacqueline," said Percival.

Seeing the room made him miss Dai Jai, but wasn't that all the more reason to allow the life and light of a mother and child to fill it? Dai Jai's next letter, which arrived soon after Tet, ranted that his father was a "puppet lackey of the American oppressor." Dai Jai hoped through service to the working people to "atone for the sins of his shameful landlord family." By filling his room, was Percival trying to fill the empty space that Dai Jai had left? he wondered. Meanwhile, however angry he might be at the disrespect in Dai Jai's letters, Percival concluded that it had been right to send him. What if the boy had been in the army during the recent offensive? All the cities in the South had been attacked. Dai Jai might have been shot by the communists, or later could have been targeted by the South Vietnamese. They would need people to blame, in order to distract from their military humiliation.

Police Chief Mei came to speak to Percival. "If the newspapers ask, can you say some good things about me, maybe that I spent the night of Tet protecting the school? I'm getting a hard time from Saigon." The newspapers had published a photo of Police Chief Mei taken on the day after Tet, wearing the dress uniform that he had donned for

Percival's banquet. The servants said that he had put it on as soon as it was clear that the battle had turned in favour of Saigon's soldiers. In the photo, Mei stood above the four dead bodies of the Viet Cong assassination squad, his .38 Colt in his hand pointed down at one of their shattered skulls. It looked like he had just shot the men.

"But aren't you a hero for having shot those Viet Cong?"

"I would have been, except that the newspaper photo was shown in America. Some reporter wrote that obviously they had been kneeling, that they must have surrendered before they were shot. They all fell neatly in a row. The bullets went in from above their heads."

"Let me guess, the Americans thought you should have taken the men for questioning instead of killing them."

"I didn't even shoot them. One of my men did. They were dead by the time I got there. But when the newspapers asked me, I posed for the photo. I thought it might help me get a promotion, maybe even a trip to America for a training course. Instead, the Americans are talking bullshit about the Geneva Convention."

"The Americans' problem is that they don't know what they want. Shoot this one. Help that one."

"They killed all the Viet Cong who attacked the American embassy, but I shouldn't have shot those ones in front of your school. Cold blood, they say. Bad press. I should have allowed my officer to take the credit. Now, I could be reprimanding *him* to earn my promotion."

"The Americans have no concept of loyalty. They don't stand by their friends, but then they can't tell their friends from their enemies," said Percival. "Yes, you were defending my school all night long."

"Thank you."

"Remember the favour."

"Of course."

Now, in the wake of all this, there would be disappearances, bodies found in the morning, relatives outside the gates of the National Police Headquarters. The quiet police would be compelled to show their vigilance. Yes, he might write in his letters along with some fatherly admonishment, that it was best that Dai Jai was in China.

MAK HIRED MASONS TO REPAIR THE shrapnel damage and gouges made by machine-gun fire on the face of Chen Hap Sing. He hired labourers to fill in the holes in the street left by shells that had landed in front of the school. It would be bad luck if someone rode a bicycle or moped into one of those holes. It took some time and several red packets to obtain glass to repair the shattered windows. In the wake of the Tet fighting, many people in Saigon and Cholon needed new glass. The windows of St. Francis Xavier had all been shattered, and Percival contributed to the priests' appeal for their repair, as well as giving extra alms to the monks whose monastery had been hit by a stray mortar. Schools remained closed. Nonetheless, the school inspector came to visit and said that he was renewing licences for the upcoming semester. He couldn't name an exact opening date, but said it would be soon. Percival provided a suitable sum of cash. The calls of the vendors and the chatter of trade gradually returned to La Place de la Libération.

Beyond the bullet in his chest which felled him, Han Bai's body had been untouched through the night of the fighting. Percival visited his family and mourned with them. He could not bring himself to tell them that he had sent the driver out that night, but he bought a grave site on a hill, with a view of the canal. It was a site suitable for a wealthy man. He paid for a lavish funeral, and gave Han Bai's family a year of the driver's salary. Percival worried that Han Bai's death might bring misfortune to the school, and hoped that his generosity might placate any bad feelings that Han Bai's spirit might have.

Percival asked Mak into the school office, and told him about the dark figure in his dream. Who else could he tell? He asked Mak if he thought Han Bai was haunting them, and whether the death would cast a shadow over the school's reputation. Mak pressed his lips tight as Percival spoke. Finally, he said, "I know nothing of dreams. See the fortune teller. But I don't think the danger to your school's reputation comes from Han Bai's death. I am sad like you, but if anything it makes the school more patriotic—we have lost one of our own to this war. The danger to your school's name is the student whom you insist on bedding."

"Former student. You are fixated on this small issue."

The fan slowed, its squeaking stopped. The electricity had been unreliable since the Tet fighting. From time to time, Cholon's fans, radios, and electric clocks came to a simultaneous halt, as they did now. Silence.

Mak said, "Han Bai told me you won her at the Sun Wah Hotel."

"I asked you for advice on Han Bai's death, about my dream. Not Jacqueline. Why does this matter concern you, Mak? It has to do with her mother's death in Thanh Ha, yes? Some business of yours. Look, I don't care if you have friends amongst every faction in this confusing country, which I'm sure you do. I hope you profit from each of them, but I love Jacqueline."

Mak sat forward. He put both hands on the table, fingers spread. "At the very least, send her back to Saigon. Your well-being concerns me. The well-being of the school concerns me. It is one thing for this house to know that you have taken her as your mistress. It's another for all of Cholon to see you flaunting it. At least send her back to Saigon. People will know, but they will see that you are making an effort at discretion, at behaving the way a headmaster should."

Percival did take Mak's advice on one thing. When he confided in the fortune teller about his dreams, the old man said, "Did someone leave your household when the child arrived?"

"My driver was killed that night."

"The ghost is jealous—on the night of his death, came life."

Behind him, the bead curtain rustled, and Percival was startled.

"What can I do to avoid being haunted by the ghost of my driver? I have mourned. I have paid compensation to his family. Much more than would be expected."

The box was prepared and the sticks were rattled out. The fortune teller said, "To appease the ghost completely, the child must leave." Percival left grumbling, wondering if Mak had somehow got to the fortune teller and told him what to say.

PERCIVAL LIKED TO BE CLOSE TO Jacqueline without doing or saying anything. She slept when Laing Jai slept, and woke with the baby's noises and movements so that they inhabited their own time. Sometimes, when they slept during the day, the room shuttered into a midday dusk, Percival crept into the room and watched them.

Jacqueline seldom went out. When she did, she folded her hair into a conical hat and hid her face deep in the hat's shade. She returned with magazines and newspapers and read them as she wandered the house with Laing Jai. She often wrapped Laing Jai with a length of cloth as a peasant would, so that she could carry the baby on her front or back, leaving her arms free. "Don't worry," she told Percival when he watched her curiously one morning as she wrapped Laing Jai. "There's no chance I will become a country girl. I am a Saigon flower. This is just a good way to carry a baby."

"Are you sure? I don't want to lose you to a rice farmer," he joked.

"I couldn't survive in the countryside, anyhow," she said. "I can speak like a countrywoman, but if anyone sees my face and hair, they'll think I am a foreigner. Can you give me some money for today's newspapers?"

"Why don't I buy you a record player? Or some novels? There are so many things you could enjoy. It is better to ignore the news. It can be upsetting."

Jacqueline laughed. "Like you do? I see you reading the papers that I buy, and hear you listening to the radio—both the Voice of America and the late-night Chinese broadcasts. I even heard you listening to the Vietnamese news one day. You don't ignore the news. You just find it convenient to pretend to be oblivious. The question is, what do you do with what you know, when you feign disinterest?"

"The Americans are talking about two hundred thousand more soldiers. They will need more translators than ever."

"Beyond what the news means for your business, do you have any thoughts?"

"If I did, I would keep them to myself."

Even weeks after Tet, bitter and bloody fighting continued in some cities farther to the north. Long after the last of the Viet Cong had been killed in Saigon, the communists still controlled Hue. The American and South Vietnamese soldiers gradually took the city back, fighting block by block. It was reported that much of the beautiful old city, even the royal palace, was destroyed by mortars and grenades.

Percival saw Jacqueline reading a *Paris Match* feature on the battle for Hue. There were colour photos of soldiers exhausted, wounded, of the dead residents of the city, their faces bloated like balloons of meat. Percival lingered. Jacqueline did not acknowledge him as she nursed Laing Jai and read about the mass graves. In her quiet was tension. He said, "It might turn your milk sour to read such terrible things."

"They had lists, you know? Of those who worked for Americans, or had business with American companies. Their spies had compiled them. You see these bodies? German missionary doctors—but their foreignness was enough to doom them."

Percival could not help looking at the blond victims, their hair stained with brown blood where they had been shot. He said, "But here in Saigon, everything is back to normal. Schools will open again soon. You should listen to music. It will soothe you."

"Is this what you call normal? In this country of blood, all you Chinese care about is *sang yee*, making money." She looked up at Percival. "Have you wondered why those men came down from the roof as I was about to give birth?" Laing Jai lost the nipple and began to fuss. Jacqueline adjusted him and put him to her breast again. "They were looking for you." Percival said nothing, stood unmoving until she conceded, "I like to read. You can buy me novels as well. And music too, if you wish."

Later that night, when Jacqueline and the baby slept, Percival looked for the magazine. He took it to the kitchen to dispose of it but could not keep himself from reading it. The more fortunate victims were the foreigners, army officers, and prominent local officials and business people. They were targeted on the night of Tet and shot by North Vietnamese assassination squads. Most of the Vietnamese who died in the drawn-out occupation of Hue—teachers, police, and anyone who spoke a foreign language—were bound by the hands and feet, pushed into pits alive, and buried by the shovels of those who were next to be killed. As the fighting dragged on, the Northern troops needed to conserve bullets. The graves were not deep and were easy to find, wrote the journalist, as the rotting bodies stank through the shallow mud. Percival read this, opened the coal-box of the kitchen stove, shoved the glossy magazine into it, and watched the pages burst into flames.

CHAPTER 18

THE REPAIRS ON CHEN HAP SING were ongoing, but the classrooms were useable, when, three weeks after Tet, the re-opening of schools was announced by the Ministry of Education. On the first day of classes, Percival stood at the door of the school to welcome the students. As they arrived, a dark Ford Galaxie stopped in front of Chen Hap Sing. The shirt-sleeved man in plain clothes, neatly pressed, waded through the students and stopped at the doorway of the school office. The officer held up a licence plate, which was blackened with soot, barely readable. "I want to speak to whomever this belongs." These men from Saigon all had a similar bearing and reminded Percival of one another, even when he had never seen a particular officer before.

Percival read the licence plate. "It is mine," he said, his mouth dry. There was no point saying otherwise. The quiet police had traced the plate to him. "Thank you. My car disappeared on the night of Tet—I thought it was gone for good." Percival had assumed the car was stolen. What did it mean, that this man from Saigon would bring him the plate? "Please, let me give you a gift for finding my car. I'm most appreciative."

"Don't bother," said the officer, "your car is in worse shape than the plate. It is not worth a red packet. I am from Saigon. I have questions. I am with the police."

"Is that right?" said Percival, though this was obvious. "How kind, you have come all the way from Saigon to speak to me." He thought of Jacqueline, wished he had given her some instructions, some emergency funds, in case of his arrest. He had been too engrossed in their new child to think of it.

"Where can we talk, Chinaman?" asked the officer.

"Won't you come in for tea?" He hoped this was the normal kind of police visit, that which had a cash price. Percival showed him into the school office. Percival used the delay to calm himself. He poured tea from a flask.

"What do you know about this?" said the officer. He tossed the licence plate with a clank onto the desk, and delicately lifted his tea cup between thumb and forefinger.

Percival glanced at the burned plate, thought of Han Bai. "My car was stolen that night, my driver killed. Are you hungry? My cook can prepare a snack."

"I'm not hungry. You were not killed. Why not?"

"No one knows their appointed hour. I was here. They stole the car from across the square."

"Who is 'they'?"

"Thieves. Isn't it thieves who steal cars?"

"Sure. A good car, a chaotic moment. Or it could have been the people who attacked that night."

"You think the thieves were communists? Did I hear on the radio that Viet Cong were responsible for the attacks?" He should be careful, Percival reminded himself, not to feign ignorance to a degree that was unbelievable.

"And you had no idea that 'they' were going to use your car to attack an army post across the bridge?"

"Is that where it went?"

"You're claiming that you didn't know."

"How could I know?"

"It was your car."

"How should I know what happened after my car disappeared? My driver was killed."

"Unless you left it for the communists. Why did you leave it outside?"

"I couldn't very well have gone out to retrieve it that night, not in the middle of the battle."

"Then we do not need to suspect you?"

"Why should I be under suspicion?"

The officer sipped his tea. He put down the cup, and rapped the licence plate with his knuckles. "People whose cars were used by the Viet Cong are being questioned. Meanwhile, I am always suspicious of people who answer my questions with further questions."

"I'm sorry. I just have more questions than answers." Percival hated the sound of his own voice right now—did it actually sound different when he was scared, or was it just that he heard it differently?

"Like insects, those Viet Cong cockroaches infiltrated all of the Southern cities in the weeks before Tet—invisible within the walls until they came scurrying out. It looks like many of their weapons were smuggled slowly into the cities, bit by bit, in carts of vegetables, in the trunks of private cars, some of which were later used in attacks. They rented rooms, met in secret, and moved around the city to plan their assault. We ask ourselves, why would they have had access to particular persons' houses, phones, and vehicles? Some people helped them, sheltered them, gave them piastres and fed them. We must find those people. Everyone knows that the best way to wipe out insects is to get rid of their food."

"I am an educator. I have nothing to do with the food business," said Percival. "Officer, I have had enough bad luck. My car was stolen. By Viet Cong, from what you say. My driver was killed. I was fond of him. I will do anything to improve my luck. Perhaps a small donation to help you in your work?"

The officer said, "You must tell me everything you know."

"The car disappeared, that's all I know." That was the trick of innocence, Percival reminded himself to repeat a simple thing. Further explanations suggested guilt.

The officer's face was flat. "Did you know that your name was on a list?"

"A list?"

"Yes, an assassination list. It was in the pocket of one of the Viet Cong who was shot just outside of your school." Percival thought of the men who had burst into the room where Jacqueline was giving birth.

Percival had told himself it was just bad luck, that the assassination team had stumbled into Chen Hap Sing. They had seemed defeated, exhausted. Was that why they were so willing to kill, because they knew that their own end would surely come soon? "The communists were on their way to kill you. That is the reason I have not arrested you for providing your car to the enemy . . . yet." The officer laughed.

"I had a narrow escape, then. One can be so fortunate without realizing."

"Yes, quite," the officer said. "Tell me about your friend. Do you trust your teacher Mr. Mak? How long have you known him?"

"I have known him since . . . well, since this school was started."

"That's when you met him, when you hired him as a teacher?"

"Yes." He would not talk about the Japanese, decided Percival, or the Viet Minh. Even if half of the South Vietnamese generals had once been Viet Minh, the same was true of the Northern generals in Hanoi. That affiliation could still get someone arrested, or make a bribe more costly. This officer was sniffing around like a dog. Better not to give him something of Mak's to chew on. Percival must return loyalty with the same.

"Would he become headmaster if you were killed?"

"He would be well suited."

"Did he have access to your car?"

"No. Only my driver and myself had keys." Percival thought of Mak and Han Bai dashing across the square towards safety, of Han Bai cut down, and pushed aside the painful memory. The bullets could just as easily have killed Mak, who did have a key to the car, of course.

"How do you think the Viet Cong took the car, then?"

Sweat trickled down the back of Percival's neck. "My driver must have panicked and left the key in the car."

"What kind of friends does Mak have? Does he visit any friends outside of the city, in the delta?"

Mak often went alone in the car to visit his own friends, his business acquaintances, people whom Percival knew nothing about. Sometimes the car came back red with mud. Percival had seen Mak wash it carefully in the alley before giving it back. "He goes to Saigon from time to time, always strictly on school business. If he ever went in the car, my driver took him. I'm not even sure Mak can drive," Percival said.

"Someone who knows you put you on that assassination list."

Perhaps this officer, like many in the army and the quiet police, needed to deliver some arrests, some villains. Or perhaps this situation simply created an opportunity for profit. It was hard to tell which this man was after. Percival said, "I don't see why that would be necessary. Do you know what kind of school this is?"

"It is a language institute."

"An English academy. We train people to work for the Americans. Naturally, my name was on a Viet Cong assassination list. Anyone in Cholon making such a list would include the headmaster of the Percival Chen English Academy, even if they hadn't met me."

The officer's expression softened as he considered this. "And your teachers, do you have enemies amongst them?"

"They are too busy making money to be unhappy. When the fighting began, we were having a banquet. To celebrate Tet and our profits." Percival watched the officer carefully, trying to see if this interested him.

"Let me put it to you plainly. You, your school, are under suspicion. Don't think your son is forgotten either, though you've hidden him. In the papers that were found with the assassins, we saw that your roof was a rendezvous point."

"Really? I suppose my roof has an excellent view of the square." Percival told himself to be confident, to play it like a bad poker hand, with complete assurance.

"My superiors are convinced there must be an infiltrator in your house. A Viet Cong. I'm not saying I necessarily agree, but you know how it is, bosses don't like to be wrong. Mine has sent me to look for someone, and he will feel better if I bring him something. He will feel clever and satisfied."

"I see," said Percival. "But now that we have spoken, you see that everyone here is deeply involved in the war effort. You could point out a number of other explanations to your boss, for surely they exist." Percival pulled out the drawer of his desk so that the cash he kept there for this purpose could be easily seen. "Here's what you can take to your boss: everyone in Cholon knows that we've recently been given a special certification by the Americans—our students are exempt from their English proficiency tests. We are a natural target of the communists. The good side of this is that we have a lot of money. Do you want a snack now? I will go out and get my cook to make whatever you want."

The police officer glanced at the tidy sheaf of piastres in the desk drawer. "Maybe I will have a snack after all. Perhaps I will bring a bite to my superior, who may be hungry."

"Of course," said Percival, standing, and leaving the drawer open. How wise of Mak, he thought. Mak must have his ways of profiting from the connections he maintained for the school, but staying in the shadows meant that the assassination squad did not look for him. Still, Percival could not fault Mak—he had understood the risk of that night and guarded his brother until he was safe. Besides, it was Mak's arrangements that made it possible for Percival to sacrifice a drawer full of piastres to some nosy police.

WHEN JACQUELINE WAS NOT LISTENING TO radio reports of the heavy fighting in central Vietnam or immersed in the latest newspaper account of the battles on the Laotian border, she made every effort to bring light into the house. She would say that the fish that Foong Jie brought from market was the most beautiful tasting fish that she had ever eaten, and that the fragrance of the cook's meals was enough to summon the kitchen god. She would urge the sweeper to take a rest, saying that he must surely be exhausted after cleaning the house so well. Cecilia had stormed about and complained with such relentlessness that it never occurred to Percival that a lady of the house could act with Jacqueline's kindness.

Jacqueline seemed anxious to maintain Percival's favour, too. Nightly, after Laing Jai fell asleep, she crept into Percival's bed. If she came to him when he was half asleep and he suggested they might just lie together, she seemed worried. So he allowed her hands and mouth to explore his body and was soon glad that he did. In their quiet dark space of two, he often wished that she was not a former student. Even more so that she were Chinese. If she were, would he marry her? he allowed himself to wonder. The obvious answer came with an unfamiliar pain, for Percival was not accustomed to ignoring his own desires. Better not to think about it. After all, how could he explain to Dai Jai that he had married a *métisse* when he had forbidden Dai Jai's own infatuation with a Vietnamese girl? How many times had he told Dai Jai the cautionary tale of Ba Hai? It was as if he could hear his own voice echoing in his ears—it was one thing to take a lover of another race, but a Chinese man should not marry a woman who was not Chinese.

What about the assassination list? If he had been on a list of targets, he must still be on it. When he stopped to consider this, Percival was forced to conclude that it might be safer for Jacqueline to remain at a little distance. What if the quiet police made a habit of visiting, and if one day a bribe was not enough? There was her apartment in Saigon. Might Saigon be better for their son as he grew older? After all, there were more mixed children in Saigon—Laing Jai would not be so unusual there. Jacqueline enjoyed the shopping on Tu Do, and the afternoon cinema. She could hire a servant who would treat her with respect. But Percival said nothing, for even as he mulled these thoughts, he knew that he wanted her to stay near him.

A WEEK AFTER THE VISIT BY the quiet police, Percival was in the school office, reviewing a new teacher's lesson plans, when Jacqueline burst in and blurted out, "I miss my apartment in Saigon." He could see that she had been crying. "I need to go back."

"You're right. We should go spend the day in Saigon. We could have lunch at the club."

"No, I should return there. That is where I belong." She stood in front of the desk, as if she were a student who had been caught misbehaving and sent to the headmaster. "I just can't stay here anymore," she said softly, tears running down her cheeks. "Can we go right now? I've packed my things."

Percival looked at her, his throat tight, his hand poised but empty, for his pen had clattered to the desk. He knew it was his part to say that he wanted her to remain in Cholon, to confess that he did not care that she was not Chinese, to say that she meant more to him than whatever people might whisper in Cholon, and more than Foong Jie or Mak's sour opinions. Had one of them somehow interfered? Jacqueline stood waiting for him to respond. It was his part to take her in his arms, to murmur that he had found his home in her, and the child they had together brought into the world, to admit that he had never expected this love to come from an encounter at the Sun Wah, but that although it terrified him, he was ready to give himself to it.

Percival picked up the pen. He fixed his eyes on it. He heard his voice saying, "I will take you back to Saigon. Today."

"Yes," she said. "Yes, as soon as possible."

At the apartment in Saigon, Percival told the taxi to wait for him. When they got to the front door, he mumbled something about it being fortunate that she was in such a modern building. It had an elevator. The bath was lovely. She began to cry. He shoved a large wad of money at her and fled. He hurried back to the taxi and dared not look back. There was no other way he could go through with it except like that—abruptly, cruelly.

When he got back to the school, Percival signed off on the lesson plan without reading the rest of it. There was a knock. After he entered, Mak closed the door. He stood with his hand on the knob. "The police from Saigon came to question you, didn't they? About the disappearance of the car?"

Percival gestured that Mak should sit. He did this out of habit, for he wished that Mak would leave him alone. He said, "You have heard about it. Of course you have. You hear everything."

"They were curious about that assassination list. Anyone with ties to the Americans was put on those lists," said Mak.

"That's what I assumed." Percival did not move. Mak's connections in Saigon had not deserted him, thought Percival, even if the quiet police were asking questions about him.

"Yesterday the police came to my home. They threatened to arrest me. They had questions about the car. It was used as a bomb, they said."

"They asked me who had keys to the car."

Mak nodded slightly. "Yes, a friend obtained a copy of the police report. It states that I did not have a key, as per Headmaster Chen. Thank you, *hou jeung*, that saved me." Mak adjusted his position in the chair uneasily. "They are looking for hidden communists in Cholon and Saigon. They have been interviewing everyone in the square." Mak looked at Percival. "They will lose their jobs if they can't produce a few, don't you think?"

"I don't think about it."

"Of course not," said Mak. "It's not your problem, but it could have been. After they spoke to you, it seems they decided to clear your name. However, later that same day, they interviewed Police Chief Mei. He's an idiot. He said that he saw the assassins come down from your room, and that he chased them out of the school and shot them dead. Once they heard that, they suspected you once again. After all, how had you escaped death?"

"Thanks to you, and to the birth of Laing Jai."

"Well, they seemed to think I could explain, as Chief Mei said I was with you. They must have made him chief in Cholon precisely because he's so inept. So, the quiet police came to me, hoping I would incriminate you. Just as they had pressed you, hoping you would incriminate me." Mak shrugged. "They need to find people to blame. That's their job. Anyhow, I don't think Mei was trying to betray you. He's trying to get himself out of the mess he created when he claimed he had shot those men. It would have been better for him to have stuck to the truth, that he took off his uniform for as long as there was fighting."

"You explained it to the quiet police, didn't you? The assassins saw that Jacqueline was about to give birth. They took pity and did not kill me. My beautiful boy, Laing Jai, saved my life."

"You think they would believe that? They are merciless killers. They have murdered pregnant women in the National Police Headquarters.

They could never believe that you were spared out of compassion."
Mak sat back.

"Then are we still in danger?" asked Percival.

"No. I have fixed the problem." Mak folded his hands together.
"I told them that you took a country girl as a mistress almost a year
ago. I explained that at Tet, when the Viet Cong came to kill you,
she pleaded for your life. She was an enemy spy but she fell in love
with you, and became pregnant with your child. At Tet, we realized
she had been a Viet Cong agent when she was able to convince her
comrades to spare you. Even the quiet police believe in the soft-
heartedness of women."

Percival recognized Mak's look. It was the same when he was offering a clever deal or a bribe to an official in Saigon. He didn't show any
nervousness, but was very attentive, alert to the moment. Percival
said, "What are you talking about?"

"Many such agents infiltrated Cholon and Saigon, to provide sur-
veillance, strategy, and targets. The one who was here has fled. All
the teachers and servants have agreed to endorse my story." Mak put
his hands on the desk, gestured as if there were a map there. "It's
perfect. Little did you know that in the weeks leading up to Tet your
country mistress had been prowling around Cholon gathering information, helping to plan the offensive. Little did her superiors know,
she was about to bear your child. They hadn't seen her for months.
Her commanders wrote the hit list, and put you on it. But she had
grown fond of you, and convinced the assassins to spare you." Mak
was now slightly on edge.

Percival spoke slowly. "And so, if the quiet police inquire, Jacqueline
is not here."

"After their visit, she fled. It removes you completely from suspicion, hou jeung. There are many in the square who noticed a pretty
country girl with a baby coming and going from Chen Hap Sing after
Tet. Often buying newspapers, magazines. Suspicious, for a country
girl, yes? They will agree that she has disappeared. Of course, as your
mistress, she could have easily taken a key to your car and given it to
her fellow Viet Cong on the night of the attack. You are clean."

"As are you." Percival thought of Jacqueline, crying with Laing Jai in her arms when he left her in Saigon. The walls of the school office seemed unsteady. He said, "Mak, what have you done?"

"The quiet police believe it! My friend is sending me their reports. They have put out a watch for a country girl in Cholon. If they need to, they may arrest some poor innocent waif, and you will deny she was your lover. Meanwhile, case closed."

Percival started to stand, unsure what he would do. Mak pushed his chair back a little. The room floated, and Percival sat again. Mak said, "As long as you say nothing different—your reputation with the Americans as a loyal supporter is stronger than ever. Jacqueline understood all of this, and agreed to return to Saigon."

"What choice did she have, once you did this?"

"She and the boy are perfectly safe. She will not ever need to tell the story," said Mak. "No one looks for Viet Cong by the pool at the Cercle. For her part, it is enough that she has returned to Saigon."

Percival closed his eyes and imagined the room closing in towards him, compressing his anger into a tight ball. It was done. What use was there in fighting it now? Mak would have calculated this, of course. Percival stood, forced himself to open his eyes. It could not be undone. The Viet Cong mistress had already vanished into the countryside. He put his hands on his desk. The wood was worn, slightly cool under the pads of his fingers. Jacqueline had agreed to this? Perhaps she saw the wisdom of it, or perhaps she did not feel as strongly for him as he did for her. Percival moved towards Mak, who continued to talk. "I did it for your good. Believe me, old friend, I think of your best interests. You go to Saigon for your fun. It is better for you." They stood facing one another, Percival's hands shaking, then clenched into fists. He could not be sure whether it was out of loyalty to Mak or weakness in his love for Jacqueline, but now that this path was laid, what could he do except follow it? Percival nodded, and asked Mak to leave him alone for a little while.

CHAPTER 19

JACQUELINE HAD CRIED ON THE FIRST day that Percival brought her back to Saigon. After that, whenever Percival went to visit her, she smiled. She wore just a hint of lipstick—he later noticed the traces on his body. The apartment was always tidy, as perfect as a stage. Percival bought a cream-coloured Mercedes 280 SE coupe from a friend who had decided, after what Percival had taken to calling the "Tet commotion," to move to France. The coupe was suitable, for Percival drove the car. He preferred to move around alone rather than with someone who could gossip about his whereabouts.

Two months after Tet, the work on Chen Hap Sing was completed. Delicately patterned ironwork had graced the windows since Chen Kai had built the house, to keep thieves out. Now, workers had welded solid bars and steel mesh on top of that, intended to keep grenades out. It would not hold against rockets, but one could only do so much. Percival went through the house minutely, checking the new reinforcements, pulling on the bars. With metal screens over all the windows, Chen Hap Sing had been blinded. The doors were reinforced with metal plates and bolts. Short concrete posts stood at regular intervals in front of the school. These were strong enough to slow a car if it were aimed at the school so that it wouldn't breach the walls. Meanwhile, the construction of brick pillboxes by the South Vietnamese Army had turned their checkpoints in La Place de la Libération into permanent posts. The old post office was deemed beyond repair, and its damaged remains were bulldozed. That handsome reminder of the French was now a memory, an empty lot.

At first, Percival wondered if he should speak to Jacqueline about Mak's manipulations. Should he console her by saying that although it was not his idea to send her back to Saigon, that in fact he wished she was still in Cholon, it might be safer for her to be at the apartment? But if he wished she was in Cholon, would she conclude that her lover had deferred to Mak rather than doing what he himself wanted? She was in Saigon now—she was safe. Nothing could be done to return her to Cholon. If nothing could be done, there was no purpose in raising the issue, Percival eventually decided. Besides, it was a short drive to Saigon. After her initial distress, Jacqueline didn't seem upset at being sent back to the apartment. Occasionally she would seem distant, preoccupied, and Percival wondered if anger was hidden, and if it would one day burst through. He was determined to do everything possible to keep her happy.

Percival kept a tab at the Cercle Sportif so that whether he was with her or not, she could enjoy the restaurant. He still saw Cecilia there occasionally, and Jacqueline did not object to the two of them drinking tea together, discussing their son's letters, and trading barbs. Mostly, Percival spent his time at the club cultivating his American contacts and enjoying his new family. A morning passed easily playing *boules*; an afternoon by the pool was a siesta in the shade followed by a swim. Jacqueline made the apartment in Saigon comfortable for him. His favourite cognac, rice beer, and pickled hams were always on hand. Jacqueline began to take a tiny white pill daily, and Percival worried that she was ill. She was fine, she assured him, explaining that this was a new Western innovation that helped with women's monthly issues. He was glad she could afford this luxury, though embarrassed to know of it, and asked no more. Laing Jai was a happy child, who waved his arms and babbled with excitement whenever Percival arrived. When in Cholon, Percival soon missed the boy as much as he did Jacqueline. He looked forward to the warm pleasure of scooping him up, smelling his neck, squeezing his tiny arms and legs.

When the boy napped, Jacqueline and Percival made love, speaking only through skin and touch. In her lips, he sometimes imagined there was a sadness. As months went by peacefully, Percival gradually forgot to worry about these things, and became so comfortable at the apartment in Saigon that he spent as much time there as in Cholon.

The rainy season arrived. It was during an afternoon downpour while they were playing with Laing Jai inside the apartment, that Jacqueline said in a sideways voice, "And Mak is well?" She continued making play-faces at Laing Jai, who cooed happily, and who was almost able to stand.

"He is fine," said Percival, surprised.

"He has not told you anything . . . unusual?"

"No," said Percival. "Why do you ask?"

Laing Jai cried out. She helped him to his feet, and then said brightly, "I just wonder how Mak is doing. And Foong Jie. And whether everything is normal at Chen Hap Sing."

"Why wouldn't it be?"

"Of course it is, then," she said with a quick glance.

"Are you angry with me?" he said, before he could stop the words from spilling out. "I know returning to Saigon might have been difficult, but you understand the reasons. When the quiet police ask questions, answers must be found."

She caught Laing Jai as he teetered, forced a laugh, and bounced her son mechanically. "I have a wonderful apartment. It is bright and airy. Each room has an electric ceiling fan. There is a refrigerator and a gas stove. You give me money." She smiled. "I have my beautiful son. And of course I have you."

"Yes," he agreed. "You have everything. Do I give you enough money?" Naturally, she wanted her sacrifice to be recognized. Why else would she have asked about Mak? She did not answer, did not give any recognition of having heard the question, and continued to play with the boy.

Percival provided Jacqueline with a weekly allowance. Not a set sum, but always more than enough for a whole family to live very well. Each week, he put a thick sheaf of notes in a kitchen drawer.

The following week when he opened the drawer, it was empty. He encouraged her to spend and enjoy.

PETERS, IT TURNED OUT, WAS FRIENDLY with Americans in every office in Saigon. Mak had chosen this contact well. Over a couple of whisky sodas, Peters was always happy to tell Percival of important Americans who had just arrived in Vietnam and might need a secretary or a translator. Percival understood the mutual benefit—it made Peters an insider, an old hand with *gwan hai*, in the eyes of his countrymen. Although Peters at first refused bribes, he did not decline the Omega watch or the gold cufflinks that Percival presented to him at a birthday banquet hosted by the school.

The troop increases that had been discussed by the Americans after the Tet Offensive did not come. Over the following year, the Americans around Saigon began to use a new word. They talked about "Vietnamizing" the war, as if until now it had been taking place in some other country. The Vietnamese soldiers were to take over the main fighting and would be supported by American weapons and expertise. That's how the thing should have been fought all along, said the glib intelligence men who wore khakis without insignia and flew out to the battlefields in the morning. They were usually back at the Cercle Sportif by cocktail hour.

The grey-haired divisional commanders, who rarely ventured out of Saigon, and who reminisced about Korea with their gin and tonics by the pool, discussed the pace at which the American troops were being withdrawn—too fast and battles would be lost, too slow and the Vietnamese would not "grab it by the balls." Percival was familiar with them all, having been introduced by Peters. He had difficulty keeping their names straight, for all these white men resembled one another, but he nodded seriously and agreed with all their opinions, while hovering around the question that interested him most, which was whether anyone needed staff. If so, he would connect them to Mak for a referral. Sometimes, with some new American initiative, five or ten graduates were hired overnight.

Over two subsequent semesters, Percival cautiously left the price of tuition unchanged. He was relieved to see that there were still waiting lists, though now many of his graduates tried to get visas to study abroad rather than interview for jobs with the Americans in Vietnam.

After a year of living between Cholon and Saigon, Percival disciplined himself to spend part of each week in Chen Hap Sing. If he stayed with Jacqueline all the time, he scolded himself, they might as well be married. Percival forced himself to make weekly visits to the Teochow temple. When he was at Chen Hap Sing, he instructed the cook to prepare only Chinese dishes, and would only respond to the servants when they spoke a Chinese dialect. When he took his breakfast alone on the balcony, where he had long since instructed Foong Jie to remove the second chair, it was a Teochow breakfast of salted fish and rice porridge—never *pho*. The presence of St. Francis Xavier annoyed him, so he faced the other direction. He gave generously, almost lavishly, to the Buddhists, and had heard that the one-eyed monk chanted a daily prayer on his behalf. The words drifting up from the square below were Cantonese, Teochow, Hakka, Percival noted with satisfaction. He sat alone, but he was amongst Chinese.

Nights at Chen Hap Sing were quiet. Percival would often hear noises from Dai Jai's old room. Each time, as he came near to Dai Jai's doorway, he wondered if he would see an apparition, Jacqueline and Laing Jai asleep in the bed, the dark figure hovering over them. He crept close to the wall, took a deep breath before opening the door, and peered in. There was never anyone there.

After retreating to his room, Percival would pour himself a water glass of cognac and look through the letters from Dai Jai. Mail delivery had ceased for some time after Tet. Clearly, the censors had held on to everything, examined it for clues. Finally, three of Dai Jai's letters had come together—lengthy criticisms, Percival's failings towards the people. They had been opened, of course, and seemed to have passed through many hands. Now the letters had settled into one monthly page. Cecilia received the same correspondence, often identical as if copied. They were not in Dai Jai's nature, she said. Percival skimmed these brief paragraphs without allowing his eyes to focus. He would linger on his son's one-sentence description of the weather, or a list of what foods he had recently eaten in the communal kitchens—perhaps two sticks of fried dough at breakfast, four onion dumplings at midday, one cup of rice with boiled vegetables for dinner. He seemed unnaturally interested in food, Cecilia pointed out. Did it mean he was not eating enough? Percival had dismissed Cecilia's worry, saying that it meant their son had a good appetite. Alone, he was pained to think that Cecilia could be right, that Dai Jai might be hungry. In one letter, Dai Jai made a recitation of his sins against the people—that he had snatched an extra piece of turnip at lunch, had allowed his comrade to shoulder more weight than himself as they pushed a hand plough in the fields. Percival was embarrassed by these confessions, and equally so by Dai Jai's celebrations of his comrades' triumphs—their ability to work until they collapsed from exhaustion, and their capacity to sing in a patriotic Maoist spirit until their voices failed. He tried to picture his son, but could not summon an image that he could trust.

The letters no longer gave any descriptions of Shanghai, and instead detailed farm work. Dai Jai never said where he was, or why he had left school. This bothered Cecilia a great deal, and Percival suggested to her that Dai Jai had probably gone out to work on a farm for a school holiday, that it was healthy for a young man to be out in the fresh air, getting exercise. Percival wished he could decipher the relentless good cheer of the Communist Party's shortwave announcers, and the confusing letters that came from Dai Jai, but even in the Teochow temple no one seemed to have reliable sources of information about what was happening in China. There were rumours of whole classes of high school and university students being sent to work in the countryside and counter-rumours that these tales were fabrications of the CIA. More and more, people in Cholon strongly supported either Taiwan or China.

Percival wrote back to Dai Jai late at night. His letters had become rote. He told his son that he was safe and that the fighting was far away, although Dai Jai had not asked. He wrote a line about whatever Chinese festival was approaching or had just passed. He wrote nothing about Jacqueline or Laing Jai. What would he say, that he was now spending his days, and often his nights, in Saigon with a *métisse* girl? And what would he say of Laing Jai? To think of the words made him ashamed. Instead, Percival wrote to Dai Jai about the great ongoing successes of the school, which he did not refer to as an English school, and of the pet fish being healthy and vigorous.

As Laing Jai grew from a toddler into a small boy, Jacqueline bought all the things for him that she imagined a modern boy required—expensive items from the Grands Magasins Charner; a small child's bed painted like a rowboat, blue striped shirts, tiny corduroy pants, and a stuffed Mickey Mouse. Percival hated this creature—why did the Americans idolize a rodent? The boy's room was the one part of the apartment that Percival disliked, with its set of wooden trains, and books that featured blond children and their dogs. Percival would never have allowed Dai Jai to be paraded like a tiny imitation of a French boy, but with Laing Jai he overlooked these indulgences. It made the boy happy. It made his mother happy. Who was he to disagree, thought Percival, when he could not even marry the woman he loved? Laing Jai's feet beat a quick rhythm towards the door whenever Percival arrived, and he shrieked with delight, "*Baba!*"

For herself, Jacqueline also bought imported clothing, though nothing showy, all modest cuts of good cloth. She must be buying gold and putting it away, thought Percival, for he couldn't see all of the allowance in her purchases. The more guilty and lonely he felt in Cholon, the more money he gave her. Imagining her buying gold, stockpiling something for herself, kept both his guilt and regret beneath the happy surface of their lives.

PART THREE

CHAPTER 20

When Laing Jai was four years old, he was enrolled in the American School. Jacqueline insisted upon it and pointed out the obvious to Percival—how could he expect the child to go to the Teochow school, given his round eyes and chestnut hair? His classmates were foreigners and the children of wealthy Saigonese who pretended to be foreigners, Percival grumbled. It was where Jacqueline's friends sent their children, Percival consoled himself. Jacqueline spent most days at the Cercle Sportif, and if Percival was a little jealous for her attention he could not blame her for socializing. He had sent her to live on her own. The club was also good for Laing Jai. Some of his classmates were there, even a few mixed children, whose mothers took them to swim and play by the pool.

At least once a month, Percival took Laing Jai to Cholon. He led him through the markets, taught him the names of things in Cantonese and Teochow, and indulged him with *chui jia bao*, sweet dumplings filled with yam or bean paste, and fresh coconuts chopped open at the stalls. He took him to the Teochow temple for every festival.

Even at the annual festival of the dead, Jacqueline never took the boy to Thanh Ha to pay respects at her family's graves, and she did not want a shrine in her apartment. She seemed to have cut off her relations completely, which was strange, but Percival decided not to ask. Percival was quietly pleased about that, for it allowed him to show the boy these traditions as part of his Chinese rather than his Vietnamese heritage. He showed Laing Jai how to make the offerings of food and joss sticks, how to delicately arrange cut oranges before the family altar at Chen Hap Sing. On these occasions, Percival made sure that the cooks prepared special Chinese dishes that Laing Jai liked—his favourite was *or lua*, oyster omelettes, and Percival was gratified that the boy relished such a characteristic Teochow dish. He also looked forward to *hung gue* dumplings filled with garlic chives, rice, minced pork, and dried shrimp, platters of Peking duck, crab balls, and tofu stuffed with shrimp. For a snack, a big bowl of *mee pok* noodles with minced pork and braised mushrooms. The cooks made far too much, because the kitchen and house staff liked to eat the leftovers, and Percival allowed this. He indulged himself in Laing Jai's excitement at seeing the displays of food.

Percival told Laing Jai the stories of his boyhood in Shantou, the same ones he had once told Dai Jai and then Jacqueline. Somehow, in this telling, they had lost both the transparent moralizing with which he had told them to Dai Jai and some of the wistfulness with which he had recounted them to Jacqueline. Even as he shared them with Laing Jai, Percival thought they sounded very distant, like fairy tales. Laing Jai rambled them off to his mother in the same way that he told the stories from his illustrated Western books.

When he was alone in Cholon, Percival was unsettled by the thickening cloud of rumour and counter-rumour about the war in Vietnam, in which he feigned disinterest. Many hoped that the South Vietnamese would continue to fight so badly against the Northerners that the Americans would be forced to stay. Others said it didn't matter if the North Vietnamese won, so let them come. They would simply change the flags. Everything else would stay as it always was. Meanwhile, many people in Cholon chattered more about Chinese politics than those of Vietnam, but as doubts about the Americans' commitment to Vietnam grew, supporters both of Taiwan and the Communist People's Republic of China hedged their words, if not their views. Who could say how the war would end in Vietnam, and what allegiances, if known publicly, might later prove to be problematic?

Percival wrote to his cousin in Shantou, asking him to look in on Dai Jai, and to the school where Dai Jai had initially been registered asking when classes would resume and whether his son was registered. Percival's cousin replied with conviction that Dai Jai was serving the people and Chairman Mao. No reply came from the school. Percival spent hours staring at Dai Jai's now rare correspondence, trying to glean any small truth of the boy's situation that might seep between the bravado of Marxist slogans and the opaque descriptions of plain-sounding meals. The paper was tissue-thin, and the pencil was always dull.

Although he never admitted to Cecilia that he shared her worries, Percival spoke with Mak about his concerns regarding Dai Jai's situation in China. Was life hard in China? If so, would it get better? Mak seemed to appreciate Percival's worries, but reassured him, saying that societies evolved, in order to improve.

Mak managed the school, but routinely saved a few school issues and problems in order to seek Percival's guidance. They both maintained this ritual, and Percival occasionally relieved one of the teachers to give a few lectures. The students expected an occasional star appearance from the headmaster.

Once in a while, Percival took some money from the safe. It was filled with stacks of piastres, which he never bothered to count. If asked, Percival took a quantity of bills to a restaurant for a money circle, now he was a lender. To be sociable, he sometimes went along with old friends to a gambling hotel or casino, inattentively lost some money to those whose friendships the school needed, or won and found that, even if it was a good sum, he didn't care.

One morning, Percival went to look for Jacqueline at the club. From across the patio, he saw her sitting at a table, laughing with Peters. The American had his racquet on the table and he reclined in his tennis whites in the wicker chair, one hairy leg crossed over the other. Laing Jai drank a mango shake, sipped it through a straw with great concentration. To see him at a distance, a four-year-old engrossed in his treat, Percival felt the pang of his resemblance to Dai Jai. Laing Jai ran across the patio to embrace his father. Percival lifted his son and carried him as he walked.

As Percival drew near to the table, Peters stood to greet him. Peters squeezed Percival's hand, shook it up and down. Even after years of association with the Americans, Percival still disliked having their sweat, their smell, on his hands. He had to remind himself not to pull his hand back too quickly.

"How is my friend the headmaster?" asked Peters.

"Fine, and how is Mr. Peters, the high-ranking American official?" Percival put Laing Jai down in front of his drink.

"Very funny," said Peters. "I'm no big shot."

"You are *my* important friend," said Percival. Anyone looking at Peters would think that he and Jacqueline were a handsome couple and Laing Jai was their beautiful mixed-blood child, thought Percival. He sat down and resisted the urge to wipe his hand on the tablecloth. He tried to look pleased at finding Jacqueline, Laing Jai, and Peters all together. There was no reason not to be pleasant, he told himself. In the art of forced smiles, the Chinese were every bit as skilful as the Americans.

"All is well with you?" Percival asked. He told the waiter to bring a pitcher of lemonade.

"The talks are keeping us busy."

"What talks are those?"

"A real joker! Listen to you." Peters laughed, and mock-punched Percival on the shoulder—another American habit Percival had trained himself to ignore.

Jacqueline leaned over. "The Paris peace talks, love."

"Oh, I might have heard of them." It was a topic that Percival never said anything about despite it having lately been a main conversation on the patio of the Cercle Sportif. For the most part, the Americans talked about it, while the Vietnamese nodded quietly. It was fine to talk about such things if one was planning to leave in the event of peace.

"It seems everyone in Saigon is snagged to support the negotiations," said Peters. "They always want something else—village reports, economic analysis, intelligence summaries. It never ends. They're sitting in Paris, eating and drinking on the Seine, and they want detailed political maps—to know which villages are government and which are Cong. Colour coded! That's the most recent request."

"Surely you can send them maps."

"They don't understand when I tell them that the same village is government by day, Cong at night."

"I thought you were fixing that problem. Isn't that why you came back to Vietnam?"

"The past few years feels like a lifetime, but I keep on waking up feeling like I haven't moved an inch. Same old." Peters held up his hands in an expression of casual resignation. "I must have been out of my mind when I came back, thinking I could fix anything in this place." The waiter produced a tray with glasses and a sweating pitcher.

Percival wiped his own sweat from his brow.

"Mr. Peters is trying to get his colleagues in Paris to *understand* the situation," said Jacqueline.

"Oh," said Percival. "I see. They have been conducting this war without understanding it?"

"Actually, they're trying to end it," said Jacqueline.

"Ah. Peace, even without understanding, should be easier to achieve?"

Jacqueline glared at him, then turned to straighten Laing Jai's outfit. Percival poured lemonade into their glasses and passed them out. He slowly drank half his own glass, in order to suppress various things that it occurred to him to say. Since the previous Tet, when Peters had hinted for, and then accepted, a fat envelope from the headmaster, Percival had felt more free to speak his mind. Even so, he scolded himself. There was never any benefit to being rude. When he put the lemonade down, he said, "Excuse my manners. I didn't sleep well."

"No worries," said Peters. "I look at it much the same as you do. Frank talk is hard to find around here, Percy. What do they say of the Paris peace talks over in Cholon?"

"That's a good question . . ." said Percival. He tried to think of what was best to tell the American from the range of discussions he had heard on the subject, and decided to trot out the usual, "We

Chinese are most concerned with business. Politics is not our domain."

"Sure, sure, free enterprise. I'm all for it. Anyhow, peace is good for business, right?"

"We Chinese love peace and prosperity," recited Percival, though he thought that peace was unlikely to come soon, or easily. There was no reason to say to the American that peace would hurt his profits. "Chinese do not care what flag flies in Vietnam, so long as the government issues business licences."

Laing Jai said, "*Baba!* Mr. Peters promised to show us his home in America. In the winter, it is so cold that water becomes tiny pieces of ice and they call it snow." The boy tugged on Percival's hand. "You can pick it up and make balls with it."

Jacqueline said to Laing Jai, "*Baba* and Mr. Peters are talking. Listen quietly." She turned to Percival. "Mr. Peters was telling Laing Jai about his village back home."

But the boy could not contain himself. "We will go to America, where instead of Tet, they have a fat man dressed in red who brings presents," he said triumphantly.

"Bright kid. Good English. I hear you have him at the American School," said Peters.

"That's what Jacqueline wanted," said Percival. He stared at Jacqueline, who now avoided his eyes. She fussed at wiping Laing Jai's face. The boy was good with languages. He could list in four languages—Cantonese, Vietnamese, English, and French—the names of many fruits. Dai Jai had been the same way at that age, eager for knowledge. Peters seemed to be looking over Percival's shoulder. Then he raised his hand, waved across the patio at someone, and stood to go over. Good. The man would leave them alone.

"Percy," said Peters. "Come meet someone."

"I need to sit in the shade. It's so hot this morning." In fact, it was the dry season, and the air was lighter than usual.

"What are you talking about? It's hot every day in this frigging place. It's someone who needs staff. Come on. We'll find work for a few of your students." Percival found it embarrassing that lately Peters spoke so openly about their arrangement, and so without further protest he stood with Peters and looked over to the beet-faced American whom Peters had greeted.

They reached a shaded awning on the other side, and Peters made the introductions, talking in his radio-announcer way. Percival smiled amiably through the inevitable round of hand-shaking, and nodded at the newcomer with the right mix of reserve and welcome. He didn't catch whether this overweight man was a newly arrived journalist, an intelligence officer, or a staffer at the State Department. Peters undoubtedly explained this aspect, but Percival was not listening. Mak would be annoyed, for he counted upon Percival to note such particulars. Right now, his eyes were on Jacqueline and Laing Jai.

"Get this: Tet Offensive in '68, I was pinned down in a Chinatown firefight. At Percy's place," began Peters, as he often did with a new arrival in town. Perhaps, thought Percival, he should bring Laing Jai to the Grands Magasins Charner at the time of the American festival of Christmas. He had heard that they dressed up a man in a red suit. Why should the boy go to America to see that? Was it not enough that the boy had the same toys and schooling as any American child? What else could Jacqueline want for their son?

Peters described the impenetrable darkness of that Tet night, the foreboding, electric feeling in the air, the first mortars landing so close that the glasses on the table shook, the bloody South Vietnamese counter-assault on the post office. Percival nodded distractedly. All he could visualize from that night was Han Bai cut down, Mak saving his life, Laing Jai born. Whatever else had occurred was so removed that it might as well have happened to someone else. He played along with the details Peters added to the telling, which became more vivid each time—the shells' explosions louder, the screams of the Viet Cong attackers more maniacal. What could this white man offer Jacqueline? he wondered. What could Jacqueline offer him in return?

The punchline of the story was that both Peters and Percival had been on assassination lists. "Percy," said Peters, "escaped because he was about to have a baby." He always waited for the look of confusion before adding, "Rather, I should say that his radiant—ahem—*companion* was with child." He looked across the patio and tilted his head at Jacqueline.

The newcomer, wilting in the heat, asked, "What about you? How did you dodge your bullet?"

"Ah, I was on another assassination list. They had my street address in Saigon. Apartment number and everything. No way the Cong could have guessed I'd be in Chinatown at a school dinner. So basically, I owe my life to Percy's New Year's banquet. And what a meal! Let me tell you about the food that night . . ."

On it went. Peters prompted Percival to chime in about the terror and heroism of the episode, which he did, as usual, nodding gravely, smiling at the right moments. Percival thought it incredible that Peters could stand here talking, practically naked in his tennis shorts and shirt. Was Jacqueline looking over? Was she admiring the American's figure? Some women, it was said, found the hair on Americans' bodies attractive, said that it was like being in bed with an animal.

At last the fat American agreed, "Yes, I do need someone who speaks good English."

"None of this *me-take-you-cyclo-one-dollar* shit," emphasized Peters.

"No, I suppose not." The newcomer wiped his brow.

"You are in the right company," said Peters, turning to Percival.

"Perhaps if you have a card," said Percival, "I might be able to help you."

"No use putting an ad in the paper, I suppose?" said the man, fishing in his pockets for a card.

"This is the kind of place where introductions matter," said Peters. "Right, Percival?"

"Indeed. Even more important is who introduces you," said Percival, with a slight bow to Peters. Then, to the newcomer, "I can send someone around if it will help you out." The man found a card, and Percival slipped it into his pocket. Percival would go to Cholon and have dim sum with Mak, who would ask Percival everything he knew of the newcomer to Saigon—name, rank, address, hometown, friends, favourite drinks, drugs, any eye for women? The occasional one preferred young men. Mak would send an exceptional graduate of their school. Perhaps Mak got his own profits from satisfying the Americans' desires, whether for girls, boys, hash, or heroin. In any case, in a few days, this fat man would approach Percival at the Cercle and thank him for the excellent help. The graduates Mak sent were the best translators in Saigon, a credit to the Percival Chen English Academy. The American would be happy. The school could continue to charge whatever tuition it liked.

When the hand-shaking and card-trading was done, Percival looked over to Jacqueline and saw her gathering up Laing Jai's toys. When Percival reached her, she stopped briefly, pecked him on the lips, said that she had to rush Laing Jai to school or else he would be late, and that if Percival went to the apartment she would be there soon.

Laing Jai asked, "*Baba*, will you be at home to play after school?"

"Yes," he said.

He went to the apartment and waited, fuming. Why did it take her so long to return? When she appeared, she said nothing. She closed the door, brought her lips to his, her hands already at his belt. He had planned to first ask what she had been discussing with Peters. Now, he felt his annoyance fade. She was here with him, after all, and so why should he be jealous of her sitting innocently on a patio with an American man? Her hands were already within his clothes as he undid her blouse buttons. She led him to the bedroom, where they sweated into the afternoon.

Afterwards, they lay naked. Jacqueline slept. Percival lay awake on his side, watching the rhythmic movement of her chest. His body had been satisfied, but this did not completely erase his worry. The shutters were closed against the bright sun, and the gaps between the slats admitted bright knives of light into the apartment. His mouth was dry, his throat swollen. Since meeting Jacqueline, Percival had not been with other women. When he went out to gamble, even if a welcoming smile beckoned, he left alone and returned to his lover's bed. It had never before occurred to him to doubt her faithfulness.

Percival eased himself up and went into the kitchen. He opened the freezer, its hum becoming louder. He took the tin ice tray, which clung to his sweat and stung his hands. He thought of snow, something he had never seen. He twisted the tray angrily, loosened the clear, cold cubes into a glass, filled it with water, and drank it empty. He poured more water into the same glass. Behind him, the sound of her feet, the cool of her hands on his back, and he turned. He put the glass on the counter, his hands on the crest of her hips, then closed them around her back. "I used to believe that a man and a woman were destined to be unfaithful."

She put her hands around his neck to draw him into a kiss. "You don't believe that anymore?"

"I don't know what to believe."

"Believe in us," she said. "That's all there is." She drained the glass and looked at the kitchen clock. Every afternoon, Jacqueline listened to the Voice of America. She went to the radio in the living room now, turned it on. The crackling voice said that after a delay of several days, a thorny issue of the delegates' seating arrangements in Paris had been resolved. A suitable round table had been found to accommodate the mission heads of the American, South Vietnamese, North Vietnamese, French, Chinese, and Russian participants. Negotiations would resume. The first issue they would consider was a possible cease-fire, although presently the bombing of North Vietnam continued.

Percival asked, "Was it last year or the year before that there were rumours of secret peace negotiations between the Americans and the North Vietnamese?"

"Both. Some say there is hope this time," said Jacqueline, though she looked more worried than optimistic.

The report went on for a while. There was no news, only speculation—the concessions that would be sought by each side, the leverage to be applied, the political leaders and their temperaments, words spoken again and again until they circled back upon themselves. Percival reached over and turned off the radio. The silence echoed.

"What are you doing?" Jacqueline asked.

"Do you listen to the news with him?"

"With who?"

"When I am in Cholon, does he come here?" Percival had intended to sound angry, and instead heard his own fear.

"Who are you talking about?"

"How well do you know Peters?"

"You were jealous this morning at the Cercle." Her eyes softened. "You found Mr. Peters and me talking. You imagined something, but what you see is all there is. He is more your friend than mine." Jacqueline reached out and took Percival's hand to pull him down to the couch with her, but he resisted.

"Then what did Laing Jai mean?"

"By what?"

"When he spoke of going to America."

"Sit with me," she said. "I want to hear this." She reached over and turned the radio back on. She folded her legs up, rested them sideways. He looked at her soft breasts, and now wished that she was clothed. Percival went into the bedroom and slowly got dressed.

When he came back, the radio was still on. Jacqueline said with a nervous edge in her voice, "It's always the same words, the complications in the way of peace, though everyone claims they want it."

Percival sat down. "The soil in this country is red from all the blood that is soaked into the earth. When each war ends, another soon begins. The Japanese, the French, now the Americans, someone else in the future, so what does it matter what they say in Paris? The land itself bleeds."

"You are so sure that these negotiations will not bring a peace?"

"I have no opinion," said Percival. "Why should I?" Now, being clothed while Jacqueline was naked made him feel awkward.

"This war makes you rich," she said.

"English is my business. It is how I eat. It is how you eat."

"You Chinese think only of your business deals, but each time the flag changes, fresh pits are dug for the defeated."

"I am a headmaster. My students translate rather than fight. They save their blood. Some of them manage to go abroad. Do you see me in a uniform?"

"No, you don't think of the graves. Only the gold." She stood and went to the window. She pushed up a slat in the blinds, peered out into the afternoon. "Fine, if that's your only concern. But do you ever think of us? What will we do, Laing Jai and I, if the flag changes again?"

"You mean the three of us?"

"Is it three?" She turned to him, still standing at the window. "Have you ever wondered why my mother sent me to study in your school?" Percival said nothing.

"I studied English to leave Vietnam. My mother thought of it before it became such a popular thing. She knew that it was best for people like me to leave."

"Some go abroad," said Percival.

"Yes. As should we. If you think of us as three, let's leave," said Jacqueline, taking Percival's hand. "That's what I was talking to Mr. Peters about—how to escape. You ignore the dangers and make money. So the money is part of what traps you. But the Viet Cong tried to kill you four years ago. On the other side, you have friends in Saigon only as long as you give them piastres. You Chinese pretend that you stand apart, but your hands are in everyone's pockets, and theirs in yours."

"Let's talk when you are more calm."

"How can I be calm? I need to get out, and Laing Jai too. These negotiations may only allow the Americans to leave, not end the war. You know that. What will happen to us then?"

"We Chinese bend like the grass, and the wind blows over."

"Spare me your cliché sayings. I am not Chinese. And Laing Jai isn't, either. After the Americans are gone, we will be the garbage the Americans left behind."

"You worry too much," Percival said.

"In Hue, did they not kill the foreigners first?"

"This is not Hue."

"At least the Northerners shot the foreigners. Their Vietnamese brothers and sisters, they buried alive. What will happen to Laing Jai and me? How will they decide whether to shoot us or bury us?"

"If there is peace, then——"

"If these fat men in Paris find a way for the Americans to abandon us, the Northerners will soon conquer Saigon. Then you will have been the whore of the Americans, and I will have been yours."

Percival said softly, "What is it you want?"

"To leave Vietnam with my son. That's what I've been talking to Peters about."

"No," he shook his head. "That would . . ."

"With you, too. I have asked Peters to see about exit permits. He is reluctant, because he wants your graduates for translators, but I've told him that Mak could run the school."

"You asked him for papers? To go to America?"

"I've asked if he can get three visas. He says he may be able to."

He had not thought beyond the next week or month. So what could he say to Jacqueline now? Without knowing how he had arrived at it, Percival saw now that he had settled for living and loving only in the moment. When he ventured to consider the future, it felt like an empty, blank space.

"We will always be together," Percival murmured. He stroked her hair. He thought of Peters and his rubber smile. "But you must not speak to him anymore," he said.

"That jealousy."

"Please," said Percival. "If he helps you, he will want something in return. I've seen how he stares at you."

She drew away from him and laughed. "Don't be like a fragile boy. He looks at every *métisse* woman that way. Fine, that's his particular taste. The Americans are not so good at hiding their appetites, which makes them easier to read. You Chinese are no more virtuous, just more circumspect. He will help us. You have sucked their dollars for so long, but you don't know them at all."

"Sucking money is your habit, not mine," said Percival.

Jacqueline pulled away from him and went towards the bedroom, stopped short, turned, "I will speak to anyone I want! Who else will speak for me and my son?" She disappeared into the room.

"There are other ways," he called after her. He spoke into the closed door. "Mrs. Ling is getting into the departure business. She is selling visas. If we need to, we can go to her. But why rush to leave when I'm making so much money? There is no peace accord yet, and I have waiting lists at the school. I could add more classes, and raise the tuition further." He could hear her moving in the room, but no reply came. "Maybe I could send some money abroad, to Switzerland, or Singapore. Would that make you feel better? Until there is peace, nothing will change." There was no answer. He went on, "If something changes, we will decide then. After all, with me gone, maybe Peters and Mak would split the school's profits. Why let Peters take my money and send us away?"

Jacqueline appeared and shot back at him, "Sending people away is *your* specialty."

Percival felt as if a knife had entered him, had been plunged deep. He whispered, "What did you say? What are you talking about?"

"I'm sorry," she stammered, the venom gone. "I didn't mean that."

He had once confessed to Jacqueline his tortured doubts about sending Dai Jai away. Time had helped him accept what he had done. Now, what had brought this rebuke? Percival's words were fragile, his voice quiet. "I agree that we must think of Laing Jai's future. But I would be less than nothing as a yellow man in a white country."

Now, gently, "How do you know that? Besides, it would be for your son. I will love you, rich or poor."

Percival walked up to Jacqueline, circled her waist with his arms, put his hands on the small of her back and kissed her slender, arched neck. He was supposed to say that he was willing, that she was right and he would do it, but he remained silent. He ran his hands up her back. She stood very still.

Finally, he heard himself say, "Let's see what happens in Paris, first. I will do what is best for us. I love you." She put her arms around Percival and kissed him. He filled his mouth with her, lest he say something that might frighten them both.

AS THE PARIS TALKS DRAGGED ON with much spoken, little said, Percival and Jacqueline listened to the radio reports each afternoon. When the news was done, they went together to collect Laing Jai from the American School. As they walked over, they tensely circled the topic of departure, Percival hoping it would fade along with the prospects of peace. When he saw them, Laing Jai broke away from his teacher, who kept all of her four-year-olds behind the gates for fear of kidnapping, until their parents or nannies arrived. About two weeks after he had enthused about snow, Laing Jai ran to Percival, saying "*Baba!* Let's go do something fun!"

"What?" asked Percival, lifting him into the air. "Anything. You choose, my beautiful son."

"The zoo! Yes, *baba*, please!"

They began to walk the few blocks in the shade of tall acacias. Workers were whitewashing the lower part of the trunks with a paint that smelled of chalk and lime.

Laing Jai said, "They look like guards—in white boots!"

"What do you mean?" said Percival.

"The trees."

"Yes, you're right," Percival agreed, and took his hand. Laing Jai had a flair for description. The zoo was a few blocks away. Percival and Jacqueline shared a silent relief to be all together, doing something.

"The zoo!" Laing Jai let go of Percival, turned and skipped a few steps to Jacqueline. "*Baba* is going to take us to the zoo!" He ran back to Percival. "Can I have cotton candy at the zoo?"

"Of course," said Percival.

Near the entrance, a vendor with a metal drum spun sugar into floss, and Laing Jai delighted in the coloured treat. He asked to see the elephant. They ambled over, and watched the flapping giant give herself a bath from a water barrel. Then they went to find the peacocks, who were crazed by the sun and fanned their feathers in an agitated display. The birds pecked at one another irritably. Was it the weather, or were the birds in heat? Percival wondered.

There were many monks at the zoo that day, drifting and talking in their saffron robes. Was it a monastery outing? Something about them was purposeful. Some distance away, Percival thought he saw the one-eyed monk from Cholon, but then when Percival looked again, he was gone. It must be his imagination. Laing Jai pulled Percival's hand down a path and called to his mother, "*Mama*, come, let's go see the tigers."

The path led to a little plaza at the far end of the zoo, a shady area ringed by monkey cages and enclosures for the big cats. The plaza was fragrant with jacarandas. As they reached it, Laing Jai was startled by the sudden spitting clamour of the monkeys and ducked in close to his mother. A cluster of monks had gathered. An older one seemed to be in quiet, serious discussion with a clump of American men. Some of the Americans smoked cigarettes, and almost all had cameras in their hands or hung from their necks. Neither the monks nor the Americans appeared interested in the zoo animals. Instead, they watched each other.

The fluidly pacing tiger always fascinated Laing Jai. He carefully approached the bars. Boy and cat assessed one another. In nearby cages, monkeys shrieked. The tiger's tongue flicked out, his teeth bared. Just once, for show, and then he relaxed.

"You are not scared, son?" Percival said.

"No, these are steel bars, *baba*. If there were no bars, and the tiger was hungry, then I would be scared."

"Come farther away, son," said Jacqueline.

"*Baba*, the animals need to be in cages so that they don't hurt us, isn't that right?" The tiger stalked back and forth.

"That's right," said Percival. "These are wild creatures."

"Different animals have different cages," said Laing Jai. "The tigers live with other tigers. But they don't mix monkeys and the tigers, because the tigers would eat the monkeys."

"Perhaps," said Percival. "On the other hand, the monkey is clever and quick."

The muscular cat raised a paw and flicked his pink tongue. Reflexively, Percival pulled Laing Jai back a little.

Around them, the crowd was growing thick, monks congregating from all the corners of the zoo. Americans fiddled with cameras. Some checked their watches. The one-eyed monk from La Place de la Libération hurried past. He did not give any indication that he recognized Percival. Like many of his brothers, he clutched a string of prayer beads.

From beneath one of the monk's robes emerged a large red plastic container. A little open space began to clear around him.

Jacqueline said, "I think we should go."

"But *ma*, I am looking at the tiger," said Laing Jai.

"Let's go," she said softly, firmly.

A megaphone appeared from beneath a second monk's robe, and he, too, stood in the small open area. He began to read a statement in formal Vietnamese from a piece of paper. The megaphone squawked, and it was hard for Percival to understand.

"What is going on?" said Percival to no one in particular.

The colour drained from Jacqueline's face. "They say their brother wishes to make a sacrifice. Let's leave now!"

Someone dashed past, bumped into Percival, almost knocked him over without apology. Percival looked around and couldn't tell if it had been an American or a monk. He caught a few of the megaphone-distorted phrases, ". . . as his personal plea for peace . . . that the foreign occupiers leave." They were now in the press of a crowd, people milling tightly together—cameras in hands, sandalled feet rushing here and there. A third monk stood in the cleared space between the one who held the red plastic container and the one with the megaphone. ". . . A fraudulent peace process, the deceit of colonialists . . ." The third monk closed his eyes and began to chant. His lone voice was plaintive. His brothers were a circle of flame-coloured robes around him. Jacqueline pulled Laing Jai's hand, searched for a way out, but all the brothers were pushing in towards the centre. The third monk sat in the lotus position. The one with the container set it down and bowed to his seated brother. The monk with the megaphone continued to read the prepared statement, and the nearest circles of monks fell to their knees around these three.

Cameras clicked, and somewhere a police siren wailed.

Percival picked up Laing Jai, jostled to get out, but the crowd of monks was so thick around them that it was hard to move at all. Percival could see more monks running urgently down the zoo's pathways towards the plaza, pressing in ever more. As the sirens grew louder, strong young novices began to form cordons between the animal cages. It was impossible to get out. The Americans with cameras checked their watches. Had they been given a time? They fiddled with their cameras, adjusted the dials. Monkeys leaped from bar to bar, reaching out to snatch at billows of saffron robes. Jacqueline cried, "We have to get out of here!" All around them, lines of monks linked arms, chanted, eyes half-closed.

Laing Jai asked, "*Baba*, why are all the monks at the zoo? This isn't a temple."

"Come . . . hold on," said Percival. He tried again to push his way out, to cleave an opening in the robed bodies. There was no hostility, but there was no way through. Around the three monks in the open centre, kneeling monks formed concentric circles. The one with the megaphone now yelled into it, the words too crackled for Percival to make most of them out. In their cages, the tigers paced on edge, as if they were about to be fed. The middle monk sat, his chanting completed, his eyes closed. His brother raised the red plastic container and twisted the cap open. Percival smelled gasoline.

An American near them gestured at Laing Jai and said to Percival, "Hey, you better get that boy out of here. This ain't fit for kids to see." They were hemmed in, no exit possible. On the other side of the high fence that stood behind the monks, there was a commotion. On the sidewalk, uniformed Saigon police shouted at the monks to disperse. It occurred to Percival that gasoline smelled like some kind of musky, overripe flower. He pressed Laing Jai to him, whispered not to look, the boy's back to the sight of one monk pouring gasoline over his brother.

The chanting of the prayers rose and overwhelmed the voices of the police. One policeman tried to hoist another up by his feet, but the fence was too high. Several officers dashed away. They must be running to reach the gates of the zoo, thought Percival. The first monk carefully tipped the gasoline container and its contents gurgled out of the spout as delicately as good wine. The seated man's robe darkened, a streaky, spreading shadow. He sat upright now, quiet, his smooth shaved head glistening as the flow of gasoline was directed over it. The process was thorough and methodical. He did not move. Was he breathing? The monks chanted in rhythm and rocked back and forth in place. The gasoline canister was empty, and was placed delicately aside. Percival could not look away.

Jacqueline clutched Percival's arm, her mouth open, her eyes closed. The seated man took a deep breath. Around the plaza, police had reached the cordon. They shouted at the novice monks to give way, and when this was ignored, they began to club them with batons and pistol butts. The speech from the megaphone continued, now read quickly. The words condemned the oppression of the corrupt Saigon government, and the false peace talks. The megaphone voice hurried to finish, ". . . and so we cannot ignore the imperialist henchman, and in particular our beloved brother Thich Tri Huang . . . prefers to hasten his arrival in Nirvana," and put down his megaphone.

Percival pressed Laing Jai's head into his neck and shoulder. The seated monk moved his lips without sound. Those close to him rocked back and forth, caressed their beads, prayed insensible to the shouting police who beat their young brothers. The first monk handed a packet of matches to the seated monk, who fumbled to open it, hands shaking, but determined. He selected a match. He looked at this small item for a moment, closed it in the striking surface of the packet, pulled, and then erupted with the noise of a small explosion, the air sucked in. He did not cry out at first, but only hunched forward, the contours of his body and robe all softened by the violent caress of undulating fire. Flame danced as if part of the saffron garment, and the seated man's mouth was a black hole within his melting face. Somewhere within, the throat shrieked, gave agonized testimony. The colour of the fire and the fabric were one, until the fabric darkened to char. The voice was silenced and then there was only the sound of fire like water, like lapping waves.

As the police swung their batons and fists, more monks got to their feet and calmly waded in to the melee to strengthen the barricade. Percival clutched Jacqueline and Laing Jai to him. A few other hapless zoo visitors, caught like the three of them, stumbled this way and that to avoid the fighting.

Oily black smoke mingled with the smell of burning flesh. One of the tigers pressed itself against the cage paws out, clawed the air, indignant that it was not receiving its portion. Percival held Laing Jai to him, covered his face, struggled to keep from being knocked over as monks and police fought. The immolated monk's charred torso fell forward—a burned effigy. Several of the Americans stalked the remains like hyenas, crouching and circling with cameras to snatch images of the burned face, the shining dome of skull hung at a strange angle. In Percival's mind, the hysterical screams of death continued.

Someone tugged at Percival's sleeve. It was the one-eyed monk. In his other hand he had Jacqueline's wrist. All around them, the police clubbed the Buddhists. Now, both monks and novices struggled with the men in uniform. Sandals were strewn about, and prayer beads scattered, released from their strings. Calmly, quickly, the one-eyed monk began to walk, and Percival followed. He went a little to the right, and then plunged quickly left. He waited for a moment, and then hurried forward, in this way spiriting Percival, Jacqueline, and Laing Jai through the crowd. Somehow, he knew how to get through. The American journalists fumbled frantically to change film, to capture the police beating the monks, kicking them after they were cuffed, lying prostrate. Already, they had lost interest in the immolated remains. With Percival, Jacqueline, and Laing Jai in tow, the one-eyed monk moved through the melee like a spirit. His brothers parted for him, and he skirted past the fights, somehow flowing through. On the other side of it, he let go of their wrists and bowed.

"Let's go! Let's go!" shouted Jacqueline. Percival pressed Laing Jai close and ran, with Jacqueline alongside. They ran away from the monks and the journalists, the police and the caged animals. They ran past the elephant and the peacocks. Percival kept on going, past the cotton candy vendor, his lungs burning and his chest pounding, towards the exit and through the gates. As they left the zoo, military police cars arrived and uniformed soldiers dashed into the zoo, slammed the gates behind them. Percival linked his arms beneath the weight of the boy while he and Jacqueline ran down the street, kept on going for blocks, although now all around them people walked—calmly enjoying a beautiful afternoon. His legs and knees cried out with pain as Percival ran past the American School, towards their apartment, through the lobby, and into the elevator. His lungs were fires. He set the boy down, felt the elevator lift them up from the ground.

CHAPTER 21

PERCIVAL THOUGHT OF A BETTER OUTING than the zoo—a picnic in Vung Tau. He loaded the trunk of the Mercedes with the cooler, towels, beach clothing, and it swallowed more even when he thought it full. Jacqueline was in a fine mood, and wore green-tinted sunglasses with tortoiseshell frames. Percival scooped Laing Jai into the car. They stopped at the market, where Percival went from stall to stall, and found baguettes, Vietnamese smoked ham, foie gras, bottles of beer, custard apples, mangos, chilled Sauternes, and ice. Still, it all disappeared into the trunk.

As they drove past the National Police Headquarters, Percival whistled a little tune. They continued out of the city. At a junction not far beyond the city, two soldiers in ragged uniforms waved the car down. They wore giant mirrored sunglasses, carried American assault rifles and wore bandoliers of grenades. A glowing French sign pointed the way to Cap St. Jacques. It was neon, lit even in day. Where did the electricity come from? Percival wondered.

The soldiers thumped on the car and waved. Percival looked at them, but did not understand. The leaves shimmered, and then began to fall. There was something wrong with the forest. The soldiers thumped again. They wanted him to get out. He did. The silence—there were no cicadas. The soldiers seized Percival by the arms, one on each side, and pulled him away from the car. Percival asked, "Brothers, what is wrong with the forest?"

The soldier on the right barked, "Poison. Kills trees. Easy for us to kill communist scum."

"Thank you for protecting us, brothers," said Percival, and tried to step back towards the car.

But they grabbed him again. One held him, and the other selected a grenade. The soldier pulled the pin and let it fall. His mouth smiled blankly beneath silver-sheathed eyes. The soldier tossed the grenade casually like a crumpled newspaper into the driver's window of the Mercedes. Percival saw Jacqueline's face, surprised, taking a moment to decipher this black object. The vehicle ignited, an angry fireball. He tried to get to the car, Laing Jai was screaming but it was too late. He heard a voice yelling. His limbs were paralyzed, and the screams were his own.

JACQUELINE CROUCHED BY THE BED, AT his side. Sounds from the street—the syncopated horns of Vespas and Hondas, the shouting hawkers—penetrated his dreams. It was a new, fresh day, cool with the respite of early morning.

"Where is Laing Jai?"

"He is asleep. Were you having a nightmare?" She stroked Percival's forehead.

From beneath the balcony came a soft rustle of leaves. He lied, "I don't know. It's vanished."

"You have a visitor."

"So early? Say that I'm not feeling well."

"It is Cecilia," said Jacqueline.

"Why is she here?"

"I was wondering that, myself."

Percival put on his slippers and pulled a robe around himself. He went out into the living room, where Cecilia perched on the very edge of the sofa. He sat down opposite her in a chair and braced himself for an attack. Instead, she looked up and gazed at her former husband. This quiet was so rare and precious from her, frightening to him. The edges of her makeup were smeared by tears. Somewhere deep and hidden, though still reachable, Percival knew the feeling of being a boy from Shantou in Hong Kong, loving someone whom he could not understand, in a world that confused him. Did he understand more now? About Cecilia, women, or anything else? He should, and yet he wasn't sure. In an argument, he knew the twitches of Cecilia's eyes, the tensions in the corners of her mouth, well enough to anticipate what type of barb would be thrown. But he did not know what made her so openly sorrowful today.

She said, "I have a letter from him. From our son."

Jacqueline was in the doorway of the kitchen. Percival glanced up at her, and she slipped through the bead curtain, out of sight. He asked Cecilia, "Can't this wait? We can have tea this afternoon. At our usual place."

Cecilia leaned forward. She spoke softly. "No. We must speak in private." She placed her slim leather bag on her lap and from it withdrew a long envelope of rough paper. It was addressed in Dai Jai's handwriting. "It is a *real* letter from our son."

The image of Dai Jai on the morning of his departure, on the cusp of manhood, appeared before Percival. As much as he tried, he had never been able to imagine Dai Jai growing older. He knew that his son was now twenty-two years old, but could not summon an image to accompany the passage of years. Percival looked at the envelope. It was a piece of coarse brown wrapping paper that had been folded and glued at the edges. "It's not stamped," he said.

"A Chinese-American brought it for me. He happened to meet Dai Jai in China."

"An American spy?"

"He did it as a favour to Dai Jai. He pitied him."

From the corner of his eye, Percival saw Jacqueline's shadow across the kitchen doorway. She was out of sight, but as near as she could be, listening. His fingers fumbled with the letter. His eyes were clumsy as they rushed over the words. *They killed many of the professors, and then some students with foreign ties. This farm is a political re-education camp, a prison.* It was as if suddenly Percival could hear his older son speaking what was written. *Thanks to our family's land, I am in the hated class of landowners. I tell them that you gave it to the people, but it doesn't matter.*

Percival pressed his eyes shut with the palms of his hands, which burned like coals on his eyelids. *I sleep with the chickens, and sometimes I steal an egg and suck it raw. Because of father's school, I'm a spy. They beat me and accuse me of being a CIA agent. I am always hungry.* It was worse than Percival had feared. He opened his eyes and then rested on the last phrase of the letter: *Please Mother, I must escape. Find a way, I beg you, or I will die here. Your obedient son, Dai Jai.* He stared at the letter, its rough hurried characters.

"Why did he send this to you instead of me?" said Percival. Did the boy not believe that his father would help him? thought Percival with a horrible pain.

"You can ask him yourself, if you ever have a chance," whispered Cecilia. "I am leaving Saigon. I am going back to Hong Kong, where there are more snakeheads with contacts in China."

"When will you be back?"

"I won't be. I have a one-way ticket for this afternoon." She stood, picked up her briefcase, and said, "My family may have lost its ships, but I still have friends in Hong Kong who can help. I've made my money off this war. I want to leave with it while I can, and maybe some of it can help to free our son."

"How are you able to leave, just like that?"

"I bought a Taiwanese passport almost a year ago. Some people make plans in advance, *hou jeung.*"

Cecilia walked out of the room, leaving the letter with Percival.

After the front door clicked shut, Jacqueline emerged from the kitchen and sat next to Percival. He was fixated, rereading the letter in a cold sweat. "What is it?" Jacqueline asked, and looked over Percival's shoulder.

"It's a private matter," said Percival, and hastily, ashamed, he folded the envelope. "I have to go to Cholon." He stood to get dressed.

"You complain about Mr. Peters' wandering eyes, but Cecilia shows up here, and you won't even tell me what it is about?" Jacqueline turned on the radio. It was in the middle of a news report. The main story was that a string of immolations in cities across Vietnam had been started with the burning of a monk at the Saigon zoo. The

Buddhists called for an immediate ceasefire and full American with-drawal. Jacqueline quickly turned it off and watched him go.

Over the years, the once-quiet road between Saigon and Cholon had become crowded with shops and apartments, laundries and bars. It was now a busy route, and today the traffic was snarled. Percival honked the horn to get cyclos to move over, swerved past belching three-wheeled taxis, and narrowly missed a Jeep as he pressed the car through the congested lanes.

He was angry at himself for swallowing his own deception. In the end, Cecilia had been right. But what else could they have done when Dai Jai was drafted by the South Vietnamese? How could Percival have known what would develop in China? It seemed it had become a different world since Percival was a boy. When he was still small, those who came back from the Gold Mountain lands with wealth were respected. Gold bought land, and a family that owned land stood above others. Had all this truly been reversed? Percival asked Chen Kai's ghost how he could have allowed Dai Jai to return to such danger. For his part, Percival insisted to himself, he had only done what he thought was best. "No father," he told himself, "would have acted differently." He said it aloud, repeated it with conviction as he drove furiously, recklessly towards Cholon.

Mak was in the school office, grading papers.

"Headmaster Chen," said Mak. "I didn't expect to see you today." He pushed his reading glasses to his forehead. "It's such a beautiful day. I thought you would be enjoying yourself in Saigon."

Percival took the letter from his pocket and held it up. He waved it like a flag and then thrust it at Mak. "This was delivered to Cecilia. This is a true letter."

Mak read the letter through slowly. He rubbed his temple.

"We must save him," said Percival. "Cecilia is going to Hong Kong, to find a snakehead. Do you know anyone there to send her to? If it costs more money than she has, I will sell everything. I will do anything."

"Not everything is money," said Mak. "To bring someone from China to Hong Kong is extremely difficult. But to bring someone out from the political camps . . ."

"If not in Hong Kong, there must be someone in Saigon who can bring Dai Jai back to Vietnam."

"Someone in Saigon?" said Mak. "Who in Saigon could possibly do that?"

"That's what I'm asking you."

Mak looked frustrated at the request. He read the letter through again. "I'm sorry. Forgive me, *hou jeung*, but Dai Jai . . . is in China." He folded the letter carefully, and offered it back to Percival. "Perhaps it will work out for him eventually at this . . . farm. Sometimes, a thing which seems hard ends up containing good."

"What are you talking about?" shouted Percival, snatching the letter. He would not be spoken to as if he were one of Mak's slow students. "His only true letter in years is smuggled out by an American spy! He must steal to eat. I am a wealthy man, and my son suffers like an animal. He will die if he stays there."

Mak sighed, looked at Percival. "Of course, any father would be upset to receive a letter like this." His tone was cool, perhaps even distant.

Percival found himself begging, "Forgive my outburst. You must help. They have decided that he is a spy because of the English school."

"Percival, Dai Jai was in trouble here in Vietnam. He was in danger, so we sent him to your mother country. Our mother country. That was your strongest wish. It was very difficult for me to arrange. I don't know what else you expect me to do."

"To bring him out, anywhere, Hong Kong, Cambodia, here, isn't there a way? You have connections."

Percival sat very still. He gripped the letter. He was suddenly aware of his hands, of their uselessness.

"But it is not so simple, friend. I wish it were." Mak spoke in halting words, as if leaving out half of them. "This is a strange time. That is the only truth."

"For my sake, can't you find the right contacts to bring him back? For the sake of your brother, please." Why was he pleading with Mak, his employee?

Mak's expression changed. He seemed exhausted, and now he chose his words deliberately. "Headmaster, I don't know if Dai Jai can be brought back. If it can be done, it will be very expensive. Are you prepared to pay?"

"Any price. Then it can be done?"

"Really?" He studied Percival's face. "Are you sure? I'm not even sure it can be done. Any price at all?"

"All that I am worth and more."

"It could cost that much." Mak put his elbows on the table, lowered his head and pressed the tips of his fingers to his temples. "I'll see what can be done." He closed his eyes, as if it would be easier not to see. "Go back to Saigon and wait. Whatever you do, make no inquiries. What about Cecilia?"

"She has left for Hong Kong. For good."

"Fine. I don't think she'll meet anyone in Hong Kong who can help, but it would cause trouble if she fussed about this here. Tell her nothing. No one can hear even a whisper of this. I must speak to some friends of mine."

LATE THAT NIGHT IN SAIGON, PERCIVAL woke from his shallow sleep fully open-eyed and alert, although there was no bombardment, no sirens. An absence of noise had roused him. There was emptiness to his side, a glow of light from the kitchen. He walked slowly, silently, across the floor. He looked into the kitchen through the screen of beads, where Jacqueline was curled up in a chair beneath the pendant lamp's illuminated patch of light, reading the letter.

Percival's jacket was crumpled in a pile on the table. As she came to the end of the first page, she began to weep. He crept away carefully, grateful that she knew, and also that they did not need to speak about this thing, this shame of his. He went back to bed without being seen, waited for her to return. He heard the click of the lamp, the creak of the front closet, then felt her body, familiar yet secret, slip back into bed.

CHAPTER 22

THE ANNOUNCEMENT OF THE PARIS PEACE ACCORD in January of 1973, just before Tet, dampened that year's holiday in Cholon. People were happy for peace, but also worried. If the Americans did not bring dollars, what would happen to their businesses? How would people pay their children's tuition abroad? If all the soldiers left, what would become of their drivers, translators, and prostitutes, who all earned good income in dollars?

In March, Percival, Jacqueline, and Laing Jai watched a parade of departing American troops as it made its way past the front gates of the Cercle Sportif. Their uniforms were clean, and their posture ramrod straight. They carried, along with regimental flags, a few neatly stencilled signs reading, WE WILL NEVER FORGET YOU. Laing Jai was excited by the line of Jeeps and soldiers, and shouted along with the dutifully cheering Saigonese schoolchildren who lined the streets.

Several times each week, Percival asked Mak about Dai Jai. Each time, Mak told him that it was not simple. He was making inquiries. Jacqueline had not raised the idea of leaving for America again. Percival was glad she had read the letter from Dai Jai. He could not have spoken about it, but it comforted him that she knew. In her silence on the matter of America, he saw she understood his predicament. Percival did not conceal his frequent phone calls to Mak. Jacqueline knew that her lover must stay in Saigon until his son was safely returned.

In the end, there was no need for anyone in Cholon to be concerned about the Paris Peace Accord damaging business. The fighting barely paused. The black market price on the American dollar rose by fifty percent while the official rate remained unchanged, creating profitable business opportunities. Cholon was a little quieter at night, but the bars stayed open. American units were sent into battle through most of August, until news came that they would actually stop shooting. Even after the last chartered flights departed from Tan Son Nhut with their Marine units, the streets and markets bustled and did not lack sweaty, sunburned foreigners. The Poles, Hungarians, and Canadians arrived to observe the peace, and all needed translators. The Indonesians and Filipinos did not hire as many employees, but they were paid the same per diems in American dollars. The Canadians soon left, quibbling that there was no peace to observe as North and South Vietnamese units continued to ambush one another. The Percival Chen English Academy remained fully enrolled, though there was no longer a waiting list.

One day, after hanging up with Mak, Percival said to Jacqueline, who was engrossed in that day's *Saigon Post*, "Once I have resolved this problem . . . if it is possible, I will obtain four exit visas."

Jacqueline nodded without a word, and continued reading.

When he went out for an afternoon at the racetrack, Percival saw that the road from Tan Son Nhut was still thick with American military vehicles, though there were more staff cars and Jeeps than troop buses. Percival was much relieved that although American boots had been removed from the mud and the jungles, many officers remained in the air-conditioned offices of Saigon. His business must continue. How much money would he need to bring Dai Jai out from China? When a new semester came, he spent several days counting the carefully stacked piastres in the school safe. There were nearly sixteen million, a fortune. It would be enough.

By the end of 1973, Percival could not bear to return to Chen Hap Sing at all. Dai Jai's letters had stopped, which terrified Percival. He dreaded walking past Dai Jai's room or going to the balcony and seeing the dry fish tanks. Every month or two, Cecilia called from

Hong Kong. As Mak had predicted, she could not find a snakehead whose contacts extended into the Chinese political re-education camps. She continued to try desperately, but the family *gwan hai* she had counted on had faded along with their shipping business.

She would mock Percival for relying on Mak. He would ask sarcastically about her connections. She would ask Percival if he knew at all what Mak was really up to. Percival would say that he didn't care, for Mak always helped them. Where, by the way, were her American friends these days? he would ask. The conversation would go on like this until one of them hung up. Percival tried to ignore the news, but in the end turned on the radio, drawn despite himself to the world's events, hoping they would give him some clue about Dai Jai.

Late one morning, when Laing Jai was at school and Jacqueline had gone by herself to the Cercle, the phone rang. Mak said, "Percival? Can you come with me to a meeting today?"

"Of course."

"Right away, right now."

"Is it what I am hoping for?"

The phone line was silent for a moment. Then, "*Hou jeung*, you said that you would pay any price to get your son back?"

"Anything."

"Then come to the school. Bring the letter."

On the way to Cholon, Percival nearly collided with an ox cart in his rush. Mak was waiting outside the school. Percival jumped out of the car and ran to his friend, leaving the car door open. "You can get Dai Jai?"

"It can be done. It was very tricky to arrange. It will cost you."

Percival clapped Mak on the shoulders. "Thank you, brother. I knew I could count on you."

"I'll drive," Mak said. "I know the way."

"Of course." The teacher got behind the wheel of the Mercedes and Percival took the passenger seat. He saw that Mak had a bulging leather document case with him. It must be full of bribe money. Mak put the car in gear and guided it slowly down the street.

"Are we meeting someone in Saigon?"

"No. We must leave the city."

As they drove past St. Francis Xavier, Percival saw a small group of monks begging on the pink stone steps. He did not see the one-eyed monk amongst them.

"Who have you found to help Dai Jai?"

"Friends. Old friends. I warn you, this will not be an easy meeting, *hou jeung*."

"As long as these friends bring Dai Jai home safely." The hollow clang of the monks' iron bowls lingered like a scent as the car drove past.

"Do you remember when I first came to Cholon?"

"During the Japanese occupation," said Percival. "I had only arrived recently, myself."

"You remember the family of chicken hatchers—the two girls?" Mak did not take his eyes from the road. Strange, Mak rarely spoke of the past.

"How could I forget?" said Percival, and shivered at the memory.

"When I asked you for rice husks and ran up to your balcony, you didn't know what I was doing, did you?" Mak's hands gripped the wheel, the skin on the knuckles blanched.

"No."

"It was the right thing to do, wasn't it?"

"The cavalry officer deserved to die," said Percival. "It was just."

"But until it was done, I couldn't tell you. I couldn't risk you stopping me." As traffic slowed, Mak's eyes darted to Percival. "Certain things, once set in motion, must run their course. As I'm sure you know, I have always left some of my activities unspoken."

"Everyone has their private affairs," said Percival.

"At various times, I thought to tell you more—but frankly, I worried about your drinking and carousing, whether secrets were safe with you. Then, over the years, it became both more complicated and more risky for me to be open. It was better to be discreet, for both of us. In any case, you understand a great deal without saying so. Don't you?"

Percival looked at his friend. "You talk as if you are apologizing, but it's not necessary. Of course you've been making your own gains through the school, as you should."

"I have been, and it was better for us not to discuss it."

"Old friend, I hope that the school has provided everything you wanted from it."

"Then you know why the school is so important for me."

"The contacts are profitable, aren't they? You can sell pleasures to the Americans, help people obtain licences, get permits, or just sell your *gwan hai*. You have your money deposited overseas, I suppose? You are certainly discreet about it." Percival laughed. "You are probably richer than I am, and everyone thinks you are just a humble teacher. However you're doing it, I hope you're milking the Americans for as much as you can. One day they'll go and they'll take their money with them. But you know that."

"I thought you knew more." Mak glanced questioningly at Percival. "Look, if we are to bring Dai Jai back, you will need to understand what I have kept from you."

"What does this have to do with Dai Jai?"

"Sometimes, friend, the end justifies the means. Remember that."

There was honking, a shout. The light had turned green. Mak turned his attention back to the road, and began to drive.

"You speak in riddles. Tell me the price, and I will pay."

"You haven't spoken to anyone in Saigon about Dai Jai's last letter, have you?" Mak slowed to let a motor-cyclo dart in front of them.

Percival thought of Jacqueline, of the quiet comfort he felt that she had read the letter and shed tears for him, but that didn't concern Mak. "No one knows," he said.

"Then I'm sure this meeting will . . . achieve the desired result." Mak drove with his eyes fixed ahead now, through Saigon, and then west past the airport. The two men did not speak. On the outskirts of the city, Mak turned off the main road and down a narrow lane into a scrapyard—a vast sprawl of Jeep carcasses, shards of broken aircraft, and gigantic mounds of spent artillery shell casings. He put the car in neutral, delicately engaged the parking brake, and looked around. The engine was still running.

It was a strange place to stop. There was no one else nearby. Mak took the small valise from the door pocket and fiddled with the zipper.

"It is the red packet? So, you have fixed a price."

"I have. It is not a money price." Mak reached into the valise and retrieved something. When Percival saw what it was, he wondered for an instant if this was another dream. Mak held the pistol awkwardly with two hands, one over the other, as if each ensured that the other would not waver, and pointed it at Percival. No, this was real.

"Old friend," said Mak, "get into the trunk of the car."

"Mak?"

"The trunk. Forgive me, *hou jeung*, but this is the only way. Now that we have arranged this meeting, I am under strict orders. If you do not cooperate, my commanding officer has told me to shoot you."

"Your commanding officer? What are you . . . Mak, what are you talking about? Why should you shoot me?" Percival heard his own voice rise into a nervous laugh. He studied Mak as if he expected him to erupt into laughter at this strange joke as well.

Mak lowered his voice. "You've met my superior before, though you did not know it. Look, I told you this would cost you more than you imagined. Do you want to get Dai Jai back?"

"Yes."

"Then we must go to a meeting. A special meeting. To discuss the situation. You must get in the trunk."

Mak kept the gun on Percival. He took his right hand off, and the pistol began to shake. With his free hand, Mak turned off the engine, removed the car key, and slipped it into his pocket. He opened his door. He got out of the car and went around to the trunk. Percival heard him press the latch and the trunk sprang open with a creak. Then Mak came to the passenger door. He opened it swiftly, pointing the gun at Percival, waved it to urge him out. "I'm sorry, old friend." Percival stepped out. He stood next to his Mercedes, dwarfed by twisted hunks of war waste. There was an acrid smell—of burning tires—somewhere in the heap. Percival walked to the open trunk as if someone else was moving his legs for him. He stared into it, an abyss. "I don't understand . . . but if you are under orders . . . who?"

"*Hou jeung*, old friend, soon it will all be clear," Mak said. "I thought you knew more, that we both chose not to speak about it. That doesn't really change anything today. You will be told everything you need to know. I'm sorry it had to be like this. Give me the letter."

"No," said Percival numbly.

"He wants to see it—my commander, who will help you."

"I will keep this one true letter from my son." He pressed his hands over his pocket.

Mak's tone softened. "Alright. You hold Dai Jai's letter, but you must give it to my superior when he asks for it."

Percival steadied himself with his hands on the edge of the trunk, dizzy. When Mak was determined to do something, there was no dissuading him. If he did not do as Mak asked, would he push him in, or would he shoot him? Was it possible? Percival could not think of any course of action except to comply. He found himself climbing into the stale stench of oil and gasoline, lying on his side with his knees slightly bent. Here he was, somehow, in the trunk of his car.

Mak spoke with regret. "I'm sorry, *hou jeung*. Keep your arms over your head. In case the road is rough." He closed the trunk delicately, then pushed on the lid to make sure it was latched. Percival heard Mak walk away. The trunk was instantly hot, midday heat intensified within the small metal compartment. The temperature increased with each breath that Percival took, and the air burned his nostrils. He felt the need to gulp air, even as it stifled him, and struggled both to breathe and to understand. He called out to Mak that it was too hot, that he would suffocate. He began to bang on the trunk. He yelled that they were old friends, brothers. There was no reply. Better to lie still, for moving made him even hotter.

Some long minutes passed. Percival heard footsteps approach. Then another voice. "The teacher is inside, Comrade Mak?"

"Yes, sir . . . I've done as you asked."

There was a sharp rapping on the trunk. "*Hou jeung*, Chen Pie Sou, Percival Chen?"

"Who is it?" Percival asked.

"I'm asking the questions, not you!" came the mocking reply. "Why are you here?"

"To bring my son home from China."

"But China is his home, isn't it?" called the voice.

"I want to bring him back to Vietnam."

"Who has sent you?" the voice barked.

"Mr. Mak."

"Mr. Mak does what *I* tell him to. But who sent you to expose Mak?" Now Percival placed the voice, and with a feeling of sick dread realized it was Cho giving orders to Mak. Who was Cho? Percival had thought he was a South Vietnamese prison torturer.

"I don't know what you're talking about," said Percival.

Footsteps went around to the driver's side of the car.

"Get in, Comrade Mak," ordered Cho.

"Yes, sir."

There was a slight shift in the car as the seats were occupied and then the slam of doors. The engine started, the transmission was engaged, and there was a roar as the gas pedal was pressed. The clutch was let out and the car lurched ahead. Percival rolled over and his head struck metal. The car bounced and jolted, and the engine yelled full and loud. The brakes squealed, and he slammed into the back of the trunk. His ribs ached from the force of the blow. He heard the slow crunching of tires on stones as the car turned. Again, the car hurtled forward, over rough ground, throttle wide open, until the brakes shrieked and Percival was thrown once more. He remembered that Mak had recommended he keep his arms over his head.

Now Cho called out. "Is the driving acceptable, or do you need a new chauffeur? I mourned Han Bai's death as you did, because he helped me to keep very close watch on you. Fortunately, Mak has kept you reasonably well-behaved. Until now."

What was that supposed to mean, that Mak kept him well behaved? That Han Bai kept watch? "I am the school headmaster!" Percival yelled. Cho laughed in reply. The car accelerated once more, and Percival tried to brace himself, to hold on to something, but found nothing to grip. Had it been a facade? he was now forced to ask himself. Whatever side they were on, had Mak been in charge of the school—with Cho in charge of Mak? The car's screeching halt threw him forward. His head struck the wheel well, a violent blow, and Percival felt the world fade into blackness, thinking gratefully that he had managed to keep the letter with him, a good luck charm.

WHEN PERCIVAL WOKE, HE WAS WET, and his body ached. He stank of sweat, oil, filth. He felt water thrown into his face, and sputtered. How long had it been, how far had they driven? He was hungry. Hours, then? He was seated in a chair. Water dripped from his ears, his chin, and the tip of his nose. It was dark. His head pounded, and there was a foul smell—of something rotting, of bodily waste. Another jarring splash of water. He cried out, and heard a satisfied grunt in reply.

"Hello!" called Cho. "Are you awake, Headmaster?"

Percival tried to raise his hands to wipe the water from his eyes. His arms did not move. Ropes secured his wrists. His fingers were numb from the bonds. He tried to move his legs. They were also tied in place. A little light—the spitting yellow glow of a gas lantern that hissed on the table. Percival's vision was blurred by the water in his eyes, and the light shifted as Cho stood in front of it. Then there was a movement in the gloom as Cho turned and swung a bucket, smashed it into the side of Percival's head. The hollow tin sound rang out and amplified his pain. "There," said Cho. "I have woken him up, Comrade Mak. Perform your duty." The bucket dropped with a clang. Cho turned to the table. Percival saw him pick up chopsticks and prod at something. He saw the blue flicker of a flame. He heard a sizzle, and now could make out a little gas hot plate and a pan—the scent of fried dumplings and a vinegar sauce.

"Sir, here is the letter," Mak said. "You wished to see it, didn't you?" Mak spread Dai Jai's letter open on the table in the lamp's dim circle of light and waved his boss over to see it. "It is genuine. You can tell." Percival struggled against the ropes again, and realized that only now was he angry at Mak—for this, for taking Dai Jai's letter from him.

Cho read Dai Jai's account out loud in a high falsetto, through the food he was eating. Then he said, "What would the little brat expect?" Percival tried to blink the wetness out of his eyes, tears now flowed along with water. Cho continued, "Still, it could be a fake, a trick by some clever American agent who suspects the school." He turned around holding a small bowl heaped with food and shovelled it up to his mouth. "Go ahead now, Mak. I wouldn't want to think you were delaying your duties."

"Yes, sir." With that, Mak picked up something from the table, a pair of gloves. He pulled them on, spread and flexed his fingers into the tight-fitting brown leather, and drew back a fist. For the second time that day, Percival thought that this could not be real, that he must be suffering within a nightmare which stubbornly refused to end. He thought this only for a moment, an instant of confused detachment, until Mak punched Percival deep in the pit of his stomach. Percival heard himself groan, head forward, tears flowing. It was no dream.

Cho came close to Percival. "Crying already. Weaker than I thought."

Percival struggled to speak through his pain and nausea. "I remember you, Cho. The last time I saw you, you wore a green eyeshade. You looked like an idiot, and played like one. Such bad luck, too. I notice you've cut your fingernail."

"Ha! That's it, show some spirit! How is your luck today? It's Mr. Cho, to you. What are you waiting for, Comrade Mak?"

Cho used the word *comrade*; he was afraid of being tricked by the Americans. So, he was not a simple prison torturer at the National Police Headquarters. Again, Percival saw Mak raise his fist, and then it came—another punch deep in the gut. Though the violence was administered as if it were rote, the force was real. Cho gestured for Mak to continue, and he did. As the beating went on, Percival could not keep himself from allowing a sob. He could have taken the blows quietly, but the tears came from it being Mak's fists. The ropes kept Percival from doubling over, but he hung his head down. Snakes coiled up within him, the sick feeling of betrayal. The force of these fists was consistent, hard, just as breathtaking each time. Percival thought of Mak's hands, always perfectly groomed. The gloves were well worn, as snug as a second skin. Once again, Mak struck his friend, and Percival wondered if he saw sadness on Mak's face.

Cho leaned in close, shouting, "Chen Pie Sou? You think we are so easy to infiltrate?" Spittle and fragments of food showered Percival's face. "Peters asked you to do this, yes? He has become suspicious of your translators! It is Peters who has sent you? Confess! He is CIA, yes? They don't use a decorated soldier to build villages! Has he smelled the enemy in his midst? He is using you to get at us? Comrade Mak, why are you so gentle today?" Cho took a step back and picked at his food. Mak struck once more. In a glint of the gaslight, Percival saw Mak's eyes begin to tear. Percival tried to speak, but could only moan with pain. Cho shouted, "Don't pretend you don't know what I'm talking about." He kicked Percival in the shin, and through the blinding pain Percival saw him eat a little morsel from his bowl. Slumped down against the ropes, coughing, he saw the shine of Cho's heavy American combat boots before one swung back and then smashed a hard toe into Percival's other leg. "Mr. Peters has sent you to catch your friend Mak, yes? He is really a spy, isn't he?"

"I have no idea if he is a spy. You are spies? You think he is like you?"

"He is not like us. He is on the wrong side. Whose side are you on?"

"Only my own, my family's," Percival managed. "You are Viet Cong agents, then?" Percival said tiredly. "And all the students . . . my school. You send my graduates to watch the Americans, to spy for you."

"*Hou jeung*, I thought that you knew a long time ago," Mak said. "I thought you were too discreet to mention it."

"I didn't know. But *you* know I don't care! I'm Chinese, a businessman."

"You see, sir?" said Mak, out of breath from his exertion. "It's just as I told you."

"Or he acts the businessman, but has been betraying us all these years," said Cho. He turned to Percival. "Or someone else has sent you? Maybe it's not Peters? Who? Why now? Your son has been in China for years. Why all of a sudden do you want Mak to get him out?"

"I didn't know . . . I didn't believe how bad things were for him. Until this letter . . ." Percival could almost hear Cecilia's voice and her doubts about China's revolution, her suspicion of Mak. He knew all the clever responses to her criticisms, all the dismissive comebacks, and yet had not seen that she was right, both about China and Mak.

Cho said, "You are friends with all of the important Americans in Saigon. Which one sent you? Someone discovered the school's real mission, yes? They caught you, didn't they? You are the string they seek to pull, and they hope it will bring a whole net full of fish. Did they say you would be shot as a spy unless you helped to catch us, and the rest of our network? Is that it? Or did they offer something? Mak! Help him think!"

Mak punched hard from the left, this time into Percival's face, snapping his head around. Tears flowed from Mak's eyes, and he breathed hard.

"I don't know what you're talking about," Percival managed to sputter.

"Perhaps some American says he can save your son? Is that it?"

"I have come here to bring Dai Jai back from China."

"Please, don't play stupid. It's Peters, isn't it? Maybe he has promised exit papers for your sweet little *métisse* whore and the mongrel boy? We know that she has been asking. Is that your reward if you betray us? Is that the bargain? Departure from Vietnam? You Chinese have no loyalty, and your whore—"

"Don't call her that," Percival groaned.

Cho yelled, "Why so lazy, Comrade Mak?"

Another hard blow, the right side of his head. Percival felt it arrive as if with a slight delay—like something was broken within him, slowing the sensation. He retched. After a moment, he managed, "You are paranoid." Liquid trickled over his face into his mouth—he tasted the salt of his sweat and the metal tang of blood. "You spend too much time sitting in your little hut, imagining enemies."

Cho was at the table, pouring the vinegar sauce over his meal. "Rest assured, Headmaster. I have had enemies." He turned and gestured to Mak with the chopsticks to proceed. "Some of them will be with me here always, but they won't cause trouble now. Excuse the smell. The last one could have dug his own grave a little deeper." Mak had not moved. Cho waved at Mak again.

A hard punch in the side. Then Mak waited for his friend to draw a complete breath before landing another blow. As tears streamed down his face, Mak struck Percival over and over. The fists landed deep in the gut, hard on the chest, rained upon his shins and arms, smashed his face, the gloves now slick with blood. Mak, too, Percival realized, was being forced to pay. Cho observed, picked at his food, as Mak continued to beat the headmaster until his body was a steady, glaring agony and Percival was more aware of the sound of the blows landing than their individual force. Cho spat his questions, accused Percival of schemes and urged him to confess, but did not wait for answers. Every now and then, Percival saw that Mak waited for him to breathe.

Was a confession desired? If they wanted guilt, should he give them guilt? But Mak had said it was good that he didn't know anything. In that case, was it innocence that Cho wished to ensure?

Cho came behind Percival, seized a fistful of his hair, and pulled his head back. "Why are you here?"

Percival gasped, "Mak brought me . . . to rescue my son."

"How can that be done? Is there a secret tunnel in this shack? A passage to China?"

The blood in his mouth slurred the words, "Mak can do it. He can always find a way."

"Why can Mak do it?"

"He knows the right people." Percival's whole face throbbed, the skin tense, already swelling. Mak always had the right contacts. Only once he said it did Percival realize—Cho was the contact who could get Dai Jai out. Why else would they be here?

"What do you mean by that?" said Cho.

"I don't know . . . truthfully, I don't know anymore." Private friends could be public enemies, and the opposite was also true. During a rare night that they had been drunk together, about two years after the Japanese departure, Percival had asked Mak what he thought of Emperor Bao Dai. He asked for no special reason—he happened to see a newspaper with a caricature of the head of state on Mak's table. The British and the Americans had given Indochina back to the French with Bao Dai as the puppet head. Mak said bitterly that half of his Viet Minh friends were pledged to destroy the new government and half had joined its army or civil service, but that some of these were each other's cousins, and still celebrated festivals together. Then Mak warily asked Percival what he thought of Bao Dai. Percival told him that he did not care about Vietnamese politics. He was Chinese. Mak nodded quietly and they drank to friendship, that their loyalty would always be that of blood brothers. The next day, it occurred to Percival through his hangover that Mak had not told him which half of his friends he was with, or what he actually thought of Bao Dai. Percival resolved not to ask again, concluded that it was best not to know or care.

Cho slapped Percival on his swollen face. "And that's what the American pig spies want, isn't it? The right people? Let us end this quickly. Save yourself the misery."

Was there no hope? "Mak, you tell him, I am no spy," Percival begged desperately. "We are friends, almost brothers, save me now. Save Dai Jai." Was this the same hut? Was this the hut inside the bamboo grove, the Chinese graveyard waiting outside? He thought of Dai Jai's bruises and how little he'd said when the boy returned home after the arrest. "I must see my son again."

The shack was quiet except for the lamp's hiss. Percival did not hear the clacking of the bamboo outside. Was the air so still today? Cho said, "Now you know who Mak's real friends are." He stood close enough that Percival could smell the vinegar on his breath. "Do you understand now?"

"All this time, I made American friends so they could hire your spies." Percival thought of all the sweaty hands he had shaken, all the pompous white ghosts he had endured, tolerating their back-patting and arm-punching. The graduates that Mak sent all seemed particularly intelligent, and perceptive, whenever Percival had encountered them in Saigon, at work for some American. And, now that he thought of it, they were especially earnest; Mak had chosen young people who could be drawn to a cause. They must be good spies, thought Percival with some satisfaction. He had thought he was doing it for the school. He was, of course, and for the money. He thought of Jacqueline, hoped that she had been hiding away some of the piastres he had given her.

Cho was at the burner again, cooking some more food. He laughed over his shoulder. "The certification was Mak's most brilliant move. The special students of the Percival Chen English Academy go straight to the best American jobs . . . and you really believed that Mak cared so much to place them in Saigon just to justify your high tuition? Anyhow, the money has been convenient. It has become a source of funding, for our activities in the Saigon area."

"But there is peace now."

"There is no peace until Vietnam is united." Cho laughed out loud. "Now that the Americans are trying to get out with the least possible embarrassment, we have a chance—to liberate all of Vietnam—but it's not done yet. Until the foreign occupiers and their capitalist collaborators are humiliated and expelled, it isn't over. Your Chinese emperors had centuries here, but in the end you were also defeated."

"Why should I care, Cho?" Percival shouted. "I'm not for or against anyone in this country. I wanted money. Now, I want my son back. Name your price and I will pay."

"Listen to you, speaking as if you were talking to a Saigon official," Cho said. "As if all that was needed was to find a price. I am naturally against bringing Dai Jai out, because he is in China receiving political education. I am a great believer in such instruction." Cho finished the last dumpling and threw the vinegar in Percival's face. It burned. "Mak convinced me that we could not ignore the situation. He said that you are emotional about Dai Jai, that in trying to get him back you might do things which could endanger the school. I admit, you are the face of the school in Saigon. If you were asking around to find people with ties to China, communists, people like us, then what would the quiet police think? What would Peters think?"

Mak said quietly, "You see, *hou jeung*, there can be no disruption, for—"

"You are more stupid than Mak thought," Cho interrupted. "He thought you must already know about the spies we were training in your own school. But even without knowing, you could have endangered us, by looking for a way to rescue Dai Jai." Cho punched Percival square in the face. Percival heard his nose crack and felt it begin to bleed. Cho walked out. A fragile light entered the shack from the open door. Percival could not tell whether the light was frail because they were in deep jungle or because it was dusk. His sense of time was gone. Mak took out a handkerchief and wiped Percival's face. He poured a cup of cool water from a flask on the table and held it to Percival's lips. The gloves smelled of old sweat, of dried blood, of vomit.

"I think the worst is over. I'm sorry, *hou jeung*," he whispered. "I've been pulling my punches, as much as I dare. If Cho thought I was going easy on you, he would beat you worse than me. I haven't forgotten you, brother."

"Why, old friend?" Percival sobbed.

Mak dabbed at his wounds. "Dai Jai is in Communist China. Our usual friends in Saigon cannot help. It must be through the other side, the same people who got him to China. I was hoping Cho would agree to bring him out, just as a favour to me. But once I mentioned it to him, he became suspicious. Helping Dai Jai could expose our contacts, he said. Undermine our activities at the school. Then he began to speculate that as we have used you to see inside the Americans, someone might wish to use you to trap us. He began to imagine that the letter from Dai Jai might be fake, a ploy."

"But the letter is true," said Percival. "I'm not hiding anything."

"I know. Cho has been a patriot since the time of the French. He has survived by being suspicious, and he wants to be sure that what you say is true."

"If he is such a patriot, why was he gambling at the Sun Wah?"

"Every man has weaknesses. It's one of the reasons he put you on the assassination list in 1968—he reported that he only got five hundred taels from you, that you shorted him on the ransom. He lost some, kept some. He was only a colonel then. His superiors would have shot him. Now, he is a general, so that doesn't matter anymore."

"Then why should he let me live now?"

"He can't kill you now. I've thought it through. The school is too valuable to disrupt anything. He just has to know he's in control of it."

"That's why he makes you beat me. To know he controls you."

Mak's face tightened. "I'm sorry. But I'm doing this to rescue Dai Jai. I'm doing it for you."

Percival thought of Dai Jai, Jacqueline, and Laing Jai. If he died here, they would not know where to look for him. Would they always wonder if his ghost was wandering unsettled, just as he had always worried about the spirit of Chen Kai? "If . . . old friend, however this ends, you promise to tell Jacqueline what happened, yes? And you will help her? She wants to leave Vietnam. She is right. She and the boy must go. If I don't return, then you must help—"

"Don't talk like that."

He stumbled over his words, spoke like a frantic child despite himself. "But you promise, because she is right! They can't stay, and you must—"

"No, you will tell her yourself," insisted Mak, straightening up. Footsteps approached the door. "Listen to me: You will see Jacqueline. Be angry with me when General Cho comes back. He wants to know that I am loyal to him. He wants to see our friendship split apart. We will rescue Dai Jai."

Percival felt tears coming freely. "Yes, you brought me here to pay for it."

As Cho entered, Mak struck Percival in the belly, so hard that Percival felt he would collapse into the ground if it were not for the ropes that circled him. He wept openly, without inhibition or exaggeration. Cho lugged a car battery with him. He placed it in front of Percival's chair. From the table, Cho collected some twisted wires, rubber-coated, frayed at the exposed ends. Percival thought of relieving his bladder, which was almost full to bursting. He could not bring himself to do it, even though he was already a mess. With the care of a tailor, Mak rolled up Percival's pant legs. Gently, he tied a wire around Percival's left ankle.

Cho leaned on the table and drank water from the same cup that Percival had drunk from a moment before. He turned to Percival. "Do you know why we are bothering with this?"

"Because you enjoy it," said Percival.

Cho snorted. "Because your school has become so important to us. It is terrible, that a school run by a greedy Chinese would be so crucial. But it is, thanks to Mak. We know the orders that are given from Saigon even before they reach their own soldiers. The Americans are so persistent—they say that the war is over, but their advisors in Saigon still tell the South Vietnamese generals what to do. Your graduates translate. Comrade Mak, the wire is too loose."

Under Cho's watch, Mak tightened the wire so that it bit Percival's skin.

Mak had told him to show a split between them. Percival summoned a shout. "Mak, you have betrayed me!"

Mak yelled, "I am a patriot." He slapped Percival across the face.

Cho waved his hand, indicating that Mak should proceed. Mak took the wire tied to Percival's ankle and attached the other end to a battery terminal, screwed it down. Then he attached another wire to the other terminal. He grasped the rubber casing and touched the loose end to Percival's right leg. Pain shot through Percival's legs, hot and burning. The invisible flame of electricity seared through his groin and genitals. Mak took the wire off after what felt like an eternity, though it was perhaps a few moments.

Percival felt real anger rising. "But you are *Teochow*. Why are you mixed up with these Annamese and their squabbles?"

"It is different for me, *hou jeung*. I was born here." Mak crouched near the battery.

From the table, Cho produced a coat hanger. He donned gloves. Cho took the wire from Mak and twisted it around the hanger. He pulled it out to make a wire flail, with which he began to beat Percival's arms, legs, whatever was exposed. Percival felt his thigh muscles, his arms, his torso spasm beyond his control. Cho spoke calmly as he beat his victim. "I would have preferred to arrange your accidental death, but Mak thinks there is a risk in that. You and Peters are friends. He trusts you, and hasn't seen Mak in years. The school's connection to the Americans might be lost, Mak tells me." The electricity seared from within. "Meanwhile, if you were going around Saigon, clumsily trying to get in touch with Chinese communists to rescue your son, it would be a disaster for us." The hanger whistled as it fell, crackled when it landed.

Through the pain, Percival said, "Ah, I see, so you are stuck with me!"

Cho held the hanger aloft, and punched Percival in the face. Cho's knuckles tore the fragile, swollen skin. "Don't be confused. You are the one who is stuck!" he said. "If we bring Dai Jai back, he will also be our security for your good behaviour." Methodically, he struck Percival again, then shoved the hanger into the waistband of Percival's trousers.

Percival gasped. "If Dai Jai can be rescued. I will keep your secret!"

Cho pulled the rusty, crumbling hanger out and stood holding it. In the hollow, quiet respite, he said, "What I want is simple. You make no inquiries. You attract no attention. There is one more thing that you must know, if you want your son."

"Just bring him home."

"And if we do that, Dai Jai will return to Saigon, and he will certainly try to find the girl whom he loved." In the absence of being beaten, or shocked, each word sounded more acute to Percival. Cho said, "And Dai Jai will find his lover, and his son."

Percival remembered the closed classroom doors after school, but he had not wondered about the boy's girlfriend since Dai Jai had left for China. Percival had almost forgotten that youthful infatuation. Dai Jai's son? Long ago, while Dai Jai was still recovering, Foong Jie had all but confirmed his trysts with a fellow student. Percival had decided to ignore it, to allow the boy this comfort after his ordeal at the National Police Headquarters. What would Cho know about it?

Cho raised the exposed end of the hanger and stabbed it through the trousers deep into Percival's right thigh. "You are sure that you will make no disturbance, attract no attention?" The electricity burned from within, and Percival felt that he was floating above the scene, blubbering, denying that he was an American spy, claiming ignorance, raging and begging for mercy. Percival was leaving himself, heard himself screaming, "Yes! Your secret is safe! I will pay anything, Mr. Cho! I don't care if my son has a child!"

Cho yanked the wire out, and said, "Good, because Dai Jai will find his lover and son *with you*." Mak looked shocked, caught off balance that Cho had said this.

Percival heard his own voice, "Jacqueline and Dai Jai . . ."

"Now, Headmaster Percival Chen, do you feel something worse than the electricity?" Cho stood holding the wire in his hand. "The truth is more painful, yes? My luck was not so good when we gambled together, but perhaps you were even more unlucky. How much simpler for you if I had won the girl's introduction." Cho jabbed again with the hanger, pushed it hard into Percival's flesh. Between Percival's legs, now, the soft release of his urine came almost pleasurably. One tension was relieved. He felt his vision fade and heard Cho asking, "Are you sure you still want your son back?"

"Yes," said Percival, "yes."

HOW MUCH TIME HAD PASSED? IT could have been hours or days. The wire gone, only a puncture oozing blood marked his throbbing leg. He had shit himself. Was he alone? There was one sound only, a dripping. He called out to Mak. No reply. He called again, still nothing but the drip. Water, of course, Cho had once explained it to him.

Alone, Percival summoned denial. It was a lie. He had seen Dai Jai's girlfriend himself, if only a glimpse of her slim silhouette through the flame trees before Dai Jai's arrest. No, it could not have been Jacqueline. This was some strange torture of Cho's, just like the beating. Perhaps he could think his way above it—it was a revenge because Percival had won that game of mah-jong, taking both the money and Jacqueline. What did Cho want from it? From the beating, he wanted a guarantee of Percival's innocence and his loyalty. From this hateful claim, he wanted . . . Percival must try to think of the motive. Then he would not feel it so much. It was difficult to think. Rising out from the dull pain that occupied his whole body, Percival felt the pin prick on his head. Water, yes. The cold water dripped on his head, each drip a sharper jab. Despite the way he met

Jacqueline, Percival had always drawn such reassurance from Laing Jai's resemblance to his eldest son.

There was a little light from below the door, but was it any different from the glow that had been there before? Had dawn replaced dusk? Or the other way around? More dripping. Percival's tongue was crusted with dried blood. If only he could quench his thirst, refresh his mouth. It was so close, the water, falling on his head.

He leaned back and tried to catch a drop. It was too dark to see the bucket. It must be hung high. He craned his neck, and the drips were daggers in his eyes. He strained and arched, but the closest he could get was that the water fell on the bridge of his nose, and from there a small drop followed the curve of his upper lip, trickling to the side, where he caught it with his tongue. He sat forward, the dripping continuing on the one spot. What could Cho wish to extract by telling this lie, he thought defiantly, this ridiculous assertion that Jacqueline had been Dai Jai's lover? The ice melted drop by drop. He could picture his scalp red, imagined it finally splitting like an overripe fruit.

A car approached, its engine familiar, then stopped. Car doors squeaked open, then slammed. Footsteps, and the clank of metal as the door of the shack was pushed. Then, silence. The open door was a rectangle of weak light. It could be late evening. But he heard a bird, was it a morning bird? The gas lamp had been snuffed out, so the interior of this place, the centre where he sat, was a black pit.

Then a bright light shone in Percival's face, searing. Cho wielded it, a flashlight? He examined the top of Percival's head. "You must be anxious to end this. Confess your mission!" Cho's breath smelled of sour alcohol, and his words were slurred. "Mak is such a good friend. To me, and also to you. We went for some noodles and rice beer, and I had a girl. He didn't feel like one, but he treated me. Have you remembered yet who sent you? Which American are you working for?"

"None. My father came to find the Gold Mountain," he heard himself mumbling. It was hard to form words with his swollen lips. Another person entered the shack, it must be Mak. Where were the ancestors' spirits now?

"You have such a sentimental friend. If it were up to me, you would have been killed at Tet in 1968. Mak prevented that." Cho lurched a little to one side, then turned back and struck the top of Percival's head with the flashlight. "Your head is ripe. Sometimes I help to peel the fruit. Look up. Sit up." He gestured like an orchestral conductor. Percival struggled to keep his head up. "If you had been shot in 1968, Mak would have become headmaster of your school and we would not be enjoying this time together. Granted, you have been a perfect stooge. The Americans who employ your students have no idea that Mak even exists. *You* are the person who sends translators and typists. But I am worried about Mak's sentimentalism." He struck Percival once more, whistled, and shone the light in his eyes. "What a mess you are." He paced unsteadily in front of Percival. "What a night that was, you winning your son's lover from me in a game of chance. I didn't know who she was either, when I placed my bets. A lovely slut, I thought. A lucky night for you. So it seemed. What shall we do now?" Cho inspected Percival's head. "This is becoming tiresome."

"Please, save Dai Jai," Percival managed to say, "Mr. Cho."

"That, again. You've had a pleasant time in this country, haven't you? With your big house, your money, your sweet girl, and your sons, or one son and a grandson, I should say." Cho continued, "There is a saying, that the *métisse* belongs to the last man she slept with. Have you heard that saying? Tell your son that one." Percival lunged in his chair, almost fell over.

"Comrade Cho, I know Headmaster Chen better than he knows himself," Mak hurried to say. He crouched down next to his friend. "I assure you, he will not betray us to the Americans. When Dai Jai returns, nothing will happen with Jacqueline to jeopardize the school. Everything will be handled discreetly, yes, *hou jeung*?"

Cho addressed Mak in a low tone, slowly, as if with pity. "Why do you still call him *hou jeung*?"

"Excuse me, sir, out of habit." said Mak. His voice was hoarse as he crouched by Percival. "Swear that you will betray nothing to the Americans, that you won't make any scene whatever happens with Jacqueline when Dai Jai returns, that you will keep your American friendships as always, that you will preserve the school exactly as it is. That's all you need to do, *hou je* . . . Chen Pie Sou." Mak spoke as if it were true, about Jacqueline and Dai Jai. Why would he do that?

Cho pulled Mak up. "I have come to a decision about the prisoner," he said.

"Thank you, General Cho," said Mak.

Cho went to the table. He turned back to them with something in his hand. He held it out to Mak. "Do your duty, Comrade Mak."

"What?"

"Your duty."

"But sir, I thought you said that—"

"As I said, I have come to a decision." Cho thrust the gun at Mak.

Percival saw Mak's pleading mouth, his desperation, but could not hear the words. Instead he heard a sound, he had once heard it in a different place. Mak was shouting, distressed. Percival had never seen Mak so upset, and yet a *hushing* grew to drown out the room. The sea? He would die here, in the Gold Mountain country. Would the same end find Jacqueline and the boy, when the communists took Vietnam? They would do so, he was now convinced. Were they all like Cho? Mak tried to turn away, but Cho seized him and spun him around by the shoulder, pressed the gun into his hand, took the safety off for him.

Mak would tell Jacqueline his fate, and take care of her. His old friend would honour this wish, and maybe she could still somehow find a departure, an escape. Mak's right arm hung limp with the weight of the pistol. He continued to talk. "But I have been faithful to the revolution. Since you've known me." Arm trembling, saying to Cho, "You see big brother, Comrade Cho, General Cho . . . I am also loyal to my friend . . ." and shaking his head.

Percival thought of Jacqueline with Laing Jai. As a newborn Laing Jai had looked so much like Dai Jai. Percival invited the noise to drown this thought, instead picturing only mother with child. Cho slapped Mak, yelled at him, screamed that his only loyalty was to the cause. Mak walked over to Percival with stiff legs. He stood close by, close enough to embrace. He raised his arm unsteadily. The sound was the ocean at Vung Tau, the waves on the beach, a welcome. Percival could smell the oiled weapon, the gunpowder. Things needed to be carefully tended to, otherwise everything rusted, disintegrated, in this country of decay.

"Since this is my fate, I'm glad it's your hand," said Percival.

The gun's muzzle pressed cold on his temple, he could feel Mak shaking through it. "*Hou jeung*, I'm sorry." And now the sharp, definite, and solid thing came.

A strike of metal on metal.

It was as if he could see his blood flowing down from his shattered head into the earth, mingling with the human waste that already soaked that place, with the stench. It was as if he could watch the skull fragments blown apart, fallen like cracked seashells. As if he could look into his own eyes, their last flicker. But he was able to think, to fear it.

There had been only the hard metal hammer falling in the gun's empty chamber.

Cho seized the chair and knocked it to the ground. Percival thudded on his side and felt his raw scalp split open, the blood flowing from his head. It was like Cho had once described, a relief.

Mak fell to the ground next to Percival and struggled to lift up his chair, to raise him back into a sitting position. Mak sobbed, thanked Cho for sparing Percival, begging forgiveness from the headmaster. In the dark, Cho laughed as if he had played a small practical joke. He held the flashlight in one hand and extended the other. "Here, Mak, give me my gun back. I had to be sure." He turned to Percival. "We will bring Dai Jai back—that is my favour to Mak. Everything will continue as before—that is the price of your life, all of your lives. We will send our eyes and ears to Saigon as long as the foreign scum is here. If a word is betrayed, if you attract any kind of attention, Laing Jai first, Dai Jai, and then Jacqueline. In a room like this one, you will watch them die, slowly, painfully, before you join them."

Cho came close, and Percival could smell the rotten teeth in his mouth beneath the sour stench of beer. "Comrade Mak will take you back to Saigon. If anyone asks about your injuries, you will say that you were kidnapped by some Chinese gangsters for ransom. Your American friends won't care about a kidnapping amongst Chinese." As he stood up, he said, "Remember, I am letting him live in order that everything remains the same! Do you both understand? One wrong step, you Chinese dog, and I know Mak will do as required. As for you, Mak, I'm glad you pulled the trigger, otherwise I would have had to bury you both."

"Yes, sir," said Mak.

"I'm going my own way," said Cho. He left the hut, and then after a moment his footsteps faded away.

"Let's get back to Saigon," said Mak. "It's almost night."

Insects rushed in through the open door, buzzed and attacked them. Mak struggled in the dark to untie Percival. He ran his hands all over his friend's arms and legs, grasped for the knots, the ends of rope, and pulled them loose. He struggled with the cords and yanked them in frustration. Cho had taken the flashlight.

Percival felt the ropes on his legs loosen, and he moved his feet as if trying them for the first time. Then the arms, and soon he was free. Percival felt Mak lift him and take his hand. Mak stood, and Percival was a limp sack against his friend. Together, they staggered forward, towards the faint outline of a doorway. Outside, the bamboo stalks rubbed each other in whispers. The moon cast a pale glow, the narrow footpath disappeared in shadows. Mak tripped and stumbled with Percival towards the sound of flowing water. He lowered him into a stream, and bathed him.

"Is it true, about Jacqueline?"

"Yes, *hou jeung*."

"All these years, you knew?" said Percival, his own words shattering the quiet.

"I'm sorry, *hou jeung*, I tried to send her away. I didn't know about it until I saw you with her at the club. By then, you were already in love. I tried to stop you. You would not be discouraged, so it seemed kindest to hide the truth about Dai Jai. And then the baby . . . I thought if I could get her further away, back to Saigon, you would lose interest. You usually do. You didn't. I saw how much you loved her, and finally I just let you go on, for while she was in Saigon it didn't seem like anything about it could threaten the school. At least you were taking care of your grandson."

"I wondered about her mother's death in Thanh Ha, if somehow you were mixed up in that."

"I don't know a thing about that. I just wanted to help you, friend."

"And now?" asked Percival.

"When this issue of Dai Jai came up, I had to tell General Cho everything. I had to. We needed to think of risks, of all the dangers that might upset our school. Its work is so precious for us. But we had agreed not to tell you tonight; I told him we could use it as one final point of . . ."

"Leverage. You wanted to keep it as leverage over me, if you needed it."

"And I also thought that before Dai Jai got home, maybe I could help you send Jacqueline and Laing Jai away to America. I thought I could save you the pain of that truth, I thought I could work it all out for you . . . but you see, General Cho likes to inflict pain. I should have known he would tell you."

The water was mercifully cool, and Mak's hands scooped it over Percival.

"Will Cho bring Dai Jai?"

"I think so. Yes. Yes, he will."

"Thank you, old friend."

Mak took off his own shirt, ripped it into strips, and washed the strips in the stream. He bound Percival's head, and then the wounds on his arms. The insects swarmed furiously. Mak struggled and half-dragged Percival along the footpath to the car, and then helped him in. Each step was pain, every part of his body scratched, or cut, or bruised. Mak eased Percival into the passenger seat and closed the door. He went around to the driver's side. Percival sat in the car, dripping, and stared ahead.

"I understand something now," said Percival. "It is something important."

"What is that, *hou jeung*?"

A breeze caressed the leaves. There was that sound again, was it waves? Did they carry all this distance from Cap St. Jacques? Perhaps they did in certain winds. This must have been the sound he had heard, the sound of the sea. The bamboo clacked. Percival said, "That you knew about the gun . . . that the gun Mr. Cho gave you was not loaded."

Mak's hands were on the wheel. He stared straight ahead. The car was a dark refuge. "Yes. Of course, you are right. Thank you, *hou jeung*, for observing that. I knew." Mak put the key in the ignition and turned it. The car came to life, and they drove away.

CHAPTER 23

THEY DROVE INTO SAIGON IN A roundabout way. Mak deftly guided the car through districts that were unfamiliar to Percival, sometimes doubling back, threading through narrow alleys, pausing for a moment before turning down a boulevard or through a quiet market lane.

"You are trying to avoid checkpoints?"

"Your condition would provoke questions," said Mak, checking the rearview mirror.

Percival said, "If you are trying to be invisible, why don't you turn out the headlights?"

"That would make us stand out."

"Of course. You hide in plain sight." The car hit a bump, and Percival groaned.

"You understand."

"More and more. What should I say if we do come to a checkpoint?"

"Don't say anything. I will explain that I am with the quiet police and that I have been questioning you. It will be a hassle, but I have friends who will back that up."

"Of course, you play both sides."

"Yes." Mak's eyes were on the checkpoint up ahead. "It may not seem honourable, but it is a necessity in my case." Mak maintained a steady speed, neither slowing nor accelerating as they passed a darkened Jeep parked at the checkpoint. As they went by, they saw that the soldiers inside were asleep. Mak breathed a sigh of relief. "It is still best to be unnoticed, not to have questions to answer."

"I don't even know what to ask you anymore. You have a whole other existence."

Mak said nothing. As they came towards the centre of Saigon, Percival caught sight of some American soldiers outside a bar and instinctively shrank into his seat. Mak seemed to take no notice. Closer up, Percival saw it was just a cluster of bar girls and soldiers, teasing, grabbing, a night-time courtship of price and desire. As the car went past, Percival saw that the soldiers were not Americans. Of course not, they were peacekeepers, Hungarians? They had the same big frames as GIs, and spent dollars in the same loud way. They were almost at Jacqueline's apartment. Percival realized that he wished to be home with Jacqueline, in spite of the truth about her and Dai Jai. As Mak drove past the apartment, Percival felt panicked and said, "Where are we going, Mak?"

"To the hospital."

Percival looked down at his blood-crusted wounds, felt the throbbing of his arm, his screaming leg. They drove past the National Police Headquarters. Percival asked, "Were you involved in Dai Jai's arrest?"

"No. I was as surprised as you were."

So Dai Jai had indeed brought that upon himself, he thought. Or Percival had done it. "But once he was arrested, it was a chance to profit. You were involved in the ransom."

"Cho insisted we use the opportunity. In Saigon, he directs an interrogator at the National Police Headquarters, a low-ranked civil servant in Saigon, a comrade of ours."

"I see, a government jailer, in reality Viet Cong, to extract confessions from the innocent, free the guilty."

"But who is innocent and who is guilty? No one can say . . ." said Mak. His words trailed off, as if he were very tired. Then he perked up, as if shown his script once more. "North and South should be united. This is one country. Anyhow, you are right—Dai Jai's ransom was just a way to get gold, which we needed very badly for our operations. Nothing more."

"Except that Cho took some for his own enjoyment."

Mak looked uncomfortable. "I shouldn't have told you that. Don't repeat it."

"Then why did they beat Dai Jai, if that sum of gold was just a . . . profitable opportunity?" The words stuck in Percival's throat.

"Dai Jai could not simply have been released without being touched—someone would have been suspicious. Our man was very easy on him, you know. He marked him up, but I impressed upon him that Dai Jai must not be seriously hurt."

"They did not cripple his body. But his spirit . . . they told him he would be killed." Percival thought about his first visit to the hut with Cho, about Dai Jai's nights of screaming back at Chen Hap Sing. The torture had continued, even after the boy was released.

"A way to make him disappear without the other jailers suspecting anything. They beat people daily in the political section. That is the routine. They kill people from time to time, when ordered. It is also Cho's way of rescuing our own spies if they happen to be arrested. A good show of torture is followed by a jungle execution."

Percival thought of the fresh bruises, the scars, on his son that had taken so long to heal. He wished he had found the thousand taels faster. Did it matter that he had prayed to the ancestral spirits to save the boy, when Dai Jai was already a pawn in a larger game? Percival tried to recall if he had consulted the ghosts before sending Dai Jai back to the motherland. He felt his anger towards Mak leaching out of him, replaced by his disgust with himself. "And now this is happening in China. The prisons, the interrogation. People have whispered about it in Cholon for a few years now. I didn't want to believe it, until this letter came from Dai Jai." Words from Dai Jai's true letter came to him, "*forced to crawl like a dog over broken glass.*"

"I—I'm surprised," said Mak. "The new society is supposed to be for everyone's good. I suppose there are . . . class enemies. Enemies of the people, after all, must be re-educated . . ."

"Like Dai Jai?"

"I don't know what to say, *hou jeung*. I sent him to China because . . ."

"As a favour to me."

"Yes." Mak kept his hands firmly on the wheel. "Mistakes happen. Some innocents suffer . . . we will get him back. That's what we've ensured today." Both men were quiet. Mak parked outside the night-time entrance of the Gral Hospital. He went around to help Percival out of the car. As Mak heaved him up, Percival felt all the wounds in his body cry out. Percival dragged his right leg along, barely able to put weight on it. He raised his hand, gasping, gestured that they must stop.

"We are almost there, *hou jeung*."

When he was able to speak, Percival said, "Mak, please don't call me *hou jeung* anymore."

MAK HALF-CARRIED PERCIVAL THROUGH THE HOSPITAL doors. When the young night duty doctor saw them, he sighed. Both of them were filthy, their eyes bloodshot in the stark electric light. They looked like wild men. The duty doctor called a nurse. Mak and the nurse gingerly helped Percival to strip and laid him down on a stretcher.

"Is Dr. Hua on call, by some chance?" asked Mak.

"That rich bastard? Long gone. A private practice in San Diego."

The doctor asked the nurse to open a suture tray, and to send the porter out to fetch him an iced coffee. He pulled up a stool, sat alongside the stretcher, and first began to repair Percival's split-open scalp, soaking gauze pads with thick blood as he worked. He sewed impatiently, like a harried seamstress. The doctor did not use any freezing, so Percival felt each jab of the needle, but it was nothing— an irritant compared to the blows that had already damaged him. Then the doctor began to close the other wounds. The porter came in from the night with iced coffee, and the doctor stopped from time to time to sip it as he went from one gash to another. His fingers left delicate bloodstains, like flower petals, on the tall coffee glass, and he complained that the hospital was out of gloves. Finally he closed the lacerations on Percival's face, and the jagged tear in his ear. It took the doctor over an hour, and when he was done, he shouted for the porter to take Percival for some X-rays.

When those had been done, the doctor emerged from the X-ray reading room and told Percival that his left arm was broken, that several ribs were fractured on the other side, that his right collarbone was snapped, but his skull had not cracked. The X-ray could not prove it, but the doctor suspected a liver laceration beneath the broken ribs. A fragment of metal was lodged in the right femur. The end of the coat hanger must have broken deep within him. "You will need surgeries for both your arm and leg," the doctor said. "Perhaps tomorrow."

Mak looked stunned to hear this catalogue of injuries. He took out his wallet, gave the doctor twenty thousand piastres, and said, "Thank you so much, Doctor. Can you please arrange a quiet room for my friend?" The doctor looked at the money, both surprised and pleased. He pocketed it. Mak said, "He needs to be alone to recuperate."

The doctor cleared his throat, his hand caressing the money in his pocket. "We are under orders to reserve the private rooms for government officials and army officers—you understand, if they are injured by the Viet Cong. Ah, those scoundrels continue to fight, even though we are at peace."

"I'll bring you another twenty thousand tomorrow."

The doctor smiled. He and the porter wheeled Percival to a small but pleasant room that looked onto the hospital grounds, and the nurse opened the windows to allow the cool night breeze.

"The pain is severe, isn't it?" asked the doctor.

Percival's whole body was a territory of pain—here sharp, there burning. He nodded.

"I will give you some relief," said the doctor, and produced a vial and syringe from his lab coat pocket. "I still need to put a cast on your arm, a temporary splint before your surgery, and I need to move your bones into a better position." He withdrew some drug from the glass vial with the syringe and tapped out the bubbles. "It is better that you don't feel me moving them." He injected some of the fluid into the intravenous. Percival felt the warm comfort seep through him. The soft hands of exhaustion and narcotic laid him back in the bed. The world became dull, and then he just managed to turn to the side, to vomit on the floor. He spat blood. The nausea gave way to a soothing, dull cloud of euphoria, and he drifted away on it.

—

PERCIVAL WOKE INTO A FRESH MORNING and surveyed his own body as if it were a wrecked foreign landscape. The bandages were caked with blood. A cast hung on his left arm like a stone, and the wound in his right leg throbbed. Mak was sprawled on the floor, snoring. In the new day, the wounds were freshly whetted knives. To lift his arm, or shift his torso, was agony. When he lay completely still, there was momentary relief. To take a breath caused stabbing jabs in his chest.

He must continue to breathe, he told himself. He wanted to see Jacqueline and Laing Jai. And Dai Jai. He did not want them to see him like this, he thought at first, but could not get Jacqueline out of his thoughts. She had seen Dai Jai when he returned from his imprisonment, and now she would see his father. Did he look worse than Dai Jai had upon returning from the National Police Headquarters? he wondered. Yes, he thought. His injuries were more severe. If Mak had not been pulling his punches, he would likely be dead. But this penance eased none of his guilt. And how did Dai Jai look now, suffering in China, his motherland? If Jacqueline could see Dai Jai today, would she go to him, comfort him? She would—she should. And then he could not keep out the thought—when she touched Percival for the first time, did she imagine Dai Jai?

An urgent desperation filled him. He must see Jacqueline. Mak must fetch her. Yes, Mak must bring her. Percival called Mak, who startled awake. "*Hou jeung?* What can I get you?"

"Jacqueline." Percival touched his face lightly, traced the ridges of sutures and the hills of swollen deformity. "Bring her here."

Mak stood up. He appeared shocked to see Percival's condition and looked down at his own hands. "Wait until you heal," he suggested. "I will get you the best doctors, the best food. It will be like this never happened. Then, you can see Jacqueline."

"Please, fetch her. I need to see her, Mak."

"Why don't you think about things a bit, regain your strength, and then—"

"Mak!" he shouted.

"You remember . . ."

"Yes, yes, I know."

"Mr. Cho . . . feels very strongly that—"

"Everything with the school must remain the same. It will. But bring Jacqueline to me. Not Laing Jai, a boy shouldn't see his . . . I couldn't bear him to see me like this."

"Nor should she," said Mak. "It would be better for her to see you once you are healed. Why don't I just tell her that you are safe, in case she is worried?" It was strange to see Mak unsure of himself.

Percival said, "I will remember what Mr. Cho wanted. For our friendship, please bring her."

"Cho would tell me not to, to wait for you to calm down, but I am still your friend, *hou jeung*. Do you really want me to bring her?"

"Yes."

After Mak left, the doctor came, took Percival's temperature, and found that he had a fever. He examined the right leg, poked and pressed around the wound where the fragment of coat hanger was embedded. Every touch was excruciating. It was more red than the day before, and the flesh was swollen tight.

"It is becoming infected. You need surgery to open your leg, clean it out properly and remove the metal."

"Will you operate this afternoon?"

"There may be some delay. On account of supplies."

"My friend can bring piastres."

"Yes, of course he will have to," said the doctor. "But even so, we have a shortage of the drugs we need. Are you in pain? Would you like some medicine, some relief?"

Percival nodded like a compliant child. The doctor fished out the vial and needle from the pocket of his white coat and prepared a dose. He injected the liquid into the intravenous. The warmth in Percival's arm was an expanding presence. When it reached his centre, Percival vomited dark, coagulated blood into a small basin before being gathered into the drug's rising balloon. Percival thought of his father, desperate for his opium pipe. Chen Kai had been angry with him for withholding it. Now, Percival understood. He accepted the high feeling along with the relief of pain, and closed his eyes.

When Percival woke, he was not alone. She had come. He peered through the slow light of the morphine, at her face streaked with tears. He wanted to reach up, to embrace and to be held. He shifted towards her, agony stabbed through his leg, and he stopped himself. How long had she stood there at his bedside, waiting for him to wake? Now he remembered about Dai Jai, and envied his drugged, sleeping self, attended by his lover in oblivion. Jacqueline bent down to kiss him, her mouth more perfect than ever on his bruised skin.

He wished to forget everything except the present, to ignore the knowledge that wounded him more than his injuries. Percival inhaled her scent, held it in, wondered if he could stop breathing now. Jacqueline traced her fingertips over his chest, stroked his limbs. He was compelled to exhale. She whispered, "My love. What has happened?"

Mak answered quickly. "He was kidnapped yesterday morning. Chinese bandits. For ransom." He had his hands clasped behind his back. "It has been paid."

"I thought you had gone gambling and maybe went with some other woman. I was suspicious." She stroked Percival's hair, and he closed his eyes. The hospital air smelled of antiseptics and chemicals. "Now I feel so sorry for thinking that." He thought of his first glimpse of her at the Sun Wah Hotel. She had gone out to find a man of means who might be convinced that Dai Jai's child was his own. She had seemed hesitant, uncertain, when he looked at her at first. By the time she was in his car, she had been determined. Why had fate led Jacqueline to him? Or him to her? He regretted his blindness, but Laing Jai felt like his own. That feeling was indelible. Even if it could have, he realised he did not want it to go away.

She stroked his hands. Percival tried to think how he might have offended the ancestral spirits, for them to inflict this. In the early days, whenever she had crept into his room at Chen Hap Sing in the afternoon, he had feigned surprise. Would it be so difficult to feign ignorance now?

Percival spoke at last. "I learned something . . ."

"They came to me for the ransom," Mak jumped in. "They came to me rather than you, Madame Jacqueline, because they knew the money was at the school." He had never addressed her as *madame* before.

"But why? Why did they do this?" Jacqueline looked from Mak to her wounded lover. "If they got their price, why did they have to hurt you?"

"We . . . we are in cruel times. It is nothing, to beat a man. Don't think of it anymore," said Mak. "The bandits have their price, and the headmaster is safe." He looked to Percival now. "What is done, is done."

"Yes, you are safe now." Jacqueline knelt next to the bed and brought her lips to his damaged face again. "You are here. You will heal."

Percival forced himself to speak, made himself do it. "Before I met my kidnappers, I was blind."

"Shh . . ." she said.

"I thought that everything about you was genuine and true. I loved that."

She drew back a little. "I don't understand."

"They hurt me with blows, but also with the truth."

Mak jumped in, "He is confused, the drugs, maybe you should go, madame."

"Shh . . . You need to rest," said Jacqueline, and stroked Percival's forehead, kissed it tenderly.

Mak put his hand on Jacqueline's shoulder to urge her away, but she shook him off. He spoke to Percival. "Ah, Chen Pie Sou, you don't make sense. You must be in pain. Should I get the doctor to give you some morphine?"

Percival whispered, "Tell me . . . on the night you went to look for a father for your baby, did you hope to find a man who would love you and keep you, or one who would pay you to go away?"

Jacqueline stiffened and took her hand from his head. He craved her touch, hated her for it. His eyes flooded. "And what did it mean to you that we chanced upon each other? Were you happy to seduce your lover's father?"

"Oh . . ." she said. Her mouth and eyes were frozen open.

"Weren't you angry with me for sending him away?" Percival thought of Jacqueline curled up that night, secretly reading the one true letter from Dai Jai.

After what felt like a long time, she said, "I was, at first. But what could I do about it? You sent Dai Jai away, so I was alone. You won me, so I went to your bed. I didn't have time to find another man. Then, once we began to know each other, I saw that you missed Dai Jai too, that you had sent him away for his safety, because you loved him, and that you worried about him in China. So, I was able to forgive you."

"Did Dai Jai know you carried his baby?"

She shook her head with a very small motion. "By the time I knew I was pregnant, and that I would need a man, he was in China." Jacqueline spoke in a soft voice. "My life felt strange at first, but I grew accustomed to it. You reminded me of Dai Jai, which was a consolation. And then when Laing Jai came, I saw that you loved him. We are happy together, aren't we?" She squeezed Percival's arm, causing him excruciating pain.

Mak fumbled to say something about drugs, and the confusion of illness, and how he must speak to Jacqueline alone. He implored Percival to rest quietly, to say no more.

"Were we happy?" Percival ignored his friend and spoke to Jacqueline, anger seeping in now. "Dai Jai is returning to Vietnam. Mak is arranging it. I have promised Mak that I will keep it a secret, so you must not tell anyone either. I'm sure Mak is very distressed that I have just told you."

Percival saw her face fall, and said to her, "Maybe you would like your first lover back?"

"*Hou jeung,*" she said, a form of address she never used. "We can, we can, surely there will be a way to—"

"A way to do what? A way for you to get out of here! To disappear from my life!" All his emotions—tenderness and fury, betrayal and desire—were at the surface, equally available. He did not know which ones to choose, felt love and hatred all within reach.

"I had to find someone," she said, tears on her cheeks. "It was confusing for me at first, when chance brought us together, but in the end I was happy it was you. Maybe with a little time, you will—"

"This is over. We are done!" As he said this, Percival longed to see Laing Jai, longed to embrace him. Meanwhile, his eyes were dry as he shouted, "Get out of my sight!"

Hurried footsteps approached, attracted by the commotion. A nurse burst in, and Percival was aware of her mouth moving, words emerging, the patient must rest. There were more feet, urgent voices in the hallway. Mak hovered to the side.

"You see, I was surprised . . ." Jacqueline clung to his hand, petted it. Her hair lay over his arm. She whispered, "*Hou jeung*, what I didn't expect is that I would fall in love with you."

"Go!" he screamed.

"How could I know, you see, that I would love you so much? Why don't you get better first, and then—"

"I never want to see you again."

The doctor walked in, the syringe already poised in one hand. He laid a hand on Jacqueline's shoulder. The doctor inserted the syringe into the intravenous. She stood, apologized, begged forgiveness, but already the nausea and soft warmth washed into Percival together, like a wave, and her words tapered away. She retreated towards the door, her face blank. The doctor and Mak stood at the bedside. She fled into the hallway and was gone. What were Mak and the doctor saying? Percival heard his own words as if through a fog, yelling at Mak, "You go as well!" More words, curses, his own muted voice drifting through the soothing blanket of a narcotic sleep, and Mak stood steadily at his side while the room went dark.

CHAPTER 24

AS DAYS BECAME A WEEK, THE operating rooms remained closed for lack of supplies. Mak offered piastres, but the drugs were still not available. The wound in Percival's swollen right leg began to leak thick pus, and the skin around it was tight and sensitive. He could not tell whether he was delirious from fever, emotion, or the morphine, and each bled into the other. Thankfully, there was plenty of morphine. When Percival kept perfectly still, his left arm was tolerable, but even the slightest movement was excruciating. The doctor explained that it was healing in the wrong position. It would have to be re-broken and put together with plates in the operating room.

Mak finally told the doctor, "Give me a list of the drugs you need. I will find them somehow."

The doctor wrote out a list of the anesthetics and surgical supplies that would be required if they were to operate. He said, "I'm sorry, it is not like before, when we had plenty of American supplies that I could sell to you. Back then, it was just a question of money. Now, we genuinely can't get some things."

"But this is a government hospital. You still have American support, yes?"

"The Americans promised they would continue to send us medical supplies, but perhaps that was just the polite thing to say as they were leaving. Or perhaps the supplies are being stolen, long before we see them." The doctor shrugged. "My brother is an army helicopter pilot. Same thing. Half of the choppers sit on the ground, needing a part which the Americans promised to send."

Percival was soon in constant need of morphine. When one dose wore off, he shook, became soaked in sweat, and his muscles cramped. His bowels loosened, and he yelled for the nurse. He needed more and more. A small dose did nothing. He insisted upon large doses, with which he slept, and dreamt of Dai Jai, of Cap St. Jacques. Sometimes, as he drifted in and out of sleep, he heard himself, "If I could just see my son, I will recover."

The doctor's private stock of morphine ran out, and Mak somehow obtained morphine, the glass vials stamped with Chinese labels. The fevers were constant. Mak checked in briefly, and disappeared to search both for the required surgical drugs and supplies as well as more and more opiate. He could barely keep up with Percival's use. The doctor cautioned both men that an overdose could kill him. Percival thought nothing of this warning, and sometimes injected himself until he passed out. His leg now smelled like rotting meat.

Sometimes, Percival felt sorry for himself. He missed Jacqueline, and wondered if he should have kept his knowledge of the truth from her, at least until he had healed. If she were here, she would comfort him, nurse him. But then his pride returned. If she were here, how could he pretend? After a week of searching, Mak had obtained all the necessary surgical supplies. The operation was scheduled. The doctors explained that the infection might have entered the muscle. They would see what the flesh was like inside the leg. If it was badly infected, they would have to amputate.

On the morning of the surgery, Percival said, "Mak, if I die, you will still rescue Dai Jai, yes? You will take care of him, won't you?"

"Don't be ridiculous," said Mak. He had slept on a cot next to Percival that night, guarding the box of precious supplies, and was exhausted. "You will have your surgery and soon be in recovery." He took a vial of morphine from his pocket, cleaned the top, and drew out a dose.

Mak injected the drug into the intravenous, just enough for Percival to reach a comfortable, lucid calm.

"When will Dai Jai be here, Mak?"

"He is on his way, friend. For his sake, you cannot die."

He felt distant from his own pain. "Dear brother Mak, you're always right."

The nurse came and said they were ready. A porter wheeled Percival into the operating room.

PERCIVAL OPENED HIS EYES. IT WAS night. The edges of the bandages were stiff and white, newly changed. The doctor was explaining the operation. Percival tried to concentrate, but the words kept drifting away . . . *That they had re-broken the arm to set it properly. That the leg had been full of pus which was now drained. That he was lucky. That the bone was not infected, the muscles intact. That now, he would surely heal.* Percival heard it as if it were someone else's operation. There was a sharp pain from the leg, but the deep throb was gone. The tightness of flesh had been relieved, though it was still hot and red. A vial of antibiotics hung above him, the intravenous line snaking into his uninjured arm. It hung in a convenient position, thought Percival, for him to inject himself. The damaged arm felt comfortable in its new cast. The doctor declared himself pleased, the operation was a great success. At this, Mak produced a fat red envelope, which he gave to the doctor, and the doctor bowed slightly, accepting this further reason for happiness.

Percival heard his own slurred voice. "You must give him gold. A bar of gold."

"American dollars are fine, *hou jeung*, you rest now." The envelope disappeared into the doctor's pocket.

"Go on a holiday, then, to the coast, Saigon is a dying patient." Even as he heard his own words, Percival knew they did not make sense.

Mak bowed to the doctor. "Thank you, Doctor, thank you."

When the doctor left, Percival said, "Where is Jacqueline? Why is she not here? Tell her I would like to go home, as soon as possible."

"You will go home once you are better. To Chen Hap Sing."

"No, to Saigon. I would like to see Laing Jai. Where is my little boy?"

"Friend," said Mak. "Good news came to me while you were in surgery. Dai Jai is safe. He is out of China, safe in the North, in Hanoi."

"In Hanoi? Why Hanoi? They say the enemy is there, in the north." Percival began to giggle.

"How do you think we got him out of China? Beijing and Hanoi are friends."

Then Percival slowly remembered why Jacqueline was not there, and would not be coming. He felt the loss as if new. "When will Dai Jai be here? How will you bring him from Hanoi all the way to Saigon?"

"We will find a way."

"Thank you, Mak," said Percival. "This news is better than any medicine."

Mak prepared a dose of morphine, tapping the bubbles out of the syringe. Percival thought to protest that he wanted answers more than painkillers, but the clear liquid invited him. Just the sight of the brown glass vials filled him with anticipation.

THE DOCTORS WERE PLEASED WITH THE wound's progress. The stench of decay dissipated. Mak spent less time at the hospital, and he told Percival that he must turn his attention to the school. Neither of them mentioned Jacqueline. Now that Percival was healing, Mak's visits were regular, cheerful, and brief. Every evening, he brought food, and morphine with labels in Chinese. Each vial had a delicate neck, with a small bulb above and the drug in the tiny flask below. Percival quickly mastered the trick of tapping any stray drops from the bulb down into the flask, of breaking the neck without cutting his fingers, of drawing up his dose and injecting it. He knew how much to draw up just by looking—and did not need to examine the markings on the syringe.

The food Mak brought was plain but rich—rice and pickled eggs, noodles and barbequed pork. He gathered up the dishes afterwards and rushed away. Mak had always been a friend, but never a nursemaid. In his eager solicitations, Percival saw the burden of his guilt. As much as Percival needed Mak to take care of him, Mak was anxious to atone for what had happened at the shack. Gradually, Percival's appetite returned.

As long hours passed, alone in his hospital room, he longed for her, and wished he had never met her. She must have some money, he hoped, for she had never seemed to spend all he gave her. Then, he mused bitterly, had she foreseen that this situation would arise, that the truth would come out and she would need to be financially prepared? That must be it. Now, in the next moment, he found himself worrying, what if she did not have any piastres left? How would she live, and care for Laing Jai? He did not want her and Laing Jai to be forced from the apartment for lack of funds, as she and her mother had once been forced out by her father's abandonment. Should he send her some money with Mak? No, it was best to keep him out of it. Every time he saw Mak, Percival asked him if there was any news of Dai Jai. He could not help asking. Dai Jai was safe, Mak always said. He was on his way. Mak offered nothing more, and Percival did not wish to make himself even more dependent by pressing for information.

In lucid moments, when there was less drug in him, Percival rehearsed his words to Dai Jai. Would he apologize? But for what? he thought indignantly. For sending Dai Jai to China? It had been to protect him—he could not have predicted what would happen there. For loving Jacqueline? He had loved Jacqueline without knowing the truth. If he hadn't, who knew what would have become of her. So, perhaps no apology was necessary. He was a good father. Now that he had discovered that Dai Jai was suffering, he had arranged to bring him out of China. When he discovered the love between Dai Jai and Jacqueline, he had sent her away. What more could he have done? Besides, how could a father ask forgiveness of a son? However numerous these justifications were, the guilt was unchanged. He craved morphine. Hated himself for it. Thought of Chen Kai's addiction.

A week after the operation, Percival said, "Mak, bring me some of my clothes."

"You aren't going to flee the hospital, are you? You are still not well," said Mak.

"The doctors won't even let me get out of this bed. I just want to be dressed like myself."

Mak complied with Percival's request and brought him several shirts and pants, though no shoes. Percival said nothing of it. In fact, the doctors had pronounced his leg sufficiently healed for him to stand, and encouraged him to do so. The first time he tried, his legs were so weak that he stood for a moment and then half-fell onto the nurses helping. Gradually, he was able to get up on his own. When Mak was not there, Percival forced himself to stand for as long as he could, and sat, caught his breath and stood once more. Several times, he almost fell to the floor, but managed to end up on the bed. He continued until exhausted.

Each day, Percival exercised his legs as much as the slowly healing limbs allowed. He traded two vials of morphine with a porter for a pair of brown loafers and hid them beneath his bed. Meanwhile, by careful dosing, he built up a stockpile of narcotic. He ate all of the food that Mak brought and asked for more. Mak exuded forced cheer, excessive enthusiasm for feeding his old friend, though he never stayed for long. If he happened to come when Percival's dressings were being changed, Mak briefly glanced at the wounds but quickly summoned a smile and a greeting.

Percival thanked Mak for helping him, apologized for being such a nuisance, and lamented the fact that he was still too weak to stand. Mak told him to take his time, reassured him that all was well at the school. When Mak was gone, Percival walked unsteadily across the room and back. At first, he had to rest on the bed after doing this once, but he made himself do more. Finally, he could walk in circles for five minutes before being forced to sit. His legs were weak, but did not give way on him. One idea haunted him whether he was sober or drugged—the idea of being in the same room with Dai Jai and Jacqueline, all three unable to look at one another, unable to speak. He knew what he had to do, the one solution that would keep this from happening.

During the siesta one day, Percival dressed himself, put on his shoes, and pocketed a needle, syringe, and all of the little brown glass morphine vials that he had accumulated. He checked that the hallway was empty, and slipped out of the hospital. He had come to a decision. He would ensure that Dai Jai never confronted the triangle that included his lover and his father. Outside the hospital gates, the city sprang upon Percival—yelling vendors brandishing food, gesturing beggars, former soldiers with limbs missing, and beckoning cyclo men advanced towards him like shock troops. He waved at a cyclo driver and half-fell into the chair as he gave the address of the Saigon apartment. He was both exhilarated and terrified to be out of the hospital, on his way to Jacqueline and the solution to his problem. He was scared of what he was about to do, but he could not inflict on Dai Jai the pain of returning to Saigon to find the truth.

Percival went up to Jacqueline's apartment in the clanking elevator. He knocked on the door, his knuckles making a hollow appeal on the wood. There was no answer. Perhaps Jacqueline had gone out for a walk. Laing Jai should be at his school right now, he thought, grateful for the boy's absence. He knocked again and called her name. He fingered the morphine, the syringe and needle in his pocket. Should he go out into the street to look for her? The apartment was quiet, yet she felt close.

Then Percival thought he heard the tone of her voice within, a low word. His imagination? He banged at the door, "Jacqueline!" He thought of her smell, the comfort of her arms. She might just be waking from a siesta. Seconds, a minute, passed. The door did not open. Had his ears tricked him? He was near collapse from this effort, his heart pounding, or was that from his fear of what he must do? The frosted window at the end of the hallway glowed silently.

Perhaps he should go through the market. At this hour, Jacqueline might be buying food for dinner. She would be surprised to see him on his feet. Would she embrace him? He wanted to hold her one last time. What if she had moved away to a cheaper apartment? What then? How would he find her? Perhaps Mrs. Ling would know, he thought, with a sinking stomach.

These thoughts tumbled along as Percival stood exactly where he was. His fingers lay flat on the door. He banged at it again, heard himself breathing. He leaned against the door frame, unable to tell whether seconds or minutes or years had passed. Then he heard feet on tile. Jacqueline appeared. She wore a silk robe. Without interruption of thought, he kissed her, embraced the solidity of her body, his hands instinctively slipped within the robe, felt her warm hips.

She stepped back, turned her mouth away. "What do you want?" She gathered up her silk robe and wrapped it around herself.

"To make things right." He shoved his hand in his pocket, clicked the vials of morphine, reminded himself that there was only one solution to this problem.

The apartment looked exactly as it always did, but something was different. Was it the smell? Perhaps it just seemed new to him after weeks in a hospital bed, as the city itself had.

"You can't make things right," she said. Firmly, Jacqueline eased Percival back towards the door.

"Wait," he said, stumbling, realizing the frailty of his injured body. "Listen to me. I have thought of a solution."

"I don't understand."

"You can have what you have always wanted." He braced himself against the door frame.

"Please go, don't make it worse." But she did not move to push him out. She crossed her arms over her chest.

"I have been thinking about this difficult situation."

"Is that all it is?"

"Dai Jai will be back soon. I want to have my son back. But I love you more than I ever imagined I could."

"There is no use in saying these things," she said, eyes wet.

"I have the solution—a way for you to be happy, and for me to have Dai Jai back."

"You had better go." Jacqueline glanced back towards the bedroom.

"I will pay anything, any price, to buy you and Laing Jai a way out of Vietnam. I have connections with the Americans, and money. You have friends at the Cercle. Mrs. Ling sells departures. The price does not matter. I will mortgage the school, if needed. We will find a way."

Now she pulled her robe tighter around herself. She did not come closer. Percival had expected that she would be happy, or at least grateful. Instead, Jacqueline seemed shocked. Was she thinking about it, he wondered, what was there to think about? It was what she wanted. Slowly, she shook her head. "It's too late. A long time ago, I pleaded with you that we should all leave. You should have done it then." Her face began to crumple.

Percival reached for her shoulder, but she shook him off. He said, "I will not go, but I will send you. Don't you see? Whatever happens in Vietnam, you will be safely in America. Dai Jai will return here, and I will have my son. He will not hate me for loving you. I'll even send you with money. Take it all, what use is it to me?"

"As if I was never part of either of your lives," she said.

"It's a solution," he said weakly. "It's the best I can think of."

"*Hou jeung*," she said, "I am paying for my own departure." She turned and went down the hallway. Percival followed her towards the bedroom. In the doorway, he stopped. Jacqueline stood next to the bed, lost. The sheets were jumbled on the floor. On the near side of the bed sat Peters, fumbling to do up his belt. His feet were bare and his shirt open.

Peters froze. He said quickly, "Percy, there's some misunderstanding here. If I had known you were still—"

"I understand," said Percival.

Jacqueline slumped on the bed. "Mr. Peters is going to take us away." Then she added, "We have fallen deeply in love." She looked at Percival. "I will be Mrs. Peters. We will raise Laing Jai as our own son in America."

Percival closed his eyes. A storm of words battered him nonetheless. Peters was struggling with an apology, saying that Jacqueline had told him that it was over between herself and the headmaster. The scent of sex on the air made Percival feel as if he was being suffocated, his chest squeezed. Peters stammered about not wanting to jeopardize the State Department's relationship with the Percival Chen English Academy. Had Percival been unwell? he asked. Why the bandages? Not to worry, he added, Mak was handling employment referrals. Percival opened his eyes, half-expecting that Peters might have vanished. He was there, still talking. Percival went around to the side of the bed where Jacqueline was huddled. He knelt before her. He said, "I love you." She continued to cry. "Dearly, truly." He went on, "And perhaps this does not matter. Maybe this has all been nothing more than a strange dream . . ."

Peters was gathering his things. Jacqueline's eyes met Percival's for an instant, and then she reached across the bed for Peters. She took the American's hand. "Stay, my love. The headmaster is just leaving."

Percival turned to go, stopped, said into Peters' ear, "Do you know that I won her in a game of mah-jong?"

"This is an unfortunate moment." Peters pulled Jacqueline closer.

"I won her like a pile of money."

"Now, Percy, I think you're upset with me, so—"

"No! I'm angry with myself. I thought it was a lucky night. I somehow forgot that she is a whore."

Percival walked out of the bedroom, down the hallway to the door, forced himself not to look back at the apartment where he had been most happy, and continued out. His leg ached. His hands shook, and his belly cramped. How long had it been since his last morphine? If he felt bad now, he told himself, it was for lack of a drug, not a woman. He pressed the elevator button. He heard the rumbling of the gears and fumbled in his pocket for a vial. The details of the bedroom floated before him: the dark hair on Peters' bare chest, the spoiled bed. Percival managed to break open the vial, a little of the precious liquid spilled. Still he saw the spent condom on the floor near the undergarments, the gleaming black dress shoes and patterned men's socks. The elevator door opened. Percival half-fell into it and sat on the floor, slumped against the wall. He pressed the button for the lobby. As it descended, he barely managed to get the trembling needle into the vial. He drew up the drug with the syringe, his whole body shaking like a plucked wire. He closed his eyes, but he still saw Jacqueline on the bed. Saw Peters pulling her to him. In the gesture he could see that their bodies were still awkward with one another. That would change. Summoning his strength, Percival plunged the needle into his vein and pushed the dose into himself.

He ordered himself not to think of Jacqueline anymore. He would not think of Laing Jai, either. Dai Jai would be back soon. The past few years, his mistake of loving a *métisse*, the illusion of a family, must all be discarded. The elevator opened and he stumbled out into the lobby. He would need to find more morphine. Many gambling dens sold heroin, morphine capsules, and other diversions. That world was a faithful friend to anyone who could pay and it had been waiting patiently for him. Percival walked into the brightly steaming day, hailed a cyclo, and told the driver to take him to Le Grand Monde.

PART FOUR

CHAPTER 25

1975, CHOLON, VIETNAM

On the eve of Tet, Percival shook a handful of morphine capsules out of the pill bottle in his desk drawer. He broke one with his teeth and let the bitter powder spill over his tongue, felt the warm relaxation begin to dissolve into him. He washed one down whole with water so that the drug's caress would filter more slowly into his body. The rest he slipped into his shirt pocket for later. From the school safe, he removed a thick bundle of piastres. Enrolments were down somewhat, but there was still money in the safe and morphine in the desk. Percival called the driver, a dour Northerner, Trinh, whom Mak had insisted be hired, to take him to Le Grand Monde. He would welcome the New Year there, inviting both good luck and pleasure. He would drown out the old year with the noise of celebration.

Lights strung over the door of the casino greeted him, winked blue, red, and white. In the old days, they had all been white. As he entered, he was swallowed by laughter and shouting, by the promises of women's flashing thighs, by the soft glow of amber-filled glasses, and the chatter of the gambling tables. Percival entered a game of *pie gou*, threw a wad of money into it, won a fast round. It was good luck, an early win. A girl in a yellow dress kissed him on the cheek and fed him an oily morsel of duck from a platter. She whispered in his ear, something explicit in French that Percival half-understood. Her legs were like Jacqueline's, an elegant length. Had he already taken her to bed? He couldn't remember. Weeks and months folded in on themselves behind him. There was only the present. He leaned to kiss her, closed his eyes, a flickering tongue. The taste of duck clung to his mouth. He bit her lip gently, then harder. She slapped him lightly, flitted away. Now he lost a sum of money at *pie gou*—he wasn't sure how much, more than he had won. He drifted to the roulette table, where he ate roast pork with one hand and placed his bets with the other. The dealer offered him a highball glass full of cognac. He settled in, drank to his wins and washed down his losses.

As Percival played, a *métisse* girl in a tight blue dress smiled at him and laughed from across the room. He had a weakness for blue. Then he saw Huong making his way over through a clutch of gamblers. Since he had cast off Jacqueline, his old gambling friendships had been renewed, at least with those who were still in Vietnam, and who were still alive. Huong, who had become bald and heavy over the years, had been forced out of the Italian shirt business by cheap Indian tailors. He managed to scrape by selling Thai marijuana and hashish, mostly to the white ghosts. His gambling luck had not improved. Huong's outstretched arms welcomed Percival. "The headmaster is here! I hope you've brought your luck for me. *Hou jeung*, old friend, what will you have? A Martell and Perrier? Champagne? I'm so glad to see you. Listen, I've had a run of losses tonight." He clapped Percival on the shoulder. Percival reached into his pocket out of habit, not looking, handed over a fistful of bills. "Just thirty? Give me fifty thousand, as a loan, just for an hour. I'll pay it back." Percival reached into his pocket for more. Then Huong was gone, already shouting out a bet on the game of thirty-six animals.

In profile, the girl in blue reminded him of Jacqueline. He beckoned her with a slight motion of his little finger. The dress was tight, and as she walked towards him he stared openly at the swaying of her lower ribs, the points of her nipples moving with her exaggerated steps. She came close and smiled. Straight on, close up, the resemblance to Jacqueline evaporated. He took a big swallow of cognac. Percival offered her his glass, and she drank from it. He asked her to stand to his side, kissed her cheek, and told her to sing an old Chinese song.

She asked, "You like me?"

"Why shouldn't I?"

Waiters circulated with platters of food and crates of Champagne for Tet. Percival emptied his cognac and took a bottle of Champagne. Corks began to pop, a chorus following the explosions outside, and the Year of the Rabbit had arrived. So much noise that he only saw her mouth forming words, did not hear a single one, didn't care. A conspiratorial wink, and he said, "You are pretty, and I'm sure even nicer from behind." He could not tell if she had heard.

He thought she said, "What song should I sing?" though she might have said, "How long is your thing?" A lewd stare.

"Sing 'The Maiden at Sea,'" he replied.

Her laugh was lusty, nothing like Jacqueline's. "I don't know any Chinese songs, *hou jeung*. I know Bee Gees, and Elvis." She swayed her hips back and forth, as if to demonstrate the music she knew.

The stereo blared the first song of the New Year, and the girl began to mouth the words. Some American rock song—it made his ears hurt. She twisted her hips, and Percival pulled her by the hand, installed himself at a mah-jong table and sat her sideways on his lap. His fellow gamblers cheered his arrival. Percival poured a round of Champagne, drained a glass himself, caught a waiter by the elbow and ordered shark's fin soup to be brought for the table on his tab. The players washed the tiles and began to build the walls. Making reckless, uncalculated bets, Percival soon won a big pot. Everyone shouted over the rock music as the play continued. He won another pot, and the girl leaned in to kiss his lips. He pushed her away, a reflex, but then put his arm around her and pulled her mouth to his. He lost a sum and felt lighter. She rubbed her ass on his groin, slipped her tongue into his ear, which, when she took her tongue out and blew into it, felt cold and ticklish. Percival laughed out loud, felt the tightness in his centre. Jacqueline would never have done such a vulgar thing. The girl's hand on his back was grasping, eager. She whispered that she liked him.

Percival said, "Then come home with me. I want to see how beautiful you can be."

That evening, before setting out, he had asked Mak again about Dai Jai. He had been waiting almost two years. Now he asked only from time to time, as seldom as he could bear. It was humiliating to get the same meaningless reply. "Dai Jai is coming," Mak had said, as he always did. No, he did not know exactly when. The boy was on his way. He could provide no details. Things were complicated in Hanoi, said Mak, as if Percival would be sympathetic. Percival must not worry, Mak said, he should try not to think of it.

There had been one letter since Mak had reported that Dai Jai had been brought out of China to North Vietnam. It had been a brief note, smuggled south. "I have arrived safely in Hanoi. I am eating well.— Thank you, Father." Was it true, that the boy was safe in Hanoi? Percival sometimes wondered. He did not allow himself to press that question upon Mak, for he did not want an answer that would cause him any further doubt. He must believe that his son was safe. At his lowest moments, Percival asked himself what did it matter whether he believed it or not? How did that change anything for Dai Jai? The impotence of this thought infuriated him, and inevitably led him to another dose of morphine. Percival now roamed the family quarters of Chen Hap Sing for hours, tolerated only Teochow cooking in the house, and left only to gamble and bring home a girl.

At some point, Percival realized Mak had fully taken over the American contacts on behalf of the school, and in any case he was in no state to represent the Percival Chen English Academy. For a while, Mak had been busy with new friends—the peacekeepers. Percival had seen Mak with books on his desk—*Basic Polish*, *Hungarian for Beginners*, *An Indonesian Phrasebook*. When President Thieu declared in January of 1974 that the war between South and North Vietnam had resumed, it was the American advisors who became important to Mak once more.

This was the second Tet that Percival had endured without Jacqueline, or his younger son. He could not stop thinking of Laing Jai that way. He would be seven today. Was he having an American birthday, with balloons and costumes? Or were costumes for a different occasion?

After winning another round, Percival put his hand on the girl's thigh, slid a finger under the edge of her dress. In the old days a girl might have drawn away, out of real offence or at least the attractive pretense of shyness. There were no such girls at Le Grand Monde, perhaps not even in Saigon anymore. The girl in blue took Percival's hand from her skirt. She fondled his middle finger, lifted it, and then sucked it into her mouth from the tip down to the base. The other gamblers laughed, but no one beyond that table noticed the gesture amidst the rippling noise of celebration, the open swirl of words, flesh, money, and bluish smoke that was a sweetly mingled haze of marijuana and opium.

Later, in Dai Jai's old room, Percival asked the girl not to speak. He half-closed the shutters so that only the most faint grey moonlight entered. He said, "Go on your hands and knees." He asked her to turn her face to the side, to see her in profile. He lifted her dress, pulled off her underwear. He rubbed her gently, tenderly, until she was swollen wet and her scent rose. The smell was different—always it was different—from Jacqueline. If only he could find a girl with the same scent, he could close his eyes and the shutters and simply breathe while making love. This girl asked if he was only going to pleasure his hand, and then gave a drunken laugh.

"Shhh," he said, and drew close, the skin of his thighs sticking with sweat on her buttocks. When he entered her warmth, there it was already—the disappointment. His own naked loneliness. Some distant voice mocked him, did he think he could fool himself? He willed himself to stay erect. The girl arched her back and began to squirm and writhe theatrically. He said, "Don't move so much." She stopped. Now, she was too still. He fumbled, undid the buttons on the back of her dress, pushed it up over her shoulders. She lifted it off her head. His hands stroked her hips, explored her body. Her back was too muscular, her breasts too firm. He grabbed her pelvis on each side, and went deep inside, pulled her onto him. He swung her back and forth, her body swaying on her knees as she moaned.

Being high and horny was his excuse, his justification, but somewhere deep, no matter how furiously he copulated, he knew this was a mockery of what he longed for. He threw his weight into the girl, screwed her to push out his thoughts, fucked her to make himself disappear, slapped his body on hers and with each thrust, each blow, he tried to know only what animals knew, and moaned with the rhythm, begged his excitement to eclipse his sadness. She reached back and grabbed his legs, dug her fingers into them. Where the old coat hanger wound had healed, he felt a stab of pain and gasped. She called his name, mistook his pain and frustration for passion.

He grabbed her hands and roughly crossed the wrists behind her back as if she were his enemy, his prisoner, pushed her down into the bed and forced himself onto her, ground his pelvis on her ass, felt her sex contract. Her face was sideways against the mattress, but now, even in the dim light, he could not pretend. Angry, he pushed himself over and over into her wet centre, his leg hurt him but he did not slow, for now it had begun and might as well be finished.

He heard her moan, felt her spasm grip him, and his sex discharged the angry fluid of his body. His animal rush was its own death; it did not set free a moment of abandoned pleasure, as it once had with Mrs. Ling's introductions. Instead, the sorrow of absence entered and occupied him whole.

There was no fooling himself, no erasing the shame of having taken his son's lover for his own, and no way to push out his longing for Jacqueline. The ancestors' spirits would curse him, crouched over a whore in his son's bed, in his father's bed, a bed where he had loved Jacqueline. He pushed away the girl. Guilty disgust. He rolled onto his back. He thought of the morphine in the desk drawer. Perhaps he should have taken some. The sex might have been better. Or at least he would have felt it less. He heard himself mumbling sheepishly, apologizing. She wouldn't know why.

She breathed hard for a few minutes and then slowed. She turned, sat, looked at him inquisitively but without words, and then crouched over him. She began to kiss him, slowly, down his chest and belly, took him into her mouth. He let her continue, for a while. He stroked her head gently and lifted her mouth from his shamed organ. He said, "It's too hot," and turned away.

Percival went over to the desk and fumbled in the drawer. He found a capsule and bit it, let the bitter powder dissolve on his tongue before swallowing. He sat on the edge of the bed. He should take all the morphine, one last time. But then what? If Dai Jai was truly on his way, should he find his father dead? He must wait.

Outside there were small rapid explosions. It was fireworks for Tet. He lay down, very still for a long time. Now that the screwing was done, even peering through the gathering cloud of his drug, he lamented the pointless theatre. It was a condemnation of himself to bring a girl here like this, as it was every time he did it.

Should he pay her now? Show her the door? But that would be unkind. He had done enough wrong. He listened to the firecrackers, to the girl's breathing, until he heard her relax into sleep. Then he got out of bed and opened a shutter, allowed the moon in. Outside, the square was empty except for some soldiers drinking on the steps of the church. From their accents, they sounded like Hmong from the mountains—it was said that they were the bravest fighters, usually thrown into the worst battles, but now the South Vietnamese government had withdrawn several of those units to Saigon. Whenever he looked out the window, he imagined Dai Jai's familiar frame appearing across the square. Would he come by day or night? There was no choice but to believe that he would come. Here he was, Mak's prisoner of silence. Percival reached into the desk drawer for the bottle of pills.

SINCE LEAVING THE HOSPITAL, PERCIVAL HAD not gone to the Cercle Sportif. At first, he did not wish to run into Peters or Jacqueline, and even after enough time had passed that they would have departed for America, Percival did not want to see any of his American contacts. Mak must have also decided that this was best and had convinced Cho of it. Percival returned to the casinos and gambling houses at night, where he took particular pleasure in winning money from *gwei lo*, and in the afternoons he played mah-jong at the Sun Wah Hotel with a group of old faces. It was a little group that gradually grew smaller and smaller, as one person's French papers finally came through, as another's daughter was able to sponsor him to Canada. Chang, who had become an importer of Swiss watches, stopped coming to play. Everyone suspected that he had boarded a boat one night and would re-appear in Hong Kong. Later, they learned that he had been kidnapped and then killed because the family was too slow in raising the ransom. Mei went to America for a police training course and did not return. He bought a liquor store in Florida, it was said, paid with cash.

During an afternoon downpour in the middle of March, Huong sat opposite Percival on the covered patio at the Sun Wah Hotel, and shuffled cards for a game of gin.With only two players on this day, they were forced to take up cards. Huong said, "*Hou jeung*, I have a contact who can arrange departures. I'm going to leave. Why don't you buy a departure too? The price is a little high, but this guy has good connections, it will be a smooth deal."

Percival swirled the ice cubes in his whisky. "Some of the old-time Chinese traders say it doesn't matter if the North Vietnamese conquer all of Vietnam. It is just a new army, they say." He looked past Huong to a skinny boy standing in the rain, staring at them from just beyond the edge of the patio. Percival sipped his drink. He said, "They have seen new uniforms many times. We have, too, but they have seen even more. There will always be *sang yee*, business. So what reason is there to leave?"

"The North Vietnamese have overrun Hue."

"You are confused. President Thieu ordered Hue to be abandoned."

"True. Last week's order was retreat. Then he changed his mind and ordered it to be held at any cost. It fell two days ago. An American helicopter pilot told me that many Southern soldiers had civilian clothes under their uniforms. As soon as they were out of sight of their officers, they became civilians and disappeared. Flying above he saw them doing it."

"Are you still hanging out with those white ghosts? Is that one of those CIA pilots? Those guys are paid a lot, and they are reckless gamblers. You are still selling them hashish, I suppose. Nice fellows, that bunch, I win money from them."

"Former CIA. They call themselves Air America."

"Of course, as they are out of the war."

"Anyhow, this pilot warned me to get out. He says the communist troops will be in Da Nang by the end of the week, and the president is keeping a plane for himself on standby, loaded with gold. Thieu will flee to Taiwan and let Vietnam hang."

"*Sang yee*, old friend, there will always be business. Maybe I can open a Chinese school, since the North Vietnamese are so friendly with Mao. We Chinese will always find something to make a nice profit." Percival took a long swallow of his drink.

"Those who say that are so old, they don't care if they are killed," said Huong. "Besides, you think the Vietnamese communists will love us Chinese in Cholon? Even in China, you and I would be shot as capitalists, old friend. Don't you remember 1968? The Northerners buried their prisoners alive, didn't even bother to shoot them first. That is the reason to leave."

Having caught Percival's eye, the boy smiled brightly. He was soaked by the rain without seeming to care. After the fall of Phuoc Long province to the North Vietnamese Army in January, a flood of refugees had arrived to live on the streets of Saigon and Cholon. Across the street, a banner hung from a deserted government office, declaring, "Phuoc Long Will Be Retaken!" though there had been no counter-offensive, and already the Northerners had pushed far deeper into the South. The rain plastered the boy's shirt over his collar bones and shoulders. His eyes were dark and intense, his two hands outstretched. Percival waved the boy over. He gave him a hundred piastres. The boy bowed deeply, and scurried off.

"But that was 1968," said Percival, sipping again.

"And you think that the communists have grown more kind since then? Five thousand American dollars each gets us to Manila."

"What? Ten thousand dollars? We could buy an airplane. And who is this snakehead?"

"It's my friend, the Air America pilot. It's easy—he'll sign papers that we have been employees of theirs, logistics or administration, something like that, and we fly from Tan Son Nhut in two days. They have started getting their non-essential staff out."

"Ah, Huong, you see? *Sang yee!* Even your CIA pilot sees an opportunity! These Americans have learned how things are done in Vietnam. Saigon is so good at spreading her legs and selling herself that the Northerners will soon be paying up just as the French did, as the Americans did. Even now, as they wait to be conquered, Saigonese are trying to decide whether the best profits are in hoarding food or fuel. Food might spoil, but fuel could explode during the fighting."

"I know, I know what people say. Some think Saigon will be left alone by the communists, a gateway to the outside, like Hong Kong and Berlin, but why take the chance? Let's get out now, you can always come back."

Percival took a big slug of whisky. "I say food and fuel. Let's invest together in both. Let's fill Chen Hap Sing with sacks of rice and drums of gasoline."

Huong leaned forward. "*Hou jeung*, it is different this time. This is the time to leave. You can afford it. You have lots of money."

"But to go where? I have everything I need here."

"Everyone knows that in the towns the North Vietnamese have taken, they begin their arrests and executions with those who supported the Americans. People like you. And me."

If Dai Jai did not come, Percival thought, he would not care if he was killed by the invading army. He would not wish for Jacqueline and Laing Jai to die with him, so perhaps it was best that they had long since escaped. Percival reached into his pocket, extracted a medicine bottle and poured some liquid morphine into his whisky. "Just because the Americans use me here, you think they will welcome me in their country? I won't be useful to them there."

Huong said brightly, "Fine. Maybe you don't think the communists will win. Alright, let me get right to it. You stay here. Lend me the five thousand dollars. It's nothing for you."

"Sure. How much is that in piastres? I'll give you whatever you want."

"*Hou jeung*, I need dollars if I am to pay for my departure. Or gold, a hundred taels."

"I can lend you piastres. You will have to find the dollars or gold yourself."

"Ah, *hou jeung*." Huong threw up his hands. "You haven't put any away in your safe? Don't you know? In the past few months, gold and dollars have become more rare than a true patriot in Saigon!"

Percival shrugged. "Deal the cards."

Dejected, Huong began to deal, and as he laid out the cards, a little group of refugee boys ran towards the Sun Wah Hotel, their feet patting the wet mud. They each held out two hands, grinning widely. Percival drained his glass and beckoned them all over. The little gang rushed to him, reeking of sweat and garbage. He opened his wallet and took out all his piastres, several thousand, which they seized and grasped at, and then they fluttered away, thanking him and bowing as they ran.

CHAPTER 26

IN FRONT OF CHEN HAP SING, the square grew louder and busier. After the fall of Da Nang to the North Vietnamese Army at the end of March, more refugees appeared each day, squatting in the open, lying beneath the orange canopy of the flame trees' blooms. By mid-April, Cholon's streets were more crowded than Percival had ever seen them. The square was dotted with shelters hastily built from bamboo and plastic sheet. The soldiers stopped dismantling them, and instead collected bribes to leave them alone. These structures grew like mushrooms from the side of Chen Hap Sing, a few families jammed into the space where the egg-hatchers had lived during the Japanese occupation. Some building owners chased the squatters away, but Percival did not care. Monks circulated amongst the refugees, handing out bananas to children, taking sick people to doctors.

The casinos had only cheap local rice wine. Quieter than usual, they invented a new bet. A dealer explained it to Percival one night. "We have a new wager—a one-week bet on the takeover of Saigon. It pays out five to one, so a thousand-piastre bet will pay five thousand in a week if there is a communist flag hoisted at the presidential palace."

"They will come," said Percival.

"Then this is a bet for you," said the dealer to Percival. "Give me your money! If you think the Northerners will defeat us within the next month, lay a weekly bet and you will at least break even. If they come fast, you will win big." Percival put ten thousand piastres down, and did the same the following week. He could no longer find morphine on his own, and so he had to sheepishly appeal to Mak, who managed to supply him with the drug.

From the school to the church, people ate and slept outside, tried to buy what they needed and sell what they could. Young men from the countryside milled about, oblivious to cars honking angrily to get through and porters shouting curses in order to pass. When they saw soldiers, they vanished, for fear of being pressed into uniform. Families displayed belongings in front of their shelters to sell—an iron pot, an army canteen, a sullen young girl in lipstick. At night, the reverberation of distant explosions from the countryside north of Saigon rolled across the square like gentle thunder promising rain. In the morning, ragged lines of helicopters trundled low over the city, making their way out to the battles. They went out flying slowly, like angry dragonflies, laden with new soldiers for the fight. They came back more quickly, lighter.

It became very difficult to get from Cholon to Saigon. The road teemed with people the whole way. Most were not going anywhere. What were they waiting for? Percival wondered. The lucky ones had settled under the shade of tall acacias. The less fortunate suffered in the sun. Now, seeing all these people out in the heat, Percival noticed that many trees along boulevards had been cut down. Roadways that had once been shaded had been widened, the asphalt pushed out to the walls of buildings and the tall canopies of leaves banished. It was not recent. The pavement was already cracked and worn, but somehow Percival only noticed it now. On quieter lanes, banyans still stood, and in La Place de la Libération, the flame trees had been left alone.

Gasoline was more expensive than liquor, and harder to get. One afternoon, after hours of searching in the market, Trinh reported that he had found only enough fuel to fill the car half-way. Percival told him to lock the Mercedes safely within Chen Hap Sing and leave it there. That night, it occurred to him that he could go to Le Grand Monde by cyclo, but why should he? He anticipated no pleasure in gambling. In fact, he had lost it long ago, had been going just because there was nothing else for him to do. In the past few weeks, the casino girls paid more attention to white men, desperately hoping to screw their way out of Vietnam. Their first question to any *gwei lo* was, "You want nice wife make you so happy?" Huong had disappeared at the beginning of April—he must have found the money for his American snakehead, thought Percival, or perhaps had paid in pot.

Mak managed to obtain narcotics for Percival, but this gave only soothing dullness. Drifting from pill to pill was to live underwater, a false life beneath the surface of the real one, intruded upon by distant words and coloured shadows. Day became night, and day again, as the flowers of April bloomed with an exuberance that made them unreal to Percival, and the occasional noise of heavy artillery kept time, beating gradually closer.

Sometimes Mak disappeared for days. At other times, Chen Hap Sing was a gathering place. Men knocked on the door of the school at night, rapping with distinct patterns, codes, before being admitted. Percival heard them talking downstairs, tense discussions, urgent planning. Some had northern accents, some southern, some sounded like they were Cambodian, others Chinese. They spoke seriously and excitedly—a mixture of languages, most often Vietnamese. Percival did not know when Mak had moved into the school. Vaguely, he remembered Mak saying that he had suspended classes, paid the teachers bonuses, and helped the foreign teachers get good prices on airfares home. One day, the house staff all fled except Trinh, who was now always at Mak's side. Mak explained that the staff did not want to be associated with the Percival Chen English Academy, a notorious haven of American-lovers. The staff ransacked the pantry before leaving. Foong Jie wordlessly showed Percival where she had hidden a crate of tinned fish and a twenty-kilo bag of rice as an emergency supply of food. He tried to get her to take it for herself, but she patted her bundle, indicating she had already taken what she needed. She accepted the thick sheaf of piastres that Percival offered her, bowed, and left by the kitchen door.

One morning, about a week before the end of April, Percival woke and discovered that his flask of liquid morphine was empty. He rifled his desk drawer, but there were no more pills. Mak was normally so good at keeping him supplied. Percival went down, found the school empty. He climbed the stairs to the balcony, thinking that he might see Mak coming across the square. It was impossible to spot individual faces. People milled about and argued, scolded children, squinted up into the sky, agitated each other. There was the sharp crack of an explosion. Children in the square began to cry. Percival heard the door behind him and turned.

Mak was there with a tray of food. "You must be hungry."

"These are our liberators?" Percival asked Mak.

"Yes, we are almost free." Mak set down a round bamboo container, food from a vendor. He sat a teapot in the middle of the table, put out two small cups, and then poured cold tea. He placed a familiar pill on the table. Percival ached to consume the drug immediately, but he did not want to display his eagerness. He pressed his palms on the balcony railing to quell them. Below, saffron-robed monks chanted monotonously into their megaphones. They called in Vietnamese for all to submit peacefully to the liberators, but no police or soldiers clubbed or arrested them. The army observation posts seemed to be abandoned.

"I see priests circulating in the crowd as well."

Mak uncovered the bamboo container and arranged the dishes and chopsticks for both of them. "The Catholics are urging people to confess their sins—before it is too late. They suffer from colonialist religious delusions, the flawed lessons of the French Jesuits—but they have the right spirit. A little re-education and some of the priests will serve the revolution. Soon, everyone will confess their sins, against the people, not the white man's god."

A breakfast of cold *bun* noodles sat on the table—a Vietnamese breakfast. The noodles were as white and light as clouds, crowned with crushed peanuts and a few chopped green onions, carefully arranged. There was no roast meat or fish. Percival thought of the morning meals he had once enjoyed with Dai Jai. Mak stood by the side of the table, awkwardly still now that he had arranged Percival's food, long enough that Percival could no longer pretend he thought Mak was about to leave. There were two chairs—at some point

Mak had put the second one out once more. Finally, Percival said, "Teacher Mak, please sit."

Mak said softly, "Thank you, comrade. You may wish to take up the habit of calling me comrade." They both took their chairs and, once they sat, looked instinctively past one another, into the distance.

Over Mak's shoulder, from the direction of Tan Son Nhut, an airliner rose. A silver ship like this one had long since carried Jacqueline and Laing Jai to their new lives, thought Percival with some relief. The only thought he had of the future was Dai Jai. Percival tried to pick up the noodles with his chopsticks, but his shaking hand dropped them. He could not wait any longer. He took the pill, washed it down with cold tea, and already felt a little better. A moment later, with the morphine settling him, he realized how hungry he was.

"When will they be here?" asked Percival, swallowing a gulp of noodles.

"It will be a few days, at the most a week. We must be ready for the people's victory. You must be ready." Mak clicked his chopsticks together. "It is time to be free of your addiction, *hou jeung.*"

Percival poked at his noodles. "You mean, my medicine."

"Opium was an instrument of colonial domination," Mak said.

"Your domination, you mean? You have been bringing me the pills to keep me quiet, so I don't reveal your spies."

"I have been trying to help you. I know you've had many reasons for pain . . . but now, I have very good news for you. I want you to enjoy the new society when it arrives, so this is the last time I'm bringing you morphine."

Percival drained his tea. "Why should I care about the new society?"

"Although for a period of time I kept certain things from you, I always thought of your well-being. When Saigon is liberated, you will have been on the side of the victors, a revolutionary hero. I may be one step ahead of you, old friend, but I will not leave you behind."

The noodles were half gone already—Percival felt embarrassed for eating so quickly. He said, "You are so far ahead of me, that I can barely recognize you. Did I ever know you, really?"

"The facts have been adjusted," said Mak. "You have been part of my work from the start, a loyal agent of the Viet Cong intelligence network, and will be well placed in the new society."

"I want to see my son. That's all I care about."

Mak lifted a clump of noodles and ate them with slow pleasure, as if they were a fine dish he, himself had prepared. He swallowed. "Dai Jai is near. That's my good news. He is very close to Saigon." He leaned forward and said, "We are near enough to liberation that I can tell you. Wait a little longer. Dai Jai will soon arrive."

"He will be here soon?" It had been so long since he had felt hope that Percival experienced it like a new emotion. "He is near? But why wait? Where is he?" Percival wanted to embrace Mak, to tell him that he forgave everything if Dai Jai was home. He put down his chopsticks and stood. "If he is near Saigon, let's go get him. I've kept gasoline in the car for this situation! Call Trinh to get the car."

"No, be quiet," said Mak, glancing around at the balconies within earshot, "not so loud. He will arrive at the right time, in a victor's uniform. Don't you understand?"

"I don't understand a thing anymore," said Percival, looking down into the square. A frail boy of six or seven years lay motionless in the sun, a mother trying to rouse him.

"All these months, with the North Vietnamese Army advancing south, you have not suspected my plan?" A distant explosion, then a child began to cry. "Your longing for Dai Jai will be satisfied with victory and peace."

Percival's dejection was as complete as the brief flash of hope had been. He gestured out at the crowd of refugees with his chopsticks. "Do you think they expect peace? Is that why they have come?" Another round landed a little nearer, like footsteps approaching. The noise of the crowd grew.

"The shells are on the city's outskirts. Parts of the Southern Army are foolishly stubborn. These peasants don't know what is happening. They have fled here in panic. If they understood, they would be happy for their liberation," said Mak. Both men ate, silently, until this last comment had drifted into the breeze. Mak leaned forward and said, "Headmaster, I put Dai Jai in a North Vietnamese uniform to cleanse his background, as I have yours. He and his comrades are becoming the heroes of Vietnam, as we speak."

"Dai Jai is a soldier?" Percival bundled the tablecloth in his fist. "I sent him to China to avoid the South Vietnamese draft. Now you have him fighting on the other side?"

"He is on the right side of the war, just as you and your school have been part of the struggle. I have adjusted your past, and Dai Jai's."

Percival released his grip. "And Mr. Cho agreed to this? So I am a Viet Cong spy, and Dai Jai is a Northern soldier. If we adjust our memories sufficiently . . . they will suit the present, yes?"

"The future, actually. I have convinced General Cho that it makes him look even smarter, for he had an agent who was well known in Saigon society, frequently seen at the Cercle Sportif, deeply connected with the Americans. I've made sure that he wrote you into his reports. You are Deep Cover Agent B. You have been with me from the time of the Japanese." Mak handed a small plastic bag of painkillers to Percival. He said, "That's the last, Chen Pie Sou, I can't get more."

"And when will I see Dai Jai?"

"Soon. Be patient. I've told you too much already, but I wanted you to have hope." Mak stood, bowed, and slipped away.

Percival opened the bag and took another pill, felt a little relief. He was tempted to take one more but forced himself to close the bag, rallied himself, and went out to the market. He hoped to find cognac, but instead settled for a case of vermouth, for which he paid ten times the normal price. In Dai Jai's room, the room that had been Chen Kai's, Percival poured the pills, such perfect white pebbles, from the plastic bag into an empty cognac bottle. Percival filled it up to the neck with vermouth and watched the pills become a cloud of drug. It took a few hours for them to be fully dissolved, and the light was already failing when the solution was ready. Then, Percival poured himself a teacup full. The bitter elixir helped his craving, dulled its sharp edge. Percival closed the shutters of Dai Jai's room and sat on the bed. He did nothing except allow time to pass. When darkness came, he drank another cup, stripped to his underwear, and slept.

OVER THE NEXT FEW DAYS, WHENEVER Percival felt the shakes and sweats coming on, he drank a teacup of the drug-infused vermouth and topped up the bottle with fresh liquor. The mixture was not enough to completely ward off withdrawal. As the solution became more dilute, he spent hours in bed trembling. His belly cramped and his leg throbbed until he was so exhausted that he drifted into fitful dreams. He saw blood and battle, flashes and screams of death. He saw Chen Kai dressed as a soldier. He tried to make out what kind of uniform, whether Chinese or the plain garments of the Viet Minh, or was it a Japanese uniform, a disguise? When Percival woke, gasping, the dream was gone, but his father's spirit was no less present. If anything, it was stronger, as Percival lay doubled over in the same bed that his father had lain in while withdrawing, fumbling for a sip of his remedy.

Percival thought of his father's cure from opium, wondered if fate had decreed that he must re-enact it. Perhaps Chen Kai's spirit had returned and entered Percival to replay that time. Details, particulars that he had forgotten, became vivid. Or was it just a trick of his mind that he could see Chen Kai's trembling lip, smell the diarrhea and vomit of his father's suffering? But then, no trick was necessary, for Percival himself shook, and ran again and again to the toilet.

By the time Chen Kai had got to the last of his infusion, there was hardly any opium in it, only a faint haze in the mixture. One evening, Chen Kai took the bottle from his son, uncorked it, and poured the dregs out the window into the street. It was done.

Chen Kai's appetite returned voraciously. He ate noodles, rice, and soft buns filled only with a spoon of crushed peanuts—nothing else was available. It was hard to supply enough food for his appetite, even simple fare, on account of the Japanese occupation. Chen Kai began to do daily tai chi—twenty-four forms, then thirty-six. From dawn until dark he exercised with the same fervour with which he had recently demanded his opium pipe. Over several months, strength and weight returned to his body. He ignored Ba Hai completely, despite her efforts to anger him by flaunting her lover. He must have built his rice business in the same determined, relentless way, Percival realized, oblivious to everything outside a focused cone of attention. For the first time, he saw his father with adult's eyes—he admired his single-mindedness, and was wounded to understand that Chen Kai must have, at times, been capable of forgetting him and Muy Fa in Shantou.

"Father," Percival had said, "rest a little. You have just recovered from your opium illness. Now you can regain strength gradually."

"No, I must be strong to travel," he said. "I yearn for home. I will return to Shantou, to your mother's grave."

Percival stared at his father, happy that he remembered his first wife, shocked at this suggestion. "It's impossible. The Japanese control the ocean from the Philippines to Manchuria."

"I will go by land," Chen Kai said.

Did his ears deceive him? Had his father recovered from opium only to lose his mind? They would almost certainly die trying to make such a journey. Cecilia might refuse to go—and she would be right. Percival said, "We are lucky in Saigon, because the French kowtow to the Japanese, so they are less vicious here. But there is a war under way, Father."

"There is no choice."

"The countryside is a battleground. My new wife is making me crazy, but I do have to think of her safety."

"Oh, no." Chen Kai got to his feet. "You cannot come. You must stay and be a good husband. Protect Chen Hap Sing. If we are both gone, Ba Hai will steal everything. I must return to China and worship at the grave of your mother or my soul will never rest. It is my duty."

Percival was unsure what bothered him more—that his father wished to travel through a war, or that he had no intention of taking Percival with him. He did not know which to protest. He said, "Very well, Father. As you wish," thinking already of how he might sabotage the trip before it started. An old man travelling north by land was ridiculous. The talk in Cholon was of heavy fighting between the Japanese and the Chinese armies in the north. Refugees from the countryside said that in the villages, Japanese Kempeitai kept control by mutilation and public execution, while at night the Viet Minh assassinated those suspected of collaborating with the Imperial Army.

Months passed, and though Chen Kai continued his daily tai chi, he said nothing further about travel. Percival assumed that the idea had evaporated, a brief fancy. One night, having returned to his bedroom with Cecilia, Percival heard a door creak and footsteps hurry down the stairs. It took a moment for him to realize what he had heard, to rise, and then to run through Chen Hap Sing's dark hallway to Chen Kai's room. His father's bed was empty. He rushed down the stairs. He stood at the door of Chen Hap Sing, stared into the night. The square was empty. Drifting wisps of cloud danced with a wavering moon. He called for Chen Kai. Only crickets replied. He felt the same loss as when his father had first left Shantou.

Over a week, Percival's withdrawal diminished to the point where it nagged rather than tortured. He drank a glass of water with each teacup of vermouth. He found he could venture briefly onto the balcony in the day, for his eyes were no longer pained by the light. If he stayed too long, he got a headache. One night, Percival watched as flares arced high and then floated down in burning, phosphorus speckles. They were close. From the direction of Saigon, explosions flashed up against an overcast sky. There was a helicopter, its red darts of tracer fire. Percival sat and watched as if they were festival fireworks. He was transfixed by the display, but too exhausted for emotion. The air stung with sulphur. In the light of one flare, Percival saw a pillar of grey smoke that rose from the direction of the airport. From that quarter of the horizon, artillery roared like storm clouds. After several hours of this, there was a noise closer by, on the stairs of Chen Hap Sing. The liberation had come. Percival wondered placidly if he would be arrested or shot. Boots clattered through his bedroom and the balcony door burst open. It was Mak.

"Oh, you have come to see the fireworks," said Percival.

Mak said, "Big brother, I have great news."

"Shouldn't you call me comrade?"

"Dai Jai is here."

"Where is he?" He listened for another set of feet. Tears began to stream down his cheeks. "Thank you, friend. Is he downstairs resting in his room?"

"No, I am going to fetch him."

Mak wore a green jacket of the Northern army that did not fit him well. "As a special favour to me, General Cho has agreed to use his rank to remove Dai Jai from his unit, which is fighting near the airport. There is a battle for Tan Son Nhut."

"Then he is in danger."

"It is almost over, but the 11th Airborne are holding out." Then he added, "Soon, we will cheer the victory of the people. Give me your car so that I can collect General Cho, and we can pull Dai Jai out before the final assault."

"Where is Trinh?"

"He has a new assignment."

Percival hurried downstairs with Mak behind him, found the car key, ran to open the clanking exterior doors. He got in the driver's seat and started the engine. The headlamps shone into the square. He was glad he had conserved the gas.

Mak reached into the car quickly, shut off the car's lights. "No, you stay here, *hou jeung.*"

"I'm coming with you."

"You can't come."

"How can I not go? He's my son."

"There is a battle. I can only move around there in uniform."

Percival got out of the car, its engine thrumming, the lights off. Mak got in, released the parking brake. Standing beside the car, Percival wondered when he had become so compliant, so dependent upon Mak. Or had it always been that way? Mak put the car in gear and very slowly eased ahead. Percival yelled, "Please, bring him home quickly."

"I will keep my promise to you, brother," said Mak, smiling confidently—pleased with himself. A rare display.

Percival brought the last dregs of his foul vermouth mixture up to the balcony and had a miserable sip. The night felt stuck in time, a darkness disturbed only by explosions that spattered up from the direction of the airport. Percival prayed to the spirit of Chen Kai that he help Mak and General Cho to find Dai Jai quickly. The noise of fighting continued, and Percival told himself that at this distance it was impossible to know if the explosions were actually from the airport. Perhaps it was fighting in a nearby neighbourhood, and Tan Son Nhut had already been taken. It might be farther back in the jungle, and Dai Jai might be safely out of harm's way. How long would it take them to return? Each time a car approached, his hopes rose, but it was always a darkened army Jeep creeping through the streets rather than his Mercedes coupe—in the night it was impossible to see if it was a Northern or Southern vehicle.

Percival meant to stay awake, but after several hours put his head down on the table, intending only to rest for a moment. Now he was a boy standing before his father. In this dream, Chen Kai sat on a carved rosewood bench, drew on a black opium pipe, inhaled the drug and kept it in for a long time before exhaling the sweet smoke from his nostrils. He mumbled around the pipe that the boy must pay his respects, must honour tradition. Percival tried to approach the bench in order to kowtow, but his leg was swollen and grotesque. Chen Kai saw his son's pain and held out the pipe. Chen Kai called him by name—Dai Jai. He called him Dai Jai. Percival looked up and saw Chen Pie Sou, the *hou jeung*, sitting on the rosewood bench, weeping, straining to pass the pipe but somehow unable to rise from where he sat. He was Dai Jai, throbbing in pain, and just managed to seize the opium pipe in his hand, but as he put it to his lips it burst into flames. Still, he wished to smoke it, raised it burning to his mouth. Percival woke drenched in sweat, fumbling for the teacup, the bottle of his bitter elixir, took a mouthful, but now the taste made him nauseous. He spat it out, eased his head onto the table, was rewarded with dreamless sleep.

Percival woke clear headed. He felt no desire for morphine. His tongue was thick, dry. He drank water. A bright morning shone. The horizon was dotted with exclamation marks of sooty smoke rising from fires scattered throughout the city, but there were no explosions. There were no rockets, no mortars. From one side of the square, Percival saw an army truck lumber along without urgency. It was not a type of truck that he had seen before—it was tall and angular. From the cab flew an unfamiliar red and blue flag. In the back of the truck, instead of troops or guns, was a loudspeaker. One soldier stood next to the loudspeaker, reading into a microphone from a piece of paper.

"There has been an uprising, a joyous people's revolution. Crowds are welcoming the liberation. The forces of the National Liberation Front are now masters of the city. Henceforth, Saigon is renamed Ho Chi Minh City. Do not be afraid. Respect order and discipline . . ."

Just an inch of liquid was left in Percival's cognac bottle. He ignored it, poured a glass of water instead and drank it. Then another. His craving had been expelled. A column of unfamiliar vehicles rolled into the square. The Northern army's tanks and troop carriers entered the city in clanking lines. The soldiers atop were sinewy and tough, some barefoot. The vehicles were layered with branches and vines, as if they had risen from the jungle and now dragged it with them into Cholon.

Percival went from room to room in Chen Hap Sing, called out, searching for Mak and Dai Jai. He wandered each classroom, confronted by silence. He returned to the balcony. Would Dai Jai be here soon? The empty fish tanks glared at Percival in recrimination. Would his son be disappointed that the fish were gone? He waited for the door to sound, for footsteps, and imagined the voice of Dai Jai. Instead, he was harassed now and then by the chatter of the loudspeakers on the Northern army trucks. *"Women must dress decently, all must wear modest peasant clothing—black or brown. Clear the streets for the National Liberation Front Army. . . ."*

There was no sign of the cream-coloured Mercedes. The horizon above Tan Son Nhut was marred by a steady column of grey smoke, a jagged charcoal stain on blue. Occasionally, a Southern army helicopter darted into the sky from the direction of Saigon's city centre and flew straight and fast for the ocean. Why had he not gone with Mak last night? Now, with a clear morning mind, Percival was furious at himself. He could not wait any longer. He must go now. Percival went to the school safe and stuffed his pockets until they bulged with piastres. Even if there were military roadblocks, surely the new conquering soldiers would respond to money the same way the old army had. He hailed a cyclo and offered the driver a thousand piastres to take him to the airport, ten times the usual.

The driver waved refusal at the banknotes. "Those are worthless."

"This is good money."

"For starting fires. The Northerners have cancelled our currency. Do you have food to trade?"

"I will give you two tins of fish."

"Two? Forget it. Five to the airport and back."

Percival ran into the house, retrieved five tins of fish, and went out to clamber into the seat. Soon, they were rolling through streets that were well known to Percival but were already made strange by the occupying army. The new blue and red flag was tacked over the doors of post offices and banks. At some corners, Northern soldiers searched vehicles. At others, they stood with long scissors, singling out men for haircuts if they judged it necessary. Twice, Percival's cyclo was stopped, and soldiers asked in their Northern twang whether he had been a soldier, policeman, or a puppet of the Americans.

"No, I am a schoolteacher," Percival replied in Vietnamese, and was waved on.

As they got close to Saigon, a boyish soldier directed the cyclo to detour away from the Hotel Duc. Percival objected at first, because it would add more time, but the cyclo driver simply began to pedal in the direction in which the soldier had pointed, smiling and bowing his head at the Northerner.

"Are you crazy?" the cyclo driver exclaimed, when they were out of earshot. "Don't get me killed." From the direction of the hotel came the rattle of a machine gun, and then a few single shots.

"I won't pay extra for the detour," said Percival.

"Never mind that. The American spies forgot to send helicopters for their Vietnamese agents billeted at the Hotel Duc, so they are fighting to their deaths, which will soon arrive."

"Saigon's new masters are here," said Percival.

"You mean Ho Chi Minh City, comrade!" the cyclo driver piped up with a wry wink. "Oh, yes, we are liberated."

As they rolled along, Percival searched the faces of the Northerners in uniform, so young but hard from battle. The cyclo passed a tank parked on the road, where a slim Saigon girl joked with a pimple-faced tank gunner. She wore a long, respectable dress that did not diminish her attractiveness. The seduction of the newcomers had already begun. On Rue Truong Minh Giang, the cyclo steered around a dozen or so young men stretched out on the ground in South Vietnamese uniforms, hands bound behind their backs. People walked delicately around the pools of blood that seeped from their heads. Percival looked away, and the rest of the street appeared much as it always did.

As they neared the airport, Percival told the driver that he was looking for a Mercedes coupe, that some friends had come out here in such a car during the fighting. The cyclo driver muttered that Percival's friends must be crazy and Percival equally insane to think he would find the car. This district was littered with the debris of battle. Some buildings were burned down, others had been shelled into rubble. The bodies, or only portions, lay in the sun—a shredded torso tangled into a shirt, a leg in trousers. An old woman called out names in a daze. Survivors picked through rubble. What could they be looking for? Percival wondered. What was left? Someone could ask him the same, he realized with a shock. They approached an armoured personnel carrier that was as black as a lump of coal.

"The Airborne was dug in here. It was the most vicious battle," said the driver. "Whatever your friends came for, they probably turned away."

"No, they came here."

"Then they might not be here anymore. I'm an idiot. Huh. Five cans of fish." The cyclo driver huffed with breathless resignation, eyes forward. Through the back hatch of the personnel carrier, Percival glimpsed a charred torso slumped against a useless machine gun. A helicopter had crashed into a house. Its tail section hung over the street and its rotors were folded like blades of grass broken in a storm. The air stung with acrid smoke.

At first, Percival didn't recognize the Mercedes, and the cyclo driver almost pedalled past it. Percival called, "Stop!" as he stumbled out of the cyclo towards the car. The windows had been shot through, or had burst in the blaze that had consumed the car. The vehicle sat on its wheel rims, the rubber of the tires having burned away. He stared at the torn-open hood for a long time. It had been penetrated by a shell, or a rocket? From another world, barely audible to Percival, the cyclo driver called at him to get back into the cyclo, to stop wasting time if they were searching for a light-coloured car. In some places, curls of cream paint had been left by the flames. The car emitted a stench of burning rubber, gasoline, and burned flesh. Percival went around to the front to read the licence plate—his own.

He forced himself to look through the space where the windshield had been, and then to walk around the car. The driver's door was open, a blackened corpse sprawled half out of the car. Mak's glasses lay on the ground near the skull, lenses shattered into cobwebs. On the other side of the car, still in the passenger seat, was the charred husk of a man slumped over. A burned hand still held a pistol, the arm out the window, flesh seared onto the weapon. Percival drew closer and saw the metal stars of Cho's rank on the shoulders.

The third figure was in the backseat. Hands clawed at the window, frozen there by flame. Face burned beyond recognition, the earthly opposite of a ghost. Percival fell to his knees, silent. A faint smoke still wafted up from somewhere within the car, where something inside continued to smoulder.

"We are almost at the airport, mister," called the driver. "Isn't that where you wanted to go?"

Percival pulled himself up and stared. The neck was bare. He laughed through his tears. He turned to the driver and yelled, "It's not him, he's not wearing the charm!" If only saying it could make it true. "It is not my son! This is not really my car!" He was unable to pull his eyes away from the figure. No, it could not be. Percival stumbled back into the seat of the cyclo. "Go back, back to Cholon," he wept. "He does not have the lump of gold on his neck." Percival beat the frame of the cyclo with his fists. "Go!"

The driver shrugged. "Even if we didn't get to the airport, you are paying me the same." He stood on the pedals and pushed the handlebars hard to one side to turn them back to where they had come from. As they began to move, Percival glimpsed his licence plate, but surely one could not be certain of the numbers after such a fire. He kept his eyes open, for whenever he closed them he saw the blackened remains of the car's third passenger, distorted by pain, struggling for escape. "The lump of gold was not on his neck," he said to no one.

CHAPTER 27

AS THE CYCLO ROLLED AND BUMPED him back to Cholon, Percival searched the faces of the soldiers. Again and again, he thought that a profile resembled Dai Jai, believed at a distance that a soldier was his son, only to be disappointed when he saw the face clearly. At a checkpoint, the cyclo driver growled at him to sit back, to quit staring at the Northern soldiers lest they become angry.

"Don't make trouble, mister." The cyclo driver pedalled along, eager to deliver his passenger. "Remember, we are nothing, the defeated."

As they neared La Place de la Libération, Percival was determined to hope. Mak was too canny to be killed. Any three soldiers could be dead in that car. Mak and Dai Jai might be at Chen Hap Sing already, waiting for him. They passed an army truck whose loudspeakers droned, "*Collaborators with the Americans must write confessions and present them to officers of the people's army. Former police and security forces must register and surrender their weapons. Confess now, and you will be treated leniently. If you fail to confess, penalties will be severe.*"

When he got back to Chen Hap Sing, Percival prowled from room to room, flung open the doors of the echoing classrooms, searched the long-vacant family quarters, called for Dai Jai, and for Mak. After combing the building twice over, Percival sat in the school office. Dai Jai could appear at any moment, he forced himself to think. Should he go out and look for pet fish? No. He must be here when his son returned. Percival had given the charm to Dai Jai. It had been passed down from Chen Kai, from a line of ancestors, and it kept the wearer safe. The third dead figure, its image seared in his eyes, did not wear the lump of gold. It could not be Dai Jai. To displace this image, he tried to picture the vast empty sea at Cap St. Jacques, where he had once believed Dai Jai was lost to the water, only to see him walking down the beach, saved by the charm. It was hard to summon the feeling of the hot breeze, the wet smell of salt. He found himself desperate for the details of that day.

The phone on his desk rang. He jumped to answer.

"Hello!"

"Percival, you're alright?" Jacqueline's voice rang clear from so far away.

"Yes."

"I'm worried for you," she said. "They haven't come to arrest you?"

"I'll be fine. Mak has fixed it up."

"Of course he has . . ." she said.

"Are you calling from America? How is Laing Jai?"

"He's doing fine. You're safe? What is happening there?" she asked.

"I'm waiting here . . . just waiting for someone," he said.

"For whom?"

Could he share with her the pain, the burned bodies? Talking to her made him feel naked, and it was harder to circumvent the truth. He longed for Jacqueline to help him carry this. But he was ashamed of the truth.

Percival said, "I'm waiting for Dai Jai." It felt so good to say that.

"Oh."

"He is in Saigon. Nearby."

Her voice was kind, generous. "I'm happy for you, and for him."

"I haven't seen him yet. Mak is bringing him." Percival felt he could use a pill or a drink. Neither was at hand. "Any moment, I'm expecting him . . ." Whatever the truth was, why should he weigh Jacqueline down with sadness? Yes, he would permit them the indulgence of speaking and hearing these words. Unknown to him for years, she had also shared the weight of Dai Jai's departure for China. But now, she and their son were safely in America. She had loved Dai Jai too, let her imagine his safe return. His voice cracking, Percival said, "He is a hero, one of the liberators, as Mak says. When we last saw him, he was barely past being a boy, and now he has grown into a man." There was a long silence on the line until Percival said in a broken voice, "What should I do, Jacqueline? You see, I'm confused. I don't know what to do." Tears flowed down his cheeks. "I love you."

"You must welcome him," she said. "I will not come between you . . ."

"I'm glad you loved him—"

"Nor between you and Laing Jai. Without me, Laing Jai could be Dai Jai's half-brother."

"What do you mean?"

"Laing Jai would like it . . . if you took him to the zoo today. Be at the zoo entrance at three," she said. "Let him be Dai Jai's half-brother. You love them both. It will work."

"I don't understand."

"I have to go now." Now it was her voice crumbling. "I'm so sorry, everything has changed."

"Has it?" he said. Why was Jacqueline calling? Where was she? "Wait."

"I love you, and I have to go."

"I'll do whatever you want. Don't go."

"At three. It's the best thing, my love," she said, and hung up.

He held the telephone, heard the hum of the dial tone, and put down the receiver. Silence stretched out. Percival was unable to stand or look around, aware only that he continued to breathe, waiting. He wanted what he had said to be true, that Dai Jai was coming, and he said it again aloud, just to hear the words. It was not the same without someone else listening, believing. There was no knock, no arrival, and still he sat, hours later. Had he really heard Jacqueline's voice? he wondered. Or was that also just something he wished for and had imagined? The office door was closed. The room was very hot. Percival realized that the ceiling fan had stopped. The air was suffocating. He was hungry—but the thought of eating nauseated him. He did crave his drugs, a lingering need, and hated the craving. He picked up the phone to call the Saigon apartment. Was she there? The line was dead now. Had she really called?

Yes, that had been real, he thought with a start. He checked his watch. It was past two. In the car, it would take half an hour to reach the zoo. But the car was gone. In a cyclo, it would be almost an hour. He took a few tins of fish to pay for the ride and rushed outside.

As the cyclo creaked its way towards central Saigon, Percival saw that since morning some pockets of the city had become strangely festive. North Vietnamese soldiers sat on their tanks and armoured vehicles, and vendors gave them free snacks, addressed young foot-soldiers as 'big brother.' Here and there, piles of uniforms and flags burned, the insignia of the old power cast into flames. Many of the Northern soldiers now wore American boots, and Colt sidearms. The newcomers examined the streets of the city, as curious and lost as tourists. Percival was stopped at checkpoints and asked if he had been a member of the police, the army, or a collaborator. No, he mumbled, he was a simple teacher.

They approached the zoo. Percival saw Laing Jai standing alone just outside the gate. Jacqueline was not there. Percival stepped out of the cyclo and was almost struck by a black Lambretta scooter. He crossed the street, ran towards the zoo gate, and lifted Laing Jai up in his arms, hugged him close. The boy was not wearing his imported clothes. Today, instead, he wore very simple blue pants and a blue shirt, which appeared to have been carefully chosen for their plainness.

"You've grown! I'm so happy to see you. Your mother called. At first I thought she was calling from America. I don't understand—what happened?"

"I was scared you would not come," Laing Jai said, and he released the tears that he had held inside while waiting. It had been almost two years, and the boy was taller, more solid, and just as beautiful.

"Shh, I'm here." Percival held the boy for a long time, amazed that he was real. "I thought you had flown away, both of you . . ."

"Mr. Peters said to stay in the apartment, he would fetch us, but when we didn't see any more helicopters taking off from the embassy, we knew the Americans were gone. *Mama* said that you would be at the zoo today, but I was scared you might not come."

Percival did not know what to say. "Shall we visit the animals?" He wiped away the boy's tears.

"Yes, *baba*." Laing Jai gripped Percival's hand tightly.

There was a handwritten sign over the gate. WELCOME TO THE NORTHERN LIBERATORS! PLEASE VISIT FREE OF CHARGE. Percival and Laing Jai wandered the grounds slowly, without speaking. The animals went about their business as usual. Turtles splashed in their shaded pool. Elephants blinked and occasionally batted their ears. Percival steered Laing Jai away from the monkeys and big cats. He longed to see Jacqueline. If she was in Saigon, he realized, he would have to tell her the truth about Dai Jai. Would she hate Percival for what had happened?

They sat on a bench to rest under the heavy limbs of a banyan tree. Percival asked Laing Jai, "When did your mother say she would come for you?"

"*Mama* isn't coming."

"She isn't?"

"She said she has another way to escape, but that I couldn't go with her. *Mama* said I must stay with you from now on." Laing Jai's eyes began to fill with tears again.

Percival put his arm around Laing Jai. "Didn't Mr. Peters promise to take you both away a long time ago?"

"*Mama* asked him all the time when we would leave for America. She gave him all the gold she had saved, to buy air tickets. He always said it would be soon but he had to stay a little longer for his work. But now he is gone."

"The American broke his promise."

"*Mama* cried so hard when the helicopters stopped. I must go with you, she said. She would see me in a better place. *Baba*, does that mean you are taking me to America? Is that where we will meet *Mama* again?"

Percival forced himself to breathe. "We must go to the apartment."

"*Mama* said that I must not go back. She made me promise not to go back there."

Percival pulled with gentle urgency on Laing Jai's hand. He said, "Yes, she's right. You must wait downstairs, but I forgot something there. I must go and get it."

When they arrived at the apartment, Percival hugged Laing Jai and told him to wait in the lobby. The boy sat cross-legged in a corner on the cool tile floor. The elevator was not working. Percival laboured up the stairs, his shirt soaked through with sweat. Once upon a time, they had been pleased to find an apartment on the eighth floor, a lucky number. His leg screamed. He stopped at each landing, but then pushed through the pain up the last two flights. Percival went down the hallway and tried the door—it was not locked. He eased it open.

Jacqueline's shoes sat on a woven mat inside the door. Percival called her name. So often he had come here anticipating the pleasure of the woman he loved. But the last time he had found betrayal, humiliation. He pushed open the bedroom door. The bed was empty, and had been made. He peered into the living room. It was tidy, the shutters all closed. He felt that he was intruding upon the careful order of an apartment that was no longer his home. Yet while it was, he had tried so hard to pretend that it was not. He looked into the kitchen, empty.

Percival found Jacqueline in the bath. She wore no makeup. She was most beautiful that way, he thought, with a bare face. Her hair radiated around her, softly drifting. She was dressed in a white *ao dai*, the colour of mourning. Her eyes, peering out from beneath the water, were eternally still. Percival put his hand out, disturbing the water with his fingers, and closed them. He stroked her face. Her skin was the same temperature as the water. Did it contain her last warmth?

Ripples emanated out from Percival's fingers. The cord of the hair dryer snaked from the outlet over the edge of the tub and into the water. The dryer itself had slipped from Jacqueline's hand, submerged. She wore a thin, finely woven gold chain. Resting in the soft indentation of Jacqueline's neck was a rough, unshaped lump of gold. He brought it to the surface, rubbed it, and knew it by touch. Percival's sobs rose as if he were being choked from within, but he wept silently, afraid that a neighbour might hear. He undid the chain and clutched the charm in his hand, sank both of his arms into the water, held her cold form, and hoped for the return of the electricity.

And then he heard a voice, calling, "*Baba!* Are you here?"

It had taken Percival a while to climb the stairs. The boy must have become scared and followed him. Percival yanked his hands from the water as if scalded. He must not abandon the last person he loved. He stood, put the charm in his pocket, walked out of the bathroom, and closed the door quietly behind him. The living room of the apartment glowed with diffuse light from the bright edges of the shutters.

"Wait there. Don't come in. *Baba* is coming."

"*Baba*, I was afraid to wait alone," Laing Jai called from the hallway.

Percival ran to the door, folded the boy in his arms, forced himself to bury his own tears. Laing Jai was small but strong, so much like Dai Jai had once been.

"*Mama* forgot to pack you a suitcase. We must bring some of your nice clothes. You wait here, stand near the door and I will pack for you. *Gwai jai*." A good, obedient boy.

Percival found a valise and filled it with Laing Jai's plainest, sturdiest clothing. He searched for Laing Jai's identification papers, found them in a bureau and put them in his pocket. About to leave, Percival remembered what was going on outside and thought to check the kitchen. He found painfully little food—a half-kilo of rice, a small pickled ham in the silent refrigerator, a little packet of dried pork. He shoved all of it into the valise and hurried to the front door.

At the threshold, Percival stopped and said to the boy, "I have something for you." He took the gold charm from his pocket and put the chain around his grandson's neck.

CHAPTER 28

IN THE LATE AFTERNOON, THE CYCLO drivers slept in their vehicles at the corners of the broad avenues. Percival offered the single can of fish in his pocket, and the drivers said that this was not enough to take a man, a boy, and a suitcase all the way to Cholon. The other scraps of food did not persuade them. Percival lugged the suitcase in one hand and clutched Laing Jai's hand in the other. They stayed on the shaded sides of the streets and made their way slowly. They had gone down these roads many times with Jacqueline, to restaurants and cafes, around the market roundabout. What if this morning he had told Jacqueline that Dai Jai was dead? Would she be walking with them now?

Laing Jai looked tired but did not complain. He asked about the unfamiliar things he saw, an artillery piece with a red star on the side, the thin soldiers in green uniforms, the hastily painted banners that hung on homes to welcome the victors. He had many questions, but Percival had few answers. A group of soldiers stopped them, and the officer asked to see their identification. He asked who Laing Jai's father was. When Percival said that he was, the officer looked confused, made a sour face, and examined the papers for some time. The officer waved them on and muttered, "American dog." As they walked past, a soldier sneered at Laing Jai and spat on the ground. Laing Jai shrank closer to Percival.

"Just keep on walking," said Percival, taking Laing Jai's hand.

Halfway to Cholon, cyclo drivers still refused to take them even this shorter distance. One driver said, "Eh, mister. No one is going to take the little *métis*. Not worth the trouble." He cocked his head at a nearby patrol.

When they finally saw Chen Hap Sing, it was almost dark. Laing Jai cheered up and asked what dishes the cook was making tonight. Could they have oyster omelettes? "Everyone has gone," said Percival. "It is just the two of us now."

In the kitchen, Percival figured out how to light the burner, measured out a small amount of rice, and put it on the stove. When it was done, he put two salted fish on top. He watched the boy eat. He put Laing Jai to bed in his own room on the third floor, then lugged in another mattress and put it against the wall for himself. He went out to the balcony. Last night, the sky had been full of violence, now it was quiet. It was the same city as the day before, but washed new. He thought of Jacqueline's voice on the telephone. Percival went back into his room, sat watching the sleeping boy breathe. His duty, and guilt, stood like a wire fence around his sorrow, hemmed it in.

The next morning, the army trucks' loudspeakers blared, "*People of unified Vietnam, welcome the liberating soldiers with warmth and obedience. Illegal migrants from the countryside must return to their homes. People of unified Vietnam, welcome the liberating soldiers with warmth and obedience . . .*" Each day, the same messages were broadcast. The ham and dried pork were soon gone. Soldiers went from house to house, searching and questioning. Percival went through the school's books and hid a collection of them along with Dai Jai's kung fu novels and Marvel comic books, under a loose floorboard in the family quarters. He hid the remaining cans of fish there, as well.

A week after liberation, Percival heard banging on the doors of Chen Hap Sing. It was a group of soldiers. The officer in charge had no rifle or sidearm. He was armed with a notebook. He introduced himself to Percival as the new local *can bo*, the North Vietnamese political cadre, and offered no name. He asked Percival where he would like to conduct the registration interview.

"What am I registering for?" said Percival.

"For the right to exist," said the *can bo*, and waved his soldiers into the school.

Percival led the way to the school office. The *can bo* sat down at Percival's desk, and Percival took the other chair. He heard the soldiers help themselves to the house, wandering through the halls, laughing and talking. The *can bo* lit a cigarette, did not offer one, put his notebook on the desk, opened it to a blank page of thin blue lines, and shot three questions at Percival—name, birthdate, occupation. He wrote the answers down in a small, neat script.

"So you are a teacher, eh? How did you get this house? Why is it so large?"

Percival said, "The house was my father's. It became my school."

"Ah, then you were a business-owner."

"The headmaster of the school."

"Now it belongs to the people. It is Revolutionary School Number Thirty-Seven." He flicked his cigarette ash on the floor. "You must have a lot of money. Did you steal it?" The *can bo* smiled.

"My father built this house."

"Then he was wealthy."

"He built everything with his work. He started with nothing . . ." Percival felt an impulse to say that Chen Kai had left China poor, with nothing but his desire to search for the Gold Mountain, that somewhere along the way he had lost his true home while finding great wealth. He stopped himself, and said, "He was a poor farmer by birth."

"Who became rich by exploiting his brothers!" the *can bo* said triumphantly. "A capitalist! Your background is problematic . . ." He looked down and wrote in his notebook. "We will use the building for the good of the people." The *can bo* stood and examined the finely worked window frame. "Were you a collaborator with imperialists? A war profiteer? Beware—already, your neighbours have told me a great deal." He tapped the notebook with the pen. He motioned to the school's safe. "Open it." Percival spun the dials and opened the door. The *can bo* grinned, eyes wide at the stacks of money. He pulled them out, bundle after bundle, set aside the worthless piastres. Finally, he snapped, "Where are the dollars? The gold?"

"I have been a loyal Vietnamese, a servant of the revolution!" Percival's voice rose, and he hoped it sounded patriotic rather than fearful. "I have no interest in dollars or gold."

The *can bo* paused, surprised at this claim. He continued, "You Chinese! You are capitalist enemies of the working people who sucked the blood of this war."

Percival thought to point out that China itself had been communist for decades now, a circumstance Percival had once mistakenly chosen to ignore. Something in the way the *can bo* spat the word *Chinese* stopped him. Instead, he said, "Comrade, I am a servant of Vietnam."

"You may have been a servant of the *old* Vietnam. It is my job to make you a servant of the *new* Vietnam. I am told by your neighbours that there was an English school here, and that you charged a great deal of tuition." The *can bo* sat at the desk, swept the piastres to the floor.

Percival also sat. "I can explain."

"And that many of your students went to work for the Americans. Don't you know that English is an imperialist language? Don't you care about the history of the foreigners in this country, or even in your own land—China? You ignored this and collaborated with the white oppressors?" The *can bo* stubbed out his cigarette on Percival's desk. "There is a two-week amnesty for confessions from police, army, and collaborators with the old foreign enemy. If you confess fully to your bourgeois crimes, you will be treated leniently. If we find after the amnesty that you hid anything, things will be more . . . uncomfortable for you," said the *can bo* breathlessly.

The door behind Percival opened. He recognized the footsteps. The *can bo* looked over at the boy in the doorway. Laing Jai slipped over to Percival and stood behind his chair, one hand gripping Percival's shoulder. He said, "*Baba*, there are strange soldiers all over the house, I'm scared."

"Shh."

"Who is this?" said the *can bo* with disdain, craning his neck to see the boy. "Houseboy?" He spat on the floor. "Saigon is full of these half-breeds—we'll fix that."

Laing Jai's breath was quick as he buried his face in Percival's neck. Percival said in a quavering voice, "I am a patriot, sir. I have been for years. I have been known as Deep Cover Agent B. It is in your own intelligence reports." Now he would see if Mak had really done him this last favour, if he had sufficiently cleansed Percival's background.

The *can bo* laughed. "What is that riddle, Chinaman?"

As Mak had intended to adjust Percival's past, Percival must now complete the revision of his own history. Summoning the courage of luck as he would at the casino, Percival leaned forward, but not too far. "This school was a special intelligence project for the revolution. I ran it with my comrade, Mr. Mak. Top secret. How would my neighbours know? In fact, I'm not surprised, comrade, that you didn't know I am a Viet Cong intelligence operative." The *can bo* stopped writing and looked up. "Your rank is not high enough for you to have been briefed. Comrade Mak and I both joined the Viet Minh over thirty years ago, to oppose the Japanese. Later, we created the Percival Chen English Academy in order to place Viet Cong spies in the Americans' Saigon offices." If anything would save Percival and Laing Jai, it was Mak's work. And Cho's. Percival tried to channel Mak's deft confidence, and the vocabulary of recent loudspeaker broadcasts, as best he could. "In Tet of 1968, we had such high hopes of victory. We cried bitterly to see the flowers of revolution wilted, and so many of our comrades slain by the imperialists. With that temporary setback, however, our resolve to overthrow the oppressors only grew stronger. We continued the patriotic fight against the corrupt capitalist puppet regimes."

The officer's expression softened a little, and he selected an unlit cigarette, said nothing.

Percival continued, "Thank you, comrade, for coming to complete the liberation. I have dreamed of this day." He told the *can bo* of their most inspired initiative, to gain special recognition from the Americans for the Percival Chen English Academy so that they would have direct access to all the most sensitive American jobs in Saigon and could place spies everywhere. He added, "With such good connections, anyone would have found it strange if we did not charge a very high tuition."

"Hmm . . ." said the *can bo*.

"How I rejoice to see the armies of the people in victory. This is a joyous day!" Percival grasped for the right language. In the sea, one must swim. He hoped the trickle of sweat down his temple did not betray his fear. Percival kept on talking, reminded himself to speak slowly lest he stumble over his own words, lavishing the account with any details that came to mind.

Finally, the *can bo* interrupted and asked, "Where is this supposed comrade, Mr. Mak? I would like to debrief him also."

"He has been missing since the liberation." Percival pushed down the image of the burned car. "He might be deep undercover, rooting out any remaining counter-revolutionaries. I look forward to celebrating with him."

"We will look into it," said the Northerner. His pen scratched the notebook. He lit the second cigarette. This time, he held out the pack to offer one. Percival refused. The *can bo* filled a page in his little book with notes in a tiny hand. When he finished his second smoke, he said, "The things you say are intriguing. They will require verification. Everyone in the neighbourhood says that you lived an indulgent capitalist life."

"Part of the ruse. How better to avoid suspicion than to live like those who were American puppets? In service of the revolution," said Percival as if this were the most obvious and trivial thing. He felt the same shiver that he knew from laying down a large bet on a bad hand. He smiled. "I am certain," Percival continued, "that in your patriotic intelligence branch of the North Vietnamese Army, there are many reports referring to our work as Southern Viet Cong spies. These will confirm what I am telling you, comrade."

The *can bo* took out a sheaf of papers that had been mimeographed in purplish blue ink. He wrote Percival's name on one, signed it, and handed it across the desk. "This is your residency permit. You will need it for food. Without a permit you are subject to deportation to the countryside. We will get rid of most of you Chinese, because Saigon is for the Vietnamese. Ho Chi Minh City, that is. If you are really a patriot, perhaps we will have to allow you to stay. If you lied to me, you will regret it. Don't lose your permit."

Percival looked down at the paper and read his name. He held it out. "Comrade, do the names of children go on the permits as well?"

"We do not register half-breeds. They have no place in the new society. Tell your houseboy to get out of here, to vanish."

"He is my son."

"What?" The *can bo* snatched the paper back.

"I have served the——"

He held Percival's permit up, taut between two hands, about to rip it in half. "In any case, I don't think you need him registered, do you?"

"General Cho would be so upset if anything happened to him," Percival said, "for he is very fond of Laing Jai." He felt the tingle of doubling up a wager on a bad hand. Sometimes this was the trick, to take a bet too far, so far that no one could think it a bluff. "Whatever—I don't care. Rip that up. I'll get another and have General Cho speak to your commanding officer."

The *can bo* relaxed his grip on the paper. "General Cho?"

"Laing Jai is his great favourite. Cho was in command of our special project. Mak and I reported directly to him." Percival spoke as quickly as he could think. "My son often delivered our briefings to him—who would suspect a young boy of carrying intelligence papers? Cho always gave him sweets."

"I've heard of the Viet Cong General Cho, that he has a temper."

"Yes, then you know who I mean?" said Percival. The flush of good luck was palpable. "A bitter temper. My son is one of the few people he has a soft heart for, I don't know why."

The *can bo* put the paper on the desk, scrawled Laing Jai's name, and handed Percival the residency permit. "Consider this permit temporary. We will verify your story." He stood. "You may keep one room, after I choose one for myself. I am going to tour my new school." He left the office and went down the hallway. Once he was gone, Laing Jai threw his arms around Percival. He did not cry, but only held on to Percival tightly.

Percival whispered, "It's alright. *Baba* will take care of you."

The *can bo* chose Percival's third-floor room with its handsome balcony overlooking the square. He took the old school office for his own. Percival and Laing Jai retreated to Dai Jai's room, and the *can bo*'s unit of special political soldiers occupied the rest of the building. The next day, they carted out the English schoolbooks and American magazines and burned them in a bonfire in the square. The loudspeakers directed everyone who had American and French books or magazines to bring them and burn them in the fire or face harsh penalties later. Percival secretly removed his hidden stash of books and canned fish to Dai Jai's room. He saw that the soldiers wrote down the names of everyone who brought books for burning, lists for future reference.

THE MIMEOGRAPHED RESIDENCY PERMIT ENTITLED PERCIVAL and Laing Jai to a weekly ration of food, one kilo of rice and a cabbage each. At the site of the old post office, which had been made the food depot, Percival lined up at dawn to be sure to get their ration. The cabbages were often rotting. There were usually stones in the rice. Percival read books with Laing Jai, hoping that his grandson might lose himself in the pages, careful to put a Vietnamese cover over English books in case one of the soldiers who now lived in the house happened to come into their room. Percival went out once a day—he had no money to buy anything, no reason to see anyone, but he loitered around the cafes to hear the gossip. If he recognized someone from the old days, they might exchange a quiet nod at a distance. Since they had known each other as capitalists and profiteers—though they had once called themselves businessmen—they did not acknowledge one another openly.

He wrote to Cecilia, to explain what had happened to Dai Jai. His story was safe for any censor to read. Their son had died as a soldier of the liberating Northern army. For a while there was no response, and Percival wondered whether this was because she had written something that the censors had seized, or simply that she had found nothing to say to her ex-husband. Then, after a few months, Percival received a brief note to thank him for his recent correspondence, nothing else. His mail had been forwarded to Cecilia in America. There was a return address in Brooklyn. He penned an equally short note wishing her all the best and saying that he was glad she was pursuing her dreams. Percival did not write about Laing Jai's true paternity. If he ever saw Cecilia again, he would explain the rest.

Jacqueline had been right about Vietnam's fate. Percival kept Laing Jai in the house. Abandoned *métis* children scurried in the shadows of the streets and alleyways, filthy and skinny, begging and stealing to live. In the morning, they were often found dead from the army patrols' night-time abuses.

Once in a while, Laing Jai asked about America, whether his mother had sent any letters and when they would go to join her. "Soon," Percival always answered. "Very soon." The boy spoke as if he were certain that Jacqueline was waiting for them in America. Percival was unsure whether Laing Jai actually believed this, or whether he said it because it was the best thing for him to believe. He did not contradict the boy.

When Percival saw that Laing Jai's spirits were low, he would open a can of fish for him in their room, and remind him to keep it secret. Later, he would sneak the empty tin out in order to dispose of it discreetly. Week after week, Percival and Laing Jai saw trucks arrive in the square to be loaded with people who had been told to report for re-education in the countryside. The Northern soldiers checked names off lists, slammed shut the tailgates of the trucks, and drove away. A few former teachers from the Percival Chen English Academy were assigned to teach in the new Revolutionary School Number Thirty-Seven. Others, those who had larger houses or came from more prosperous families, or perhaps just spoke with a little too much confidence, were ordered to report for re-education. Some mornings, Percival watched as someone he knew, a former teacher or student, peered at Chen Hap Sing from the back of a North Vietnamese Army truck, a wordless goodbye in their eyes. He dared not wave. He wanted to turn away, but felt obliged to at least watch them go. Meanwhile, Percival heard occasionally of other former students who received good positions in the new government—they were those who Mak had placed as Saigon spies.

In Chen Hap Sing's classrooms, the new Revolutionary School

Number Thirty-Seven taught Marxism, classical Vietnamese poetry, and political confession to the neighbourhood children. There was no question of sending Laing Jai. In political confession class, the *can bo* sat and took note of the things children said about their parents.

By autumn, no one had returned from their two weeks of re-education in the countryside. One did not ask after people who had not been seen for a while. Such queries led to a re-education order. By the anniversary of the liberation, everyone knew someone who had fled by sea, or who had either died or been arrested trying to do so. In the old days, trouble could be avoided by slipping away to Phnom Penh, but now Percival heard that the killing was even worse in Cambodia than in Vietnam.

Once the lists of the politically questionable were exhausted, the *can bo* turned his attention to deporting would-be escapees. He began to fill the trucks with people who had tried to ride bicycles out of Cholon towards the coast at night, people who had attempted to engage snakeheads who were really political soldiers in disguise, families who hid themselves in the trunks of cars heading east, or those who had sought out coastal charts or waterproof compasses. Their gold was confiscated, their houses given to soldiers and officials, and they were put on trucks bound for the jungle camps. Even so, there were the whispered rumours of escape, that someone's uncle or brother had sent word, having escaped by boat to Thailand and found his way to San Francisco, or Montreal, or Marseille.

One of the teachers who had been assigned to work at the Revolutionary School snuck up to Percival and Laing Jai's room one day, when the *can bo* had gone to Saigon. He did not knock, he simply opened the door and crept in. In the old days, this teacher had been jovial and amply fed. Now, he was nervous and thin.

"*Hou jeung*," he said. It was jarring for Percival to hear himself addressed that way. "I have come to ask you for help." The teacher glanced uncomfortably at Laing Jai, who was reading a book in the corner. Laing Jai had read all the books several times, but turned to them again and again. It was known in whispers that Percival's *métis* son lived in the house, and Percival was unsure whether the teacher was simply discomforted to actually see the boy or that something else bothered him.

"He will not betray anything," said Percival. "But he doesn't speak Teochow, if you want to talk in our old language."

The teacher peered out of the door, and then closed it softly. In a near-whisper he said in Teochow, "They will send all of us Chinese away, bit by bit. They are just doing it gradually, so that we don't resist. It is still possible to leave by boat. One must get to Vung Tau, or Nha Trang, on the coast. I've decided—I would rather risk the pirates and sharks than to wait in Cholon to be taken away. The going rate is twenty taels of gold."

Percival said, "I've heard there are communist soldiers who pose as snakeheads but will arrest you."

"One must find the right snakehead," whispered the teacher. "There have been successful voyages. A student of mine escaped to Thailand and eventually made his way to Australia. I need your help, *hou jeung*."

"But how can I possibly help you?"

"Lend me the gold."

"How can I lend you the gold?"

"There is a benefit to you. Hear me out. If you lend me the gold, you will know if this snakehead can be trusted. I will take the risk of trying her. If I escape, then you can trust her and escape yourself. Then, I will pay you back double from wherever I end up."

"What makes you think I want to escape?" said Percival. He added in a loud voice in Vietnamese, "We treasure the liberated Vietnam, comrade." He looked towards the door.

"*Hou jeung*, I wasn't sent by the *can bo* to trap you. But you must be thinking of escape, yes?" The teacher glanced at Laing Jai. "For a boy like him, to be here in Vietnam . . . there is nothing for him." Laing Jai had become thin. Percival could see how his clothing hung off him. The cans of fish were long gone. Percival gave the boy more than half of their rice and cabbage, but they both were wasting away. "He cannot stay here like this—they hate the mixed children."

Percival knew the pain of this truth, but shrugged as if it did not concern him. "And if you don't escape? What if you are betrayed and sent to the countryside?"

"Then, I will not be able to honour my debt. But then, you will not have taken the risk of going with that snakehead. I will have paid you back with my life to spare yours and the boy's."

"That is a fair bargain," said Percival, rubbing his chin. "You should have been a trader, not a teacher, as you've offered me something from nothing."

"If I had been a trader, I would be dead already. If you help me, *hou jeung*, and I succeed in getting out, not only will I pay you back double, in dollars or gold, but I can help coordinate your escape from the outside."

"I don't know," mumbled Percival. "I have made too many mistakes. Laing Jai is everything to me. I won't do anything that endangers him."

"Staying here endangers him." Laing Jai was not reading but stared at the book to be polite in the company of adults. Percival was glad they were speaking in a language which Laing Jai did not understand.

"Old friend, I would help you, but I don't have any gold."

The teacher's face fell. "But all those years, all that money . . ."

"Is gone. Stacks of worthless piastres. The soldiers who live here have used them to start cooking fires."

"How can that be? The tuitions were so high. You didn't put gold aside? Dollars? What about Mak? He was always looking ahead."

Even now, an old teacher thought that Mak would have made up for the headmaster's shortcomings. "That's the way it is, old friend. If I had the gold, I would lend it to you."

"Then I am sorry for bothering you," said the teacher. "You won't . . ." He suddenly looked very worried.

"Betray you to the *can bo*? Of course not. But tell me, who is this snakehead?"

The teacher hesitated, "Mrs. Ling."

"The matchmaker?"

"Some say she is the best smuggler, but that she plays all sides. She provides girls to the highest communist officials in Saigon."

"She is well connected."

"It may make her an especially good snakehead."

"Or she betrays her passengers. But it's probably better business to get them out." Percival smiled despite his worries. "Ah, it is always possible to do business, *sang yee*, isn't it? Do you have her address? She is an old friend."

The teacher gave Percival an address in Saigon. "Really, you swear to me, you don't have any gold? Mak didn't put some aside? It's hard to believe, *hou jeung*." Mak had been so careful in every respect but this one. But of course, Mak could not have imagined a need to put aside gold, Percival realized, for he had believed that the Northern victory would bring a new and golden Vietnam.

"I have nothing. I'm sorry."

"Then I had better go before someone sees me here," he said.

That afternoon, Percival told Laing Jai that he would be out for a few hours, and began the long walk to Saigon. Mrs. Ling had always been a straightforward business person, Percival told himself. Naturally, she had found ways to make money after the change of power. He went slowly. His leg still pained him if he rushed. The streets and squares were naked and scorching, for the trees had all been cut down for fuel soon after liberation. He had not been to Saigon since then, when he collected Laing Jai at the zoo. What if the teacher had told him something untrue, whether by design or by accident? He needed to be careful. There was no one to look after Laing Jai if Percival was sent to the countryside. Snakeheads were sometimes arrested, though many re-appeared after an arrest. They shed gold to escape in the way some real snakes shed tails. It was said that the political cadres realized it was more profitable to let them go and grow new tails.

By the time he reached Mrs. Ling's house, the light of afternoon was softening. The house stood on a quiet, well-proportioned cul-de-sac off Rue Pasteur. Except for the flags of the Provisional Revolutionary Government that had been tacked up over every door, the lane appeared much as it might have during the time of the French; porches obscured by climbing plants, the copper door knockers gone green. Percival lingered outside the address he had been given. The house was overgrown with honeysuckle. Part of the handsome verandah had been occupied by a wire pen within which chickens squawked and pecked. He began to doubt the risk he was taking. Many good houses had been taken over by officers and officials from the North. Could the teacher have been sent by the *can bo*, to see if Percival had gold hidden away? He looked up and down the street and saw that all the houses had their drapes drawn, even if the shutters were open to allow air. He wasn't sure if this should make him more comfortable or worried to be standing here.

There were cooking sounds from inside the house—the hiss of a gas stove, the clank of a utensil. There was the pop and the scent of fritters in oil, there were voices of women. Percival listened carefully for one particular voice. He heard laughing, teasing, splashing water. He stood there for a while, then thought he heard the voice that he was looking for. He waited a bit longer, and then was almost certain he heard Mrs. Ling scold a girl for making a mess of the kitchen. So now she was keeping girls here. She had previously kept them in apartments and hotels. The liberation had changed her way of doing business.

He came close, and the chickens made a racket. When he knocked, there was some hushed talk, some giggling over whose turn it was. The door opened, and there was a middle-aged woman in a plain brown pantsuit. She was well groomed, wore precisely applied lipstick, and her hair was cut short in a severe communist fashion. Her eyes darted around before she settled them on Percival.

"You are still making introductions, Mrs. Ling?" said Percival.

"Capitalists, communists, men are all endowed with the same organs."

"Aren't you going to invite me in?"

"I didn't recognize you at first—you have become so skinny. Come in."

Percival entered the front room and accepted Mrs. Ling's invitation to sit. She went into the kitchen and then brought him a cup of good oolong tea. It had been so long since he had drunk a sharp, fragrant tea. His stomach grumbled loudly at its taste, and at the scent of frying dough.

"With all the departures you arranged before liberation, you are still here?" said Percival.

"I was too greedy," she sighed. "I was making a fortune, and I didn't think it would end so fast. I had a ticket to Paris, booked for June. By the end of April, it was all over." Mrs. Ling looked healthy and vigorous. She ate well, despite everything. "Bad timing. I thought the Southerners would fight harder."

"Well, at least you are earning a living."

"The girls are still having breakfast, so you will have to wait a little. What do you have to pay with? Gold? Silver? I don't take paper, you know."

"I'm not here for a girl."

"Then why have you come to see me?" she said warily.

"I need your help."

"Ah, you want to borrow money." A teasing look crept over Mrs. Ling's face. "Haven't you heard that gambling is one of the Great Evils in the new society, *hou jeung*? Comrade, I should say."

"It's not that. I have heard that you are still in the departure business, and that you are good at it."

Mrs. Ling studied Percival. "You are bold to ask me like this, openly, here in my house. Turning in snakeheads is also good business," she said.

"Mrs. Ling, if you are a snakehead, I will pay any price."

"These people from the North, they love confessions and betrayals." Her smile disappeared. "I'm not even sure what you are talking about."

"I'm not a Northern informer," said Percival. "I've said enough that you could turn me in, too. All I care about is Laing Jai."

Mrs. Ling tapped the arm of her chair. Percival noticed that she no longer wore nail polish as she once had, but her nails were still long, carefully rounded and groomed.

"The boy is still here? Why didn't he leave with Jacqueline and Mr. Peters?"

"She is gone," he said. Percival noticed that Mrs. Ling did not refer to Laing Jai as his son. "She left Laing Jai with me."

"Ah," she said. "Then I see. You have a serious problem. The new government is unkind to the mixed children."

"An understatement. What will it cost to leave?" said Percival. "Do you have a way to arrange a boat escape?"

"I'm not saying that I do, but it is dangerous, old friend, even with the best snakehead. There are pirates, storms, boats are lost. Many who leave never arrive."

"But some boats must be safer than others, right? I will pay any price. The boy means everything to me, I can't fail him."

"What will you pay?"

"You can have Chen Hap Sing."

Mrs. Ling stared for a moment, unable to speak as if from disbelief. Percival persisted, "It is the house that my father built. It is strong, and spacious. You could use it for your business, for . . . anything."

Then Mrs. Ling began to laugh out loud, then doubled over, her hands on her legs. Finally, she sat up and wiped the tears from her eyes, waved at Percival to stop. "You don't have Chen Hap Sing to give me. Your house is now a political school. Are you still oblivious to everything that happens around you, just like in the old days? And why would I want it? If I had a big house like that, I would be the next person sent into the jungle."

Of course, Percival had known all this. He felt embarrassed for having offered her Chen Hap Sing, an absurd suggestion. At least she took it as naivety rather than a trick. He said, "Is there a way to escape? I have nothing, but I'll owe it to you."

Mrs. Ling pressed her lips together and looked down at her nails. In the kitchen, her girls were laughing and teasing one another. Finally, Mrs. Ling said without looking up, "I do have an idea. In one week, bring Laing Jai to see me. We'll see if my idea can work."

"Why should I bring Laing Jai?"

"We are done talking for today. Say nothing to anyone about this. Instead, win my trust." She stood, and tilted her head towards the door. Percival finished his tea in a gulp, ashamed at his greed for a good cup of tea, and got up. He was about to leave, but he stopped for a moment and said, "Do you remember when you introduced me to Jacqueline?"

"She is a beautiful girl."

"She was."

"Oh. I'm sorry."

Percival said, "Laing Jai was a month early."

"Yes," said Mrs. Ling.

"Did you know?"

"*Hou jeung*," said Mrs. Ling, in the frank way that one old friend could speak to another when there was no business to conduct, "there are only a few reasons why a beautiful girl who is attending a good school comes to me and suddenly wishes to be introduced to a man, saying that she is not picky, she must meet someone as quickly as possible."

"A short list of reasons."

"Perhaps only one. It may have been some strange fate at work." Mrs. Ling looked at the door. "I didn't put it all together, at first, even though she told me that you reminded her of the boy she had lost. One day, I saw Laing Jai at the Cercle Sportif, the image of you. Then I understood what had happened. But all of you were happy, and Dai Jai was in China. It would have been cruel to tell you."

Percival nodded, and went out. The light was fading fast. He hurried back to Cholon, struggled with his leg to get back before the curfew. A week later, Percival and Laing Jai slipped out of the house early in the morning and took a long and circuitous route to make sure that they were not followed. When they got to Mrs. Ling's house, she offered excellent *teet goon yum* tea for Percival and a cold Fanta with a straw for Laing Jai. His eyes lit up as he took the precious treat in both hands.

Mrs. Ling regarded Laing Jai. She said, "Do you remember me?"

"No," said Laing Jai. Percival cringed. Laing Jai had met Mrs. Ling at the Cercle Sportif, of course, but that was a world away. The boy took a tiny sip of his soda, determined to make it last.

"Good," said Mrs. Ling. "It's better that you don't remember me from before. I was a friend of your mother's."

"I miss her so much," said Laing Jai, his face now lit up. "If you are her friend, have you heard from her? Tell her I love her, and I wish she would write from America."

"*Gwai jai*," said Mrs. Ling, and then pursed her lips. She donned a syrupy smile. "Your English is good, for such a young boy."

Laing Jai waited for her to say something more, and when she did not, he looked down. Percival thought Laing Jai might begin to cry, but instead he contained the emotion he was feeling and sipped his Fanta. He gave his attention to the drink, held it with two hands.

"Do you want cookies?" Mrs. Ling asked. Laing Jai nodded, and Mrs. Ling brought coconut biscuits from the kitchen—a luxury Percival had not even seen in the market since liberation, never mind being able to offer them to Laing Jai.

Mrs. Ling produced a thick envelope. She shook the contents out on the table. There was a set of American dog tags, photographs, and letters with American stamps.

"These are some mementoes of Lieutenant Michaels, U.S. Marines helicopter pilot. He had a lover, Pham, and they had a son, Truong. Lieutenant Michaels served from '67 to '69—two tours, highly decorated. Then he was back and forth between America and Saigon, working for an American bank. Soon after the Paris Peace Accord, he was killed in a car crash in Michigan. So sad, to be killed at home after so many dangerous missions in the jungle. It is doubly sad, for he had planned to bring Pham and Truong to America. He promised to do so, in the letters."

She handed a photo to Percival. "This was taken a couple of years ago. This boy certainly could have grown to look like yours."

"Yes," said Percival, as he examined the image. Truong and Laing Jai both showed their foreign blood. Both had slightly wavy chestnut hair and soft, rounded eyes. He leafed through the stack of letters, little bundles of photos, documents in official envelopes. "What is all this for?"

"I even have love letters that Lieutenant Michaels wrote—very sweet and touching. I bought this, at a high price," said Mrs. Ling, "from Pham's parents. She and Truong were killed in the last days of the liberation. These documents will not help them. You see, there are some Americans who do care about their bastard children. They have learned how bad things are for their soldiers' offspring, how the North

Vietnamese beat them to death. So they help their *métis*, whom they call Amerasians. To make themselves feel better. Children fathered by Americans can leave on airplanes, and so can their mothers."

Mrs. Ling pointed out a photo, this with Truong in the arms of a burly American, Pham tiny beside him. "She is pretty, isn't she? She and I look alike, don't we?" The girl was younger than Mrs. Ling, but the bones of their faces had a strong resemblance. Mrs. Ling looked younger than she really was, and the war would have aged Pham. It could be pulled off.

Percival put his tea down. "You have everything, except a boy."

"Yes," said Mrs. Ling. "I will be Pham, the child's mother. He will be Truong. I have been waiting for the right boy, and perhaps you have brought him to me."

Percival thought of switching to Teochow, but then continued in Cantonese, which Laing Jai understood. "So then the price I would pay for Laing Jai to escape safely on an airplane . . . is Laing Jai."

Mrs. Ling nodded. She turned to Laing Jai. She spoke to the boy in English, and asked him to describe Mr. Peters. Laing Jai did so— spoke of his blue eyes, his loud voice. She asked him what Peters liked to eat in the morning, and what he liked to drink at night. She asked him what kinds of things Peters said when he was happy, or upset. Laing Jai answered precisely in good English. Laing Jai chose one biscuit at a time, trying to be polite, and yet he had almost devoured the whole plate already.

Mrs. Ling turned to Percival. "There are thousands of *métis* boys, but I need a boy like yours, not some poor wretch from the street. They conduct interviews to make sure they are evacuating the right people. Even in charity, they are picky. I need a boy who can remember an American, describe an American, and speaks English as well as Truong would have. Most children who would be suitable have a mother here. Laing Jai is perfect." She turned to Laing Jai. "Do you think you can play a game of pretend?"

"What is it?" The plate sat empty.

"Pretend that everything you remember of Mr. Peters is what you remember of Lieutenant Michaels. He was an American who loved me. You are our child. You pretend that I am your *mama*. If you can play this game, we can leave by airplane."

"But I have a *mama*," said Laing Jai, his voice fading at the end. Laing Jai looked at Percival to see if this was what he wished.

Percival nodded at Laing Jai with both sadness and hope. "If you can play the game well, we will go to America."

Laing Jai said in English, "Just by playing this game?"

"Yes," said Mrs. Ling. "As long as we pass the tests. This game has tests, called interviews. But it is easy—you don't have to study. Just remember, until we are on the airplane, I am your *mama*. Lieutenant Michaels is your *baba*. Whatever you remember of Peters—"

"Is Michaels." Laing Jai swirled the bottle of soda, in which he had rationed the last sip. The orange fluid spun around at the bottom, fizzing as it circled. "And what about my real *baba*?" said the boy, turning now to Percival. "How can he come with us, if *baba* Michaels is dead in America?"

"He is very smart, isn't he?" Mrs. Ling drummed her nails on her chair. She said to the boy, "Would you like another soda? Go into the kitchen. Ask one of the girls for a Fanta. Cookies, too." Obediently, Laing Jai went.

She looked at Percival. "If you agree, you will come to America later. By boat."

"How can I trust you?"

"Do you have a better option?"

Laing Jai darted back into the room towards Percival with a fresh soda and a plate of biscuits, sucking on a straw. Percival clasped the boy to him. "You see, there are not so many seats on the plane," said Percival. He must be as brave as the boy and hold back any tears. "I will come later, by boat, and you will go by airplane. I will meet you in America. It's a good game, a wonderful game. You will play it perfectly."

Mrs. Ling held out her hand, beckoned. Laing Jai shrank back and hid behind Percival's chair. He said, "If that's how it is, I don't want to play that game, *baba*."

"It's what *Mama* wants you to do. It is what she wants, and what I want. It's the best thing, I promise," said Percival desperately. He pulled Laing Jai around and put him on his lap. "I will go on the boat, which is a little slower, but it goes to the same place."

That night, as Percival put Laing Jai to bed, Laing Jai wept and pleaded that he didn't want to go without *baba*. Percival shushed him, and settled the sheets around him. He said, "Maybe you are scared to be alone?"

"Yes."

"Here's a secret. Whenever you dream, I will be with you. If you go to sleep every night and think of me, I will see you in America every night." Laing Jai gripped his hand tightly, and eventually it relaxed. Once the boy was asleep, it was Percival's turn to weep.

CHAPTER 29

LAING JAI LEARNED THE ROLE OF Lieutenant Michaels' son perfectly. Percival snuck him out to Saigon several times a week during the siesta, and when he was practising, Mrs. Ling fed them well. Percival was happy to see the boy gaining weight, and felt some of his own strength return. Laing Jai and Mrs. Ling underwent three rounds of interviews with the USAID officials, and each time Mrs. Ling reported with satisfaction that the boy had been clear and charming in describing Peters' quirks as those of Michaels. "An all-American boy," she laughed, and tousled his hair.

After round three, the USAID officials were satisfied that they were dealing with Pham and Truong, the surviving family of Lieutenant Michaels of the U.S. Marines. American visas and air tickets were issued for Pham and Truong, complete with new identity papers that had officially stamped photos taken by the USAID photographer.

As she had promised, Mrs. Ling arranged and paid for Percival's escape by boat. She fixed it so that Percival would be smuggled out of Saigon on the night that he left Laing Jai with her. It was safest to do it this way, so that when the *can bo* thought to look for them, they would all be gone.

On the appointed day, when the afternoon classes of the Revolutionary School were in progress and Percival judged that the *can bo* was having his siesta, he roused Laing Jai from his afternoon nap.

"Let's go—quietly," said Percival.

"Yes, *baba*," said Laing Jai. "Are we going to an interview?"

Percival took Laing Jai's clean white shirt and blue cotton pants from the armoire and placed them in a rough sack. Laing Jai had dressed in plain clothes for the interviews, but Percival wanted him to arrive in America properly dressed.

Percival had not told Laing Jai that he and Mrs. Ling would be flying the next day—it was safer that he didn't know, in case they were stopped and questioned.

Sewn into Laing Jai's good pants was the letter Cecilia had sent from America. In a concealed pocket that he had sewn within his own trousers, Percival had the one true letter from Dai Jai and a photo of Jacqueline. In his jacket pocket, he had the residency permit for himself and Laing Jai, but that was just in case they were stopped on the way to Saigon. Soon the boy would become Truong, the child of Pham and Lieutenant Michaels, and Percival would be making an escape attempt from which no document could rescue him if he was discovered.

Percival closed the door of their room silently behind them. Pulled it tight. They slipped down the stairs, down the hallway, to the front door. They stepped out. Percival eased the front door shut, grasped Laing Jai's hand, and they walked along in the shadows of buildings, alongside the barren square. The church's doors were chained shut. None of the priests had returned from their re-education. A few monks stood on the steps, though people were wary of them now, for some said they informed to the *can bo*. Since the incident at the zoo, Percival had not seen the one-eyed monk of whom he had once been fond. On the site of the old post office, a drab cinder-block cube now stood as the neighbourhood food ration office, built without windows to prevent theft. There were no rations today, and it was quiet.

Percival kept his eyes ahead, did not look at the houses and shops that had all once belonged to people he knew. Now, many of the voices that came from within them were unfamiliar. The Chinese owners had been sent away and the houses given to Northern Vietnamese. The strangest absence was the lack of vendors and hawkers in the square. Something pulled at Percival and he had a peculiar thought, that the Gold Mountain was behind them. At the corner, seeing that no one was nearby, Percival turned back once, saw Chen Hap Sing, already small from across the square. He looked at the house that his father had once built. It came as a surprise, this sharp ache, that he would miss the house, Cholon, even Vietnam. Then they turned the corner and walked away.

Laing Jai said, "Are we going on our trip, *baba?*"

"Shh . . . *gum laik.*" So clever.

They went in the direction of the market, away from Saigon. Percival had planned a cautious detour. There was hardly anything for sale in the stalls, so he knew it would not appear suspicious that they did not buy anything. When Percival was satisfied that no one was following them, he and Laing Jai took a circuitous route to Mrs. Ling's house. It was dusk when they arrived.

She opened the door with a relieved smile. "You are later than I thought you would be," she said to Percival. She turned to the boy. "Tell me our game."

"I am Truong Michaels," said Laing Jai. "My father was Lieutenant Michaels, Marine helicopter pilot. He loved to dance the twist. After his tours in Vietnam, he worked in banking, here in Saigon. He went home to America and was arranging to send for my mother and me. He died in a tragic automobile crash. Now, my greatest wish is to go to the land of my father."

Mrs. Ling clapped excitedly. "*Gwai jai!*" She showed them into the neat side room in the back of the house where they had practised Laing Jai's game and where he would sleep for a few hours. Their flight was early in the morning. She brought them big bowls of food—barbequed pork and vegetables on rice. When they had finished, Laing Jai said, "*Baba*, there is only one bed here."

"I won't be sleeping here," said Percival. "I have to set out tonight, to meet the boat. You will leave before dawn. I will see you in America."

Laing Jai's face collapsed. "But *baba*, I don't want to go on the plane without you."

"But that is the game. You remember."

"I don't want to go. I'll come on the boat with you."

"But the plane is much better than the boat." Percival felt his eyes begin to water. "Get to sleep now. Remember your game. You are the son of Pham and the late Lieutenant Michaels. You are an American." Percival let down the mosquito net and sat by the side of the bed.

"I don't want to go without you, *baba*."

"I will meet you there. Until then, I will see you in sleep. Think of our special story, our secret."

"Yes, *baba*," Laing Jai said.

"Tell it to me."

Percival reached into the mosquito net and found the gold charm around Laing Jai's neck. He rubbed it in one hand and took one of Laing Jai's hands in his other. Laing Jai began to recite, "Many generations ago, our venerable ancestor left Shantou to go searching for wealth in the land of the Gold Mountain." Laing Jai yawned with the familiar words. "He went to make his fortune, and in that faraway land, he found this piece of gold. Whoever wears it will be safe wherever he wanders."

"And there is no design on the charm because . . ."

"Because one never knows what form wealth will take." Laing Jai touched the gold lump around his neck and grasped Percival's hand. "*Baba*, did he ever return home?"

"Who?"

"Our ancestor, who went to find this gold." The boy's voice was already tiring.

"Well, of course he did. He brought this gold back to China. This is the proof."

"*Baba*, if it is good luck, you take the charm." Laing Jai's voice perked up. "I don't need it. The luck has rubbed off on me."

"Shh . . . sleep now."

"*Baba*, when will we return to Chen Hap Sing?" The boy's words were drifting off.

"Once you have left a place, you can never go back. I made that mistake. I thought it was possible. If you come back here one day, that house will be changed, or it may be gone. The place of your memories will have vanished, and you will have new memories. They will make the old ones feel different."

"I'll miss all the good things the cook made," the boy yawned again. "The oyster omelettes and the *mee pok* noodles."

Somehow, Percival realized, the boy recalled pleasures that were already years away in the past of Chen Hap Sing. He was glad. "But don't worry, it's inside you. Take the good luck with you, and go. The people who love you, and whom you love, remain always. Everything else vanishes. The gold lump doesn't even matter, except for what it helps you to remember."

The boy resisted sleep and turned from side to side. Night grew until darkness was complete. Percival waited. Eventually, the boy's breathing became heavy and regular.

CHAPTER 30

Chen Pie Sou was at the age of growing tall, but was still skinny as a reed. He was playing after school with friends, near the railway siding. That day, he bet the pickled duck egg in his pocket. His overseas father, Chen Kai, had not been home in years but sent enough money that his son could eat an egg every day. He wagered it against an older boy's triangle of bean cake that the train would pass through without stopping.

The train had speed at first, when it appeared far away. It laboured towards them with the steady grumble and fire of an earthbound dragon. The boys stopped and watched it keenly. The odds were on his side, Chen Pie Sou reminded himself. The shelves in the town shop were well stocked, and mail had been delivered the day before. As it came near, grew large, its brakes squealed. Even as the brakes sounded, he counted on the beast to exhale its smoky trail of breath and speckle their skin with black soot as it passed through and continued onwards.

It did seem to be slowing.

The older boy, of similar height but with almost an adult's weight, said "Ha! Give me the egg."

Raising his voice above the shriek of brakes, "It has not stopped."

"You are trying to run away from your bet." The older boy attempted to shove his hand in Chen Pie Sou's pocket to grab the egg, but he danced away. The train soon overwhelmed their voices as it ground to a stop. The older boy ran at Chen Pie Sou and tripped him before he could get away. Chen Pie Sou kept his hands up and tried to deflect the punches that came for his head. His mother would be upset if she saw more bruises. Everyone knew that Chen Kai was far away. This allowed them to attack Chen Pie Sou, and it made him fight harder. The other boys envied his eggs and resented his bragging about being a landlord. Fortunately, he picked his bets and won more than he lost. The eggs were a tempting prize that allowed him to make profitable wagers. The older boy was fast, straddled him now, and had the upper hand. Chen Pie Sou was hardly able to land a blow, and struggled beneath the older boy, who pummelled him with both fists.

An adult's voice yelled, "Stop!" The taunts of the gang of boys grew distant as they fled. A man walked from the train and stood sternly over the combatants. The older boy rifled Chen Pie Sou's pocket and snatched the crushed egg before he jumped to his feet and ran. The man who drew close wore a well-cut suit and a crisp felt hat.

"Why are you fighting?" asked the man.

"I lost a bet. For my egg."

"If you lost a bet," said the man, "then you must pay."

From behind the man, the railway porter brought two handsome leather suitcases and placed them carefully beside the passenger. The Western-dressed man gave a tip that must have been generous, judging from the depth of the porter's bow. His shoes shone like the smokestack of the locomotive. He fished a gleaming watch from his pocket, checked the time, and replaced it. Chen Pie Sou had never seen such a watch, or such a man, glowing with wealth. Though the man had Chinese features and spoke Teochow, in clothing and manner he was exactly like a gwei lo. He must have come directly from the Gold Mountain. He stared inquisitively, softly.

"Why did you bet your egg?" asked the man.

"I wanted the piece of bean cake."

"But you had the egg for a snack."

"I wanted more."

"Yes," he nodded, "I understand."

"I thought the train would pass through. I wanted to win, and I felt very lucky today. I was wrong."

The man had not touched his baggage. He stared. What did he mean by this? Perhaps he would pay to have his bags carried. Perhaps he expected them to be carried, whether he paid or not. Chen Pie Sou went to pick up the suitcases, but then he did not know what to do with them. He waited for the man *to tell him where to take the bags. The man said, "You were wrong about the train," his eyes twinkling, "but right about the luck."*

Chen Pie Sou stared at the man, at his clothes of a foreigner, at the soft cleanliness of his hands and the roundness of his well-fed face. It contained something familiar. Then he dropped the suitcases to kowtow at his father's feet.

IT WAS A NIGHT WITH NO MOON, chosen for darkness. Along with the others, Percival lay in the sharp, tough grass of the dunes above the beach. He guessed that they were somewhere a little north of Vung Tau.

After Laing Jai had gone to sleep, the smuggler collected Percival from Mrs. Ling's house. This man was a sergeant of the North Vietnamese Army, and he packed Percival into the back of an army truck crowded with other passengers. Over the days that followed, they took a meandering route through the countryside, heading east from Saigon. The smuggler knew the soldiers at the checkpoints, told them casually that he was deporting counter-revolutionaries to be re-educated, and pressed bills into their hands. There was a new currency, the dong, and this sergeant had plenty of them. Mrs. Ling had been good at the exit business, because she had found soldiers to do the smuggling. For several sweltering days in the back of the truck, babies nursed lethargically at the breasts of dozing women, and men kept silent as they bounced along small roads. Laing Jai would be in a new world already. Percival was glad that his grandson was not in this truck that stank of people and fear. The passengers survived on the little food and water that the sergeant provided, and finally they reached the coast.

"Not to worry," the smuggler had said, as they all climbed out of the truck. "Wait patiently. The boat will come tonight. Don't let yourselves get caught by the coastal patrol, because then you will not see morning." The man got in his truck and drove away. They hid for hours in the dunes of the desolate beach, pressed against the sand, grateful for the cover of night. Darkness shielded them, but they still kept low. The hushing noise of the ocean was the only comfort. It reminded him of his luck.

Now, beneath the open black sky, surrounded by sand grasses and low dunes falling into the sea, Percival and the others waited. The signal would come only once—three flashes. When they saw the light, they must run across the beach into the water. They were to go out into the ocean as far as possible. A small launch would pluck them out and take them to a ship.

In the starlight, Percival could barely make out the ghostly shapes of his fellow travellers crouched around him. He stared out on the water and saw nothing, heard the chop of waves. What if the signal never flashed? What if morning cracked the horizon, if the sun shone down and exposed them before the boat came? The night must be half gone. Occasionally, soldiers patrolled the beach, swung dim flashlights, their radios squawked. If daylight came before the little boat, if they were caught, the soldiers would not bother loading them into trucks. The sand was easily dug. They'd be given shovels to prepare their own graves—the smuggler had explained this.

And if the signal did come? What if, by then, the wind had whipped the waves up? Percival could not swim. Even once they were at sea, there were navy boats and pirates. Engines failed and captains became lost. But there was no point thinking any further than this moment—the one thing was to watch for the signal. Percival prayed to the ghost of his father and all his ancestors for the boat to come, for a chance to see his grandson again.

He imagined entering the water, the waves welcoming him, licking up around his legs. He would plunge ahead up to his waist and listen for the boat, for any directions that were yelled. When it was close, he would go as deep as he could, up to his neck. He could not be left behind. He must not panic, even if the waves submerged him. If the launch was yet farther out, he would rise to the surface and swim. If the fish could do it, so could he.

Then they came fast as three winks—the three flashes of light. Darkness again. There were no patrols nearby. Around him, he heard the others in the grass rising, uttering words of relief and fear, gathering and shushing children, running for the water. He ran too. He ran headlong down the dunes, legs slashed by the stinging grass, forward across the beach. His feet pushed through the soft sand, his lungs aching, the wind everywhere, guided only by the noise of the sea.

ACKNOWLEDGEMENTS

My deepest gratitude is to my wife, Margarita, who always encouraged, sometimes consoled, and often cheered me during my journey writing this novel. In so many important ways, she made this book possible. My parents helped me with generous recollections of their childhoods in Vietnam. The specific details and anecdotes that they shared with me were invaluable in my understanding of life's rhythms in that era. My late grandfather, William Lin, inspired the fictional protagonist of this novel. A number of former teachers and students of his school shared their memories with me. Portions of the story pay homage to episodes in the lives of my relatives. In particular, this book remembers my late Aunt Sophie. Echoes of history are to be found in this narrative and yet it is a work of fiction.

I am immensely appreciative of my editors in this project. Martha Kanya-Forstner believed in this book and nurtured it, even during its most impressionistic and fragile beginnings. She entered the lives of its characters with compassion, wisdom, and editorial rigor. In doing so, she helped me to carry the project through to completion, and challenged me to bring it to life on the page. Nita Pronovost peered deeply into the shadows of this book, and those of its author, to help both find their way through some difficult times. Alexis Washam asked essential questions of the characters, and her insightful editorial work helped bring clarity to the text.

Thank you to Alex Schultz for a superlative copyedit, and Shaun